The Guinea Boat

Alaric Bond

Old Salt Press

The cover shows detail from a painting by
William Anslow Thornley

To Natalie and Alexandra

Two French ladies who have shown remarkably fine taste in English men.

By the same author

His Majesty's Ship

The Jackass Frigate

True Colours

Cut and Run

The Patriot's Fate

The Torrid Zone

Turn a Blind Eye

CONTENTS

The Guinea Boat

Chapter One

Nat's story

There is much I would change now, but that must be the same when looking back on any life: you always remember missed opportunities, while those taken and fully exploited somehow slip the mind. I probably hurt a good deal more than I healed, but that was never my intention, and if I looked out for myself whenever possible, it surely doesn't make me so very unusual. The main point is, I never set out to do any real harm. Some, who came off badly, might not have been my enemies to begin with, but certainly became so afterwards, so I can probably say in all honesty that I never hurt a friend.

And youth had a lot to do with it. The young long to grow older yet cannot understand that, by doing so, they must also alter. There is no doubt I changed, and can now see how, and almost exactly when, but that is with the gift of hindsight. Along with grey hair, wrinkles and even knowledge itself, hindsight is a thing old men acquire without effort. And, again like knowledge, it is often confused with wisdom.

But then I was far too young to look back: the only thing that concerned me was the future, and mine in particular. I had plans, many of them: all equally inspired and far too good to be challenged, compromised or modified in any way. Some were quite mundane, others more fanciful, but at the heart of every one was the very real need to avoid spending any more time in some stuffy office, which was what my father wanted.

He trained as a book-keeper and could cast an account like a witch might spells. That was where his commercial skills ended, however; there were a number of small businesses he dabbled in that never did terribly well, and I put this down to an inability to get out of bed. To some extent this was counteracted by his working during the evenings, although even that eventually stopped. Frankly he always seemed to be in the house, and doing precisely nothing.

We lived comfortably enough, due mainly to money inherited from his own father, but I did not rate his head for business at all, it being obvious to me that he lacked both motivation and the courage to take a risk. At first he had a family to support and probably this was a good enough reason for caution. But my sister married early and when mother died, and her position as wife was swiftly taken by another, I knew my days at home were numbered.

My stepmother was an apparently doting little hussy hardly ten years older than me. Towards the end I would watch the two of them make eyes at each other while sitting out much of the day in the garden and most evenings at some more private haunt. Frankly his lack of enterprise appalled me.

On reaching seventeen I felt more than able to fend for myself: I could work hard, had a fine head for figures, and considered myself to be a potential man of business. My aim was not just to be outrageously rich, but also more successful than my father. More to the point, I would become so by clever dealing and very obviously taking chances. I was determined to show him that none of his laziness or lack of ambition had been inherited by me.

So, rather than spending any more time in the dank, dark clerks' office at Ashburnham's cannon foundry where I had been placed, I began to look elsewhere, and finally set my sights on the nearby south coast.

It was the January of 1803, and England was at an uneasy

peace with France. All knew it might end at any time but the Royal Navy was not so hungry for hands, and a man might visit even substantial ports without finding himself pressed. I knew I was not the right material for the cut and thrust of Royal Naval life, but the sea still appealed. My initial intention was to find a coaster and sign myself aboard. It would be as sure a way as any of saying at least a temporary farewell to Sussex and, after two or three short trips about Britain's shores, I might then feel inclined to lend my newly acquired skills to something a mite larger – maybe a deep sea merchant, perhaps even an Indiaman.

It was common knowledge that substantial riches were waiting for those who sailed in John Company vessels, and I wanted my share. There was talk in the clerks' office of a local joiner who left the area some years back to ship as a carpenter's mate. Two Eastern trips later he returned with a pile big enough to set up a fine house and, by all accounts, now spent his days like a pig in butter. I'd never met the cove, and word was the riches had come through a good deal of personal trade, some of which might not have been strictly legal. But keeping to the narrow path had never been a great concern for me: if the temptation were strong enough, I would usually stray.

Of course, my main concern was money. It didn't take long to work out that to follow the joiner's example would require an initial investment, and I had little, apart from a handful of cartwheels and one silver groat. But, as I slipped silently from the house at first light that winter's morning, at least I knew that opportunities did exist and the knowledge, together with my blatant disregard of his wishes, already seemed to have put me one step ahead of my father.

I would make for Rye: that had been decided long ago and, as I started along the track in a light and chilly mist, there was no reason to change my mind. It sounded a pleasant enough port and not much more than a day's walk from our village. A cross-country path headed almost directly there, but I was eager to get to the sea as soon as I could, and chose instead to go by way of Hastings; a fishing town that was far closer.

There were no Indiamen waiting for me when I arrived, or

viable coasters for that matter. The walk to Hastings had taken longer than I anticipated and, though nothing had really been expected from the place, it still disappointed. A small and rather sad collier was run up on the eastern side of the beach, but she was clearly in want of something more than an inexperienced hand. Apart from that, little caught my attention. There wasn't even a harbour, or a wharf, or a mole. Several small huts had been rather crudely constructed, some made from the hulls of old boats sawn in two. These were assembled in untidy groups towards the top and one side of a long shingle beach that I was later to know as the Stade. There was also a profusion of nets and untidy piles containing rope, spars and cork floats, all topped by the very domestic sight of washing blowing on lines in the steady breeze.

It was early afternoon and I had been hungry since mid-morning, but still I wandered along the high water mark, just to see if the effort taken to get there had been worthwhile. A group of men in loose fitting smocks, baggy trousers and sea boots were attending to a spread of netting. One smoked a clay pipe, which he tapped against the wooden frame as I walked by. I nodded in his direction and received no reaction, but neither did he appear particularly unfriendly. Further along, what looked like a mother and two daughters were pegging small fish to lines strung between wooden tripods. One of the girls waved at me and I smiled in return, but the woman called her back to work. The air was cut with the smell of wood smoke and something familiar yet undefined, while all the time the call and cry of gulls and a regular roll of rushing water filled my ears, blocking out much of the muted conversations. The birds ranged in size from small doves to one great beast that, to my naïve mind, could easily have been an albatross. It was all interesting enough in itself, and definitely a change from the mundane inland life I had known, but only as I reached the end of the beach and stopped, did I remember the real reason for my being there, and finally looked out to sea.

There were no fishing boats in sight. Instead what I took to be a Royal Navy ship was several miles off and steering to the east. I could see her three masts, and the single line of gun ports, but had no idea as to her purpose or type. Even then I was able to appreciate beauty, though: the way in which the onshore breeze filled her canvas, pressing the hull down until a cloud of spray was forced from beneath her bows touched me somewhere deep inside. She was not apparently moving fast, but still crossed my small horizon before I had realised it. Within minutes she started to fade from sight and soon disappeared completely behind the nearby headland.

I say disappeared, but in my mind that ship never truly left. I still think of her now and the freedom she enjoyed. There were few limits: she could go just about wherever her captain pleased, even if the wind were against her – I already knew enough to appreciate that. And it was then I decided my life would definitely be spent on the water. Not necessarily in a frigate – as I now guess she must have been – or even the Royal Navy, where the rules and restrictions would not suit my maverick nature one jot. But on the sea, a medium which knows no bounds. I was later to learn of shoal waters, and tides; contrary currents and sudden, unforeseen squalls but the magic was strong then, and it remains so now.

My stomach began to rumble once more and, rarely being able to ignore such a call, I turned and began to head inland. There was a small pot house directly opposite the wooden huts, and it looked friendly enough from the outside, so I stepped in.

The place was empty, but smelled strongly of beer, sweat and fish so I guessed it usually did a good trade when the fleet was in. I sat at a table, and presently a girl of sixteen or so approached. She was pretty, with dark hair and a purposefully nonchalant manner: I straightened my back.

"It's quiet," I said, after ordering food and small beer. Hers was a pleasant enough face: nice eyes, a slightly over long nose, and she was definitely a year or so younger than me.

"Most folk is workin'," she looked at me as if I was somehow strange. "It will be busier later."

"The fishermen?" I asked, sensing warmth but guessing that conversation might become hard work. "Expect them soon, do you?"

"By sunset, or just before," I was told. "The boys ashore will be here afore then, 'case any gets in early. Sometimes a few of them drops in."

"Boys ashore?" It was a strange term: where I came from boys didn't just drop in to pot houses.

"Most boats have at least one in their crew what they leaves on land," she explained, unbending a little more. "They sees to the launching, then mend nets and tackle while waiting for them to return. We've no harbour here, and it can take a fair bit of effort to beach some of the bigger ones. Then there's the sivver to be dropped and taken to auction."

"Sivver?" I questioned.

"It's what they calls a catch hereabouts," she explained.

"And they're boys?" I asked.

"Well a couple are women," the girl almost laughed. "But that's more a way of saying really. Some might be lads, and a lot are retired fishermen, or those what can't take to life at sea."

"Any chance of my joining them?" I chanced, treating her to one of my hopeful looks.

She seemed to size me up, and this time did give a slight smile. "What, with you being such an expert?"

I think I took the rebuff well and hope no one could guess the effect her words had on me. Back then I was rather more the optimist, and felt most things to be within my powers. Such an attitude usually worked well, and pumping myself up with aspirations that were too frequently based on lies could often swing things in my favour. But a simple word of truth could also deflate me, and I may even have blushed.

She was right, though; I had never worked in the fishing trade, either on land or afloat, and had only been on the water as a river boat passenger. And as for fish, well, I couldn't stand the things: apart from being forced to eat them when young, I knew little.

"I'm willing to learn," I said, adding, "and am known to be able," with a not so subtle wink. The girl regarded me for a moment, then gave a slightly different look, before moving away without saying more.

Within a few minutes she was back with my drink and food. It was really quite a substantial meal, a lump of cheese and the heel of a loaf together with one whole onion that had been neatly peeled, as well as some pickle and a carrot.

"If you want work there's nothing to stop you askin'," she told me as I was examining the plate. "But we ain't short of men at present, not with the war being ended."

"Do you really think it so?" I looked up, surprised. My father was in a syndicate that subscribed to a newspaper and, from what I had read, the current peace was showing distinct signs of failing.

"It will last for as long as it does, and not a moment more," she replied wisely, and it was my turn to smile at the queer logic. "There ain't no point in trying to anticipate such things," she added hurriedly, noting my reaction. "Folk spend too long trying to guess the future, when what they really should be concerned with is the present."

My expression faded; I didn't agree, but then neither did I argue. She was clearly sensitive and we had only just met: I did not wish to upset her. Even then I was well practised in not making enemies, and felt she may prove useful later. Besides, whatever folk might say, I never really set out to hurt anyone. But if I had only known my future, her statement would have had my full support.

* * *

She left me to eat my meal and said little else when I paid and left. For a while there had been the noise of something being kicked against the pot house wall and as I stepped out into the bland winter sunshine I saw a ginger haired lad of about my size but a year or so younger with a bladder ball at his feet.

I was wearing what roughly comprised my Sunday best, while he was far more scruffy, with a woollen hat, plain canvas shirt and cotton trousers cut short to just below the knee. He was also barefoot, whereas I wore proper shoes that were shaped slightly differently for right and left. Such things were of little importance, though, and his feet were so heavily stained, any deficiency was not immediately obvious. As I yawned and stretched, the ball came rolling towards me. I considered it for a moment, before booting it back easily enough. It was returned straight away, and at a far higher speed. I failed to trap it with my foot, but fortunately the mis-shapen thing hit my calf, and bounced towards him.

It didn't take much more for us to be kicking the old bladder back and forth in a way that was sporting and only mildly aggressive. At one point he captured it, and tried to dribble past me, but I flipped the thing away, and took possession, only to lose it again when he tackled rather roughly, despite his unshod state, from behind. We played for a good quarter of an hour before, by unspoken agreement, stopping to settle on the nearby sea wall.

"You're not from round here," he told me, and I think they were the first words either of us had spoken until then.

"From Ninfield," I said. "Small village to the..."

"I know where it is," he interrupted. "We've a cousin from round there. He's mad, of course," he continued, with strange authority. "But then they say everyone thereabouts is."

I glared at him and was expecting a fight when I noticed he was grinning, and found myself smiling in turn.

"So what brings you to Hastings?"

"Looking for work," I replied. "Do you know of any?"

"Oh, plenty," he grunted. "That is if you don't mind watching others. Should you want to do it yourself, it's another matter."

As well as being something of a wag, I guessed he was one of the boys ashore the pot house girl mentioned, so persevered.

"Is there any at all hereabouts?" I asked, seriously. "I'm not so fussy."

"Not much on the water," he said, after thinking for a spell. "Else I'd be out there now. Billy Danton's lad is off with the measles at present, but it's a large boat, one of the biggest, and they have crew enough to cover. Besides, most round here employ local folk – that's not to say anything against Ninfield," clearly the time for teasing was over. "But if you've grown up with the fishing, there ain't so much to learn; so mostly we relies on Hastings families, and each other."

I nodded. That made perfect sense, but was of little use to me. "What about anything not connected with fish?" I would have far rather been involved in coastal trade or perhaps passenger transport.

8

He seemed unusually cautious, and eyed me carefully before replying.

"Not a lot," he said. "Some of the boats might be used for other purposes from time to time, but I wouldn't know about that, and they don't take kindly to strangers asking, so best not to." His tone was firm and I could tell this was more than idle conversation. "As for anything else on the water, well the choice is limited for those what don't like fish. How do you feel about lobster?"

It was getting late and would soon be dark, while there was still a fair way to go if I was to make Rye that day so I decided to move on. He apparently sensed this and stood up when I did.

"Look there's nothing to stop you helping the day boats when they lands; we all muck in and another hand is always welcome. Can't promise a job, or even payment, but you might get to hear of a berth or, if you're really unlucky, earn a few fish for your supper."

It didn't sound like much of an opportunity, but I was pretty cocky in those days and usually reckoned on getting something out of nothing. Besides I had already made two acquaintances, and one almost seemed keen to help. It's amazing how far you can go with a few gullible folk to lean on.

Chapter Two

We spent the rest of the afternoon kicking the ball about and yarning. The lad's name was Alex: his uncle and two older brothers ran their own lugger, and he was very much an unofficial boy ashore; I gathered that money and regular employment were both rare commodities in Hastings. Then the ball was taken from us rather roughly by a bunch of new arrivals who wanted a proper game. Some of the lads treated Alex with a measure of disdain which frankly puzzled me, although he took little notice.

"My uncle's boat is one of the larger ones," he told me, when they had gone. "Though she's gettin' on a bit now. Seth, he's my older brother, has a notion to buy his own, in which case I'll be joining him. Might be a space for you then though, if Seth's involved, don't expect anything this side of Christmas."

That was almost a year off: far too long for my plans. But the offer did at least show the local folk weren't so dead set against newcomers. Rye was all of ten miles away; less than three hours walk on a good path admittedly, but I knew no one there and had already half decided to stay the night in Hastings. Then a shout went up, and the first of the fishing fleet could be seen coming in with the breeze.

I gathered it wasn't the entire fleet; there were about ten boats in all and they had been fishing off Newhaven; the rest were still at sea although Alex was reticent as to where. They were not expected to return immediately, however, and would take care of themselves when they did. All on the beach assembled to see the arrivals in safely, and I got the impression that fishing was very much a shared industry.

The boats ranged in size from smaller vessels, less than twenty feet long, to monsters almost twice that length and probably four times as heavy. I could make out little difference in the rig; most had two upright masts, and a collection of triangular and misshapen square sails spread across what looked like a muddle of spars; nothing like the beauty or symmetry of the warship seen earlier. The arrangement appeared to work though, and the boats made for the shore at quite a speed, as if taking part in some madcap race, or a shared desire for self murder.

The crowd on shore gathered round in a practised manner, flocking forward as the leading boats charged towards the hard, dark band of sand that marked the lower beach. Those aboard then appeared to see sense and began taking in their canvas as the hulls entered the surf, to eventually ground under bare poles. Some of the younger boys waded into the water to meet them; lines were passed, and stakes driven into the beach further up, where the sand gave way to loose shingle. The rest of the shore party divided between the boats and sought for a purchase on their hulls. The sea was far too eager to reclaim them, and each had to be wrenched free of its grip. This was clearly not an easy task, although there was no hint of anger or frustration; the very reverse, in fact: all seemed remarkably good humoured, despite many being pretty much soaked to the skin, and I could see then why Alex was so content to be barefooted.

As they were hauled up to the firmer pebbles, the boats righted onto their shallow, flat bottoms. Then there was a moment of relief and rest while two horses were led down to meet them. The animals were attached to the largest of the beached craft. Meanwhile one of the smaller boats had been fastened to a rope that ran from a windlass mounted near the upper road, and rows of what appeared to be round fence posts were laid down at regular intervals up the beach. The tow lines were soon drawing tight and, riding on the wooden rollers, the first two vessels began a slow and stately progress up the gentle rise.

I watched, fascinated; all was running so well there was no need for an inexperienced hand, and I was far too interested to interfere. In each of the fishing boats, their crew were passing open, wooden boxes down to eager hands. Seagulls screamed overhead as chains of lads collected a crate each and raced each other up the beach to where a line of wagons waited to receive them.

The boxes were filled with fish, some still very much alive and even contriving to escape. Those that did were picked off the shingle by groups of even younger children, most of whom were hardly more than toddlers. Each carried a large leather bucket, almost as big as themselves, and gave squeals of delight whenever a fish was captured for the second time that day.

Apart from caw of the birds, the shriek of youngsters, an occasional greeting and general laughter when one of the older boys tripped and fell headlong into his box of wet fish, little was said, and no one appeared in overall charge or gave instructions. The whole procedure had the air of a military operation, despite being carried out by civilians of all ages, some barely free of the cradle, others a long way from it. I might have been idle, but Alex was busy enough, and ran from one boat to another, apparently knowing exactly what to do with each and where he would be most wanted. By the time the last was in place a good way up the beach, and all the catch was on, or being taken to, the carts, he turned back to me with a grin on his flushed face.

"Been a good sivver, by all accounts."

I puzzled over the word for a second or so, then remembered the pot house girl's earlier explanation and knew Alex was referring to the catch. He was carrying a large flat fish which must be his payment, holding the thing with his finger pressed up the beast's gill in a way I found quite disturbing. "Mostly plaice and cods, though a fair few turbot as well, and the flats always get a fair price this time of year."

"Where's the sivver bound?" I asked, using the word for the first time and hoping the question did not sound too stupid.

"Auction house'll be their first stop," he told me, with the air of an expert. "But that won't take long; most'll be on their way to London within the hour, and probably on some rich man's plate by midnight."

I fell in step with him and we crunched up the beach together. Until then I had not imagined the intricacies of fishing to be so terribly complicated. I also felt a little embarrassed about not helping in any way. "Will you be waiting for the others to come in?" I asked, but Alex shook his head.

"I dare say they'll stay out a good while, yet," he told me. "And won't want the likes of us about when they do return. There's one more due in, though: he tends not to sail with the others an' can usually look after hisself with the landing. In fact, here he is now."

I followed his gaze and, in the last of the light, could just make out a smaller craft coming in.

"Old Ned Coglan," Alex told me as the boat neared the beach. "His family's been fishing these parts an age or more; it was just his misfortune to have no sons."

The boat came in far slower than any of the others, and was considerably smaller, probably less than sixteen feet in length.

"She's showing less sail," I said, hoping to sound like an expert.

"Aye, naught but a punt," Alex confirmed. "Similar to a lugger, but a far simpler rig; Ned needs it as there's only him to manage."

My ears pricked up and Alex must have sensed something because he turned to me. "And you can forget any thoughts of joining him," he said. "Besides being bloody-minded, he's the meanest man afloat, and only makes enough to cover hisself, and his daughters. There'll be nothing spare for a landsman."

I accepted what he said, but was not put off in any way: it was still the best chance of work all day and, as far as being bloody-minded was concerned, I felt I could handle that. My father was not the easiest of people; stubbornness being a common trait amongst poor men of business. On the other hand, I had excellent commercial sense, and knew myself to be a positive pleasure to deal with. Already I could see the potential for a good little team – and the sound of daughters was also encouraging.

* * *

But Alex might well have been right. Despite only the two of us bothering to help the old man in, he barely acknowledged our existence and, when we had pulled the boat safely off the sand and my new friend offered to fetch the rollers, he accepted with a distinct lack of grace.

"Don't think I'm payin' yer for your trouble, young Combes," he shouted after him. "Your uncle still owes me for those two pints of linseed he borrowed last October."

Between us, we rolled the poles down the beach; I found they did so surprisingly easily, and had to run to catch one that went faster than the rest, only stopping feet from the prow of the fishing boat.

"You've not done that too often," Ned informed me as I manoeuvred the thing into position in front of the boat's stem.

"No, it's my first time," I said. "You're honoured."

"You'll be honoured if you scrape any paint off *Katharine*," he grunted.

Alex was on the other side of the boat, and together we heaved the bows up onto the smooth wooden pole.

"No need to get your feet wet, Ned." Alex muttered as the hull began to run freely towards the next roller.

"It's Mr Coglan to you, young Combes." The old man was fussing with his catch. I looked inside the undecked boat and saw three full crates, but far more empty ones.

We were well onto the shingle by now and in danger of losing the first of the rollers. I went to go back for it, but Ned was ahead of me and swung himself over the side with surprising agility. He picked up the length of wood easily enough and straight away tossed it in my direction. I saw it coming, and knew it would be heavy; part of me wanted to jump clear, but I had reasonable bulk for my height and decided to catch it instead. The roller landed square against my chest, fortunately high enough to avoid winding me, which I think might have been the intention. I had to take a step back, but held it, and for a moment our eyes met.

There was the hint of a smile on Ned's face, and he even went to speak, but we had left Alex in sole charge of the boat, and he was calling for assistance.

It was dark by the time the punt was fully secured at the end of a line of far larger boats. Alex and I had taken the catch to the last of the wagons, and Ned was chalking something on a slate when he broke away and considered us.

"Obliged to you both," he said, in a voice that was slightly muffled. "Can't pay you, mind, but if you'd care for a bite of supper there'll be some spare."

"Thanking you, Mr Coglan, but I have mine here," Alex replied, collecting his payment from earlier. "This'n might take you up on your offer, though," he added, glancing in my direction.

Ned regarded me again with those same sad eyes. "Well if that's the case, we'd better get movin'," he grunted.

Chapter Three

"You won't find any work round here, not that'll pay," Ned said as we walked through the dark streets. "Best you can do is try and borrow yourself something small, but you'll need your wits sharp: there's no guarantee the owner'll see his boat back – or you, if it comes to it."

I realised this was a long statement for Ned, and one that seemed to sap him of energy, as he said little else for a while. He was carrying a cluster of small fish tied together at their heads and, despite the crisp evening, either they, or he, smelled strongly.

"I don't mind hard work," I said, repeating the phrase yet again, and almost starting to mean it.

"Good of you," he snorted.

Not another word was said for the rest of the journey. He had promised me a meal, and we both knew it could be stretched to a bed for the night. But there was nothing further for me in Hastings, and certainly not with Ned or his family. Tomorrow I would be setting out for Rye: that was definite.

His house was small, just two windows at the front, one above the other, and with a door at the side. It stood at the end of a terrace, and had an area next to it filled with various pieces of fishing tackle as well as a pile of wooden boxes, similar to those that had held his meagre catch. A small boat, probably no more than eight feet in length, rested against the wall; looking at it I remembered our recent conversation, and wondered vaguely if Ned would be foolish enough to lend it out, before guessing the answer. He tapped loudly on the door, then pressed it open and walked inside. I followed.

We entered a small back parlour; it was surprisingly well lit by three separate lamps, and welcomingly warm – a dark leaded range that glowed on one side saw to that. There was a plain wooden table to the centre. A woman sat at it with her back to us and an enamel bowl on her lap. Ned placed the fish on the table and she glanced up, mildly surprised, before standing and turning to meet us. I saw she was quite young, not more than nineteen, with long, light auburn hair and a pleasant expression. But something about the way she looked at us was unusual.

"This is Jenny," Ned told me, adding, in a firm voice: "She don't see so well, so you'll treat her with respect." Something seemed to strike a chord with him, and he glared at me. "As you will both my girls. You're a guest here, but that don't mean you won't be thrown out if I catch you misbehavin'."

I nodded and grinned at Jenny, even though she could not tell: her apparently perfect green eyes were actually staring at a point about a foot from where I stood. "What cheer? I'm Nat Audley," I told her. "It's short for Nathaniel."

"Nathaniel?" Jenny repeated brightly, as if trying the name out, before fixing her attention on my exact position.

"Nat," I corrected. "The only time I'm called Nathaniel is when folk aren't pleased with me." I meant my father, but avoided saying so as it made me sound like a child. Creating a good impression was always very important to me.

"From the Bible," Ned almost sounded approving. "One of the Apostles."

"Actually it is Nathaniel, Jacob," I added, determined to capitalise on every available asset. "Jacob's Biblical as well."

"Aye, and so it is," Ned conceded, although his face had fallen somewhat. "Weren't he the cove what wrestled with an angel?"

I was taken aback slightly; it was my name, so I knew a good deal of the background, and he was quite right. The Old Testament Jacob was also a mother's boy who duped his brother out of what was rightfully his and went on to be renamed Israel, but that was about as far as my religious knowledge went. Ned, it appeared, was way ahead of me.

"Amongst other things," I replied, hesitantly.

"Well there'll be no wrestling while you're staying under my roof." he declared. "You've been helpful enough and I'm grateful, but that's where any obligation ends."

Jenny gave a short laugh. "Don't worry, Nat, this might be All Saints Street but you won't be finding many angels hereabouts." I'd moved slightly but her gaze followed and she was still looking in

17

my direction. "Not in Hastings, and certainly not in this house."

The old man snorted, but his expression softened as well, and he pointed dismissively at the cluster of fish on the table. "That's as maybe, so he won't have no cause to go looking. There's sprats for supper; nothing more I'm afraid."

"They will be fine," the girl said, feeling for the fish. "Mrs Combes dropped some early springs in, and we've plenty of potatoes left."

"Did she now?" Ned asked. "That were good of her."

"She left more than enough for a decent meal," Jenny added, smiling at me, and I'd have sworn our eyes met.

Ned murmured something about going to clean up, then stomped back out through the door so I guess he must have trusted me to some extent. He needn't have worried; I'll admit to having an eye for a pretty face, but looking was mostly as far as it went. And never would I have taken advantage of a blind girl: there are limits.

"Can I help you there?" I asked. Jenny had collected the sprats and cut the string connecting them with her paring knife, before guiding the separate fish into the bowl.

"No, I have them safely; thank you," she said, picking one up again, and neatly cutting off its head as if lopping the end from a carrot. "Father gutted them aboard the boat, so we just need the final trim."

I have to say I found the sight rather unpleasant and looked away.

It is not something I am particularly proud of, but dead things affect me. I might have spent my life in the country but always hated working with meat. Of course, I'll eat most of what is given once cooked, but never particularly enjoy the stuff, and don't care to see a whole animal, or any recognisable part of one, on my plate. I put that down to being soft hearted and at various times have tried to conquer my feelings. They remain to this day though, and must have been apparent that evening.

Instead I stared at the wilting Christmastide decorations on the far wall feeling both mildly disgusted and more than a little ashamed. Jenny was blind of course, and I was almost glad, if only because her condition allowed me to hide something of my naivety. But she must have sensed it and turned back to me grinning.

"My, you truly are a stranger, Nat – are you from the town?" she asked.

I muttered something about coming from nearby, but frankly was too surprised to elaborate. Being found out so easily, and by a blind girl, was disconcerting on many levels; I must have been blushing by then, which was unfortunate as her sister chose exactly that moment to come tumbling into the room.

"Oh, my word," she said, bursting through the two light doors that masked the stairs. "Visitors!" She swung round and hurriedly began buttoning up the shirt that had been gloriously open. "Jen, you should have warned me!"

"This is Nat," Jenny replied, with a sister's innocence. "He's been helping Dad and is staying for supper. Nat, meet Susan."

Susan looked back, hot faced through anger and embarrassment. She was younger than her sister and about a year older than me, I would have said – but with the same light tawny hair as Jenny, although hers was tied back in a bun. She also had a longer face, but with a similar, slightly turned up nose. Susan's cheekbones were more defined, however, while her creamy white skin owed nothing to the ruggedness of her father's. And yes, I couldn't help but to have noticed: she had a fine figure.

"Sprats for supper," Jenny called behind her as she walked towards the stove and reached up confidently to collect a massive frying pan from a hook in the ceiling. I stepped forward to assist, but Susan stopped me.

"Jen'll manage well enough," she said softly. "Try and help and you'll only confuse her."

"And I confuse easily," Jenny added, unabashed.

When Ned came back, Susan and I were sitting facing each other a little awkwardly at the kitchen table, while Jenny did battle with a searing pan at the stove. We had empty plates in front of us and the smell of fish was overpowering, but it was some time since my mid-day meal and I felt in need of food.

"You going off to *The Cutter*?" Ned asked the younger girl, who nodded.

"I said I'd be there for eight and would stay to close up. Shouldn't be so busy midweek, what with half the fleet being out."

"Aye but there's still enough to cause mischief," Ned replied guardedly.

"Is that the pot house by the beach?" I asked.

"No, *Cutter*'s further up from Rock-a-Nore," Susan said, assuming I had more than half an inkling of where she was talking about. "You're probably thinkin' of *The Anchor*, Tilly Medcalf works there; we were at school together."

"I might have met her," I said, with the air of one who knows all.

"So what brings you to Hastings, Nat?" Jenny asked, as she planted two enamel dishes on the table which were clearly too hot to be carried for long. Susan removed the lids to reveal steaming potatoes and what looked like cabbage.

"Well, I'm not actually staying," I began. "I come from Ninfield, but am on my way to Rye."

"Then you've come by a strange route," Ned informed me gruffly. "Must be true what they say about Ninfield folk."

"I came here first because I wanted to see the sea," I replied, as Jenny lowered the hot pan in front of us and seated herself to face her father. The fish were cooked in their skins and still appeared far too realistic for my liking. But they didn't smell quite so bad now and I was almost hungry enough to have eaten them raw.

Ned muttered what I took for a grace, and there was a couple of seconds pause afterwards that almost fooled me. Then the two girls made a dive for the food.

"So the sea interests you?" Jenny repeated, spearing a sprat with her fork and dropping it on to her plate. "Isn't that a little curious?"

"Curious is one word for it," Ned murmured.

"Only 'cause you're on it every day," Susan countered. "Planning to travel are you, Nat?"

She was looking at me with interest, and I felt the urge to impress, but then it was obvious anything I said would sound trite in the company of a proper seaman.

"Well, I don't want to stay in Britain," I began. "And would like to go to sea..."

"If you want to leave Britain there's little option," Ned added, and the girls laughed.

I'd taken my first bite of a sprat, which was far hotter than expected; that and the speed of his remark, floored me for a second. But both girls were regarding me with amused benevolence and even the old man seemed to have softened somewhat. In such company, and with the food already making me feel at home, I elaborated, and soon was telling them just about everything.

"So you don't see yourself as a man of business?" Ned asked, when my story finally dried up and I had revealed my wish for a different path from my father.

"Oh, I do," I assured him quickly. "But not a clerk; not in some stuffy office."

"Men of business work in offices," Susan pointed out.

"I suppose so," I admitted. "And wouldn't mind, as long as it were on my own terms."

"It's the difference between crewing a boat and owning one," Ned reflected with an element of understanding. "Never liked being third hand m'self," he continued. "Mind it were necessary, if I was to skipper my own craft eventually."

The way Ned put it made him sound as if he captained an Indiaman, but I was not so much the fool as to make fun of him.

"I don't mind putting the work in," I assured them instead. "Though a clerk's job has no opportunity: no future."

"No future in fishing," Ned said. "Best we can do is make it pay its way, and I've never asked for more."

"You've just the one boat?" I asked and he looked at me suspiciously.

"Only the one sea-going."

"The others on the beach are far larger," I continued. It was an innocent enough remark, but the girls obviously thought it funny and laughed again.

"It's big enough for what we wants," Ned stated. "I don't need no crew, and I don't need no help with it neither, if that's what you're thinking."

It wasn't. In fact helping Ned could not have been further from my mind.

"Dad's very protective about his boat," Jenny informed me. "Plenty of women go out but he won't let either of us, even though we'd both be capable enough, and willing."

Ned shifted uncomfortably in his seat. "The fishing's no place for ladies," he said defensively.

"Neither's *The Cutter* on a Wednesday evening," Jenny responded. "But you let Sue go, right enough."

"I wouldn't, not if there were a choice," Ned replied.

"If you made more from your boat there wouldn't be the need for choice." I said. A long period of silence followed my words, and I realised I had touched upon a sensitive subject. The pleasant atmosphere had fooled me into allowing my mouth full rein, and it wasn't the first time it had got me into trouble.

But my words were well meant: I'd spoken more from instinct than anything else. Whatever folk might say about me, I can usually spot a business opportunity, and there was something about Ned and his tiny little punt that simply screamed potential. It had been the wrong thing to say though, and all stopped eating as they considered me. Then Ned spoke.

"I'm not saying I won't listen to advice," he said, and I was surprised at the moderation in his tone. "After all, it's rare the likes of us gets to speak with one so well versed in commerce. Just remember that none of my girls will be involved, not if it means them going on the water. Now, what's on your mind?"

I could feel their eyes upon me and knew even Jenny was concentrating intently, and had already penetrated my façade once that evening. I swallowed and drew breath – this had to be good.

"Those with larger boats," I asked at last. "How do they manage?"

"Most have sons," Jenny spoke slowly. "That or cousins; Dad was unlucky; he was landed with girls."

"I'd not change my luck for the world," Ned said softly.

"But the fact remains," Jenny continued. "Round here, the

fishing is kept in the family or done on shares: whatever a catch brings in being divided between boat and crew. If Dad had help aboard there would be five shares: one for the boat, one for the tackle, two for him and one for the hand; it's how we do things."

"So an extra man on board would cost you a fifth of your take," I said, quick as a cut purse. "And would chance you're not making twenty per cent above break-even to be able to pay that."

All three looked at me as if I had suddenly slipped into Latin but, for probably the first time that day, I was on home ground. "What does your average catch bring in?" I asked, and the old man shrugged.

"Impossible to say; I might be going after cods, tunny, or flat. They all sell for differin' amounts, depending on what the other fellows have caught, an' the time of year. An' sometimes I comes back with nothing," he added almost triumphantly. "So there's no numbers needed then."

"On average," I persisted. "How much more would a lugger turn compared to yours?"

"A big boat would deliver three to four times; maybe more," he replied. "But most carry at least one hand, so I'd be losing a fifth, and that's assuming they accepted the share system. Some want a set wage, and we can't afford to pay one." He turned to me, clearly thinking he had made some sort of point.

"Does a lugger cost more to maintain?" I persevered.

"Costs more to build, or buy. Upkeep is about the same – maybe a little extra for oil and paint. And harbour dues are more if you go into a different port. Tackle costs are higher of course; much can be mended, though that will take longer as well."

"A hand could help with that," Jenny added. "And if you were properly crewed, there might not be so much damage."

"Then you will have to get a lugger," I said – to me it was simple.

"Buying a bigger boat would cost more than we have," Susan explained. "Dad would be lucky to get a hand on the share basis, and a set wage works against you when pickings is low."

"You could always marry Danny Corridge," Jenny said softly, but Susan chose to ignore her.

"I don't want no bigger boat, and I don't want no help with crewing," Ned stated in a voice rich in both anger and defiance.

"Then what are we going to do when you gets older?" Susan asked.

Yet again, I sensed I had touched upon something purely private, but it was also a subject my presence had brought to the fore, so I felt an entitlement to be there. And, rather than making me uncomfortable, there was a distinct warmth from the others – well the girls at least. It was as if I had been allowed temporary membership of a family; a feeling that had been notably missing in my own home for some time.

"I'll work till I drop," Ned said. "You all know that."

"We know it, but it won't do us a great deal of good when you do." Susan replied coldly. "Oh, there'll be a bit for the boat, and maybe something for the tackle, but that won't pay the rent on this place, not for long."

"And Susan could find a husband," Jenny added. "But I might not find it quite so easy." The other two seemed shocked by her statement, although Jenny was not in the least perturbed. "If you really are concerned for our future, you're going to have to think about it."

"There ain't no money to buy a bigger boat." Ned said, with the air of one who had done so many times before.

"You could borrow," I chanced.

"We don't borrow – not in this family," he said, looking at me directly.

"I could," the words shot back instantly, almost without thought.

"No one knows you," the old man batted in reply.

"You know me," I returned. "You could speak on my behalf: besides, we're not talking about tomorrow. If I stayed a while, people would get familiar with who I am, and that I can be trusted." I was strangely certain about the last point.

"Well, I don't know," Ned said, after a moment or two, and then he started to pick at his food once more. But Jenny was clearly pleased and, from across the table, Susan treated me to a smile. It was the first sign of a breakthrough: the first sign that my own particular magic was starting to work. That small success truly delighted me, and it wasn't until much later that I began to wonder quite what I had let myself in for.

Chapter Four

I slept in the kitchen. There had been no question of my not staying the night; it was as if they expected me to: again, like I was already part of the family. Looking back, I may even have felt slightly sorry for them, not knowing quite what they had invited in. But, with the way I was starting to feel about Susan, it was a sentiment only a fool would discourage. When I woke the next morning I did have second thoughts, though; as well as the unmistakable feeling I was sinking deep into a problem hardly of my making.

The place still smelt of our previous night's supper, but I was already getting used to that particular aroma. What bothered me more was the prospect of spending the day, and possibly many more after it, tossing about on the water under the instructions of a grumpy old man.

Along with the location of my sleeping space, strict regulations regarding the use of the outhouse, and a complete and absolute restriction on going upstairs, Ned had also decided I would be working for shelter and board alone. There might be something in my pocket at the end of the week, but a lot would depend on the effort I put in, and what we were able to achieve. The arrangement suited me to some extent; I still had some laid by, and was never one to undervalue an education. If Ned really could turn me into a half decent fisherman, time with him would be well spent, as I must then find it easier to get employment elsewhere. Even the Honourable East India Company should look more kindly on a hand with seagoing experience. Somewhere, at the back of my mind, the idea of Eastern travel remained, although the dream had been modified slightly: I would still come back with a pile, but now there might be someone to spend it with.

I decided to head for the outhouse before the rest of the family stirred. The old man might make strict stipulations to protect his girls but, in reality, I was equally shy about myself. I'd shared a home with a sister, knew how much privacy could be expected and was in no rush to commit a similar gaff to Susan's of the evening before. When I returned, Ned was about, although there was no sign of either girl. He barely greeted me, but pointed instead to a half loaf of bread which lay on the kitchen table. Next to it was a small saucer of butter, and I sensed this was somehow a test.

I collected the bread, and spread a minute amount of butter on the cut end, in the way mother used to. It was scraped thin, so the face of the slice was covered, but could in no way be called greedy. That done I placed the loaf back on the table, and cut off the newly buttered end. It was a thin piece, but stayed together when I lifted it. Such a slice would have been impossible to spread with butter, had I cut it first.

Ned seemed satisfied, which was a relief, even if I also knew a single piece of bread was not going to carry me far on a day filled with physical exercise.

"There's clothes and boots for you in the yard," Ned said, as he repeated my performance with the bread. "Some might be a touch on the large side, but we'll find others if you prove useful."

I thanked him and stepped outside. Sure enough a pair of old leather boots that looked as if they would reach up to my waist lay by the back door. There was also a baggy, oiled canvas smock, an apron and a hat; the latter had seen better days, and came down to my nose when I tried it on. I was still wearing Sunday clothes however, and appreciated the gesture. Kicking off my shoes, I tested one of the boots. Although worn, the leather had been properly cared for, and folded down upon itself until it felt more like a legging. The door opened behind me and Ned came out as I was stepping into the second,. He was already wearing both his boots as well as oilskins, and clearly had no time to wait around. Slamming the door behind him, he strode off for the road. I hurriedly wriggled into the second boot, flung the jacket across my shoulders, and rushed after him.

We reached the Stade as dawn was properly breaking. Neither of us spoke throughout our journey, and Ned may well have been having second thoughts about my presence. I couldn't care either way; it was a shame neither of the girls showed themselves before we left the house but, until the previous evening, I had not known of either's existence. Susan had a winning smile, a more than pretty face, and I still had every intention of claiming her, but I also knew if we never met again, she would eventually be forgotten.

In those days I regarded such an attitude as an example of my acute mind, which tended to give everything a value and mere personal relationships attracted very little. Should I learn a bit from Ned, it was worth staying, and I would woo Susan at every opportunity. But if that day proved a disaster for us both, then I would be gone by the same time tomorrow, leaving Hastings, and all those who lived there, in my wake.

The rest of the day fleet still lay beached, and there weren't any extra, so I guessed those out last night had yet to return. There were men a plenty about though, mostly attending to individual boats and odd pieces of tackle. A small fire burned on the pebbles and several crowded about it as one of them cooked breakfast on the face of an old shovel. Some shouted or waved a greeting at Ned who grunted a monosyllable reply, but he made no effort to stop, introduce me, or explain my presence in any way.

"I'd be setting drift nets ordinarily," he told me, when we reached his boat. "Only that might take all day and half the night, and I can't be sure I wants to waste so much time on the likes of you."

I made no response. It was hard to take offence at what was such an honest statement; besides, I didn't know if I could stand being in a boat for any period with him. Ned was hauling a great bundle of netting out of the punt, and proceeded to carry it away. I stayed where I was; he had given no instructions and I was certain help would be asked for if required. Instead I turned my attention to the boat.

This lay exactly where we'd left her a few hours back, and in the fresh winter daylight I noticed the name *Katharine*, painted on the prow. As we had discussed, she was considerably smaller than any of the others, although the rig also appeared a good deal more simple. I could see now that, though she might be old, her equipment was well maintained, and understood why Ned should wish to keep such a personal tool under his control. To allow an unknown hand aboard, especially one who freely admitted no expertise and must appear little more than a boy, was probably quite a concession.

Once more, the impression came to me that it was a decision he might be regretting; things said in the warmth of an evening's conversation can feel very different in the cold light of morning. That would explain his gruff manner, although it was equally clear he had no intention of going back on his word. This both relieved and worried me in equal measure: whatever I had let myself in for was not to be easily avoided.

When Ned returned a few minutes later he was carrying another net. This one was smaller, and mounted on a short wooden beam. It also contained an assortment of cork floats within its folds. He laid it on the ground, collected several lead weights from inside the boat, and began attaching them to the net with knots tied far too quickly for me to follow.

"We'll go for a trawl," he said finally standing up and brushing his hands together. "There ain't a lot of wind, but enough, and we may find some flats off The Hards – or even cods, if we's in luck." He paused and appeared to sniff the breeze before continuing.

"But whether we are or whether we ain't, we'll know within a few hours, so that's all the time we're going to waste." He caught my eye, and stared straight at me as if for the first time. "First we gets yon boat on the wood," he said, indicating the nearby pile of poles. "Then chawk her down the beach."

It must have been the longest speech he had addressed to me since the previous evening, and I was quick to act upon it, laying out a short line of poles spaced about four feet apart, as we had done last night. The stern of the boat was heavy, but together we eased it up, while Ned kicked a pole at the head of my line under it. I straightened the wood in time for him to lift the prow completely on his own. Then, still unassisted, he began to steer the craft over the shingle beach.

It struck me this must be the regular start to his day and to do everything alone would take ages, as well as a good deal of effort. There were other men about and, remembering the co-operation of last night, he could doubtless have asked for assistance. But no one was taking any notice, and I guessed Ned to be one of those who chose not to seek, or give, help if such a thing could be avoided.

The boat made steady progress towards what I judged to be considerable oncoming surf, with Ned holding her firmly at the bows and me collecting those poles passed over and running down to replace them at the stern. I felt like someone involved in a frantic and solitary relay race and was immediately out of breath, but soon *Katharine* was lying on wet sand, with the seas lapping inquisitively at her hull.

Ned clambered into the boat and began attending to her rig, so I took the initiative and collected the wooden rollers, returning them to their spot higher up the beach. When I had dumped the last, I saw Alex's mop of red hair coming over the brow. Behind him was the odd collection of buildings below the cliffs that I now knew to be Rock-a-Nore. He saw me and waved; I waved back, but knew instinctively that pausing to speak with him would not go down well with the old man. Instead I raised my hand once more, before pointing at our beached boat, then skipped back down the beach. I'd only met Alex the day before, but already felt I could trust him to understand.

Ned greeted me with a surly look on my return. "You done with the yarning then?" he asked.

I said nothing in reply, but noted he had the boat's largest sail spread out, apparently ready to raise.

Despite what he had said, there appeared to be little wind, and I wondered vaguely what use the sails would be. Just how we were going to get the boat through the surf was also a mystery; the waves were steadily beating against the sand with a rhythm I was finding mildly hypnotic, but there was apparently no time, or need, for explanations. Ned swung himself back out of the boat, before grasping hold of the prow, and began pushing her for the water.

I joined him, and the boat was soon properly afloat, although it was not deep enough for Ned, who insisted on taking her well into the foam. The sea began coming up at a height that ranged from one to almost three feet, and we were in danger of allowing it to lap over our boots when he finally relented. Nodding briefly at me, he began to turn her, hand over hand, until the bows were aiming for the open water.

"Keep her be," he said in rare instruction. "I'll raise the main, and will hold us long enough for you to board."

The last part was added almost in condescension, although Ned's attitude had softened slightly now we were actually in the sea. I hung on gamely to the punt's upright stern. The small craft bucked and wallowed badly enough as Ned boarded and locked the rudder into position, but grew far more unstable when he raised the upper spar that carried the mainsail. He glanced back at me, and I guessed it to be the nearest I would get to guidance so, waiting for the time when the boat was at her lowest, and dodging the horizontal boom to the rear that was perfectly placed to knock me into the water, I pushed myself up and over the stern.

I almost made it in one go and would have, had my unaccustomed boots not held me back. But there was inertia enough to allow the inevitable fall to be forwards, and a solid pile of netting caught my weight. Ignoring Ned's roar, which might equally have come from humour or disgust, I clambered upright.

In fact the wind proved quite sufficient. Now we were on the water and with what, to me, was a vast expanse of sail raised, I could feel the boat powering forward. Already we were passing out of the breaking surf, and I needed to cling on for fear of being thrown out. Ned was half standing by the foot of the sail and looked far more secure. He still held the line running from the main's lower corner, and appeared fascinated by the boat's motion.

"Set the jigger," he muttered without turning, I guessed he meant another sail. The only option seemed to be the small affair on the boat's stumpy mizzen mast. There was also a bowsprit – I already had the term chalked up from reading pirate stories as a boy – but it was not run out, and lacked canvas, so I duly turned my attention aft.

The boom at the stern was not dissimilar from the bowsprit, and every bit as long. It too was unrigged, with the far end almost touching that of the forward spar. There was another, shorter, pole lying with it, and the two were joined by a length of tanned canvas. I eased the boom further over the stern, and went to make it fast, although Ned was there ahead of me and, bending over, had it secure in a trice. A line, connected to the spar, ran up the mast, and it took no great insight from me to realise this must be the means of raising it. The yard ran freely at the first pull and, once more, Ned fastened it, before fussing with another line that brought the sail round slightly, apparently forcing it to become stiff.

The whole procedure could not have taken more than a minute: two at the most, but now we were sailing reasonably sweetly, and the shore we had so recently left was already a fair distance away. Ned had secured the line from the mainsail and was stepping over piles of net and rope, and soon had the bowsprit out. A small triangular sail of a slightly lighter hue was run up, and the boat quickly settled, then began to move with true purpose. Ned was still forward and, steadying himself on the mainmast, looked back at me. Then, for the first time, the set expression relaxed slightly.

"That was done well enough for a first effort," I was told. "So, why not ride your luck, and try a trick at the helm?"

Chapter Five

Alex's story

As soon as I met Nat, I had him for a chub. Not of the first order and, don't get me wrong, I liked the cove. He had a good sense of humour and it was a change for me to be on social terms with any fresh face.

To be straight, I didn't have so many friends and could not afford to be choosy. And I enjoyed being in the know for once: despite being a year or so older than me he clearly had a good deal of learning to do and, though he might consider himself the man of business, actually was as bobbish as they came. Men of business don't turn up in out of the way fishing towns expecting to find work, especially if they know nothing about fish.

Still, I was glad he got off all right with old man Coglan; for all their faults they were good people. I'd known he would get a decent meal and probably a bed for the night. It was surprising to see them together the next morning, though: by then I'd have thought Nat would be well on his way to Rye, or wherever he fancied his fortune lay. As it was, he obviously intended to crew the punt, which almost made me laugh out loud.

Ned Coglan was not one of life's natural teachers, he hardly suffered fools and was incredibly protective about anything under his care. This included his boat, his tackle, and especially his daughters. And that was another area where I didn't expect Nat to make much progress: if he were interested in either girl, he was set for trouble, and not just with Ned.

Jenny was as sweet as they came, but somehow I couldn't see them pairing up. Maybe it was to do with her blindness but, despite appearing vulnerable, she exuded a barrier strong enough to deter any casual enquiry. To put it bluntly, Jenny was too damned independent. Susan, on the other hand, was far more conventional, but even she had hidden defences.

The other lads called her Sniffy Susan, and she always was a stuck up old trull. Like most of the kids in the area, we had gone to the same dame school in Grange Street, but she kept herself very private. I was a couple of classes below her and, in those days, young and sweet enough to avoid much of the trouble my father left behind. I might even have been regarded as relatively popular, but Susan Coglan wasn't. Of course, we all felt sorry for her, losing her mother as she had, but the Coglans weren't the only kids in such a scrape – before long, I was also down one parent, and there was no need for her to be quite so aloof.

Gave herself airs and graces, she did, and it was clear we were all decidedly inferior. I don't think anyone liked her then: apart from Tilly Medcalf, of course, but then Tilly could never think ill of anyone.

The older lads used to wonder what Sniffy Susan was hiding and, a few years later, several tried to find out. They all came back disappointed though; even Shaky Johnson, who considered himself quite the stag. He became frustrated to the extent of actually proposing, but still never got further than snatching a kiss and a bit of a squeeze. If Nat had any ideas in that quarter, he was due for an uphill climb.

Apart from that, there was nothing actually wrong with the Coglans, and they'd have probably done well enough if Ned's wife hadn't died young; especially if the boy everyone supposed her to be carrying had been born. As it was they were suffering, and no one likes seeing a family in distress. I'd offered to crew for the old man a number of times, but Ned always turned me down flat, even though we both knew a punt could only be made to pay with two hands aboard.

He was probably worried about my family's problems or, more to the point, that they would rub off on his, and he may have been right. I survived in Hastings, but no more than that, and had to choose where I went, and with whom I associated. Most of the day fleet accepted me, but some people, and some places, were definitely off limits. In effect, I needed to be careful pretty much all the time. Such a way of life is not particularly easy, so I understood Ned's concern but, had I been able to crew, we would have both benefited. Whenever I approached him on the subject though, he was adamant, and eventually I gave up asking.

It was a shame: sailing with Ned would have been the ideal berth for me, and I'd have done anything to get afloat. But I didn't take offence: with half the town set against me, rejection was common and easily borne, although watching the two of them sail off together did feel a touch galling. It was good to have made a new friend, and I didn't begrudge him landing a job, even if I'd lived in Hastings all my life, whereas Nat had hardly been in the place a full day.

I made my way slowly up the beach; the day stretched out ahead of me, and looked like being no better than any other. Then I remembered Tilly.

She would be working from noon at *The Anchor*. Her parents were pretty strict, and didn't usually let her out before then, while I was not a welcomed caller. But there was a market being held that day, and it might be worth my passing by on the off chance.

And I was in luck; she came out of the side door ahead of me and began walking up the street. She was wearing her mother's old coat, and carrying a trug, so I knew I had been right. I did not call out, as that would have attracted attention from passers by, but soon caught her up and we turned right into a side street, taking the route we had used a dozen times in the past. It was one that, whilst still ostensibly heading for the market square, would actually take about five times as long: luckily neither of us was in any hurry.

It was one of those rare sunny days in winter that are particularly pleasant. There was hardly anyone about, so Tilly put her arm through mine, which I always thought was splendid. I told her about Nat, and the Coglans, and she said she'd seen him, and what a rum cove he appeared. But there was nothing nasty in it; Tilly was never one to judge people. And then, just as we were coming out of Winding Street and finally getting nearer to the market, it all went horribly wrong.

She'd had to drop her hand from my arm as there were more people about, but we were still happy together. I was telling her some nonsense or other, and we were thinking of a way to meet up again that evening when I heard the footsteps from behind. There wasn't even time to turn, just a searing pain as someone's boot connected with my spine. My jaw closed with a snap and I found myself flying forward, landing painfully on one side and in the dirt.

I knew from their laughter it was the Luck brothers. They had done the same, or similar, on countless occasions and I grudgingly admitted they had more cause to hate the name of Combes than most. Any damage caused to their family had been done by my father though, and in the course of his duty. Now he was dead, I failed to see what purpose was being served by persecuting his sixteen year old son. But then some folk just can't be explained.

Despite all of the Lucks being older than me, I could have handled any one of them easily enough on their own. They hunted in packs however, and were annoyingly partial to solitary ginger haired lads for their prey. I rolled on to my knees and dodged the stones that followed, then saw Tilly looking down at me. She wore a dreadful expression of pity that no lad should ever see on his girl. The Luck brothers called out a few more insults but soon left, as was their style, and Tilly helped me up and began knocking the dirt from my clothes. My back hurt and I had a small cut to my lip, although mainly it was the indignity of it all which really hurt. That and the fact such things happened all the time.

Tilly continued brushing off the dust; I tried to stop her, as people were starting to look, but she was not to be dissuaded. By then it was getting late and I had to leave: we could never have gone to the market together. I was usually safe enough in crowds although to openly associate with me would have done nothing for Tilly's reputation. And so I went, but did so with the hurried promise of a meeting later that evening. I'm not sure if the Luck brothers' attack had persuaded her but, if so, it might almost have been worth it.

Nat's story

Ned and I began by working an area of rough ground a little way offshore. It was, I gathered, one of the many local fishing spots that included such places as Cliff End Hard, Shelly Bank, Hole in the Sand and what sounded like simply The Mud. None of this was told to me directly, of course: I had to work it out from Ned's cryptic comments and the occasional monosyllabic grunt. But, ignoring the old man's gift for communication, it soon became apparent a different language is needed when speaking of the sea, or fishing in general. Whether this is to confuse, a means of exclusion, or simply out of spite I never discovered. Basic terms, such as left and right, require translation while specialist names for anything from parts of the rig, the weather and even types of fish, glory in titles such as Mitch, Sammar and Flukers. Even words I recognised and was comfortable with like cod, which could be singular or plural in Ninfield, acquired an additional S when a Hastings resident referred to them in bulk.

Actually releasing the net, or shooting the trawl, turned out to be relatively easy; everything was laid out ready and Ned handled the procedure with little assistance from me. We then spent the best part of two hours sailing towards the incoming tide in what turned out to be bright, if crisp, sunshine. There was little conversation at first, but the old boy's attitude softened slightly and his presence almost became companionable as the little boat pressed gently through the water. At no time did the punt create more than a ripple at her bows and slowed further as the morning wore on, so much so that I started to sense it was turning into a successful day. And that was even before Ned became communicative.

In stages, I learned the history of the boat, that she had been passed on from his father, yet was always called *Katharine*, which had been his mother's name, as well as his late wife's. From there we easily moved on to families in general. I elaborated on mine, telling of my mother's death and then it felt completely natural for him to speak more of his wife who, I gathered, died whilst carrying a child. The law of averages dictated it would have been a boy, and the pain of losing both her, and an unknown son, was still with him. I also discovered Jenny to have been blind since birth and, more importantly for me, until recently Susan had been betrothed to a young man in the town.

My ears pricked up at the last point. She would have been marrying into one of the largest families in the area; they already owned two luggers as well as a part share in a third and I guessed the proposed wedding would have been the end to most of the Coglans' money problems. Even if Ned himself were not taken into the family firm, Susan would have been provided for and, in turn, be in a position to look after her sister. But the relationship was brought to a close quite suddenly, and by his daughter.

Ned said he was sorry, but I could see no evidence of disappointment. Indeed, I'd already judged the Coglans to be a close knit unit and, whatever the loss of financial security, guessed him glad to keep Susan at home. The time spent trawling was by far the best of the day; I learned much, and not just about fishing.

Hauling in the catch was more complicated. The sea seemed reluctant to give up its own, and the last stages of landing what had the makings of a considerable catch all but turned us over on two occasions. The boat needed to be kept with her stern towards the net, but our wind, which had been reliable if light until then, chose that time to turn playful. Ned cursed it, me, the fish and much of the world in general, although when the last of the load was eased over the side, the net released and everywhere was suddenly filled with slipping, slithering bodies, he became truly elated.

Moving about was more difficult though; there was no place to stand that did not wriggle beneath your feet, and a good deal of weed, rock, numerous crabs and other sea life also came aboard, and filled every vacant space. But, by working methodically, we stowed the net to the stern, collected what shellfish were worth keeping, and set about sorting the sivver.

There were fewer of the flat fish, but any deficiency on that count was more than made up for by some truly strapping cod. Ned was more than satisfied and, in his benevolence, even credited me with partial responsibility.

I had yet to learn a major truth about fishermen; living both close to the elements and with the threat of death constantly about them, they tend to hold a strong faith. Some follow conventional religion, others rely more on superstition, while more than a few, like Ned, wander from one to the other like spiritual harlots. But it was clear he felt I had brought him luck, and my star was very definitely in the ascent. And it was then that the worst part of my day began: the knives appeared, and I all but disgraced myself as we turned to gutting the catch.

Anything Jenny had done to those dead fish the previous night was nothing in comparison to what was asked of me then, and my fundamental instincts came to the fore. Fortunately Ned was too distracted by his own work and, as we were using separate boxes, I thought I was getting away with the few creatures I was forced to slice to a painful death. The flat fish were ignored by me completely: I could see that any form of precise surgery would be impossible on such apparently meatless carcasses, although the cod turned out to be no more obliging.

They were wet, wriggling beasts, far larger than sprats, and still holding enough life to deal a hefty blow – my nose throbbed from an uppercut delivered by a monster determined to carry his fight on to the very end. After half an hour I was covered in gore, yet had contributed surprisingly little to my personal stash, whereas Ned seemed as clean as he had been all day, and was already starting to fill his third box.

"We can leave the rest for the auction house," he said magnanimously as *Katharine* drew nearer to the shore. "They'll take 'em whole as easily and there ain't no sense in wasting good fish. That one offend you, did it?" he added, glancing at my current effort.

I was silently grateful, both that the gutting was over and he had not taken the opportunity to chastise me.

It was clear we would have our work cut out bringing in the sail with so many fish still flapping about our feet. Alex was standing on the last of the sand; the tide had obviously altered, and we must come in higher up the beach, which I considered to be a good thing, as the boat was heavily laden. Ned had other ideas though, and appeared far more concerned.

"Would have been better to have caught it lower," he muttered, his face creased in concentration. "A few more hours, and there'd be no trouble. But we'll get a fairer price, being the first in, and it don't look like so many have sailed."

I was now more certain than ever the rest of the fleet had not returned from the day before, so was silently hoping our outing would prove truly profitable. Then Ned said the words that chilled my heart.

"Take the helm. We can't keep her locked in this breeze, and you're gonna have to steer mighty careful."

I looked at him in horror, but could see reason in what he said. The wind was continuing to dodge from one point to the next, so setting the rudder would be of little benefit and only one of us was skilled enough to take in the sail. My last attempt at helming had not been a total disaster, but the breeze was more reliable and Ned stayed beside me most of the time. Now there was so much more at stake, and it would have to be me alone that held the boat straight as we neared the beach.

"Take it steady, and make sure to keep yon bows aimed so," he muttered, fumbling with a sheet. "If you allows the wind to catch our beam we'll be over. Then you can wave goodbye to all we caught, including those you've been a murderin'."

I settled myself next to the tiller and released it. For a while, little was required of me but, when Ned dropped the mainsail and jigger, the boat became far less easy to manage. The wind whipped past, one moment over my right shoulder, the next my left; then, for one horrifying period, died completely, and we began to drift round, no matter where I placed the helm. It returned soon enough, but by then we were at a disadvantage, and the boat remained determined to lie beam on. Ned shouted, and I knew the punt was in imminent danger of capsize. I fought to bring the head back, but could make no progress until a lucky gust corrected us, and I had her on course once more.

I was vaguely aware of Alex shouting as we drew closer to the shore, and felt the boat rise and fall when it entered the surf. The jib came down, then the tiller lost all effect, and our stern began to creep round yet again. I tensed, but felt the solid thump of land hitting our prow. In no time Ned had skipped over the side to join Alex and then we were being held firm in their grip, with both being securely rooted to the wonderfully solid ground that I had never fully appreciated until that moment.

I learned a bit more of the size of our catch as Alex and I began to carry it to the top of the beach. Rather than the meagre boxes of the previous night, there were more than twelve stuffed full with cod alone, a further five containing flat and other fish, as well as two leather buckets of crabs.

"Glad to see no spiders," Alex said, staring into the latter. I noticed his lip was cut, but didn't like to enquire further. His statement intrigued me though, and I asked him to explain. "Get a couple of spider crabs in your trawl, and you can be days mending the net," he said, adding, "worse than a bunch of cuttlefish, they are."

"Do they cut up the nets as well?" I chanced.

"Na, cuttlefish are more likely to stain the whole lot black," he replied. "Makes it worthless."

There was so much still to learn, and I felt my spirits sinking. Ned seemed unusually chipper though: he was even whistling softly as he chalked the amount up on a slate, and signed off his catch.

"Best old man Coglan's landed this year," Alex told me as we went back down the beach and finished securing the boat. "Got to be ten stune if its one. Trawled The Hards, you say?"

I nodded, knowingly, even though I had no idea what a stune was.

"You were fortunate the rest of the day fleet weren't about to get in your way, but there's usually a good sivver to be had round there. And catching cods and flat together is quite a feat." Alex considered for a moment as he showed me how to release the trawl, and lift the net free of the boat. "Old Ned was lucky you were with him, else he'd never have got it landed safely."

I felt a little reassured by what he said.

"Any damage?" Ned asked, approaching.

"Nothing more than a couple of tears," Alex told him.

"Very well: leave that with me, you two can take a stroll," he said gruffly, before handing a half filled bucket to Alex. "Give that to your mother with my regards; some are a bit mangled: they were gutted by a proper chub, but all will cook up well enough. Besides," he added, considering, "She's a sensible woman and was never too fussed by appearances."

Chapter Six

The early release came as a wonderful surprise, although I was far too hungry to think of doing anything other than finding something to eat. Alex suggested we take the fish back to his home and I agreed, in the hope it might lead to a meal. His house was actually along Rock-a-Nore and stood rather perilously with the rest, under several hundred tons of cliff that appeared only too ready to crumble.

The building was compact, plain but solid, and one in a series of eclectic dwellings and small businesses that lined the road. We passed the pot house where I had eaten lunch three doors further down. It came as a shock to realise that meal had only been the day before. I wondered vaguely if the girl there might remember, and be willing to feed me again, but Alex was chattering nineteen to the dozen about the size of our catch, and wasn't to be diverted. Instead he led me towards his own front door, which opened directly onto the street, and charged inside.

I followed, and heard a more gentile reply to his shout. The sound came from somewhere deeper within and I was hurried through a formal sitting room furnished with chairs and tables that were inexplicably covered by white sheets. Alex continued to what was a combination of back parlour and kitchen. A middle-aged woman who I took to be his mother stood in front of an ironing board with a table to one side that was heaped with laundry.

"Alexander Combes, what have you done to your face?" she asked. Now that I looked properly I could see a bruise as well as the busted lip, and felt mildly guilty about not mentioning it before. This wasn't the kind of thing lads comment upon, though: mothers are inclined to be different.

"Walked into a door," Alex told her blithely. "Didn't like it, so I won't be doing it again. Meet Nat, he's helping old man Coglan out in *Katharine*," he raised his thumb to indicate my presence. "They been going after cods."

There was that strange plural again, but I was getting used to it by then.

"Ned Coglan taking on a hand?" the woman, said in wonder. She was older than I expected, but still very attractive, and with a welcoming look that exuded warmth. "Well, there's a thing. Experienced are you, Nat?"

I went to answer but Alex thrust the bucket of fish under her nose saying: "No, he don't know nothing, he don't – take a look at what he did to these."

His mother glanced down, pulled a face and then said, "Oh dear," followed by a somewhat wistful, "but lovely fish."

"Have we any proper food?" Alex asked. "Nat's one of those who keeps wanting to eat, and won't shut up about it."

"Your uncle and brothers are going to try for the last of the herring tonight, so we'll be having a meal first, and early," his mother told him firmly. "Until then there's apples in the store or you can have a slice of poor man's wedding cake – no, I tell a lie: Seth finished all the bread pudding. Apples it will have to be." The woman was obviously going to say more but Alex had already disappeared through the back door.

"Ned all right is he?" Mrs Combes asked conversationally, although I noticed she was listening intently for my answer.

"Ned's fine," I replied, not actually knowing him well enough to truly be certain. "He sent his regards with the fish."

"Did he say anything else?" she persisted, and I shrugged.

"Only that you weren't one to be bothered by appearances," I added lamely.

It had clearly been a throw-away remark, and I only repeated it because she asked, but Mrs Combes laughed out loud, as if I had just related some tremendous joke.

"Ned's an old dog," She told me with the air of a confidante, adding, "send him my best, do," and I promised I would.

She nodded, apparently satisfied, then asked: "So, what brings you to Hastings?" I could tell she judged it to have nothing to do with my skills as a fisherman.

I tried to look nonchalant. "It was while on my way to Rye," I said, as if important business were involved. "Fell in with the Coglans and thought I might help them out for a spell."

The woman smiled politely before placing her current iron back on the range and collecting a fresh one in its place. A small explosion followed as she spat, expertly, on the face of the hot metal, then more steam as it was plunged down upon her current piece of laundry.

"An' he ain't made a bad start," Alex informed her, returning to the kitchen and lobbing an apple in my general direction. "More fish than old man Coglan's raised in many a long time. I'd say there was at least ten stune, if not more."

"I caught the apple and wondered if rubbing it on my shirt would be considered rude.

"Ten stone of fish?" his mother repeated, far more clearly, and another mystery was solved.

"Cods, was it?"

"Mainly cods," I replied casually, before biting into the apple. Really, I was getting rather good at this.

* * *

"Dad said the sivver weighed in at nearly fourteen stune. An' the price was good, as few went out today. We had the early London cart almost to ourselves: ain't that a thing?"

It was late, Susan had returned from her work at *The Cutter*, and I was lying in my makeshift bed next to the range.

"Yes, we did well," I said, hoping she would join me on my level. I had taken my trousers off to sleep, and it was only an old blanket that kept me decent.

"Well? You probably saved us," she replied and, as if in agreement, sank down on the rug beside me. "It's been a bad winter for the herring and things were getting more than a little seedy. I've not known it as tight as this: we were down to my wedding guinea!"

"Wedding guinea?" It was an odd expression, and one I had never heard before.

She flushed slightly. "It's a local custom, probably don't have it about your way." She spoke softly, as if of foolish things. "When a couple have a daughter, they puts a shilling aside every year.

45

Then, when she reaches twenty-one, she has a guinea. It's supposed to be a dowry, or maybe pay for her wedding; I don't know."

"But you already have your guinea." I pointed out. I knew she was older than me but had thought the gap to be only a year or so.

"Yes, but that's a refinement. Dad could see we might become short of money after mum died, so he made over our guineas when he was able."

"What about if she's ugly and doesn't get married?" I asked.

Susan looked rather shocked at that, but nothing had been meant by it.

"Oh, I don't know," she replied. "Maybe she just keeps the money."

I'm not the most perceptive of folk, but sensed that a bubble may have been burst somehow, and hurried on.

"So, how much would you have, if your father hadn't advanced the money?" It was a cheeky question, but was meant to bring her smile back, which it did.

"Ah, that's for me to know, and you to find out." she told me playfully. Then her face fell again. "But it's a silly custom and all a bit irrelevant. We had to spend Jenny's guinea just before Christmas. And mine – well, let's say I regard it as temporary."

"Now I'm here, that might change," I chanced.

"Indeed it might," she agreed and we laughed together, although I was way ahead of her, and already spending the money.

"But I really can't thank you enough," She continued more seriously. Her eyes were looking deep into mine and I was feeling aroused and uncomfortable at the same time. As a matter of fact she could have thanked me easily, and I would have shown her how, but was far too green. Instead I lowered my head and broke the trance.

"I've learned quite a bit from your father," I said.

"Well, I know he appreciated your help," she was still gazing straight at me and I looked back, almost reluctantly, as she continued. "He can be a bit crusty sometimes, but means well. And he's taken a liking to you."

Now I felt embarrassed and actually a little guilty, knowing only too well exactly what sort of a liking, if Ned caught me talking to his daughter without my trousers on. But suddenly I was prepared to take the risk, and clearly so was she.

"Were you serious, about getting a bigger boat?" She asked next, surprising me by the change of subject. "Do you really have such a thing in mind?"

I wasn't sure what to say; to me it was the logical solution to their problem, and I was prepared to help out for a while. But the enormity of it all was starting to sink in.

After that evening's meal I had taken a turn alone along the front. It was dark and the first time for me to be properly alone since arriving in Hastings. I had time to think without distractions and decided it would be good to learn how to sail, and even fish, if my inherent dislike of the things did not turn out to be too great an obstacle. Living in the same house as Susan also had its attractions but, were I to get a larger boat, it would effectively mean committing my life to one family.

Foreign travel still beckoned and, however well the Coglans might prosper under my care, I sensed there were no fortunes to be made in Hastings. Consequently I had more or less made up my mind against staying too long. Now though, with the two of us alone, barely inches apart, and her lips so tantalisingly close, it was a different matter.

"A boat's not out of the question," I said, temporising. "But I would need to make sure I truly want to be a fisherman. And, in time, your dad might not find me the ideal hand." Even then I was aware of my somewhat selfish tendencies, and could have been trying to warn her.

"There is no real rush," Susan replied, and I was a little uncertain as to what she meant. "In fact, if you bring home a few more sivvers like today, we'll be able to wait forever – or not at all."

The last part confused me further; I went to reply when she lent forward and kissed me long and firmly on the lips. I was startled or, to be more accurate, shocked. She had made the first move: something I was completely unprepared for.

Susan was obviously of a totally different calibre from any woman I had met before but, by the time I realised this and was thinking of ways to use it to my advantage, she was standing and making for the door. I almost followed, but remembered the need for that damned blanket just in time.

So I stayed where I was and watched her go, while the last thing she had said stayed in my mind. Did she mean she could wait forever, or was that 'not at all' significant? Her touch remained on my lips as I settled back in the bed. One thing remained indisputable: whatever was on offer, I had no intention of waiting any longer than I had to.

Alex's story

I had no intention of waiting any longer than I had to; eleven o'clock was the time agreed, and I was there well before. The door opened bang on time though, and Tilly slipped out, closing it behind her in one swift, silent movement. We began to walk along the street. It was cold, but dry, after such a glorious winter's day, and now quite quiet. Sober folk had been in bed for several hours and most would be asleep, but still we did not talk. *The Dolphin* was ahead of us and I grew wary as we approached; the place was still very much awake, and was one of those where I was not welcome. But we did not have to pass; the Tamarisk Steps were close by, and led up to the east cliff: that huge mass of rock which hung over all our houses. Tilly guided me to the left and we began to climb, hands held tight and our breath appearing as steam in the crisp night air.

As we reached the top it was obvious we were totally alone. There was no moon but the stars were bright and, by their light, we moved away from the cliff edge and on towards the nearest thicket. There it was soft and dry; the young bracken had yet to break through, but we had grass and some higher brush that sheltered us from any wind. Her mother's coat was so much larger than mine and made an excellent bed on which we both settled: our eyes not meeting in sudden embarrassment. Then we turned to each other, and I saw her regarding me in an odd, dispassionate manner; as if I were food about to be devoured, or an article of clothing that might, or might not, be worn. Finally she leant forward and held me in an embrace that took over my entire body. And suddenly life in Hastings became a good deal happier.

Chapter Seven

The days ran into weeks, then months; spring came and I grew used to crewing for Ned. I also improved, almost to the extent of becoming quite cocky. He could always outmatch me in boat handling and general fishing skills, but I think I brought something else to the partnership that was, grudgingly, accepted.

It did not take me long to realise the old man's natural disinclination for social contact could work to our advantage. The main fishing fleet relied upon their combined skill and experience for mutual support. Together they would discuss the day, taking into consideration a vast number of factors such as weather and the time of year, and their collective minds gauged where the best catches would be found. Ned, being the grumpy old soul he was, never involved himself in such gatherings but, wherever the day fleet went, he was inclined to follow, if only at a suitable distance to prove his independence. It took a while, but eventually I persuaded him on a totally different tack and, one morning when the fleet set out for haddock off Newhaven, we tried for flats on our own, and further to the east.

It began as a disaster: the two of us returned with barely half a load of plaice, whereas the other boats were filled to capacity. I was decidedly in the dog house but, when it came to pricing, Ned's spirits picked up. The value of our sivver was boosted due to its rarity, and the difference more than made up for any defect in bulk.

And after that it became easier. We would discuss the options on our way to the boat, see where the main fleet was heading and decide upon our own destination, which was usually at odds with the common consensus. He had the ultimate say, but I was learning a good deal about the habits of fish and occasionally would be listened to. Of course, if we were successful, it usually turned out to have been Ned's decision in the first place, but I was not particularly worried. The team worked: we were making money, and that pleased us both.

As I grew better at my work, I also became stronger. Arms that had never exactly been scrawny, started to develop sizeable muscles, while my waist slimmed down, and managing the nets or swinging gloriously full boxes of fish out of the punt became just another part of the working day.

And I discovered more about my adopted town and its various areas: the Pier Rocks that ran out to the south-east, providing the nearest we came to shelter on such an exposed beach. Then there were the Tamarisk Steps; a thin stone staircase set off the street that apparently rose up almost vertically to the cliff above. And finally Rock-a-Nore itself: I gathered the name originally referred to 'rocks to the north' – presumably the huge cliffs that towered threateningly over much of the Stade, its small businesses, net huts, fishing fleet and houses alike. Those cliffs were especially evocative and, I felt, symbolised Hastings and the tenuous hold it had on existence.

The massive craggy formations dwarfed all beneath them, appearing solid and dependable, but were actually liable to crumble at any time. The town gave the impression of being equally strong, with a vibrant fishing industry and many inhabitants who were on the verge of affluence. But, as with the cautious farmer who only plants one type of crop, much depended on a single enterprise. Take that away, or deplete it significantly, and everyone would starve.

I learned about the Hastings folk as well, especially my new friend, Alex. More to the point, I learned about his qualified acceptance in the area. We had taken to each other immediately, and he was obviously well liked by some, being a genial, hard-working and capable cove. But there were a defined few who went out of their way to avoid him, while some carried their apparent antipathy even further.

This surprised me at first, especially as those who expressed a dislike seemed to share no common ground, and ranged from local traders, through neighbours and even included a few of the fishermen. A greeting, or some request from Alex would be ignored, or spoken over; open doors were left to swing back into his face, or an ostensibly benign passer-by could accidentally trip or barge into him. At other times things were not so subtle; he might find himself being shouted at in the street, and once we were both assailed by a hail of the finest Stade pebbles thrown by a bunch of louts. They stopped as soon as we turned on them of course, but plenty of folk were about, and no one intervened, or even apparently noticed.

I soon came to realise there were places he and I could go and be welcomed, and those better avoided: locals who would be civil, and others that looked studiously past us both, for when I was with him, I became included by association. And in time I grew to accept this, especially when I realised the Hastings fishing fleet itself was divided.

Some of the boat's crews gave and accepted assistance from all, and were happy to include us both, while a few of the larger vessels ran to no set schedule and kept very much to themselves. It was pretty clear the elite made a smaller contribution to the auctioneer's carts, and no great hardship to deduce that smuggling was rife. From there I went on to realise Alex's late father, or rather his chosen occupation, had much to do with the ill will his son encountered.

It was something he and I never discussed in detail, but Jenny told me Mr Combes had been a minor Customs official who died in circumstances that were, at best, doubtful. Whether or not this had been an accident, or the result of action by a local gang, was still unclear, but such an occupation was liable to attract local contempt. Of course, transferring the ill feeling to his sixteen year old son was unfair on several levels, but I was also starting to learn that Hastings folk were like so many small and insular communities; they had selective memories, and were not particularly rational in their thinking.

Alex had two older brothers; stout lads with jet black hair and not the kind to be messed with, while his mother was safe in the protection of their uncle, Saul Robbins. He was a sour old puss, quite undeserving of Mrs Combes' openly affectionate nature. I gathered the avuncular title was used loosely, and that he was not the first to have earned it. But Alex's Uncle Saul was also a man of influence, so it was only his young, red-haired, supposed nephew who took the punishment.

Happily the situation did not appear to worry my friend unduly and he took it in his stride. We soon settled into a routine that included the many glad to associate with us, while all but excluding those who were not. For two young men there was plenty of interest to be found in Hastings and more than enough safe places to go, so we spent much of our free time together. After a few weeks, Ned had been shamed into allowing me a decent proportion of the new found wealth my presence brought, and we were able to spend most Saturday nights in a pot house. There we could drink and yarn like the two old chums we had become, and let those who didn't approve of Alex go hang.

We never went to *The Cutter*, where Susan worked; it was one of the places Alex was not welcomed, and I was secretly glad. In any drinking establishment the serving girl is liable to end up the butt of japes, or an object of drunken fancy, and I could not have tolerated Susan being treated in either way. She and I had an unspoken understanding: our relationship was yet to develop beyond the occasional kiss, and there was little basis for my overprotective behaviour, but I had no mind to spoil things.

For roughly the same reason, we avoided *The Anchor*. Alex was developing an eye for Tilly Medcalf, the girl who served me that first lunchtime. I was reasonably sure she had yet to return his advances, but neither was she discouraging them, so most Saturday nights were spent at a neutral tavern at the end of All Saints Street. It was known as *The Stag*, a name that was to have a deeper significance for us both later, but then simply represented a place to relax after a hard week's work – somewhere we could play skittles or crib, and mix with the more amiable fishermen of Hastings.

But on one particular evening, Alex was not with me. He could be a clumsy oaf, and always seemed to be taking the odd trip, or tumble. Most times this happened while he was alone, and I used to wonder why: the cove was as sure footed as a mountain goat when with me. This time it was a simple slip, but he must have landed badly, and had injured his back. I'd teased him about it of course, but actually think he must have been quite hurt; in any case he took to his bed, forcing me to drink alone.

The evening was not the same without him. I'd stowed two lonely pints and was about to drop back and see how he was when a couple of men entered, and I heard one ask for me by name. I had rather grown used to being anonymous in my newly found world, so the first thought was they must be friends of my father: both looked unusually presentable in clothes with the mark of town about them, and lacked the distinctive bearing of seamen. But they were also well known and even respected in *The Stag*. I was pointed out, and quite a few heads turned as the couple made their way to where I sat alone at my table.

"Mr Audley?" one asked; he was the better dressed of the two, and also slightly podgier. The other appeared far more powerful and looked as if he would be happier in some form of manual labour.

"Name's William Bennett, though you can call me Billy," the chubby one informed me. "Word is you might be looking for a larger boat, and I'm in a position to help."

My suspicions were instantly aroused. The fishing industry was new to me, but I already had a reasonable handle on commerce. Billy Bennett was presenting himself as a man of business but, if such were the case, I sensed it to be business of the worst kind. Then he went on to say more and, despite myself, I became intrigued.

"My family have an interest in the Phillips' boatyard; you've probably seen it, at the far end of Rock-a-Nore." I had, and knew most of the boats on the Stade were built there. "We got a lovely little vessel almost ready for delivery. Not too large, and set up proper. Sad thing is, them what ordered it are unable to honour their commitment."

Billy was noticeably scant on details, but it was clear the cancellation was causing him problems. I wouldn't have wanted to be in the buyer's position – Billy and his friend were not the kind you would purposely upset. He suggested we took a brief walk to inspect the boat "And then maybe I can buy you a real drink," Billy continued, looking contemptuously at the dregs of my pint. "Somewhere a little more exclusive and suitable for men of business and taste."

It was early spring but still light, and I had nowhere particular to go. There was also money in my pocket; it had been another good week, and I was feeling mildly prosperous. Of late the idea of getting a larger boat had become more attractive, especially as Susan and I were obviously growing closer, so I agreed. After all, little could go terribly wrong if I just looked the thing over, and I have never been adverse to anyone buying me a drink.

As decisions went, this turned out to be one of my worst.

Chapter Eight

An hour later I was comfortably installed in what were indeed far more select surroundings. We had walked a fair distance through the back streets of Hastings and were now a good way from the relatively crowded Rock-a-Nore area that I was starting to regard as mine. From the outside, the place hardly appeared a commercial establishment at all; it blended perfectly with the other quietly prosperous houses in the street, and carried no sign or indication it was open to the public. But inside there were all the usual beer parlour fittings, and they really did appear to be a cut above.

Polished wood gleamed back at me at every opportunity, from the furniture and picture frames to large areas of dark wainscoting that covered most of the walls. And the tables were not just left bare. We had lacy cloths, and small slate coasters for the drinks, while one was topped entirely in stone and held a selection of cheeses and cold meats. Underfoot, a series of thick rugs quietened our step, as well as adding a muted quality to the entire room, and there were far more than the expected number of candles burning.

Despite all this, it was quiet for a Saturday night. Three men sat about one table in the corner playing cards, and there was a larger, central, party who were heads down and deep in discussion. One girl was there to serve, with another sitting by herself in the corner. The second might even have been a guest, except that no woman would enter such a place alone – in a town like Hastings, the very act could sully a reputation forever. But this was clearly no ordinary pot house, and the woman concerned; pretty – well dressed, and only a few years older than me – appeared quite content and attracted no obvious attention.

At the time, I remember thinking it would be a fine place to take Alex: for far too long he had been the one who knew all the Hastings haunts; I longed to surprise him and prove I could also find my way about. But then I was also under no illusions; with him I rarely got the upper hand. Besides, I was not entirely sure of the route and with no indication outside, we would probably get terribly lost.

But the brand new boat had been impressive. Not as large as most, but a good deal bigger than the punt. And well made from fine wood, that included outer strakes of seasoned elm, which I already knew to be the best of sea going timbers. Most of the upper works were even payed or painted already. There was a minimal amount of attention needed to the palarum – the small hold that would contain a catch – in itself a refinement I found particularly attractive, and the twin masts had to be stepped and rigged; otherwise she was ready to go.

I knew a boat of such a size would need another hand, besides Ned and myself, but I had been chewing the idea over vaguely with Alex, and he was pretty keen to join us, should something materialise. Having him as additional crew might not fit entirely with Ned's plans, of course, but I was starting to get just a little bit ambitious. Besides, the old man had done all right with taking me on: why not one more?

The evening was pleasant, spring was on the way, I had a good amount of beer inside me and was having serious thoughts of taking the craft for myself. Alex could be the third hand, with Ned, though skipper, effectively in my employ. Even finance was going to be easy: Billy, who claimed another appointment, had left me with his older brother, Robert, and it appeared a lack of money was not the stumbling block it might have been.

Rob Bennett was older, leaner and, I should say, brighter than his brother. His thin face made him look slightly shrew-like, and narrow eyes, with a perpetually damp lower lip hardly adding to his beauty. But there could be no doubting he was a man of consequence, and blessed with a sharp mind I was quick to respect. Consequently I decided to allow him a little more of my time: but then any of us can make mistakes.

"You'll need three in total aboard, including the skipper," he told me with all the airs of an expert fisherman, even though he looked nothing like one. "So that'll be one share for the hand, two for the captain, and two for the owner," he looked pointedly at me, to make sure I was keeping up, before ending, "then a share for the boat and one for the tackle."

I nodded vaguely. I had been sticking to beer, despite the offer of gin or brandy, but still my head was swimming.

"All we does is add another share for the financier," Bennett told me, as if it were the simplest thing in the world. "But even that has a limit. You pledge we see a guinea a week: no more, no less. And a guinea's nothing – there's not a boat on the Stade that couldn't do that. Otherwise you can make what you wish: take on two crews if you feel so inclined: fish herring at night, and cods by day – it's all the same to us. As long as we see our weekly bean, there's no restraint."

My mind ran over the figures; it meant eight shares, and would effectively rule out taking on a fourth hand. But Rob was right; I had already learned a good deal about the economics of fishing: a boat of that size and in such good condition should not need more than three, and was bound to bring in a reasonable return. We might easily do away with a permanent boy ashore: between us, Alex and I would manage, or there was even the chance Susan could give up working at *The Cutter* and help out. It all seemed perfect, and certainly worth exploring further: I was interested.

"How long would this last?" I asked, conscious that any such arrangement should have a time limit.

"Oh, it goes on," Bennett told me, almost sadly. "We have to make something out of this as well, you know. As it is, my brother and I will be putting out for the boat, so there will be a goodly time before we even see a return on our investment. You're a man of business, Nathaniel, and must understand."

In the face of such a compliment, how could I not? But, in truth, it sounded reasonable.

"You can buy us out at any stage, of course," he continued.

My attention was roused further.

"Current building costs are just on the hundred and fifty guinea mark. We'll set a price of two hundred, and that won't change: it gives us a healthy return on our investment, which is fair on all parties. Bring us that much in gold at any time, and the boat will be yours, no questions, and all drawn up legal."

Again that seemed a decent arrangement: frankly I was

astonished and not a little impressed.

"But don't decide now," he said, surprising me yet again. "You've had a glass or two, and it is Saturday night; enjoy the rest of your evening." He looked around and raised a hand, attracting the eye of the woman sitting alone in the far corner. She was far more attractive than I had realised, with long fair hair and a pleasant dress that showed a good deal more white skin than I was used to.

I knew the last point should not shock me; everyone said the fashions were changing and, even when the French were our enemies, anything appearing in Paris was immediately copied in Britain. The girl also wore more rouge on her face than was customary in Hastings, but I was quite prepared to allow for that as well: this was a decidedly better class of drinking establishment after all.

"This is Caroline. She's a good friend; she likes the same things I do – the same people," he explained, winking to me alone. "Caroline, why don't you get Mr Audley here another ale, and something for yourself? I'm sure you two will have a lot in common."

It was an odd request. Even when in company, women never bought or even ordered drinks. But Caroline appeared eager to comply and turned towards the servery without question.

"She's a nice girl," Bennett told me. "All mine are, that's why I choose them. And let's be realistic for a moment, Nathaniel: they does as they are told – anything they are told – so you'll be having no trouble there." I was momentarily taken aback as his meaning became clear and he patted me paternally on the shoulder before turning to go. Then, as if remembering something, he paused and added, "the truth of it is, I'm one of those lucky people, and trouble is something I rarely encounter."

* * *

"What do you know of Billy and Rob Bennett?" I asked Alex the following morning as we were filing out of the morning service. Although attendance was not compulsory, most of Hastings went to one of the two main churches and the division between them was almost as wide as that of good and evil. St Clements, in the High Street, looked after the gentry, or those with aspirations in such a direction, whereas that near the Coglans' house in All Saints Street was for more humble fishermen and their like. With a deceased Customs official for a father, and an uncle who owned a lugger outright, it would have been far more fitting for Alex to join his people at St Clements. But Tilly Medcalf's family went to All Saints, and so, of late, did Alex.

I had been particularly careful to attend that day as well; there was a decided chill in the air during breakfast: my staying out late the night before had been noted and not approved of. None of the Coglans knew any details, of course, and nothing so very terrible had taken place: I'd left Caroline after that one ale. She was a pleasant enough companion and I'm sure would have proved every bit as compliant as Rob Bennett intimated, but I had a lot to think about and, rarely for me, did not feel the need for female company. Besides, I also had an absurd impression the offer would remain open, and could be taken up whenever I wished.

"The Bennetts?" Alex repeated, before whistling softly to himself. "Not a lot, but enough to treat them with caution. Some say they've roots in the Ruxley Crew – a bunch of roughs what plagued us a few years back. But the truth is the Bennetts have an operation every bit as big, even if it ain't so obvious. An' not much of it is good."

The crowd outside church was especially noisy; there was talk of an important international treaty being in danger, and some of the men were in quite a lather. But I needed to speak more with Alex: specifically I wanted to know about the Bennetts.

We eventually found a quiet spot overlooking the Stade. Despite being asked, Tilly had not come with us and I guessed her parents' refusal to allow the two of them to meet was to blame. Such an embargo made no sense to me, especially when Alex came from a reputable family. Revenue work might not be universally popular, but at least it was a respectable calling – I completely missed the point that, rather than his late father, it might be Mrs Combes, and her succession of gentlemen friends they objected to.

In those days I was rather too keen to judge people quickly, and on my own assumptions.

"I've been offered a boat," I told him, when we had finally found a patch of grass that was soft and dry. Alex was still suffering from the after effects of his fall, and was treating himself as if he had been seriously hurt. It was a good spot: we looked out on an empty blue sea and the March sun was starting to warm us properly. "She's brand new, from the Phillips' yard, and all but ready for work."

"That'll cost," Alex said, easing his legs into a comfortable position and resting back. He pulled a face but I could tell he was interested.

"There's no money needed up front," I continued. "We would normally have to commit an eighth share, but they are willing to accept a guinea a week."

"A guinea sounds like a fair enough deal," Alex replied. "You'd be unlucky not to clear at least ten yellow Georges in most big boats. But you mentioned the Bennetts, and if Rob and Billy are involved, I'm not sure if I likes the sound of 'we'."

"I've spoken with them both," I assured him, in my best sophisticated man of the world demeanour. They might have other interests, but this is a legal matter, and all seems reasonable enough. I'd judge them to be above board."

At this Alex began to choke and it took a deal of coughing before he finally got his breath back. When he did, his face was red and neck quite swollen. "First time I've ever heard the Bennetts called so." he told me, gasping. "Tilly's folks deal with them, so do most of the traders round here and, don't get me wrong, both can be trusted up to a point. But they play by their own rules, which ain't the kind most folk recognise. And legal don't usually come into it."

"Exactly what other kind of business are they involved in?" I asked, after digesting this.

He shrugged, and recovered some of his equanimity. "Where shall I begin? Smugglin', owlin', anything a bit off the level. They even run the local nuggin' house in George Street."

I was surprised, not so much by the range and areas of the

brothers' enterprises but more the nature of the last. Was it even possible I had spent last night in a brothel, and hadn't realised it?

"But basically smuggling's where they specialise. The two of them can supply pretty much anything." Alex continued. "Spirit, tobacco, dry goods, lace, works of art – if that's what you fancy. Ask me, there's little Rob and Billy can't get hold of, and none of it comes duty paid."

This was all news to me, and I was feeling a bit less sure about the arrangement, although still could not see how their other interests could affect my buying a boat.

"They think no one knows," Alex added blithely. "More to the point they think the Treasury don't know, but the Revenue men would be fools if they didn't. Fact is, there's booty everywhere in Hastings if you look, an' little that can be done about it."

Alex rarely spoke of his father; and this was the first time the Revenue had ever been mentioned directly, so what he said amazed me all the more.

"But if the Customs are aware of dealings in smuggled goods, surely they must act?" I said, all thoughts of my venture temporarily suspended.

"It ain't as easy as that," Alex replied. "There's little use arrestin' those what carry the stuff; most magistrates maintain the possession of contraband is not a crime, else they'd be roastin' half the population, including theirselves. They only start handing out fines when it's bought or sold. No, it's the suppliers, like the Bennetts, that are the problem, and they're the very devil to catch.

"Dad disrupted quite a few landings in his time," he continued, his eyes now set on something in the far distance. "Some were arrested, maybe a few fined or transported and Charlie Luck was even scragged. But he was just a lander; there was never sight nor sound of Rob or Billy, or any of the others what put up the money, come to that. So when the dust's settled, they just go out and hire a load more men, then carry on as before."

I shook my head; it all seemed incredible.

"They mainly work from *The Cutter* and *The Dolphin*; both are warehouses for their gang."

"I had no idea," I told him.

"It's why I'm not welcomed thereabouts."

"But your father's dead," I reminded him, with the delicacy of youth. "They can't carry on a feud, not on his family."

Alex shook his head sadly. "Don't believe it," he told me. "The old man was particularly good at his job. Charlie Luck weren't the only runner he saw swing, and he shot Stoner Catt dead with his own hand."

I was quiet for a moment. What he said made sense and also answered a lot of questions: in a community like Hastings, bad memories might be inclined to fester.

"What about *The Anchor*?" I asked. "Do they work there?"

He laughed and shook his head. "No, Tilly's father buys for certain, but he won't store for them. Yet still he thinks the Revenue might close him down, even though he's nothing to fear on that score." Alex sighed. "In truth, even *The Cutter* and *The Dolphin* are pretty safe. All raiding them would do is put your Susan and the other honest ones who work there out of a job. The trade might be disrupted for a while, but it would only be driven elsewhere. And the Revenue would prefer to know where it was, rather than needing to guess."

My mind was reeling, not so much at the extent of the Bennetts' interests, but the Treasury's apparent acceptance of them.

"But in the end Rob and Billy are only men of business," Alex continued. "And as straight as any in that line," he said, looking directly at me. "You can deal with them if you wish, but make sure you keeps that in mind. And if either of them shakes your hand, count your fingers after."

"So you think I should forget about the lugger?" I asked, now resigned to the fact he would put me off, and even secretly pleased.

"No, from what you say it is a deal worthy of at least a decent look," he said, surprising me yet again. "The Phillips' yard is sound, even if it does have Bennett money behind it. I know the boat, and watched it being built. The Dawkins family what ordered it are near neighbours of ours. Jack Dawkins has hurt his back, so he's not going to sea no more and the brothers aren't clever enough to skipper. Mind, I'm surprised they ain't just selling it at a loss. Doubling on the Bennetts is known to bring about the worst possible luck."

I saw his point, and couldn't think of an answer, which was a rare occurrence for me.

"Or maybe they haven't been given a choice," he mused. "Say what you want about Rob and Billy, they ain't short on finance and are always happy to take a risk or two. P'r'aps they don't actually need their money back straight away, but would rather see you stitched up nice for the rest of your life."

"Oh, I can buy them out at any time," I interrupted quickly, despite the fact that his words had chilled me. "Two hundred guineas, and the boat's mine outright."

He looked at me as if I had just admitted to believing in bogeymen.

"Two hundred beans is a pile for a boat that size," he told me. "Besides, where are you going to find such money?"

Then I became cross; Alex was probably my closest friend, and I owed him a lot. However it was getting just a bit tiring, always having to defer to him as the expert. I was a year older for a start, and the one with business acumen. And I had been educated far beyond any parochial dame school. Yet for all my expertise it was clear he actually trusted me no more than any of the other small minded fishermen on the Stade. "Oh, I can raise funds easy enough," I blustered. "And if we're talking the rest of our lives, I've no intention of spending mine helping out an old man on a rowing boat."

"Fine, then take the offer," he said. "I've not your head for commerce but will be a loyal crew, you know that. In any case, you may be right: the Bennetts have no reason to see you go under – it would be like killing the goose that lays the golden egg."

Once more I had secretly hoped he would persuade me otherwise, and now felt as if I had talked myself into a corner.

"For all I know it could even be the start of a whole ruddy fleet," he continued. "And you wouldn't be the first to make proper money out of the Bennetts – why do you think so many deal with them?" My mind wandered as Alex rattled on, and I started to think back to the start of our conversation. The two men had been quite happy to give me a legal document and, whatever Alex might say, no one could argue with the law.

"But just give it a week or two to think things over," he was speaking more gently now, and the change in tone broke into my thoughts, forcing me to take notice. "Because it is important," he looked me in the eye. "And you may well be talking about the rest of your life."

Chapter Nine

Alex's story

He was a mate and all that, but there were times when Nat really used to annoy me, and that was one of them. I'm not saying he hadn't done well; he and Ned Coglan were turning into a fair old team in that little boat, and bringing in sivvers way above any the rest of us would have credited. And he'd also beaten me to a job on the water, so I was even mildly jealous. But just because he had succeeded in crewing a half-pint punt, it didn't mean he was ready to handle bigger boats. And to get himself tied in with the Bennetts was just plain folly. Admittedly I would be there to help, and the prospect of not having to wait for Seth to get a shake on certainly appealed; we could be working Nat's lugger within a week. Being afloat wasn't everything though; the boat would have to pay its way and, however sound the agreement might have looked, it was still going to be drawn up by criminals.

But I had my own problems to think about, and left Nat to worry over his. Tilly had been strangely preoccupied at church and we only had the chance of a couple of words. She said she was going straight home, and wanted me to follow. Her family were a religious lot: *The Anchor* always closed on a Sunday, and Tilly was not usually allowed out. So I guessed her parents must have granted her permission: that or she was intending to defy them. But Nat had been so insistent in needing to talk that I felt obliged to listen to his ramblings first, despite him wasting an hour or so when I should have been with my girl.

I sensed trouble, and wanted to see her badly. What I had told Nat was quite correct; her parents always refused to store contraband. They did buy it, though, and not just from the Bennetts. Despite all his God-bothering, Jack Medcalf was a regular customer with several smuggling gangs and, even though Dad had been dead for several years, mine was never the most welcome face at their house. But still I was determined to call and see what was amiss.

And my luck was in. When I knocked a few minutes later, she opened the door herself and, without even calling to her parents, headed straight out into the street.

"Hey, steady!" I called, but she was already running down Rock-a-Nore, leaving me to close the door behind her.

There was usually no contest between us: at every age I had been able to outrun Tilly, but on the previous day I'd bumped into the Luck brothers again. They'd taken great delight in escorting me up to the first stage of the Tamarisk Steps before letting me tumble down to the bottom all on my own. It was a trick they had pulled countless times, but never failed to amuse them, although I was getting just a little tired of it and, on this occasion, had been hurt more than usual. When I tried to run, the pain made it impossible and soon I gave up and simply limped along in her wake.

I remember feeling particularly miserable as I did. It felt as if my life to date had been revealed to me in one horrible dose. I had no proper job, and was hated by half the folk in Hastings, who constantly clawed me off for no other reason than my father had chosen a certain occupation. And a newcomer like Nat could come in, find employment, make money, and, before anyone knew it, would have his very own lugger.

I went to shout again, but was worried in case my doing so would attract attention other than hers; as it was Tilly, bolting down the road in a flurry of coat tails, boots and petticoat, was drawing several eyes and more than a few comments. I watched as she turned a hard left by *The Dolphin* and began heading up the Tamarisk Steps. It was the place of my latest humiliation, but I was pleased to see her take the turning. Her destination was now obvious and I was content to follow at a more sedate pace.

I found her on the edge of the east cliff, sitting looking out to sea with both arms wrapped about her knees. She was still panting from the climb although her face looked quite washed out. I noticed she had her mother's old coat on, so had obviously been intending to leave before I called and might even have been waiting for me. For a moment I wondered if I had been wrong to follow and would not be well received but she greeted me readily enough, and I slumped down painfully next to her. Neither of us said anything at first, then she flung herself back with her arms above her head and breathed out as if she was expelling her very last breath. I eased my bruised body into roughly the same position and for a moment we were at peace. The sun was hot in our eyes and mine were closed as I felt her reach for my hand. Then, with our fingers closely entwined and both our hearts beating wildly, she spoke.

"Alex, you won't think ill of me, will you?"

"I could never think ill of you, Tilly," I told her, and it was the absolute truth.

"You may, when you hear what I must say."

I simply shook my head.

There was a terrible pause, then she spoke again and her voice was much softer, as if she dared not say the words. "I am with child."

Nat's story

The talk outside church was quite correct. On the following Tuesday a newspaper arrived at the coffee house on Market Street, and within hours most of the town seemed to have read the thing, or at least know what it contained. It appeared the French were expecting us to evacuate some island in the Mediterranean and they also had their eyes on our possessions in Egypt. It was utterly unfair, of course – the paper was adamant – simply the Bonaparte brothers throwing their weight around. And, being a London edition, it could be trusted. War would be resumed within weeks – there was little doubt of that although, at the time, I failed to see how events taking place so many miles away could possibly affect a small and insignificant fishing town in England.

But Hastings remained a mass of speculation and gossip; most traders instinctively put up their prices, and a Navy officer came down to talk to the fishermen, trying to fool us into joining some sort of volunteer defence force. I should have taken more of an interest, but had other things to consider at that moment which, being as they directly affected me, were far more important than any global conflict.

The Bennetts' offer was still preying on my mind. After speaking with Alex, there was only really the Coglans to consult, and I wanted to come to a definite conclusion myself before I did. And that was the problem; my thoughts just would not be controlled: one moment Rob and Billy were nothing but trouble, and I was dead against any involvement with such people: the next they seemed to have come from nowhere to give me the very chance I had been craving. I was desperate to lift myself, and hopefully Susan, out of that mean little house and up to the station we properly deserved. Were the boat to prove a success, there could be little opposition to our marrying. We were both under twenty-one but Ned would be all but forced to give his consent, and I should have no compunction in declaring both my parents dead. Then the old man and I could continue to work together, but as father and son-in-law. I even had wild dreams about larger houses and a place in the lugger for our offspring to take over in time: to me it was perfect.

Susan had yet to agree, of course, or even hear of the proposal but, to my tender mind, that did not present so very great an obstacle. She might have been slightly older than me, but had received far less schooling and I felt confident of winning her round.

But what did concern me was the detail in the offer; that and the thought there might be something obvious I had missed. It all appeared simple enough by anyone's standards, and I had gone over it a dozen times in my head, looking for tricks or catches and finding none. Still some internal alarm bell kept sounding, and I was disconcerted and troubled.

My fears were not based on any facts or evidence, and could easily be written off as either a hunch or simply nerves – both things that had no place in the mind of a shrewd man of business. But, however much they lacked substance, and however hard I tried to ignore them, the doubts remained. And for as long as they did, a part of me would stay convinced there must be a flaw.

I knew I could ask to speak with the Bennetts again, but instinctively felt reluctant. It might give me another crack at Caroline, but the same inner feeling told me further talking with the brothers would do no actual good. Privately I admitted to myself I had met my match there. As far as business was concerned, either could talk me under the table and I might easily find myself committed before even presenting my case to the Coglans.

So, for the next couple of days, the stumbling block remained. Each time I considered throwing the offer over, either to Ned alone, or with the rest of his family, I was afraid something hidden for so long would suddenly be revealed. With Ned's erratic instruction we had made money, and I had some bright ideas, but was by no means an expert when it came to the mechanics of fishing. Even young Jenny had a greater understanding of the art, while I was becoming so used to having most of Hastings tell me where I was going wrong that, when it came to commerce – a subject I considered myself an expert in – my confidence was starting to flag.

Any one of them might easily make me look a fool in front of the others and the same warning feeling inside told me I could not bear the humiliation. Should such a thing happen, I would have little choice other than to leave everything that had become stupidly important to me: Hastings, the boat, the house on All Saints Street and, most of all, Susan's promised love.

Ned and I had taken the punt out the day before, and on several occasions I considered broaching the subject with him then, just the two of us. That way a refusal might be easier to hide. But whenever it seemed we would have time for quiet conversation, something came up to spoil the moment. I felt the longer I left it, the harder it would be and the climax came the following Wednesday afternoon. The tides were such that Ned and I had come in before three and, being it was the one day Susan did no work at *The Cutter,* we were eating early. Consequently I knew there would be time enough to talk things through and reach a proper conclusion, however dreadful that might turn out to be.

"There's a brand new lugger ready in the Phillips' yard," I told them casually when we were finished with the food. "And I've been given first refusal."

Jenny had been collecting the plates, and Susan was in the act of rising from the table. Both froze as they considered my words, while Ned stayed pretty much motionless. He had just lit his pipe, and appeared more concerned that the thing should stay alight. For more than a second I wondered if I had truly spoken at all, then Susan flopped back into her chair, as Jenny continued collecting the crockery, but clashed the plates together in a way that was quite unlike her.

"The Phillips' yard, you say?" Jenny asked, as if she had missed my telling her the time. "That would be Jackie Dawkins' boat. They've been talking about it at the market these last two months or more."

"It might have been ordered by him," I agreed, keen to establish myself. "But it will be me who launches her."

Nobody spoke, although Ned was now hidden behind a positive cloud of tobacco smoke.

"I've been given first refusal." I repeated.

"By old Elsiver Phillips?" Susan enquired. I shook my head but said nothing and was glad when she did not pursue the matter.

"So who are you going to get to sail her?" she asked instead.

"Alex Combes will crew," I stated. "Together with myself. And I was hoping your father might skipper."

Still the old man did not speak.

"I was also a thinkin' one of you could act as our boy ashore; that is if you do not wish to sail with us as well."

"A boy ashore is no job for a lady," Ned said with emphasis, and finally breaking into the conversation. "And there will be no Coglan female going aboard a boat, not while they lives in this house. Neither do I want the Combes boy."

Nobody challenged him, but I felt it a particularly weak protest and sensed we would have few problems in that quarter. Actually I was quite encouraged; if this was his highest card, it would be easy to trump.

"How shall you afford it?" Jenny asked next. She had seated herself at the table and was fixing me with those green,

71

compelling, but otherwise redundant eyes.

"I shall be committing no more than an eighth share to the financier," I said grandly. "And there is the option to buy her outright, should I so choose." The words came out with far more confidence than I was feeling, but they had the desired effect on my audience.

"An eighth?" Jenny questioned. "Is that all?"

I nodded. "Five in total for the crew, two for the boat and tackle, then one for the man who settles with the builder – although I have negotiated a special rate, and will never have to pay more than a guinea a week."

"And who is to maintain her?" Jenny again.

"I have not decided," I replied, giving her what was probably a slightly patronising look, which was totally wasted.

"But someone else will have," Ned retorted. "If Phillips' is the builders, they will expect to keep her straight an' all."

I shrugged; that also did not seem so terribly important.

"Phillips' is the most expensive yard for miles about," he continued. "That's why they do mainly buildin'; no one can afford their prices for repair."

Still it did not appear to be a great problem. "There is the share for the boat," I replied. "And another for tackle; it is a brand new hull and should suffice."

"And if it don't," Ned persisted. "What then?"

The question hung cold in the air. I supposed there might be an instance where repairs or maintenance cost more than the money set aside; in which case...

"Then it has to be taken out of the crew's share," Ned answered the question himself.

"It should not come to that," I chipped in hastily. "The share for the boat will cover."

"Not if Elsiver Phillips has his way." Ned was almost shouting now. "Not if you're in to him, or rather those two jesters what's behind his business. You'll pay through the nose for work that's wanted, then more for any what's not. And you won't be allowed to go elsewhere, not if I knows them and their ways."

Up until then there had never been any mention of the

Bennetts' involvement, and even now I noted they were not referred to by name. But clearly all about the table knew them and their reputation.

"Jackie Dawkins showed me the boat, just afore he wrenched his back," Ned went on in a more mellow tone, and again I was relieved that another delicate point was not being pursued. "T'aint a lugger, not proper: more a puffed up three-quarter bog, though I'm sure they're charging lugger money for it. An' it's set for a dipping lug; a good enough sail, but one that needs seamen to manage it. Jackie has two stout sons what were bred on the water; how am I expected to cope with young Combes and a lubber like you?"

His words came as a surprise, and caused me a good deal more pain than I could have imagined. All the time I worked with Ned, he had been a hard master. I rarely encountered praise but, to his credit, those moments when I did disgrace myself were usually allowed to pass with no more than harsh looks, followed by a period of sullen silence. This was the first occasion when he had ever properly acknowledged my lack of seamanship, or used such an insult to my face.

"If you would prefer a change in the rig, I am certain it might be arranged," I said, shaken slightly, but still thinking fast.

"And so you begin to pay," the old man said with obvious satisfaction, before puffing hard on his pipe once more.

I chanced a look at Susan, who had been uncharacteristically quiet for some while. She did not meet my glance, but seemed more intent on examining the worn surface of the old pine table.

"What think you, Susie?" I asked gently.

She raised her eyes and turned to me. "I think you don't know what you're about," she said plainly. "You mean well, and have the best intentions for us all, but this is hardly the way, and I could not support you in it."

The silence lasted for all of five seconds. Coming from her, such a comment was utterly damning and ten times worse than anything her father might have said. My worst nightmares were being realised and I started to reel. Little was required at that point; a few words along similar lines from Jenny, or another one of

Ned's snide comments would have set me totally aback.

And I also knew then, in that brief time, there would be no returning from this little episode. Even staying on at the Coglans' house would be futile; my one effort to change things was about to end in disaster. Nothing I suggested in the future would ever be taken seriously: I may as well go that very evening – by nightfall I could even be in Rye.

And then Jenny did speak, and it was not the additional damning I had been expecting, but something else; something that took us all by surprise.

"Well at least Nat is making an effort," she said quietly, and in a manner that was almost offhand. "Which is a darn sight more than either of you ever do."

We all looked up and I noticed her expression, usually so placid and good humoured, had acquired the look of pure fury.

"Oh, you both work hard enough, we all know that, just as we know how difficult things are, and how ill done by this family has been. But you never so much as raise a hand to do anything about it."

I think we were all slightly stunned and, for a moment, thoughts of the Bennetts and my new boat were forgotten.

"Yes, life is rough, and we just about cope, but that is all we do. No one ever thinks of a way to improve. It is as if you wished to be in such a state: that it makes you comfortable and happy to remain in your tidy little ruts. Well let me tell you, life is not so very rosy for me."

Ned reached across to his daughter but she sensed his movement and snatched her arm away before he even touched it.

"You wish to know how dark things can be? Well I shall tell you. I have few prospects: no dashing young man is going to turn up on my doorstep and try to whisk me off or make my life the better." She was facing her sister now, and I noticed Susan flush slightly as the words hit home. "Neither have I known a loving partner, and neither will I – probably ever." Now she switched to her father, "Nor will I marry and start a family, or do so many of the things you both take, or have taken, for granted. Nat has not been living here more than a few months, yet we have never fared better or eaten so well. And now he has a plan to improve our lives further, one that might not be the ideal solution, but is a hundred times finer than anything either of you have ever produced."

There was absolute silence as she drew breath.

"And do we thank him for it? Or do we make him feel a fool for even trying? This isn't his family, yet he cares enough to try and help, and has already done more than anyone in that direction."

Susan and Ned exchanged awkward glances, and even I felt a mite uncomfortable.

"When Nat first walked into this house, so did the best piece of luck the Coglans have known for a many a year. And how do we repay him? Make him work all hours for a handful of small change, then sleep on a rug by the fire, like some pet dog." Her face flashed back to her father. "You may tell yourself you lost the son you wished for, but had you treated one half so bad, he would have been long gone by now."

Ned winced as if he had been physically hurt, but Jenny continued.

"Yet Nat is still here, and has the cheek to think of a way we may improve ourselves. And do we listen? Do we say thank you? Or do we find fault, and quibble with details, while making him feel small into the bargain? Perchance he should be thanked for taking the interest: frankly I cannot see why he does."

She paused, as if to think, then turned her anger on her sister. "And you, Miss Prim, holding back her favours until exactly the right man comes along. How large a choice do you want? You've already turned down half the boys in town. Dick Johnson was stupid enough to fall in love with you; he would have made a fine husband; and his family's large enough to support us all. But no, I was forgetting: you're special – superior: well, if it goes on much longer you'll also be alone."

Susan had flushed a deep red, but was saying nothing.

"Then Nat comes along, and you keep him hanging on a cotton, dealing out the odd kiss to keep the poor cove interested." She was looking directly at me now, and I must admit to withering a little under her sightless stare. "Honestly, it would do them both good to meet some true bad luck once in a while."

I swallowed, but stayed as quiet as the others. Despite her lack of sight, I wished she would turn that look somewhere else.

"Yes, mother died young, and yes, we all miss her," she continued, mercifully turning back to the family again. "But the mother I remember wouldn't have sat down and done nothing while the world collapsed about her shoulders. If Nat had not come by that evening, we were all heading for the workhouse. He saved us and, if he has an idea which might improve things further, I think we should at least listen. Listen, and support; would that really be so taxing? And don't we owe him that much?"

Chapter Ten

After Jenny's little rant I did my best to get out of the house as soon as I could. I knew Susan wanted to speak with me, and think even Ned would have liked a few words, were the chance given. Both looked extremely crestfallen, but I had no intention of delaying any longer. As far as I was concerned, Jenny's speech gave me full licence to buy the boat. Whatever Alex might have said, I now had the Coglans' support: that was all I needed, and I could not get myself to the Bennetts' place too quickly.

It was as if a strange force was powering me; I found the place first try and, once there, all was over swiftly enough. There were two men behind the door, and I boldly asked for Rob Bennett, feeling mildly important as I was obviously on speaking terms with the owner. But these were not the kind to be impressed and told me curtly he was unavailable. Billy was there though and, after I had given my name and business, I was grudgingly allowed in.

I remembered the main room from my last visit. It was a week night, yet a little busier, which surprised me. Several tables were full and each, I could not help but notice, held at least one attractive woman dressed far more provocatively than was usual for Hastings. Despite the reason for my visit, and that last, plaintive look from Susan, I found myself searching out Caroline, and was oddly relieved when she was missing.

As soon as Billy appeared the doubts began. He noticed me, and walked across with a polite enough smile, but there was another look in his eyes that was more worrying. I'd seen such an expression before, usually on a man placing kings down over my jacks, or selling stingo which turned out to be small beer. Of the two of us, Billy Bennett clearly considered himself the winner and, were it not for the momentum I had already built up, the deal might have been abandoned there and then. But it was going ahead and, despite my misgivings, I followed him into a tiny office beyond the main room.

It took less than two minutes to produce the papers:

everything was drawn up as if I had been expected. I read through the legal wording with a reasonably practised eye; my father had taught me well, as far as such things were concerned and by then I was especially cautious. Nothing stood out as being particularly unfair, however: as Ned predicted, the maintenance was down to the Phillips' yard, but there was also a three month warrant on the hull and surely a brand new boat could not need to spend so much time in their hands? The purchase clause was also plain enough; just as Rob had promised in fact, and I remembered Alex's comments about the Bennetts being trustworthy within their own rules. With nothing I could honestly raise in objection, there was little option other than to continue: all that was needed was to sign and date the papers, and the deed was done.

"You'll have a name for the boat, I am thinking." Billy said, indicating a blank space left for the vessel's title. It was something I had not considered, and my first thought was for *Susan*, but something stopped me, almost as I went to write it in. The look of defeat on old man Coglan's face came back to me suddenly. It was evident that Jenny's tirade had been both stored up and right on target. But, true or not, it could hardly have been pleasant for a daughter to lay into him so. Whatever the girl said, and however right she might have been, he was no longer married, with his wife being taken in the most tragic of circumstances. Consequently it was with little effort that I wrote *Katharine II* in the space, and then signed my own name at the bottom. It made little difference to me; I felt Susan was as good as mine already and, if it cheered the old boy up and left him feeling a mite better about the whole deal, the concession was well worth making.

By then Billy Bennett's expression had lost all trace of victory. I was just an annoying detail that needed to be cleared up before he could get back to whatever pleasure he was planning for the evening. No offer of food or drink came and Caroline certainly wasn't mentioned as I was bustled out of the door, with instructions to meet again at the boat house the following morning.

Walking through the back streets of Hastings, I felt a strange mixture of emotions. So much had happened over the last few days, yet the strongest one was of pleasant anticipation. After all, I was heading back to the Coglans' house as something of a hero; a man who was to pluck the family from the depths of poverty bringing them, if not wealth, then at least a more secure future. My copy of the agreement was safe within my coat, while my mind held the memory of Ned's look of regret and what I hoped might be an unspoken promise from Susan, so I was prepared for a good evening. Of one thing I was quite certain: it would be a different house from now on, and there would be no more nights spent sleeping on the kitchen floor.

In the past Susan had intimated she might put pressure on her father to let me use the sacred front parlour as a bedroom; nothing had happened, of course but now, even without Jenny's little outburst, I felt it might: after all, I would be providing the means to make them all affluent. By this time next week we would be working our own lugger and, with Alex as crew, making some serious money. At the end of a hard day, it was only right for me to have a private room to go back to. The last thought was especially appealing: were we to engineer the situation correctly, it could easily be a place where Susan might occasionally visit.

So wrapped up did I become in these foolish dreams that I was not paying particular attention and, when the sounds of whistles, shouts and running feet were registered, it was almost too late. Three men known vaguely from the Stade thundered past and one half turned as he went. He shouted something, but was gone before I had heard his words, or truly understood their meaning. I looked about; all seemed completely normal, then noticed a group of men at the opposite end of the street. They were moving purposefully towards me; large fellows, dressed similarly, and carrying what looked to be small clubs. A young Royal Navy officer was walking beside them and, seeing him, it slowly dawned on me what was about. The press was out.

* * *

But even then I did not immediately react. War had still to be declared. Besides, I held a protection against impressment that was currently sharing a pocket with the Bennetts' agreement. Were I to be caught, it would only need a brief interview with the officer, and perhaps a trip to All Saints Street to prove my identity, before being allowed to go free. But then I had a moment of doubt: the men who had passed me were also fishermen. They must be carrying similar protections, yet were running. And all of a sudden it seemed wise for me to follow their example.

I wasn't so familiar with that part of Hastings, but still felt confident enough to make good an escape. Doubling back, I found myself heading for the Bennetts' place once more, but there was another press gang outside as I approached, and I could hear the sound of more whistles and a door being broken down. An alley to my right seemed a likely bet, and I took it, despite the fact that my followers were now gaining.

The path was uneven and, although my time with Ned had made me physically strong, I was never one to have a great deal of stamina, and soon became out of breath. The alley opened on to a larger road that I recognised, and actually led to my usual stamping ground of Rock-a-Nore. This was a place I knew well, and common sense told me to head for the crowds it usually contained. I was halfway down the road when I saw a group of ten or more rushing towards me. I recognised some as being from the Hastings fleet, and it didn't take a genius to deduce they were also being chased.

My pursuers were close behind, and instantly noticed by the other fishermen. We all turned into Union Street, which should have seen us safe, but as soon as we rounded the corner there was yet another group of sturdy Navy types all but blocking the road. I was panting heavily by then. My companions were mainly from the smuggling boats; the ones who kept themselves aloof and were particularly nasty to Alex, but there was no distinction now: we were united by a common enemy.

"War must have been declared" one muttered, as he looked around for some means of escape. "If we splits up, a few may go free: staying together will only see every man seized."

It appeared a wise enough suggestion, but my original pursuers were now blocking the other end of the road, and there was no place for any of us to actually go. Some of the fishermen banged on nearby doors, but none were opened, even though anyone inside must have heard the noise, and be aware of our plight. One made a bold dash for the first gang and, taking them by surprise, almost passed through, but was tripped, before being quite unceremoniously bundled away. I glanced about in desperation. "Better let ourselves be taken," I said, still breathing heavily. "We've protection, so none will stay long."

"Protection ain't going to do no good," one said. "This is a hot press: all are fair game."

"But that ain't legal," I protested, and drew not a little scorn from the others.

"Legal is whatever them in government chooses it to be," another replied. "Better face it, matey: we's in the Navy."

* * *

The men that held us were a contrasting mixture of regular foremast Jacks and casual louts. None were particularly rough, but then neither did they handle us kindly or sympathise with our plight in any way. The very reverse, in fact; the Navy seamen especially treated the whole performance as something of a glorious jape, howling with joy whenever another local man was dragged into the fold. Most speculated loudly amongst themselves as to how long it would be until we saw our loved ones again, before finally supposing such a thing unlikely with feigned regret. I sensed the majority had been recruited in a similar manner, and were drawing ghoulish pleasure in seeing others share their fate.

In theory at least, we might have put up more of a fight and towards the end outnumbered our captors. The gang were all armed with short wooden staves however, and several had already shown they were not afraid to use them. In addition, every seaman carried an evil looking cutlass that swung menacingly from their waistband and, for the time being at least, appeared to have the law on their side. Consequently, apart from the odd individual bid for freedom that was countered even before it had begun, we generally behaved ourselves. One of our number, who I dimly recognised as being a friend of Alex's brothers, waved his protection in front of the eyes of the young officer who was in charge.

"Plain as day," he was saying, although it was doubtful if the fisherman could actually read. "Says I have the right to continue my lawful employment with no interference from the crown nor its servants."

The officer, who was probably the youngest person present, brushed the paper aside.

"We shall soon be at war," he said, with rare authority in such an adolescent voice. "And are ordered to press from all protections, so no such restrictions apply."

The statement induced a rumble of objections, but the lad had more to say.

"Consideration may be given in the case of foreigners, indentured apprentices, freeholders or members of the gentry; any so qualified will be given occasion to register a complaint with the regulating officer."

His sing-song words did nothing to pacify the fishermen and the protests grew until they overwhelmed anything he was about to add. I have never known such a feeling of intense and combined anger and, for a moment, wondered if all was to end in riot. But, however unfair our capture, there was no doubting who had the upper hand, and the crowd gradually began to accept it. One of the Navy men produced a hand knife and proceeded to slash through each of our waistbands in turn. His actions brought forth little more than grumbles of defiance, but no one stopped him, and soon we were being marched towards Rock-a-Nore, with every man clutching at his unsecured trousers.

We ended up at *The Anchor*, which was in danger of becoming a significant place in my life. It had been commandeered as a Rondy, the regulating men's headquarters, and looked very different: most of the tables and chairs were gone, and there was no sign of Tilly, or any of the usual serving staff. About the room several burly soldiers of the type no one would wish to mess with watched over us. I later learned I was wrong on the first point – these were actually marines – but quite right about the second. They were crisp, with highly polished metal and white leather ornamenting their brilliant red tunics. With gleaming muskets and shiny, fixed bayonets, each looked as if he had just fallen out of some giant's toy box.

An older naval officer who appeared quite senior then addressed us, and received even more respect from the fishermen. He took a moment or two to sympathise with our plight, then went on to explain that war was expected within the month, and Britain was in imminent danger of invasion. Any who had been pressed unfairly would be given the opportunity to protest but, in reality, no loyal Englishman could turn down such a chance to serve his country. He went on to list the pay and living arrangements, which did indeed sound better than the usual seaman's lot, adding that we could expect five golden guineas a piece, should we volunteer now and save the country additional expense. No one did, but the offer had the effect of mollifying the crowd further and, when it was announced that we were to be removed immediately, there was hardly a word spoken in protest.

I am not certain of my exact feelings at that moment. To some extent I was happier knowing, should things turn out for the worst, the Navy might not be such a terrible place, although I still remained in little actual fear of being pressed. My life had contained its share of ill luck by then but not much injustice and, rather naïvely, I felt no one could be forced to fight against their wishes. Besides, whatever had been said, there was a proper legal protection in my pocket: the right of law, together with every man's inherent sense of fair play, was strongly in my favour. The only mild annoyance was that I would have to find my way back from goodness only knew where, and might be late collecting the new boat. But such were small worries, and I was in little doubt my world would resume as before.

The younger officer produced a sheet of paper and began to take down our details. Some who I knew well gave false names; presumably they had their own reasons for staying anonymous but, when my turn arrived, I could see no benefit in lying, and proudly produced my precious protection. The lad, and he could not have been less than three years younger than me, copied down my true name and the Coglans' address, but would say nothing further when asked why the document was not being honoured.

"You can tell them at the Nore," a seaman who noticed my disappointment, told me, not unkindly. "We've pressing tenders anchored offshore; one of them'll get you there in two or three days. If any are here in error, it will be found out then. Don't expect 'is Majesty to carry you home mind, but it ain't so much of a stretch, an' you'll be given a proper exemption to see you back safe."

The Nore: it was a place I had barely heard of, let alone visited, but at least I knew a little more of my fate. Then there was more confusion as a fresh intake of men were bundled into the room.

I saw Alex almost immediately, but it took a good half hour, while the senior officer made exactly the same speech and they gave their names, before I could engineer a place next to him. When I did, he greeted me with a sardonic nod.

"Got you an' all, then?"

"Only for now," I said, broodingly. "I'll be damned if I'm staying."

"It's a hot press," Alex replied simply, using that same term as if it explained everything. "I'm just glad to be wearing my best boots and trousers."

I lowered my voice and asked: "What exactly is a hot press?"

He was used to filling me in on what he took to be common knowledge and often made as much as he could of my ignorance. But this time the stakes were high, and he explained everything as simply as possible.

"Only happens occasionally, but basically no one is safe. They need men for the Navy, so will take all they wants, providing they're not already servin' the king. Some might be able to talk their way free, but fishermen are pretty fair game, so don't hold out too much hope of seeing All Saints Street again for a year or so."

"But I have just agreed on the boat," I told him pathetically, bringing out the contract along with my protection. "Signed the deal with Billy Bennett little more than an hour ago."

"That so?" Alex asked, and whistled with what I took to be respect. "Must say I never thought you'd have the bottom." He took the paper from me, and peered at it for a moment, then handed the thing back. "Better keep that safe, it's worth a darn sight more than any protection."

"Will it see me clear of the Navy?" I asked hopefully.

Alex shook his head. "No, but you might be able to prove the liability is down to you, if the Bennetts try and swing something on Ned Coglan."

I was mystified. "My agreement on the boat has nothing to do with Ned," I protested.

Alex looked at me with tired and unbelieving eyes for a moment. "How can anyone be both so clever, and such a lubber?" he finally asked.

I was lost for words; besides this being a change in his usual behaviour, Alex was the second person in an afternoon to call me by that hateful term.

"You might think yourself the man of business, and probably class both Bennetts as such, but they may not be quite so foolish, and certainly aren't known for sticking tight to the law." He paused, as if suddenly weary, before continuing. "In their minds they've sold the thing, and it's Ned's address on the agreement. If you don't collect, they won't just sit back and think it all a piece of rotten luck; old man Coglan'll find a brand new lugger laid up on his doorstep, and the bills will start from then on."

The thought chilled me to the extent that I even forgot my own predicament. "But he won't be able to fish it, not without me – and you." I added, as the enormity of the problem became clear.

"Well there'll be no one else able to help him out," Alex agreed. "The number of men they took today is going to leave the entire Hastings fleet short of hands. An' with the smugglers just as depleted, money's going to be even more important to the Bennetts: they'll be relying on that guinea a week." His gaze grew distant as he considered the situation more fully. "Why there'll be boats laid up or offered for what they'll make in firewood: ask me, you closed your little bargain at precisely the wrong time."

I was quiet for a moment; all Alex said made perfect sense and, if I could have relived the last few hours, I definitely would. But then I have always been one to look forward, rather than behind, and one fact remained: I had not parted with any money.

The feeling I was both morally and legally in the right returned and I became foolishly outraged: if the Bennetts wanted to chase me for their guinea a week, they were welcome but, while I was in their care, they would have to discuss the matter with the Royal Navy first. And Ned could go back to fishing from his punt: it may not pay as much without me to crew, but the family would survive. "They got nothing over Ned," I said at again, feeling more than a little reassured by my own words. "And anyway, he could never raise that sort of money, so it would be no use hounding him."

"That won't bother Rob and Billy," Alex was definite. "I told you, they work by their own rules. Just because the lugger's not earning, they aren't going to forget their weekly bean. The agreement was drawn up by them, remember, and they can soon produce another: Ned's mark will be simple enough to copy and the Bennetts are behind most of the magistrates in Sussex."

"But that ain't legal," I protested, and not for the first time that afternoon.

Alex gave a short, humourless laugh. "You can forget legal; Rob and Billy only work so when it suits them. Ask me the Coglan family's far deeper in the mire than either of us, and it's you what's put them there."

Chapter Eleven

We did not speak much after that, although Alex's words had been noted and I found myself thinking of them when really I should have been worrying over my own plight. An officer called out a list of names: Alex's and mine were included, and an hour later we were among twenty disconsolate men sitting in a Navy longboat and being rowed towards the area Hastings fishermen knew as The Hards. There were four vessels anchored; three looked to be the pressing tenders previously mentioned; stout, purposeful little tubs, obviously built with the emphasis on capacity rather than speed. They had bluff bows and sat squat in the water, with wide hulls that tapered in steeply from just above the waterline.

The fourth was a far sleeker affair; she also sported twin masts but there any similarity ended. Both spars were of a far greater height and carried more yards than the tenders, while the hull was slim and with a much lower freeboard. She would be fast though, even I could see that: her prow was shaped to cut through the water, rather than stub at it, and there was a line of evil looking cannon peering out along her upper deck. I knew she was small compared to most warships, but the look of defiance was undeniable and I was immediately drawn to her.

We were brought alongside the first of the tenders and ordered aboard. Most of us had wet trousers from boarding the longboats and, with our waistbands still cut and such a depressing prospect before us, we must have appeared a dismal bunch. As I waited my turn, a wild thought came to me. I was a strong swimmer, and it was not that far to the shore. For one mad moment, making a dash for the side seemed like a good idea, even though I was bound to be recaptured almost immediately. Then I remembered the stories I'd heard about deserting sailors being flogged or even worse, and meekly followed Alex as he climbed over the tender's top rail.

Once aboard, we joined the line of men waiting to file below. There were eight marines on the tender's deck: all appeared far more casual than those encountered ashore and lacked their leather headgear and smart red tunics. The simple white shirts and trousers gave them an air of nonchalance; but their muskets were still purposeful, and I felt no more inclined to annoy them.

The lower deck turned out to be both crowded and dark. The tender had clearly called at a previous port, and was almost full, with lines of dejected bodies having already claimed much of the space. The entire area allotted to us spanned the width of the hull, but there were no ports or scuttles, and stout partitions fenced us off to either end. The galley, and what looked like the entrance to a store room, could be made out through cracks in the forward bulkhead, while the seamen's mess was to the stern. We were given no candles but a lanthorn was set above on a central grating, and enough light filtered through for our surroundings to be examined. One of the hands followed us down with a length of light sisal about his shoulder.

"You're not going nowhere now, so we may as well rig yer waistbands ag'in," he told us new arrivals, while removing the line and cutting through one part of the entire coil with his hand knife. The lengths were quickly seized upon, and soon our trousers were secure once more.

Other than Alex, I noticed no familiar faces and even he, who usually knew all and sundry, seemed not to recognise anyone. Some of our fellow prisoners were known to each other, though and, as we found what space we could, many bewailed their fate loudly. There was also a far younger boy who must have volunteered: he was sobbing gently in one corner with whatever heroic visions he may have held of life in the Royal Navy soundly dashed.

I was quite content for us to be left alone, and glad that none of the Hastings smugglers had been drafted into our party. The chance to think was also welcome and, even without considering the possibility of spending the next few years serving his Majesty, I was still wondering how things would be at the Coglans' house. It had been growing dark when we transferred to the pressing tender; at first I supposed the family would be wondering what had become of me but, by now, assumed them to have guessed.

After all, there could be few in Hastings who did not know of the press gang's visit: Ned may even have been caught as well – he was old for Naval service, but then no one was being particularly fussy. If the impressment men had left him alone, I assumed he would go back to fishing the punt. There would be no young fool for him to boss about, and the catch must be correspondingly smaller. That could only mean hardship for the family, even ignoring any future problems that I might have saddled them with.

I felt a strange mixture of emotions; at once both guilty, and tremendously put upon; so much so that, when one of our fellow prisoners addressed a remark to me, I was probably not at my most receptive.

"Hastings," I replied curtly to his enquiry. Then added: "I crew for the Coglans of All Saints Street," in an effort to appear more mannerly.

The fellow, who looked in his late twenties, nodded, although I doubted he knew either the family, or that area. His landsman's clothes were well cut, making him appear far more a true man of business than I supposed myself to be.

"What about yourself?" I asked, as he clearly intended to be sociable. He shook his head ruefully.

"I'm a lander for the Dorseys. It's a gang what operates about the south coast," he explained. "We had a run go down yesterday evening – do you know the Cuckmere?"

I did: Cuckmere Haven was a beach some distance from Hastings but closer to the home where I'd grown up. Even then it had been known as a place frequented by smugglers; so much so that I was surprised to hear it still in use.

"Revenue took us," he complained. "Along with a troop of dragoons, and a bunch of Navy toughs what outnumbered our lot two to one."

"That was quite a force," I said, and he nodded again.

"Reckon it were planned: we've been landing at the Haven for ages with nothing more than the occasional landshark to chase away. Soon as war's rumoured, we gets the whole lot falling about our ears; 'tain't fair, and no mistakin'."

"You were given the chance of joining?" I asked, but he pulled a face.

"Na, not voluntary," he snorted. "The only choice they gave us was this or the county assizes. We'd have probably ended up in the Navy anyways, so all took the quicker route. And this way there were no risk of the winder, or a chance to shake hands with some nubbing cove at Newgate."

I knew winder as a cant term for transportation while Newgate was renowned as a place of execution, so guessed he had taken the wiser option.

"What happens now?" I asked, as the man appeared far more worldly than myself.

"Blowed if I knows," he confessed. "It's not a position I've found m'self in afore."

I sat back against the hull of the tender, disappointed. So much had happened that the fact of my impressment was hard to take in, but it slowly dawned on me I would not be spending the night with Susan, or even curled up in front of the Coglans' fire. I opened my eyes and noticed my new friend watching me with what might have been concern.

"Don't take on so; I been in worse scrapes, and come out the other side." he said. "We've yet to be passed by the surgeon, so there's the chance they'll find you sickening from something."

I gave an ironic grin; it did not seem the best of solutions.

"An' I knows enough to make a break, should the situation present," he continued. "Besides, with the number they've taken I'd not rule out someone doing somethin' about it."

* * *

We were given food shortly afterwards; mine amounted to a chunk of cheese every bit as hard as the dusty biscuit that accompanied it. Both sat heavily in my stomach as we turned in to sleep. There were no hammocks, or bedding of any kind, and the crowded space was thick with the stink of closely packed humanity that, to my mind, beat putrid fish into an easy second. I could only hope things would improve with the morning.

And to some extent they did; we were underway – I knew that the moment I woke: the motion was unmistakable. It hardly altered our position any, but at least meant we would reach the Nore, and any chance at regaining our freedom, more quickly. Then the cover above the hatch was removed, a ladder extended into our lair, and a young officer descended.

It seemed we were to be allowed exercise and fresh air, but obviously this could not be arranged for all at one time. A short list of names was called out which included my own and, after a cautious glance at Alex who was still in the process of waking, I found myself being shepherded up to light and the outside world.

The gloriously clean, clear air filled my lungs, making me feel quite dizzy. I was right, we were properly at sea. The tender was under her fore and main, with a single jib and, even though the wind was hardly in our favour, made reasonable progress against the light chop of the Channel. Of Hastings there was no sign, but I knew the local coastline relatively well and could make out Rye on our larboard beam. That was the extent of my travels eastwards with Ned: just beyond, and off the larboard bow, was a headland that must be Dungeness, but after that I would be in doubt. I looked about; there was no sign of any major shipping: apart from a solitary fisher to leeward, we were quite alone.

"Others'll be waiting at Hastings a while longer, then probably going on to try their luck at Rye." The voice took me by surprise and, turning, I saw my friend from the previous evening. He had clearly slept as badly as me: dark shadows underlined his eyes and the smart clothes I'd noticed the night before looked far less respectable in daylight.

"Aye," a nearby seaman agreed. He sported a queue of intricately plaited black hair and was clearly one of the tender's crew. "We got our fill with you lot," he continued, coiling a length of one inch line in his hands as he spoke. "So it'll be a quick dash to the Nore for us, then back again for another dose."

The lander from last night turned to him. "With no escort?" he asked. "Not worried one of us might make a dash for it?"

This apparently amused the seaman, who treated us to a display of uneven teeth every bit as dark as his hair. "Not much chance of that, matey," he chortled. "We're three mile or more off shore, and there'll be no stopping 'till we raise Sheppey. If anyone wants to leave us they're welcome, but it's a long walk to dry land."

I glanced at my companion while the sailor cackled raucously at his own wit. The lander was not laughing, but I did notice a softening in his expression that actually gave me hope. "We reached Deal yet?" he asked. I shook my head and was about to reply when the seaman did so for me.

"Na, ain't as far as Deal. In this old tub, an' with the wind in the north east, we ain't likely to be 'till this time tomorrow."

My companion nodded, but said no more, although I could see the information was important to him. The seaman must have sensed something as well: he stopped coiling the line and his eyes narrowed.

"So what's so important about Deal?" he asked. The lander shook his head.

"It's just a place I'd heard of," he replied, weakly.

"You might 'ave 'eard of it," the seaman stated, his expression lifting. "And you might even get yourselves a glimpse. But none of you'll be going there," he chortled. "Not in many a year!"

Further laughter followed, but it was soon cut short by a more authoritative voice and our eyes switched to a stooping, grey haired officer, speaking from the stern.

"If all have taken their fill of fresh air for the morning, what say you go below and give some of your fellows the deck?" The tone was almost considerate and I sensed that transporting men forced to serve in the Navy had not been an ambition when he first set out to be a sea officer. "You'll get another chance this evening."

I drew my last breath of the fresh, cold sea breeze as my group started to shuffle towards the black hole that would hold us for the next few hours. It was hardly a pleasant prospect, but strangely I was not without hope.

Chapter Twelve

Alex's story

Nat was surprisingly cheerful when he came back from his morning exercise, and I was blowed if I knew why. We didn't have time to talk; my group were next and, as I clambered up the ladder, I tried to think of the most hopeful sight that might meet my eyes. Possibly a Revenue cutter under full sail, about to forereach on us and carrying some special order to see me free of the Navy for good. Such a miracle was not totally out of the question; I was old enough for Customs service and, with my father's record for zeal and efficiency, enlistment would have been simple enough. Once on their books, I would be a servant of the king and the Navy wouldn't even get sight of me.

It was a line of work I had always been determined to avoid though. Having suffered enough from my dad's choice, I didn't wish to inflict the same on any future family of my own. But now, when that very family was not so much of a far off vision, I found the prospect more attractive. In fact, if Nat had not landed himself with the lugger, I may even have opted for it straight after hearing Tilly's news.

On gaining the deck, I automatically moved away from the other men, and looked out to leeward. The lugger that had been following the night before was still off our stern, but there was nothing unusual there; she might be sailing to fish off any one of the major banks to the north-east, or even preparing to take advantage of the south-westerly currents and cross the Channel. Apart from her, I could see no sign of another vessel nor, when I had completely swept the horizon, anything that might have cheered old Nat up.

I slumped down in the lee of the weather bulwark. My body was still sore from the little escapade down the Tamarisk Steps and it felt good to have my legs out straight for a change. I knew the tender was likely to take anything from two days to a week to fetch the Nore but, however fast we travelled, it would make little difference to the outcome. Had Henderson, our local Collector of Customs, known of my plight he might have been able to have me freed. He was as bent as an old hoof nail, but still felt bad about dad dying the way he did, and would certainly have helped. I'd been offered the chance of training as a tide waiter several times and, if securing my release would add another to his desperately small band, I'm sure the right strings could have been pulled.

We were underway though, and it would be a different matter once I reached the Nore. That was a proper Navy base and things were bound to be far more official. Henderson might have been able to intimidate a bunch of junior officers far away from home but I couldn't see him influencing a regular port admiral.

That so, a swift trip would probably be better, if only to allow less time in which I, or my name, might be recognised by my fellow captives. I was fortunate inasmuch as none of the Hastings runners were aboard, but there were still a few I half recognised, and a couple had been eyeing me closely, although nothing had been said as yet. Were it to be discovered they had Alex Combes, son of John Combes, the infamous landshark, at their mercy my life would not have been worth the living.

The other men were yarning further forward and some seemed quite reconciled to their fate: there was even the occasional sound of laughter. I could find nothing funny in the situation: being seized by the press was bad enough, but my mind kept returning to Tilly, and her predicament. I guessed she would hear of my being taken and, whatever the circumstances, would understand: she was that kind of girl. But still I worried there might be a tiny doubt lurking somewhere. After all, I wouldn't be the first to run on discovering himself about to become a father.

Nat's story

Neither the conditions, nor the food, improved any as we continued our journey. By lunchtime a proper wind came up, the tender started to roll with the swell, and some amongst us not so acquainted with the sea began to be ill. Such a situation would not have made any mid-day meal more appealing and, with the galley stove set so near to our quarters, the stink of boiling salt beef alone was enough to set my stomach heaving. I'd touched hardly any meat, other than fish, since arriving at Hastings and did not miss the stuff one jot, having never been particularly fond of it to begin with. On being presented with a shapeless, lukewarm, glutinous chunk that needed to be eaten in my hands, and nothing other than dry biscuit and pickled cabbage for accompaniment, I was halfway to joining the lubbers bending over necessary buckets.

But our meal was over soon enough, the weather moderated slightly, and we settled down to a voyage that was already unwelcome and uncomfortable, and now fast becoming boring into the bargain. Despite the lack of light, space and air, and a deckhead that prevented most from standing upright, many of us did what we could to move about. And so it was that Alex and I were able to find a comfortable spot next to my new friend, the lander.

"You mentioned Deal earlier," I reminded him, after we had learnt he was from Shoreham, a port several miles further to the west. "That's a long way from your part of the world, why the importance?"

"No importance as such," he replied guardedly, "Just that I'd heard word of it from other runners. If there's hope for any of us, it will come from there."

"Are the Bennetts involved?" I asked, trying to say the now hated name without undue emphasis.

"Might be, I couldn't rightly say," the man said stiffly.

"But one of the gangs is?" Alex chanced.

The hatch above us opened, and the boy officer, who was hardly old enough to shave, peered down into the depths for a moment. It wasn't just us, everyone stopped talking, and the silence became forbidding. Then the lad leant back, and shut the trap once more. It was one of their periodic checks, and something we were becoming used to, but clearly the interruption had shaken our Shoreham companion, and he refused to speak further.

We left him in peace; Alex seemed doubtful of anything being behind his words although I could not agree. The two of us bickered quietly for a while, but he was his usual dogmatic self, so I let it be. I had never been as far to the east, but knew Deal as being the nearest port to the Downs anchorage. There was likely to be a goodly amount of shipping there; both the Royal and Merchant Navies used it extensively. There would also be vast numbers of fishing boats, passenger vessels and, for all I knew, smugglers. Were there any substance in what we had been told, I guessed it would reveal itself once we drew closer. And I was proved correct.

* * *

It was the following evening, in fact. We had been allowed on deck twice since speaking with the man from Shoreham, and there had been little to note, apart from a fleet of mighty Indiamen. They were anchored with various other shipping in the lee of some impressive white cliffs; apart from them, and the same, solitary fishing lugger keeping station off our stern, there was nothing of interest.

The sight of the big ships filled me with both envy and regret; should I have chosen another path, I might even be aboard one of those monsters at that very moment. Aboard, safe and employed, while looking forward to a voyage that was warranted to bring both adventure and wealth. As it was, I had nothing but years in a Navy ship to look forward to. I suppose, after my earlier high spirits, it was inevitable that I would sink back down again; then Alex returned from his evening exercise more than a little excited.

"We're still heading nor' east," he told me. "The Downs is long behind us an' we are standing out to sea, probably to clear North Foreland."

I nodded eagerly, what he said meant little to me, but his enthusiasm was infectious.

"The wind's in the east, so we're beating against it, and not making too great a progress by the looks of things."

"Where exactly are we?" I asked.

He shrugged. "There's a port just passing to larboard, though we are a good way off an' I couldn't say which. Main thing is, a lugger's close hauled and on our tail. I'm pretty sure she were there the last few times, certainly as we was clearing the Downs, though now she has all sail set an' is trying to catch us."

My mood fell once more. For all Alex's enthusiasm, I had also seen the lugger and knew her to be far too small to bother a Navy pressing tender; especially one with marines aboard.

"But you haven't heard the half of it," he continued, triumphantly. "All the while what looks like an armed brig is lying hove to and off our starboard bow. I'd say she were waiting on us."

It certainly sounded that way to me, and I began to feel better. Across from us, the man from Shoreham had been talking with a member of Alex's exercise party and now appeared a good deal more cheerful as well. In fact, there was a noticeable lifting in morale amongst all the prisoners, and I was keen to take my turn on deck.

When it came, I was amongst the last to be allowed up. Each subsequent group had returned with more news; the lugger was closing, while the brig which, according to gossip, was either a known privateer, a Navy ship, or a Frenchman, lay off our prow. And we were almost in range of her guns which, I learned, could be anything from six to eighteen pounders. Speculation was rife amongst the men, and all were in a high state of excitement. A few might have been concerned we were to be captured by a potential enemy, but the general impression was the warship would improve our lot, and I was ready to welcome anything that could benefit me.

As soon as we gained the deck, all rushed to starboard and began peering forward through the light, misty rain. Yes, a brig was clearly in sight; she was well built and riding low as if heavily laden and standing less than a mile off our starboard bow. The tender would have to turn back if she wished to avoid passing but, should she so do, the lugger, lightest of the three but still substantial for her type, was making on our stern.

Our marines were in full uniform now and the elderly Navy lieutenant in command stood deliberating on his tiny quarterdeck. In the brief time we were in fresh air he ordered two blue lights to be burned from the main and fore mastheads, and the glow reflected eerily about us as night began to fall. The only face on deck I recognised was that of the black haired seaman: he seemed not to notice me though, and had certainly lost his sense of humour.

"Very good, Mr Mallows," the lieutenant called, and there came the sharp report of a signal gun firing from our forecastle. It was probably our only armament, and the sudden crack made all about jump. Smoke billowed amongst us and the clean air was tainted with the scent of burning powder. I had the distinct impression it would not be the last we would smell that day and, as soon as we were shepherded below, sought out Alex.

"Any Navy ships in sight?" he asked, as soon as I related what had been seen.

I shook my head. "There's a couple of fishers and what I take to be a coaster, but they're a good way off and to leeward."

Alex digested the information and nodded. "Then I'd say the brig's a privateer; that or a smuggler," he said. "Either way, she'll be both armed, and up to no good – at least as far as the Royal Navy is concerned." I waited, not wishing to ask the obvious, but still dying to know. He must have taken pity on me, and it was not for the first time.

"She'll be British, if that's what you're thinking. But, though her captain might be carrying a letter of marque, those aboard will not be acting for the crown."

"But you said the brig was armed." I reminded him.

"And she will be," he agreed. "But carrying cannon don't necessarily mean she's on the side of the righteous."

This was all getting far too complicated, and I sat back as Alex continued.

"There are several ways to run your own warship, if you are rich enough to buy one," he explained. "War or no, the French will provide a safe berth, no matter where you hail from. And they will be especially generous when it comes to dockyard facilities, supplies and the like, even if they might lack them theirselves. You see it's worth it to them, especially as privateers in this area are mainly used for protecting free traders, and no one doubts it in their interest to encourage smuggling."

That made sense; for smuggling to be in any way successful, co-operation from the French was vital. They, in turn, would see such activity as both a means of income for them, and potentially detrimental to Britain, their eternal enemy.

"Of course, if siding with the frogs goes against the grain, a man can also register his vessel as a privateer in England, in which case it might be berthed in any British port, and carry two decent sides of cannon into the bargain."

"But not to protect smugglers?" I asked.

"Not in theory," Alex agreed. "They might be expected to engage the odd enemy vessel from time to time," he added, after considering. "But that don't mean they has to. And there's plenty of other ways a well armed craft can make money at sea, 'though running is still the most fruitful."

"But attacking a pressing tender?" I asked doubtfully. "Surely no one's going to profit from that."

"It could just be a means to an end, as far as our friends are concerned." Alex replied. "They're taking a terrible risk but, as long as no other Navy vessels come into sight, it's one that should pay off."

"But who are they, and why so interested in a shipload of pressed men?"

"They might be the Bennetts," Alex said dispassionately. "I've never heard of them having anything as large as a brig at their disposal, but different gangs are known to cooperate. There are a number of other free traders along this coast; some have pretty substantial vessels, while others run craft that would give even minor warships a run for their money. It wouldn't be beyond them to pool their resources."

"So they might not even be interested in the tender?" I asked, not a little disappointed.

"No, I'd say they were: extremely. We have more than a few smugglers amongst this lot," he added softly. "As soon as we left Hastings it would have been common knowledge where we was bound, as well as who were aboard. Ask me, there are a bunch of free traders out there intending to claim back their own. And with a bit of luck, us as well."

* * *

I can now see that, if I had spent more time thinking of things other than buying the Bennetts' lugger, the events of the last few days would have come as no surprise. War was on the verge of being declared, so there was bound to be a widespread press and, with pressing being such an inherently unfair method of recruiting to begin with, it was almost logical that our prized protections would be deemed useless. Then, once the regulating men had struck; once we were all safely trussed up and heading for the Royal Navy, it was equally reasonable for the free traders not to sit back and simply curse their bad luck. In terms of scale, smuggling must have been similar to the fishing industry and, with the Navy taking all their best men, they were bound to react. But my home village was a good way inland, and I found it hard to comprehend that criminals could be quite so powerful. Or so organised.

In the past, whenever I heard tell of smuggling vessels, they had always been small smacks and perhaps the occasional coaster, with their work being confined to little more than a clandestine run ashore. The night must be moonless, of course, so as to avoid attention from the Revenue men, who would be heavily armed, and really nothing more than government employed kill-joys. I had learned much since then although, even now, my perception of the free traders was distorted, and any thought of them using small warships to sail against the king seemed simply incredible.

But Alex's words had the ring of truth about them and, as if to prove them right, the tender took a sudden lurch when her helm was put across without the finesse expected in a Navy run craft. The experienced hands amongst us sat or stood tight watching, with amused interest, as the landsmen tumbled about the deck. Then all humour was forgotten: a loud crack came from the stern, and the entire hull trembled.

"Cannon fire," Alex said glumly, as the hollow sound of a far off ship's gun reached us. "We're probably safe enough where we is, much of our deck's below the waterline. But it won't take a lot to sink a tub like this, and in that case..."

He left the sentence unfinished: we could both imagine the panic and confusion of so many desperate men trying to leave through one small, locked hatchway.

The tender shuddered again as another shot struck her; the privateer must be reasonably close as the sound of muskets soon followed.

"That'll be the marines," Alex informed me. "They'll be firing from the stern. We turned, so I reckon the brig'll be standing off our tail an' taking pot shots at us while the lugger comes up on our prow. Ask me, one or the other will be boarding us in no time."

Chapter Thirteen

Alex was right, as had become his habit. The musket fire continued spasmodically, then we heard several loud shouts, followed by a grinding crunch, and the entire hull felt to be pressed to one side. Those beneath the grating were straining to see, but could only make out what was happening directly above them. At one point a seaman on deck fell back across the wooden framework, to an accompaniment of cheers and comments from below, but quite who he was, or what had placed him there remained a mystery.

"If the Navy has let them alongside, it'll just be a matter of time," Alex murmured. "Either boat could be carrying more than the crew of this little tub an' they'll take her easy, even considering the marines."

I said nothing; actually most of us were growing quiet: it was difficult to be otherwise with what sounded like the largest pot house brawl in history taking place above our heads. But all came to a close eventually and, after several shouts and what sounded like a scream, silence finally descended. We looked to each other uncertainly; one of the men tried the hatchway, but it was still secured. Then, after a rattling of keys, the trap flew open, and an impressively rigged man carrying a lantern stepped down the ladder to a series of shouts and raucous greetings.

"What cheer, cousins?" he asked, grinning broadly, and shining his light on our miserable faces. The man was well, if flamboyantly, dressed, with a long jacket over an elaborate red embroidered waistcoat. The plain white trousers were tucked into black, highly polished, boots that could almost have been japanned, and there was no hat, although his jet black hair was generously cut, and seemed to glow in competition with the footwear.

"Fine haul for the Royal Navy, you lot would have made," he announced with heavy irony. "Hey there, Hallows; thought they'd make a sailor out of you, did they? An' Milner; you'd have cost his Majesty so much in rag water, we're probably doin' Farmer George a service!"

The lander from the Dorsey gang gave an embarrassed smile, and it did appear the new arrival was generally well thought of.

"What's the scrap, Ugly Joe?" someone called from deep within the prisoners, and there was a tittering of nervous laughter. The new arrival looked through the crowd and took two steps towards the voice, although few could have been certain who had actually spoken.

"Ah, we have a jester amongst us," he gave a humourless grin. "Let me tell you, the last simkin who called me so found hisself in such a state that even his mother failed to find him attractive." The laughter was more good natured now, but the new arrival was closer to me and I could see him quite clearly. The mouth was smiling, but not so his steely blue eyes and, though the face was strong and some might say handsome, I knew him to be deadly serious.

"So yes, the scrap – as you so delicately put it." He turned about, clearly enjoying being in charge of such an audience. "Well, as some may have smoked, this vessel is now under the command of the Clipping Crew." A further rumble of approval erupted from his onlookers, but the man continued to speak through it. "For those who do not know, we are a mild mannered bunch of mateys whose only ambition is to prosper whenever the opportunity presents. My name is Joseph Prettyman, and any that calls me different is apt to find hisself mourned." More laughter, though I noted a measure of respect this time.

"Some may wish to follow us, in which case positions will be found. We're a tidy pack, and treat each other well, though those against us, harshly. Others might only yearn to be free of the prospect of shipping for the king, and who can blame them? But come with us still, and we will see you safe to shore as our honoured guests." He paused and raised his eyebrows theatrically: "And there may be those who still wish to serve his Majesty; so be it, and honour to them for their loyalty. No doubt they shall find far more space aboard this fine vessel to properly enjoy the rest of their cruise in comfort." More catcalls and screams of derision; it was clear that any who set out with ambitions of joining the Navy had changed their ideas in the course of the voyage.

"But let us not delay, for there may be government shipping about with men aboard who do not wish us kindly. Those that care to join me in my endeavours, kindly step aboard *Jessica*, the fine and warlike brig you shall find alongside. Jackie Clarkeson's lugger is joining us shortly and will deliver any wishing to be free of his Majesty to a safe and secret landing ashore."

So saying he turned and made for the hatchway, clambering up the ladder at the head of what quickly became a queue of eager bodies. I looked to Alex, who had said nothing for some while. "Do we follow?" I asked.

"Would you rather stay?" he replied.

* * *

On deck, the crew of the tender made for a sorry sight. Night was almost upon us, but the small group of marines that sat disconsolately on the forecastle could still be seen, and there were several seamen with them, all apparently unhurt. They were under the amused care of three men armed with wide mouthed carbines that they handled in an overtly casual manner; one had released his trigger, and was holding the hammer back with the very tip of his thumb as he waved the gaping barrel under each prisoner's nose in turn. I turned from the sight, only to notice the body lying face up on the grating actually belonged to the black haired seaman I had spoken with so recently. It was the first dead man I had ever encountered, and the sight sickened me far more than any fish.

I looked away, only to chance upon the elderly lieutenant, who had captained our craft, and was now amongst four who lay equally motionless upon the quarterdeck. With them was the younger officer who had supervised our mealtimes. He sat hunched and bleeding from the chest, while two of his shipmates attempted to wrap a length of canvas about him.

There were other members of Prettyman's Clipping Crew present; some were trying to force open a locker forward, while another was carrying something up from the hatchway that led from the accommodation below. Whatever it was had been wrapped in a blanket, and the man appeared unusually pleased with himself. Prettyman stood on the tender's deck, immediately next to where his brig lay alongside, passing comments and the occasional greeting to the former recruits who clambered past to board his vessel. By the time we arrived on deck, most had already joined him: Alex and I stood uncertainly amidships with twelve or so others.

"Plenty of space for those who wish for a life of adventure, gentlemen," Prettyman told us, extending an elegant hand towards his brig. "We will soon be back at war with those damnable Frenchmen, though it will not change my circumstances a jot: I shall still be living in France." He paused, to gauge our reaction although, of all present, I was probably the only one to show surprise. "And I can tell you now, the frogs are not the devils we take them for," he continued, apparently speaking directly to me.

"Better by far than the gobblers and landsharks what infest our own shores, and far less dangerous. Why, in all the time I have spent on French soil, no one has tried to place a noose about my neck. Yet I cannot walk more than a mile in England without encountering a notice encouraging such an outrage."

Some of the men guffawed, but I could tell it was servile laughter, the kind given to a bully in the hope of appeasing him. I'm not sure if Prettyman saw through the sham, or simply liked being the centre of attention too much to care.

"We berth at Boulogne and are as safe there and more welcome than at any place in Britain. Twice a week I shall take *Jessica* back to England, where we pay way above market prices for our countrymen's wool and, in return, bring all manner of luxuries the government would rather no ordinary folk enjoyed. Those with a stout heart who can hand, reef and steer will always find a place in my team. So why not ship with us, and help your fellow countrymen, while filling your hat with the Frenchmen's coin?"

One of our party broke away to join and another called out his thanks, but declined. I was in two minds; only that morning I had been dreading a lengthy spell in the Royal Navy; and now the chance to change was being offered. Despite his calling, Prettyman was obviously influential and not afraid to get things done, were it in his interest. I had learned long ago that such men were good to be alongside.

I also felt instinctively that, despite the bluster and bravado, there was an element of truth in his words. England might be on its knees, and traitors such as him were surely not needed, but was the government, who should be working in our interest, doing any better? Despite the peace, which must have saved them a pretty penny, little had been done to lessen the punitive taxes, and now war seemed imminent, they had stripped the south coast fishing industry of vital manpower.

Were I to go with Prettyman, I would at least be sure of getting well paid for my labour. In a few months I should have enough to buy the Bennetts' lugger outright, or at least settle any immediate problems Susan and her family were having with them.

I looked across at Alex hoping to sense a common purpose, but his face was deadly set and I guessed him impervious to Prettyman's words.

"What think you?" I asked cautiously.

"He is a known rogue," he replied in a slightly louder voice. "I would as easily deal with him as the devil himself."

The words, coming from someone I secretly trusted, had their effect, and I held back. But Prettyman was looking in my direction, and I hurriedly turned away, focusing instead on the dead man sprawled across the grating. The sight reinforced Alex's sentiments: I had already decided life in the Royal Navy would not suit me, but that of a privateer, where enemies formed on every side, was likely to be so much worse. Alex glanced at me, and I could tell he was wondering if I would go. I smiled and shook my head and he appeared relieved. Looking back on it I can now see that, with his late father a particularly vehement preventive man, he really did not have a choice: there would be no rosy future for him in a gang of free traders.

A shout from behind alerted us. The lugger was closing on our larboard bow and had begun to spill her wind. Someone aboard called out a warning and, as we looked to the stern, the reason became obvious. A small craft could be made out running down on us under full sail. She was still more than a mile off, but travelling at speed and raising a tidy bow wave as she did.

"A cutter," Alex muttered. "She might be Royal Navy, or perhaps the Revenue."

I nodded. It could be either but one thing was certain: she had been summoned to assist the pressing tender, and with the wind in her favour, would be with us in no time.

"Take the men who wish to leave and bear away, Jackie," Prettyman bellowed to the lugger. "It shall be my pleasure to detain the gobbler's cruiser."

There was an answering shout from the fisherman and Prettyman skipped nimbly back to his own craft as the brig made to bear away and take the wind. Alex pushed me to larboard, just as the lugger slid alongside. "They won't wish to wait," he said. "Best jump as soon as you're able."

We did, in fact the two craft were hardly together for more than a few seconds before the tender was cleared of all her former prisoners. I fell badly on the lugger's cramped deck, and was trodden on, but my friend hauled me up. Then we both ducked as the large lug sail swept over our heads, and the boat turned away. We could see our former captors on board the tender; they watched as our vessel leaned with the wind. I guessed they had been disarmed although, from their look, there was little fight left in them.

The lugger was larger than those I was accustomed to in Hastings. She was also fully decked, and a far more lithe craft than the pressing tender had been. She heeled readily as the wind was taken on her starboard beam and set her prow for the nearby land. Prettyman, in the brig, was proving as good as his word, and beating for the cutter that was still running towards him under a tower of canvas and spray.

"Them Revenue boys is in for a treat," one of the lugger's crew said with ill concealed relish. "That'll be the Deal boat. They ain't hardly got more'n popguns, whereas *Jessica* carries a broadside of twelve pounders."

Despite all that had happened to me over the last day or so, I could not help but feel sympathy for the Revenue boat. If it hadn't been for Prettyman and his efforts, I would have been heading for a life in the Royal Navy, but still my inherent sense of fair play rebelled against what I guessed was about to take place.

The cutter continued to close with the brig, but veered to starboard at the last moment, and we could see a brief line of bright flashes erupt from her hull. The smoke rolled quickly with the wind, but the brig remained doggedly unchanged. Then, as the sleek and graceful Revenue craft swept past her, Prettyman replied.

Much of the broadside was masked by the cutter coming between us and the brig but, even in the dim light, we witnessed the results plainly enough. The Revenue boat's massive sail plan disintegrated before our eyes. One moment there was the oversized main, fore and jib, along with a square topsail and royal, all braced to perfection, and powering the cutter at a truly tremendous pace. The next everything had been wiped away, and the minute craft was entirely enveloped within her own canvas.

"Got the bastard!" The seaman nearest to me screamed, and there was certainly no argument from anyone else. The Revenue boat must have been struck neatly on the mast, or some vital securing point had been destroyed. Other damage might have been caused as well; even I knew such craft were paper thin and relied almost exclusively on their speed and manoeuvrability. But Prettyman's work was done: the preventive men were now effectively at his mercy, and the action, such as it had been, was over.

Chapter Fourteen

"I'll take us as close to the coast as she'll manage," one of the lugger's men, a stocky, older man who held the tiller and appeared to be in charge, grunted. He had grey, thinning hair, a rugged face and the air of command. The small boat had turned away from the scene, and was setting her prow for the nearby land. We had the wind on our quarter, and made good progress, but I was more interested in the fate of the Revenue cutter, and made to go aft.

"I'd keep your eyes for'ard, were I you, younker," a crewman who stood close by told me seriously. Apart from the hair – his was thick and blond – he looked like a younger version of the skipper. "Ugly Joe has work to do and it's best we leaves him to it. Those what don't know can't never tell."

A chill ran down my back. Despite his bravado and flamboyant ways, I had already sensed Prettyman was not one to be trifled with. He might also have a score to settle with the Revenue men; one that I knew nothing about, and had no desire to witness. Instead I obediently returned to Alex and the other former pressed men.

"Where are we going to land?" my friend asked the younger crewman, but it was his father, at the tiller, who replied.

"We ain't landing nowhere, least not for several hours," he said. "Firs' we needs to be away from hereabouts in case we gets any more Navy ships botherin' us. Moon won't rise 'til later, and dawn's expected a short time after. With luck, we'll gets to where we're going before then, an' you lot will have daylight to find your ways home in."

"Where are you based?" Alex again.

The skipper eyed him warily before replying with a grudging, "We sail from Rye, but it wouldn't do to leave you there case any of us is seen. You'll be dropped off a good deal further to the west – beyond Ramsgate; there's a road to London an' most other places thereabouts."

"Have the press been about in these parts?" another enquired, and the old man gave a short laugh.

"Press 'as been busy all 'long the south coast," he told us.

"An' there's enough military being roused to invade France," the son added. "Whole country's up in arms; hardly a fishing boat's at sea, and every docked merchant's been stripped of her crew."

"Lunacy, if you asks me," the father continued. "No country can last long if there ain't no trade, nor no fresh food. Yet what does the government care, long as they can fight their wars?" He looked at us all, and his eyes seemed to settle on me.

"Any of you fancy some time aboard *Lucy* here, we may consider you," he told us. "We fish much of the time, but do our fair share of running as well. With manpower as it is, I can offer a decent wage to those with experience. And we have our own ways of avoiding the press."

Once more I looked to Alex, but he had the same, set expression on his face and I knew that, however small the involvement with smuggling, he would sooner have starved than join the lugger's crew.

And I must admit to having been a mite put out. For all the rights and wrongs of it, smuggling was a commercial enterprise and I was sure someone of my intellect could prosper in such an environment. But it appeared the small hesitation was enough: the old man's gaze had already swept by me and there were no other takers. It felt like a lost opportunity and I was suitably miffed. Alex might have fine ideals but he also lacked my problems. Some of us might not be able to afford such worthy principles and, just because he was a friend, it didn't mean I had to set my life to his measure.

"Well, the offer were open," the old man grumbled, "Can't say it will be again, but if you changes your mind and asks for the *Lucy* anywhere 'twixt Ramsgate and Rye, we can usually be found."

Alex had settled himself on the deck and I joined him; there was little point in standing further, but he also looked unusually tired. "Once ashore, do we make for Hastings?" I asked.

"Dished if I knows," he shrugged. "We've both got folk depending on us there, but then the Navy has our names, and knows where we live. They won't take kindly to us running from the tender."

"Country's in uproar," I reminded him. "Can't see anyone caring too much about us, not when they got other things to think of."

He was about to reply when there came a shout from one of the lugger's crew. We both clambered to our feet and followed his gaze aft.

Prettyman's brig was still in sight amid the gloom, as was the pressing tender, and neither had apparently moved significantly. But of the cutter there was no sign, although a cloud of an even darker hue hung over her last position. Clearly there had been an explosion and, as we watched, the sound reached us.

"Must have caught alight," Alex murmured through the low rumble of the eruption. "An' the flames found her magazine."

"Would that be down to Prettyman?" I asked.

"Maybe so, and maybe not," he replied. "He might have boarded and set her ablaze or the brig's original broadside could have been to blame." Then he looked at me in deadly earnest. "But one thing's for certain: a good few will have died, and the Revenue won't forget about anyone blowin' up one of their cutters."

* * *

The lugger's crew left us at a small and sheltered inlet they seemed to know well. It had grown properly dark by then, but the sky remained clear and we could see reasonably well by the starlight. Alex and I waited with the others saved from the pressing tender as the small boat grounded on white, level sand. Then we all jumped into the gentle surf, and the lugger immediately re-floated with the loss of our weight. The water was deep and cold; we waded through it and, after a final acknowledgement to our rescuers, were soon completely alone on a deserted, but unfamiliar, beach.

All about us huge chalk cliffs towered even higher than those I remembered from Rock-a-Nore. To the west, the outline of what appeared to be a castle stared down, adding to our sense of vulnerability. The place looked far too military for my present state of mind but, according to others in the group, it was also our signpost to civilisation, and we started to walk in that direction.

For the last hour or so, Alex and I had been arguing in the lugger and now seemed to have reached both an impasse, and exhaustion. I was for staying near the coast, if only to avoid becoming completely disorientated, but he was dead set against it, and wasn't to be diverted, however hard I might try. Instead he felt we should make for a large town inland, where we could remain relatively anonymous and work might be found more easily.

There was little wrong in the plan but his attitude annoyed me. To my mind he was far too used to being the clever one: full of ideas and with the local knowledge to back them up. It was something I was prepared to accept, but only for as long as my business brain was given a modicum of respect as well. I was a good year older than him, after all and, at that moment, we were both in the same predicament – both fugitives, both tired and hungry, and both a long way from home.

Possibly my recent débâcle with the Bennetts had not helped my case, but Alex would brook no argument from me. He had made up his mind: we would be heading inland, and I might as well accept it. Faced with such determination, I ceased to argue, but still inwardly rebelled. I was not so foolish as to defy him outright, but continued to consider the options as we walked.

"I know these parts," one of the others said. We had finally left the soft sand and were crunching up a narrow path that led through a gate in the cliffs; the castle was now a reassuring distance away. "Kingsgate is less than a mile to the north east."

"And it's a dead and alive hole," another added from behind. "I wouldn't stay there long."

Alex murmured in agreement, but I stayed quiet: my mind was my own, and still had to be made up.

The pull of Hastings was strong, and getting back to All Saints Street to see what sort of mess I had left behind, seemed the only course. But I would be of little good to the Coglans if the Navy picked me up once more, and Hastings must be several days' walk away. To get there I would have to follow the coast road and was bound to encounter other press gangs. Even if I were not identified as escaping from the tender, I could just as easily find myself a

Navy man once more. Meanwhile, I remembered the promises of the lugger captain and Joseph Prettyman. Both had been keen for men, and the prospect of working for either was attractive, if only in a purely mercenary way.

Smuggling might hardly be the most respectable of trades, but it was not one I would turn down just because it was illegal. There was also the chance of violence and danger – memories of the recent battle were still fresh in my mind, as was the image of that seaman's body sprawled over the grating. Still, I had grown used to dead fish in time, and could probably do the same with anything else that appalled me. And, for all its faults, free trading remained a source of good money.

My mind continued to run on that course; I knew that having my pockets full would make everything so much easier. There was bound to be a way to send funds to Susan and her family. Again, not the ideal solution, perhaps, but at least Rob and Billy would be kept from the Coglans' door until I was able to return and fix matters permanently.

I was still convinced of my ability to do the latter, by the way. The last couple of days might have held more than their fair share of disasters but, to my mind at least, I remained entirely blameless. All my actions had been carried out legally, and with the best of intentions, yet really the outcome could not have turned out worse. That being so, my twisted logic dictated that a nefarious route must surely improve matters. Of course, I was careful not to share such a philosophy with Alex; especially after our recent spat. But, at such an hour of the night, and after all that had occurred of late, it made perfect sense to me.

And so we walked in silence up the steep, gorse-strewn, path and, on reaching the crown, stopped and took stock. Three of our group were for heading to the nearby hamlet, while the other four appeared intent on striking inland. Theirs was probably the wiser course; press gangs were bound to be roaming every county, but more would be found nearer the sea, where pickings must be greater. The others walked off on their separate paths leaving Alex and me alone and strangely exposed on the cliff top.

"What say you to Canterbury?" he asked at last. The was a

note of compromise in his voice and I knew he was trying to be conciliatory. "It's not so very far, still within striking distance of Hastings, and we should be able to find shelter and work of some sort."

I opened my mouth to agree and am certain, even now, that was my intention. But the thoughts began to tumble about my tired mind and something in his look made me hesitate. Canterbury may well offer shelter, and would probably make an excellent refuge but, at that moment, it felt as if I had been hiding from something ever since I left Ninfield.

My private epiphany continued and I could then see that Hastings, the place I had been running away to, was now becoming somewhere to escape from, and the mere fact of it annoyed me. But, whatever the reason, I truly felt I knew my own mind, and it was set on a different course from Alex's.

"You may go to Canterbury," I said, noticing his look of surprise, and even drawing strength and pleasure from it. "But I have other plans: I wish you well, and trust we shall meet again sometime."

I did not wait for a reply, but turned instead and started off on my chosen path to the west. The skipper in the lugger had said where they might be found; I judged myself close enough to reach Ramsgate in not much more than an hour and might even arrive as they were docking. The press could be active there, of course, but I felt myself a far sharper man than the one captured a day or so before. Meeting up with the lugger's crew could well lead to highly paid employment; if not, they must surely know Joe Prettyman's whereabouts, and one or the other was bound to be the answer to my problems.

Chapter Fifteen

Alex's story

For Nat to go off on his own like that was the last thing I had been expecting although, once I'd given it a bit more thought, perhaps it was not so strange. I already knew him to be an impulsive type, as well as the kind who blew one way, then the other. So, as I watched him wandering off down the road, I was reasonably certain he would have a change of heart before long. But it was cold and late, and I felt hungry, even if he didn't. And I had no intention of standing about in the dark waiting for the cull to come to his senses.

The others were long gone, but the road was clearly defined and soon a strong moon rose to help me. In no time my body settled into the rhythm of walking and, as I passed through yet another small village and discovered it to be twelve miles from Canterbury, I felt I was doing well. The local church also gave the hour as five and twenty past three, which meant there was ample time to arrive before breakfast.

That was ignoring the fact I had no money, of course, and knew not a soul in the area. Food would have to be bought while, to purchase anything, I should need to find some form of paid work.

I decided this must have been the fifth settlement I had encountered, the others having ranged from tiny hamlets to one reasonable sized place that might almost be considered a small town. Most were passed through without incident. Only once had my presence been noticed: a dog was disturbed and my pace quickened until the sound of its barking slowly faded. But no one came to investigate, and I sensed this was hardly the most hostile of territories.

I was just leaving that village and bracing myself for what looked like a short climb when I first heard the cart. It was approaching from behind, and clattering along the rough road at great speed. I turned to look, then pulled back to one side as it was obviously only on the very edge of control. A pair of strong horses pulled, and two men sat atop. In the moonlight I could see them leaning forward, urging the beasts on, while the driver shook the reins down on their backs.

The cart swept by close enough for me to feel its draught, yet I am certain I was not spotted, so intent were they on their journey. A cloud of dust hung in the air for some while after, and a rooster crowed twice. The silence felt eerie, and I was cautious about moving on. But, when I did, the road and the world in general was not changed, and the incident would have been forgotten had it not been repeated almost identically.

The difference was that, the second time, there was just a single horse and no cart. Instinctively I pulled into the hedgerow once more and looked back towards the now distant village. The sound increased, then horse and rider came thundering into view at the gallop.

The beast was steaming, and I judged from the trail of foam streaming from its mouth, that the two of them had been travelling at speed for a fair while. Of the rider I could see little; he was dressed in a long coat that flowed behind as he rode, with a flat hat pulled down low over the eyes. Again, I was either ignored or simply not noticed but, by this time, was becoming accustomed to my apparent invisibility, and began to walk on as soon as they were past. The sound of hooves disappeared into the night and silence once more descended. Now though, I was not so relaxed, and my opinion of the area had also altered.

It was thick forest for the next spell and, with the moon temporarily shielded, I slowed my pace for fear of straying off the road. While I was walking quickly the cold had not been a hindrance, but with the reduction in speed, my joints began to complain, and soon I was shivering. The thought of food came to haunt me; I told myself I would be able to eat as soon as dawn broke. There was nothing to back this deception – March is not a good month for scavenging and, in reality, I knew that nothing would be passing down my neck for some while. But then I have always been the gullible sort, and was at least partly convinced.

I saw the cart again as the forest cleared and a small house came into view. It had been left unsecured in the yard outside, with the weary horses still attached and in harness. As I approached, the pair were in the process of dragging the wagon over to one side; then I noticed another horse, hidden in the shadows of a tree, that was also free to roam. It might easily have been the one in chase a while earlier, and my curiosity was aroused.

I was still just as cold and hungry, but the loose horse puzzled me and any distraction was welcome. The two harnessed to the cart would probably not go far but the one on his own was able to wander: I turned into the yard and approached. Horses had been pretty much a mystery to me until then; the only ones I knew at all were the old nags that pulled boats up the Stade and those belonging to Jefferson, the auctioneer. They were more draft animals though; friendly enough but not exactly responsive. This one was of a totally different calibre, and seemed as alert as he was fit.

The beast was still breathing deeply and probably could have done with losing his saddle, together with a good rub down. I drew closer; he nodded his head a couple of times, but was not unusually fazed. Then he let me catch hold of his reins and lead him over to a post. The other two came across almost socially, dragging the cart behind, and I wondered about securing them as well. There was no brake as such on the vehicle, but I found a length of wood nearby, and threaded it through the spokes. It would foul against the chassis were they to wander and prevent further movement. Then, as I was about to head back for the road, something on the first horse's saddlebag shone out in the moonlight and caught my attention.

It was a crest, and would have meant little to most people, but the faint lines of a crown and portcullis had special significance for me. When dad died, mum got rid of everything in any way connected with him. The only thing I could keep was a small silver badge with the same design emblazoned upon it. It was what he wore when on duty – a direct link to the old fellow – and probably my most treasured possession. I used to clutch it in my hand when going to sleep at night.

Seeing the crest again told me the horse belonged to a riding officer, or someone connected with the Revenue. That, and the fact that there had obviously been a hot pursuit, was enough to start me thinking.

I went back to the cart and looked inside. At first I thought it empty, then noticed five small barrels secured behind the driver's bench. These would be the tubs I had heard mentioned a hundred times before. They were literally half the size of an anker, the traditional container for spirits, but far more easily transported or stored, and their presence confirmed the cart was being used for running. This was becoming more serious by the second, and I turned my attention to the house.

Every window was dark, then I noticed that all on the lower floor were shuttered. Little could be seen through the cracks, but no light shone from within. The front door was locked: I might have been able to force it but that would have attracted too much attention. Besides, it was late and these were difficult times: the fact that windows were sealed did not mean that no one was home.

And I might easily have been mistaken about what I had seen – for all I knew there was no pursuit at all: the cart may even belong to the Revenue as well, and was being used for transporting captured contraband. Were I to start wandering about a darkened house in the middle of the night, I might wake the owner, and someone cautious enough to shutter his windows would probably greet me with nothing less than a face full of buck shot. But I was still unsure, and had no intention of continuing my journey until I knew exactly what was going on.

Walking round to the back it grew suddenly darker, as the bulk of the house shaded my friendly moon, but I did notice a small hut at the bottom of the garden. It was set away from the privy, and this time there was definitely a light within. I walked nearer and instinctively softened my step. The hut had one small window, and I peered inside.

A single candle burned on a small wooden table and, with its help, I could see much. The back wall was stacked high with tubs, some chalked with numbers, others left plain. There were more to one side but the light was not strong enough to show them in detail. What floor space remained was taken up by a man in a greatcoat who sat hunched on the plain wooden planks with two others standing over him. One, with his back to me and the door, was holding a horse pistol but, rather than aiming it, the weapon hung down and was pointing lazily at the floor. It was clear they must be the captors and equally that neither were Revenue men. Both were dressed in rather old fashioned seamen's garb: for anyone to wear petticoat trousers marked them as either fisherman or smuggler, and I knew which my money was on. The unarmed one was fiddling with a snout lamp – a specialised piece of equipment used to send clandestine messages over long distances, usually to vessels at sea.

That a riding officer was being held hostage seemed obvious, although what could be done about it was not so plain. At the time, my only allegiance to the Treasury was a family connection: one that had not only accounted for my father, but also caused me so much personal misery I hardly felt in their debt. But the connection remained and I knew I must act.

The cove with his back to the door was the smaller of the two, which gave me something of a lead. I was no expert in street fighting, but mixing it with roughs on numerous occasions had taught me a thing or two. Until then, I never valued the experience as every fight had been one sided and inclined to end the same way. But even that now worked in my favour: odds of two to one hardly daunted me at all, and actually felt quite encouraging.

I examined the door, noting that it opened outwards, which was a pity. Still, not being tightly closed meant it was unlikely to be locked. I also had the major advantage of surprise: whatever might be going on inside, some half starved lout launching in on them must be the last thing anyone would expect.

And so it proved. Grasping hold of the iron handle, I swung the door back, stepped in and raised my boot, almost in one movement. Kicking at the base of the nearest man's spine, I watched with satisfaction as his shoulders snapped backwards, and he gave a shout filled with shock and pain. The force sent him sprawling forwards into the arms of his companion, and both gun and snout lamp fell to the floor.

I ducked down and collected the former, feeling reassurance in the warm, heavy weapon. It was a standard, single barrelled pistol, which meant I could only have dealt with one of them, but my entry had been enough to send them into a state of mild confusion.

The man on the floor twisted awkwardly to his feet; I guessed his hands were tied, and was at a loss as to how to release him, while still being encumbered by the gun.

"You!" I said, pointing the weapon out straight and almost in the face of the man I had kicked. "Untie him!"

My voice cracked slightly as it was inclined to, but I must have made more of an impression than I thought, as he rushed to comply.

"That was smart work," the riding officer said once his hands were freed. He was younger than most of his type, not more than forty, and reassuringly calm, considering the circumstances. "Brooks and Godson here couldn't decide what to do with me; never were much when it came to thinking, isn't that right, lads? Well now you've solved their problem."

"Any what helps the Revenue is making trouble for hisself," the unhurt man told me with feeling, but he wasted his breath. I already knew the move was probably the best I had made in ages.

It actually turned out to be my first ever act in favour of the Revenue but, even then, I sensed it would not be the last. Suddenly I could foresee a positive way of striking back at those who had intimidated and oppressed me and, tired and hungry though I might have been, and even considering the predicament I had left Tilly with, I don't think my future had ever felt more optimistic.

Chapter Sixteen

Nat's story

The promised moon did indeed rise shortly after Alex and I separated, and was of considerable help in guiding me on my path. It marked out a tiny village that sat in the valley below and was far too small to be the town that interested me. But a few miles further it finally revealed Ramsgate and, as I entered the place, was even strong enough make me realise the mistake I had made.

The day had yet to begin, and the streets were all but deserted, but there was no doubting it was a far larger concern than Hastings, and actually quite a considerable community. As I walked down a gentle slope, there were rows of well built houses; small, seemingly prosperous businesses and, on finally reaching the waterfront, a properly constructed harbour that stretched way out to sea. It was large enough to give real protection to anything moored within, and there were several ships, truly deserving of the title, lying safely under the watchful gaze of a small lighthouse.

I stood at the shore end of the longest pier I had ever seen and gazed across the still water. Many of the vessels had three masts and would be capable of deep sea travel, and some even carried boats on their skids that were larger than most found on the beach at Hastings. A few had been built for fighting and boasted neat lines of cannon along their upper decks, and all appeared decidedly smart.

But it wasn't the ships, the harbour, or even the size of the place that I found oddly disconcerting. There was something else; something almost primaeval in the atmosphere. Dawn began to break and I stood there, feeling increasingly vulnerable, as the first, tentative, fingers of true light felt their way about me.

Then the streets were suddenly not so quiet: blinds began to be pulled back and there were people walking purposefully wherever I looked. From close by I heard a horse cough, and a large cart clattered past, forcing me to the side of the road. I moved away from the harbour, conscious that my grubby clothes and lack of intention must mark me out as a stranger. It would be better to retreat, I decided. Take the same path out of the town: within half an hour I should be on the coast road again. Then I could even head back and try to catch Alex. Being in such an alien and frightening place had suddenly restored our friendship: I cursed myself, not only for leaving his company but, yet again, for thinking I knew better.

However, the road which had carried me in had apparently disappeared; I tried several that pretended to be it, but all were intent on luring me elsewhere, and a feeling of panic began to rise in my stomach. The sound of a bugle cut through the still morning air, and was quickly followed by a thin rumble of drums, and then there were military types absolutely everywhere.

I took shelter in a doorway as the small road became filled with marching men. An officer on horseback passed and I looked away, trying desperately to appear casual as he glanced down at me. They were soon gone, but in my intended direction, so I doubled back, and found myself at the harbour wall once more.

It was strange, the difference light and a few minutes could make. Now the area was apparently alive with men; they swarmed through the streets while the anchored shipping was equally active. Colours were raised and a few of the smaller craft appeared to be setting sail. There came the sound of more drums, and I realised I was actually outside some sort of barracks. A group of soldiers began forming up beyond the gate, and more men started to appear on horseback. Then my heart all but stopped as I noticed a party of seamen looking unpleasantly like they might be Royal Navy.

I moved on, knowing my escape route out of town was being left further behind, but feeling unable to do otherwise. The road narrowed, people started to push past: I studiously avoided making eye contact, but knew I must stand out like the one bad pea in a bowl. Then I chanced upon the first piece of luck to come my way all morning.

A hundred yards or so ahead, and on the other side of the road, I could see a group of three men walking towards me that I recognised. Leading them was the skipper from the night before, and next to him his son, the latter's swab of yellow hair being almost unmistakable in the clear, morning light. The other must also have been aboard the lugger, I decided, crossing the road towards them, and narrowly avoiding a boy who was trundling by with a hand cart.

The sound of a whistle cut through the air and instantly my mind went back to press gangs. I found my pace increasing without willing it, until I was almost running. The lugger's crew noticed me as I approached.

"You still wanting hands?" I cried, growing nearer. The group slowed and the older man regarded me with frank surprise. "I was on the pressing tender," I all but shouted, reaching them, and was about to explain more when the skipper's son stepped forward. In a single action he wrapped a stout arm about my shoulder, and turned me about.

"What cheer, matey?" he boomed in an apparently genial manner, although the grip on my upper arm was fierce and painful. "'Tis grand to see you; what say we takes a stroll?"

"And we won't be saying much about no tenders, now, will we?" the father added in a lower voice as he caught us up. He stared at me for a moment. "Yes, I have you now," he said. "Not got your little friend with you, then?"

I shook my head and tried to wriggle out of the grip, but was held firm, and the entire incident was starting to feel very much like the fire that followed the frying pan.

"So you wants to come aboard, does you?" the skipper asked, as the other man joined us. "What say you two; room for another, have we?"

The men gathered around. They had the smell of breakfast about them and I found myself smiling in what I hoped would be an agreeable manner.

"Not got no room for one what blabs," the son said harshly, and there was a grunt that might have been agreement from his father.

"Give him to the Navy," the third suggested. "We'll take the crimp's share and be done with it."

The skipper glared at him. "And that would look fine," he

hissed. "Specially when he tells 'em how we met and what 'e were about." The older man's eyes turned back to me and, although he was shorter, with far less hair and actually sported quite a paunch, I was strangely reminded of Ned. "No," he continued. "I think our friend here might prove useful in other ways."

Alex's story

The riding officer's name was Adams, and he seemed to know his way about. Whether it was a confidence born of success or simply innate I never did discover, but it was good to be in the company of one so assured. This was despite the fact that there was something about him vaguely reminiscent of Ugly Joe, even if they followed different and opposing careers. Brooks and Godson were swiftly secured, using rope that was as plentiful as the spirits stored in the small hut, then we led them outside where dawn was about to break.

"I'd been tailing these two since Minster," Adams said, allowing me the first real piece of information since my arrival. "Lost 'em for a spell, then caught up when they was heading down the high road like the devil himself was behind them. And don't-cha know?" he added, giving me a wicked look. "That might almost have been the case."

The man clearly enjoyed his work and I would have judged him good at it, were it not that he had allowed two runners to get the drop on him.

"Ain't got nothin' to hold us, you ain't," Brooks grumbled. "That spirit is paid for, Customs duty registered."

"It that the case?" Adams asked, clearly amused. "Then there will be documentation a plenty, an' we can examine it while you're safe in Whitstable gaol. But for now we'll leave this little lot locked up until we can empty it properly. You able to drive a wagon?" he added, glancing at me again.

"Not done it so often, but reckon so," I replied. In the past, when Combes was not such an unwelcome name in Hastings, I had ridden the auction house carts and once was even allowed to drive one most of the way along Rock-a-Nore. That had only been the one horse, and she was a tired old thing, but I felt I could cope, especially as there should not be so much traffic at that time in the morning.

"Then we shall head on for town," he said, beaming still, and I assumed he meant Whitstable. "Should make it in no time; have these two locked up safe and then, what would you say to a spot of breakfast?"

It was completely the wrong direction for me, but the alternative was to continue wandering on towards Canterbury, where I might, or might not find work. I knew little about Adams but he did have the security of the Treasury about him, and seemed grateful for what I had done. Besides, the promise of food was irresistible.

Nat's story

I had been half marched and half carried back to the lugger of the previous night. She lay moored against the outer wall of the harbour and we were soon heading out to sea. My companions divided themselves easily, as if it were a practised routine; the sour faced one attending to the mainmast, the son the mizzen, while his father stood solidly at the helm. I was still unsure if I were prisoner or crew, and generally tried to keep out of everyone's way.

The skipper had been keen for additional hands before, and his prompt action may well have saved me from yet another trip to a Rondy, even if his recruitment techniques differed little. However, it was clear I was not particularly popular with his son, or the other member of the crew, and I really wondered if this had been the better option.

Still, I found myself trusting the old man. Whether it was his similarity to Ned, or the fact that he was a father, I don't know, but there was an air of calm and competence about him, and instinctively I felt he would do me no harm. The others I was not so certain of.

We spent the entire day meandering along the coast on a southerly heading that turned further westwards as the boat progressed. It was sweet sailing and the wind was in our favour although my three shipmates showed no signs of unbending: as far as being uncommunicative was concerned, they could have given old Ned lessons.

But from the little that was said, I discovered the son to be Dan, while everyone referred to the reticent and repressed third member as Shiner, which I took to be an ironic nickname. Shiner was short, dull and tight-lipped with an unfortunate expression that made him look as if he were continually sucking a lemon. As for the skipper, he remained a mystery: naturally enough, his son called him Dad, while Shiner never addressed him, or anyone else, directly, so I still had to learn the old man's name.

By mid morning, and as we were passing the crowded shipping at the Downs, he called for tea, and all eyes turned on me. There was a small spirit stove which lit easily enough and I soon had a kettle boiling. I handed out the steaming metal mugs that were almost too hot for me to carry, although all were collected and held in tough hands without comment. There was no milk or sugar but no one seemed to require either. I helped myself to a mug and swallowed some of the scalding liquid down, even to the extent of burning my mouth. I knew the others to have eaten, and felt slightly resentful as nothing had passed my lips for some while. The tea tasted good though and, while drinking it, I noticed the skipper watching me with dispassionate interest.

"Breakfast?" he asked.

"And last night's supper," I replied, defiantly.

He gave a half shrug, secured the tiller, then disappeared below, only to return a few seconds later. I was wary, expecting some trick, but now he was carrying a chunk of bread which he tossed casually in my direction. I caught it and thanked him, but that was the extent of our contact, and no mention was ever made of further refreshment. Still I guessed that perhaps I was not in such a bad position, and relaxed enough to even doze slightly as the lugger ran easily along the English coast.

As evening was drawing in, I thought I recognised the headland that was Dungeness off our starboard bow and realised with a spontaneous thrill that we were not so very far from Hastings. The place held little for me except trouble, but even knowing I was nearer what had become my home was heartening, and I rose and wandered over to where the skipper still manned the helm.

"Can I ask where we're bound?" I enquired, as the son suspiciously joined us.

"You can ask," the younger man told me, rolling his eyes slightly. I did not take this as especially rude; indeed, compared with the small amount of conversation that had been held, it was almost garrulous. There had been no oaths or cursing but they were definitely a taciturn lot. I duly opened my mouth to repeat the question, but the skipper spoke before I got the chance.

"Rye," he said, simply. "The *Lucy* berths in the outer harbour, but we've business with the town first and, unless this wind picks up, we'll be heading straight there."

I waited for more, but nothing was forthcoming, and eventually returned to my previous resting place by the mainmast. Even those few words had given me enough to think on, though. So much had happened since, but I had been making for Rye when I first stopped and fell in with Alex and the Coglans. I had never visited, knew no one there, and had singularly little prospects, but still the fact that I would finally arrive cheered me.

Alex's story

We reached Whitstable just as the town was waking, and I followed Adams as he wound his horse through streets fast becoming crowded. I was feeling a lot more comfortable about driving the wagon than at first, but less so about my companions, who were bound hand and foot, and lying in the back.

Adams had not seen fit to gag them, and they had been treating me to a litany of fates that awaited one who sided with the

Treasury. This was not so very disconcerting; much of what they said I knew to be fanciful and the rest was barely heard. Besides, I had spent the last few years as the least popular lad in Hastings; not only had I survived many of their threats but actually grown stronger for them. And now, now that my best girl needed me the most, that very hatred was apparently acting as a spur for me to create a secure life for us both.

For I too would become a riding officer such as Adams; that or perhaps a simple tide waiter or even take a job in the stables. But the main thrust remained, I would be employed; the Treasury was always crying out for men, yet I had spent so long kicking my heels, doing odd jobs and keeping my head down, just because of folk like the ones I was now carrying off for trial. Thinking of the time lost both angered me, and nullified their attempts to intimidate.

The Whitstable Custom House appeared a far grander affair than that in Hastings. Adams led me to a large, modern building with generous windows and a bold entrance that boasted an ornate frame of polished hardwood about the door. By the side was the double entrance to a yard, well protected by wrought iron gates. They were opened at his shout by a boy who waved us in to safety and I jumped down from the driver's bench as both huge barriers closed behind us with a heavy clatter. Two men emerged from the building and the lad took Adams' mount. All three horses were breathing heavily after the journey, and clouds of condensation hung in the chilly air.

"Godson and Brooks," a well dressed, older man who was one of the reception committee commented, as the side gate of the wagon was let down. "We sees your faces round here so often you must have a liking for the place. And there's some more of your booty – as if we didn't have enough already."

"Ran into them on the Minster Road, Mr Cartright," Adams explained laconically while the second man untied their legs and led the two away. "Wouldn't have paid them much notice, but it was late, and they were making a run for it."

"Never were the sharpest of blades," Cartright, who I took to be the Whitstable Collector, commented dryly.

"Well, they were bright enough to see me down," Adams continued, ruefully. "I followed them to old Percy Holworth's place, just the other side of Upstreet. It's been empty a while, and I'd checked out the building myself a few weeks back, so considered it safe. Knew I was wrong when I saw their cart in the front yard though; then they jumped me and I found myself trussed up in the back shed along with enough dutiable spirit to float a liner."

Another man, smaller, and not as well dressed as Cartright, appeared from the Custom House and, after a nod of acknowledgement to Adams, clambered up onto the cart. He stood and stared hungrily at the tubs for a second or so, before bringing out a writing block and starting to make notes.

"All of this is over-proof," he muttered. "It'll let down to twice the volume; I'd say there's enough for a tidy fine, and might even earn them an eighty-four; that's if the Navy don't want 'em."

"Plenty more after that," Adams told him. "They've been using the hut as a hide for a while by the looks of things. I should have discovered it when I checked the house."

"That's as maybe," The Collector interrupted. "But we've found it now, and likely with a deal more in store for the delay. Take Walters here and a couple of landwaiters and rummage the place," he continued. Then, considering the wagon: "May as well use their cart, as they've been kind enough to provide it. Look to the horses, though. Who's the lad?" he asked, after finally noticing me.

"This is Alex Combes," Adams told him. "It's down to him we snagged them at all. If he hadn't intervened I'd be mutton b'now."

"Is that the case?" the older man asked. "And what were you about at that time of night, Master Combes?"

I had to admit it did sound a deal suspicious and, for a moment, considered making up a story. It was what Nat would have done, after all. But my mind had always steered a different course; besides, being able to string a line had never done him that much good.

"I was running from the press," I said, surprising them, and myself, simultaneously. "Regulating men took me in Hastings a few days back; half of the town was in a tender afore we knew it. We were sailing for the Nore when a privateer intervened, and set those who wanted it ashore."

Now all three men were looking at me with a mixture of amazement and incredulity; even the clerk had stopped making notes.

"Privateer, you say?" the Collector still seemed suspicious.

"Ugly Joe – Joseph Prettyman," I corrected myself quickly. "He's well known down Hastings way."

"The lad's father was John Combes," Adams explained. "Part of the landguard in Mr Henderson's sector; he were killed a while back."

"I remember the name," Cartright said, now regarding me with interest. "Fell off a cliff, or so they said, though nothing could be proved, as I remember."

I said nothing: this was a subject I had learned not to discuss.

"Never met the man myself, but he had quite a reputation," the Collector continued. "Revenue could use a few more of his sort."

It was embarrassing, yet almost a relief to receive the men's attention. In the past my father's actions had only brought me misery, shame and perhaps a beating: this was one of the few times I felt publicly proud of him.

"But all know Prettyman well enough," the Collector continued. "An' the cove took a Navy tender, you say?"

I nodded; it had occurred to me whilst telling that the complete truth might not have been necessary; things could have been tidied up a bit, maybe a few of the facts missed out; again, Nat would have. I knew the Navy and the Treasury held differing views on the other, and could never have been accused of being on the best of terms. But still they both worked for the king, and there was little to stop these loyal subjects doing the right thing and handing me in at the nearest Rondy.

"Old Joe has the cheek of the devil, but it'll serve him bad eventually," Adams said with what might have been respect.

"An' he just came an' took you off the tender?" Cartright asked.

"At first the Navy men put up a fight," I admitted. "But his brig was well armed: it were no contest."

"They shouldn't have been travelling alone," Adams sighed. "The Navy always considers theirselves safe on the water: no matter what you tells 'em. It's like they think they owns the bloody stuff."

"Then a Revenue cruiser showed up, and he fought that as well." I continued.

"A Revenue cruiser?" The Collector's eyes flashed across to Adams. "*Sparrow*'s in dock; that would have to be Jim Werriby's boat, from Deal," he said, and now the atmosphere grew much more serious. "How did she fare?"

"She was dismasted and caught fire," I told them bluntly, hoping that the delivery of such news would not blacken my position any. "And then she exploded."

"Did she indeed?" Adams murmured, and it was clear his impression of Joe Prettyman had altered somewhat.

The two men were silent for a moment and I grew worried. But it seemed the blatant honesty of my story had come across, and they bore me no ill will.

"Are you enlisted in the Navy, son?" the Collector asked me eventually, and I could see he was looking over my rig, which couldn't have appeared too smart.

"They took my name and address," I told them.

"Did you sign anything, or make your mark?"

I shook my head.

"Then you've nothing to be afeared of," his harsh expression relaxed. "Man can't desert if he hasn't signed on now, can he?"

I felt a wave of relief wash over me and had to control the need to laugh out loud. Were that the case, I only needed to stay clear of the press until I made it back to Hastings. But Cartright had more to say.

"And we're grateful for what you have done. If there's a service the Treasury can provide in return we should be pleased to hear of it."

"I promised the lad a spot of breakfast," Adams interrupted. He too was looking at me closely, and probably for the first time in daylight. "Perchance he needs a spell of rest afterwards?"

"I'd like to get back to Hastings," I told them. Tired and hungry I may have been but, now that I knew no crime had been committed, the need to meet up with Tilly was far more important than any physical want.

"We can arrange that as well," Cartright said with certainty. "Though I was thinking more of a position in the Revenue service. We're forever on the hunt for likely young men, those who know how to handle themselves."

"Thank you, that has been on my mind and I shall indeed be applying," I said carefully, not wishing to offend. "But would prefer to wait until I am home and can be in my father's old sector."

"That is understandable." he conceded. "The monthly coaster is due in at the end of the week. She'll be collecting our returns as well as any booty that did not shift at sale. After that, she continues down the south coast; they'll drop you at Hastings for certain. You won't mind waiting, nor travelling by sea and courtesy of the Treasury?" he asked, clearly thinking my previous experience might have influenced me.

The sun finally broke through as he was speaking, and I felt its warmth on my face. "I won't mind at all," I said.

Chapter Seventeen

Nat's story

When we arrived at the entrance to what must surely lead to its harbour, the town of Rye itself seemed strangely absent. There was no sign of any substantial housing, just one or two small shacks greeted us on the headland, along with a low lying building that might have been a shore battery and some particularly mean and windswept cottages a little way inland.

A single promontory reached out to sea, guiding us to a narrow mouth that looked to have been widened of late. We entered this and, after turning sharply to larboard and passing under a small drawbridge, wide canal walls rose up and drew us into their embrace. *Lucy* sailed smoothly through the still water and all aboard began to relax. We were continuing up the channel at a steady pace under the headsail alone when my attention was drawn to another Revenue cutter moored at what was presumably her home quay. It was the first time I had looked on such a vessel close up and was somewhat surprised at the lack of size. Her hull, though broad, seemed far less substantial than the mighty spars indicated although this one appeared even more foreshortened with what must be a reeving bowsprit currently inboard. A few red shirted men were working on her deck, but they paid us no attention.

"That's the Rye boat, *Stag*," the old man told me from the tiller as the lugger passed her by, adding, "Commander makes a lot of noise, but he's no seaman."

I tried to think of something intelligent to say in response. It was good to indulge in even this small amount of intercourse, but I was sorely tired, and could hardly think straight.

"Where do the crew live?" I asked eventually.

"Aboard," he replied. "That, or in the red brick building 'longside."

I looked and, sure enough, could see a single storey structure set just down from the wharf. There was a deal of washing hung from its low roof, and children played on the grass between it and the cutter.

"An' that's our place over there," he continued, indicating a small inlet with a jetty let in to the other side of the main channel. "So you could say we was neighbours," he added with what might generously be called a smile.

I wondered about a confessed smuggler pitching so close to a Revenue base, but supposed it was little different in Hastings, where Alex's dad had lived cheek-by-jowl with known free traders. I waited in the hope the old man might say more, but that appeared to be the extent of our conversation. Despite his claim, the lugger passed the inlet and continued up channel where the town of Rye proper came into sight.

It was set on the side of a steep hill, and seemed strangely exposed to the world, with even the streets being on view between well-to-do stone and brick houses. There were folk walking about on their daily business and, as *Lucy* was made fast against a fine new quay, I sensed a pleasant feeling of normality about the town. It was a shame I had ever been diverted in the first place.

Sadly the impression did not last. Still with barely a word passing between them, my shipmates finished securing the lugger, then jumped ashore before heading inland.

There was evidently some degree of haste required: we were late for something, or someone, and I had to rush to keep up. The streets of Rye were every bit as steep as they had looked from the harbour, and I was soon out of breath. But the other three showed no sign of tiring, and powered along the cobbled surface. Then I saw a sight that made me turn cold.

Ahead of us was a party of Royal Navy men: about six Jacks in striped shirts, duck trousers and lacquered hats accompanied by two young officers dressed in gilt-trimmed broadcloth. They were approaching our group on the same path and Dan's words of that morning came back to me. Even if I were not seized, it would take little for any of the three to denounce me, and I would be back in the Navy before I knew it. Then both groups turned down the same narrow alley and, after exchanging a few curt greetings, merged into one.

My mind was now awhirl; I began to suspect the lugger's crew of working in league with the Navy. Possibly they had brought me here to be handed in for a reason; maybe a larger bounty – perhaps, purely spite. However, hard as I might try, none of it made sense: I could not even be sure if I was being held prisoner, or was now included as one of the lugger's men. There had been scant food and little sleep since my rescue from the tender, and I could barely gather my thoughts.

Then I noticed an ensign hanging above the front door of a large, purposeful, building at the end of the lane, and my spirits sank further. A similar flag had flown outside *The Anchor* a few days back and I immediately knew the place to be both our destination and a Rondy. This did not bode well, and I actually started to get angry.

So this was what all the trouble had been for; within an hour or so I would probably be back aboard a pressing tender, and heading off for the Nore, although this time without a friend for company, and far less chance of rescue. I considered making a run for it; Dan and Shiner were walking several feet behind but I was still more than desperate enough to try, even though there were regular Navy foremast Jacks to either side of me. But, just as we stopped outside the entrance and I was deciding exactly which direction to bolt, I found myself being thrust through the closed door, which fortunately opened inwards, and under my weight.

"Get in there, younker," the son's voice followed me. "It's the safest place: you don't know who you might meet on the street."

* * *

"Gentlemen, if I might have your attention..."

The sound of a dozen conversations stilled and there was respectful silence. I stood at the back of a large, dusty hall that held little furniture, with the rest of the lugger's crew about me. There must have been at least sixty of us crammed inside. Most were seagoing men; fishing folk in the main, although some wore a form of uniform and appeared to be barge or wherrymen. In addition there were a few land based creatures clad in shore rigs, as well as a fair proportion of regular Royal Navy Jacks who seemed very relaxed and greatly amused by the whole experience. But only one looked to have been wearing the same shabby clothes for the last three days, and that was me.

"I am immensely gratified to see so many return," the voice continued, and it belonged to a Navy lieutenant. He was standing behind a table at the far end and facing us, with the two young officers I had noticed in the street, seated to his left. "And especially glad you have brought so many potential recruits."

Old fears re-emerged with his words, although the atmosphere was nothing like that of my last time in a Rendezvous.

"Protections will be granted to all who qualify for acceptance into the service, and I might remind you these are Navy warrants, and will hold good, even in the current time of crisis."

At this the crowd began to mutter again, but stopped immediately when the officer continued.

"My name is Bryson, and I will be your commanding lieutenant under Captain Dalrimple, who is in overall charge of this sector. Above him, Admiral Berkeley heads the force."

There was a moment of respectful murmuring which amused me; I'd noticed before that, no matter what their station or calling in life, everyone loves an admiral.

"As members of the Sea Fencibles, you will be required to attend for one day's training every sennight, for which you shall receive payment of a shilling, plus victuals." Bryson went on, using the title of the corps I appeared destined to join for the first time.

"The tasks allotted will be various but, in short, you will be charged to defend our country in case of invasion. That will inevitably involve a number of diverse actions other than simply seeing the enemy from our beaches. You may be ordered to attack and harry hostile shipping off the coast, or even be included in our own invasions of French soil from time to time. I am certain any family men amongst us, as well those with a love for their country, will have no difficulty with undertakings such as these."

There was less of a reaction to this, and I wondered if

Lieutenant Bryson had overestimated his audience slightly.

"Any with seagoing experience may volunteer for extended service in a rated Royal Navy ship, but such will not be compulsory, and can end as soon as word is given – there will be no impressment, do I make myself clear?" He did, and it was evidently approved of.

"Others may prefer to be detailed to one of our own craft; we have but two at present, and they are not large, though there be talk of a collier being provided for Fencible use as a gun boat. We may also benefit from any captured local smuggling vessels, some of which, as you may be aware, are almost minor warships in themselves."

Now there was more comment, but I noticed that none of the lugger's crew said a word.

"Those landsmen amongst you will be given the opportunity to train for sea service, or may prefer to take up artillery duties. This coast is already protected by shore batteries but, with a French invasion becoming increasingly likely, these will be supplemented by fortresses manned entirely by the Sea Fencibles. We are to be equipped with French and Dutch cannon which are heavier than the standard British gun, throwing a shot of some forty-two pounds." He paused and grinned. "With such weapons at our disposal, I think we may make merry hell with any interfering foreigner."

The murmuring was replaced by a deep throated roars of approval; and Lieutenant Bryson grinned conspiratorially. I sensed he was the kind who could inspire, and would be a man worth following.

"You will, as I have said, only officially be committing to one day in seven, but I ask you to expect to do more. I ask you to expect to come to grips with the enemy. In the last war we took the fight to the French, with attacks on their shipping and ports led by Admiral Nelson himself, and I see this next bout as being no different. Should Monsieur Crapaud come, we will be the men to meet him, and shall have the weapons, organisation and manpower to thrust that arrogant little amphibian back across our Channel where he belongs."

The speech served its purpose. Men were now stamping their feet and slapping each other on the back in approval. One of the young officers opened a large brown ledger in front of him while the other fingered a handful of papers.

"My midshipmen shall take the addresses of any unknown to us – I regret, only those lodging locally are permitted to join. Then you may request your protections, which have been signed and only need to be made out. Our first assembly is for Tuesday evening at six, when you shall be issued with weapons, and a command order established."

There was a surge from the crowd, as men fought for a chance to sign on. I took a step back but the skipper grabbed hold of my arm and pulled me towards the lieutenant.

"I've a ripe one for you, Mr Bryson," the old man said, when we had pressed our way to the head of the queue. The officer looked at me and was apparently taken aback. I couldn't blame him: my appearance, being as it was, would hardly have made a good impression, but he nodded readily enough.

"Are you a seaman?"

"I've crewed in a lugger, sir." It was a slight exaggeration: I was never one to undersell myself.

"Well, we shall see if we cannot find a larger vessel for your talents. Is he with you, Clarkeson?" he asked the skipper.

"He is, Mr Bryson," the old man confirmed. "And lodges with my family."

"What's your name, lad?" the officer turned his attention back to me. I told him; he reached out for one of the nearest midshipman's papers, and scratched at it with a goose quill pen.

"Glad to have you with us, Audley," he told me, waving the form in the air to dry the ink before handing it across. I took the thing eagerly, then folded and pressed it into my pocket to sit with my former protection, as well as the Bennetts' agreement.

"Very good," the lieutenant said briskly. "I shall see you both on Tuesday next."

One of the midshipmen was vying for his attention, so the skipper and I withdrew. There was still much I did not understand; exactly where the old man's loyalties lay for a start, but the prospect of being included in a proper naval unit certainly appealed. There would be the opportunity to learn more, without the commitment to several years enlistment in the Royal Navy and it was a better outlook than joining up with some foreign privateer. We returned to Shiner and Dan, both of whom seemed less than pleased.

"So, he's gonna be a part of the crew is he?" Shiner asked.

"Aye, an' he has a name. It's Nat; he can take young Josh's place for now."

The son was eyeing me with more than a little disdain. "You can put up with being the boy then, younker?"

"I can do most things," I lied, jutting my chin forward and matching his stare. He was large and probably used to handling himself, but my first line of defence was always to stand up to folk such as him. Once they became convinced I was not going to be intimidated, things usually became easier. And if they never did, I could always run.

"Well if you goes back to blabbing your mouth off, I'll see to it personally that you don't do it again," he promised, and we walked out of the building.

Chapter Eighteen

A lack of both sleep and food was starting to take its toll and, as we made our way back to the harbour, I found I cared little whether I were amongst friends or enemies. The lugger was moored where we left her and I clambered aboard with the rest. Soon we were turned about, and following the course of the channel back towards the sea. The others went about their duties with little apparent notice of me, so I found a place amidships, curled myself up comfortably enough, and immediately drifted off into a deep sleep.

I woke with a bright light in my eyes, just as the boat gave a violent jerk and began to rock. Voices were being raised nearby, and someone gave a loud, guttural chuckle. I was still lying in the same spot and realised it was early morning, and must have spent the night there. Now, despite the sun, I felt an inner chill and my whole body was stiff. I stretched out, but someone carelessly kicked my leg on their way by. I drew it in again and, guessing more would be required of me, clambered groggily to my feet.

We were not at sea, as I had first thought; indeed, the lugger seemed to have been transported into the middle of flat countryside. Then I remembered the small inlet seen the evening before and, looking back, spotted Rye harbour's main channel, with the Revenue cutter still moored proudly at her quay. Our lugger was alongside something far less substantial: a short wooden jetty, beyond which were nothing but a few storage sheds and, further back, a rather mean little single storey cottage. The ground all about was low, and awash in places; I guessed it would flood easily, which probably accounted for the lack of decent housing. The only other man in sight was Dan, the skipper's blond haired son, and I wondered for a moment if this would mean another confrontation. But it appeared he had something important to tell me, and could hardly contain himself from doing so.

"You was too busy asleep to get any food last night," I was told. "And it were tripe and onions," he added with a look of triumph. But he was way off target. Hungry I might have been, but the thought of putting chopped up cow's guts into my own stomach did not appeal in the slightest, and I was able to smile benignly at his words.

"Shiner's headed off home and Dad's below," he continued, clearly disconcerted at my lack of reaction. "If you've had your caulk, you can give him a hand with the rig. I've to help Ma indoors."

I nodded; it made little difference to me, although I was surprised that a strong lad such as him intended leaving manual work for his father. I must have given away something of my thoughts, as he did not turn to go. Instead, for several seconds our eyes met, and I began to grow tense.

Despite our similarities in age, Dan was a good deal larger, and there was definitely some resentment there: should he choose, he would have little difficulty in settling my store for good. I was certain such a thought was also on his mind, but had insight enough to guess he was not so keen for a scrap as he made out. Once more, I matched his look, endeavouring to give the impression that any move he made would be more than rebuffed, while my mind worked out a viable means of escape, should I be put to the test.

Fighting is one of those activities that has never appealed to me, and I privately admit this is due to an innate cowardice. But, with a brain such as mine, it is surely foolish to waste time and risk being hurt when matters might more easily be sorted through discussion. Looking at Dan, I knew intellectual debate was out of the question, though, and was preparing to make a rush for the shore when, just as suddenly, he turned away. I waited, then drew a silent sigh as he heaved himself over the side, landed solidly on the jetty, and began to trudge towards the distant house.

He was more than halfway home when the skipper emerged from the minute aft cabin.

"Dan not about?" he asked.

"He's gone to help his mother," I said. The old man muttered something to himself, then turned his attention to the pile of netting inside the stern locker.

"We're clearing *Lucy* of all fishing gear," I was told. "I expect you'll be ready for breakfast. Help me with this, then we can both get some food inside us." So saying he reached in and began dragging a trawl net out onto the deck.

It was similar to the one I had handled for Ned, although considerably larger, and this was definitely a two man job. Together we collected the beam, corks, lines and apparently miles of mesh, and heaved the lot over the lugger's gunnel.

"Run on tonight," he commented, "so we won't be needin' this." The tone was by no means friendly, but not exactly hostile either, and I was encouraged.

Sharing a difficult load is an excellent way of learning about a man. Much can be told from how he cooperates: pauses, if you have to manoeuvre past a particular point, and maybe gives a nod in appreciation when the same is done for him. By the time we had the net ashore, and safely installed on racks inside one of the sheds, I felt a lot better about the skipper, as I think he did me. We then attended to other smaller items of gear, from buckets and floats to bobbins, booms and buoys. When we were finished, the deck was far clearer and most of the topside lockers lay empty, The old man snorted in what might have been approval then, without a word we began to walk down the short path that led towards the house.

"Ma will fix us some scran, then you can sleep some more if you wish," he told me in a voice that was almost affable. Both food and rest would be very welcome: I could have used a change of clothes as well, but was still unsure of my exact position.

"No need to thank me," the skipper replied when I had. "You'll need all your strength and energy tonight, considering where we's bound."

"Where are you going?" I asked, despite myself.

"Where are *we* goin'?" he corrected, with a slight chuckle, although I was now ravenously hungry, and the semantics didn't seem to make a great deal of difference. "You're in for a spell of foreign travel: how does that sound?"

I suppose it was what I had always claimed to want, but somehow the words did not reassure or in any way fill me with joy.

"Short trip over the water," he continued. "We'll be back

before we knows it, and a good deal the richer."

There had been mention of a run being on that night, but I had assumed we would be taking delivery, not going to collect and, as further hints were given, I gradually accustomed myself to the idea that I would be spending the next few days in France.

* * *

I discovered the family's name was Clarkeson and they actually came across quite well, once I was beyond their carefully erected façade. The small, single storey, house was good, solid and kept clean by a respected mother, who was addressed by everyone as Ma. The father, who skippered the lugger, was hard working with Dan, his son, ostensibly keen to follow the same path. On the face of it then, a worthy family, and what some might consider to be the bedrock of the English working class, even if the two men had been living rather more than double lives for several years.

In addition to fishing and smuggling, both were enlisted in the Sea Fencibles and appeared to combine all three activities without difficulty. By day, they fished, by night, and on occasion, they ran untaxed goods for Ugly Joe, while once a week both turned out for the Sea Fencibles. There they drilled, exercised, and learned all the latest methods for combating any enemy of the state, be they wicked French, deceitful Dutchmen, or the equally despicable smugglers.

I learned the force had been created by a desperate Admiralty towards the end of the last war, when a French invasion appeared more likely than not. Officially they had been stood down with the ensuing peace, but many local units remained active, their commanders seemingly knowing more about our enemy than any government. The intention was for the service to be manned by those with knowledge of the sea who were not already serving their king. Consequently any man not enlisted in the Royal Navy, or any associated force – Customs, Trinity House and the like – could be recruited for part-time service. Many were expected to be fishermen, and it was hoped that, by tapping their local knowledge, a form of naval militia could be established: one made up of men who knew their coastline well, and could defend it both at sea and ashore. Small craft would be used for the former, often private vessels suitably armed and adapted, while on land, members were trained for guerrilla style warfare, and would become expert in harassing any French who had the temerity to invade.

The idea was laudable enough, but volunteers remained hard to find, especially with an allowance of only a shilling a day: little more than an average land-worker's wage. A further incentive soon became apparent though; it was quickly realised that anyone already serving the king in an armed force must be exempt from further impressment. This was by statute law, and could not be revoked without an act of parliament. In fact, it went further: should an enthusiastic regulating officer attempt to force the point, he would be liable for prosecution. The recent hot press had been all encompassing, with many so called safe occupations proving ripe for harvesting. But every member of the Sea Fencibles had stayed immune and, for the cost of only a day's labour a week, they could be certain of remaining so, and at home with their family for the foreseeable future.

And so, by combining the three trades, the Clarkesons were able to survive. I gathered fishing remained their staple and favoured occupation, but hardly provided enough. Smuggling, and neither man tried to glorify the act by dressing it in names such as free or fair trading, was by far the more lucrative, but also held the greater risk, while enlistment in the Sea Fencibles kept them free to follow both pursuits.

The skipper's name turned out to be Jesse, but I only discovered the fact when his wife called him so; if I ever had to refer to him I did so as Mr Clarkeson, and no one told me otherwise. Their home, which was small and neat, was run by Jesse's wife, who could not claim to be either. A woman built on substantial lines, who always dressed in the same well-worn house coat, Ma Clarkeson terrified and fascinated me in equal measure. Her command was kept tidy by utilising a system consisting of constant cleaning, usually to the detriment of any comfort. It was a pleasant enough place though and, despite the obvious hard work of all, lacked any evidence of wealth.

I told them a little about myself after breakfast, and they listened politely. Ma Clarkeson even found me some fresh clothing, saying my own was as much in need of a nap as I appeared. Looking back on it, I suppose I was accepted, as much as any interloper could be in a close knit family. But I found myself missing the Coglans, and not just Susan.

* * *

When I was called upon to crew her properly, *Lucy*, the Clarkeson's lugger, turned out to be a very different vessel from Ned's punt, and I was soon bewildered by the number of sails needing to be set and attended to. We met up at the boat late in the afternoon; Shiner was sailing with us again, and appeared no more friendly than before. Clearly not a favourite of either Clarkeson, he once more stationed himself at the taller mainmast, leaving Dan to look after the mizzen, and Jesse to helm; a position that seemed unequivocally his. I was to help Dan, learn what I could, and try not to get in anyone's way. If I proved useful, they might take me again; otherwise this was my first, last and only trip, and I would be free to seek employment, and lodgings, elsewhere.

Due to the increase in the number of sails, there were also an inordinate number of lines, all apparently identical, although each serving a distinctly different purpose. And it didn't help that I was getting used to the new rig in poor afternoon light that would soon give way to dusk. After one prime blunder, when I all but dropped the mizzen gaff, I decided against trying to bluff my way though and fortunately Dan took pity on me.

"We won't be staying on this tack long, so it ain't important," he said, snatching a line I was holding in wonder and securing it to a cleat with brisk efficiency. "When you've been aboard a while, you'll know the set of the sails without having to think about it." Both his help and change of attitude were welcome. I may well have talked up my skills in the past and, if he'd the mind, it would have been easy to point out my inadequacies. He had opted for guidance rather than censure, though and the change was encouraging. I was actually starting to feel more comfortable in the lugger, and with the Clarkesons in general, when a call from Jesse at the helm brought me back to reality.

"There a cutter to larboard," he said, the urgent tone of his voice imparting as much as any words. "And by the look of her 'sprit, I'd say she's a preventive boat."

All aboard *Lucy* stared out to the east. The light was even worse in that direction, but we could still make out the dirty smudge that marked Jesse's sighting.

"And they got what breeze there is on their quarter," Dan grumbled. I already knew enough about the fickle channel winds from sailing with Ned. Most of the time anything from a south to north-westerly could be relied upon. But, during a relatively fine spell, such as the one we'd been enjoying, an easterly breeze was equally possible. And, once installed, it could blow forever.

"I'm taking her round to starboard," Jesse said, heaving the tiller back until *Lucy* was steering a similar course to the cruiser. We were a good way out by then, and unlikely to be fishing. The change of heading might not disguise our ultimate objective, but at least the goal was less blatant.

Shiner, Dan and I were quick to reset the sails, and it was a mark of my learning that we did so reasonably efficiently. But there was no space for congratulation, we were all far too intent on watching how the Revenue cutter would react to our new course.

"Will he know what we're about?" I asked, rather artlessly.

"He knows we're not here for the good of our health," Dan replied bluntly. "And heading away from the main fishing spots hardly speaks in our favour."

"But he'll also know we ain't big enough to be carrying anything outward," Jesse added from the stern. "Luggers like *Lucy* have been proving too small for owling of late; the best they could hope for is that we're running bullion."

"Gold?" I asked, amazed.

"Frenchies pay a solid premium," Dan confirmed. "We're certainly large enough for that; probably too big, in fact. It would take all night and half the following day for them to carry out a decent rummage of us."

"There's few who can finance such a venture, though," Jesse

continued. "And I can't see an entire Revenue crew wanting to waste so much time on the off chance."

I digested this, while watching the cutter continue on the same heading. She was off our larboard counter now, and steadily forereaching on us, but it was clear this could not be a hot pursuit. I knew by then that Revenue cutters had large rigs, considerably out of proportion to their hulls, and were able to carry a positive mountain of sail: certainly in winds as light as those we were experiencing. But, despite seeing the Rye boat close up the previous evening, that was about the extent of my knowledge. I could spot a thoroughbred when I saw one, though, and this particular vessel certainly fell into such a category.

She was only showing a small headsail, along with what appeared to be a reefed main, but there was no doubting her potential: the lithe little craft could have the heels of us, however much canvas we showed. Her present course and sail pattern would take her alongside within quarter of an hour, and there was no sign of the preventive men acting to make that any the less.

"We'll hold ourselves so till they passes," Jesse said. "Then see them safely out of the way, before turning for France again."

"It'll slow our arrival at Boulogne," Dan said, a little testily. "And, if the gobblers know we're out, they could be waiting for us when we gets back."

"The Revenue has bigger fish to catch than us," Jesse told him shortly. "An' I'd rather arrive late, and stay an extra tide, than risk putting the helm across now."

It was all that was needed to be said. The other members of *Lucy*'s crew accepted the skipper's words totally and even I, who knew least of all, drew comfort from his manner.

It was reassuring having such a strong hand literally at the helm. I had rarely doubted Ned, of course, but somehow there being just the two of us meant I was able to challenge any decision he took. With two trained men and myself, Jesse was facing far greater odds, yet his word remained firm, and no one questioned it. I think, like me, the others were simply glad to have a solid man in command.

Alex's story

I didn't actually have to wait for the monthly coaster: *Antelope*, another Revenue cutter, docked unexpectedly at Whitstable later that morning. She was returning to her Portsmouth base after delivering captured smugglers for a London trial. When he heard of my family connection, and that I intended to volunteer for service, the captain was happy enough for me to tag along; I boarded and we were underway before noon.

Adams had sorted out a fresh pair of trousers and shirt for me and, after being allowed the luxury of a decent wash, I was feeling a little more the thing and looking forward to getting back to Hastings. The crew of the cutter were in no rush, though. I guessed their little jaunt to London was something of a treat for all, and they made no secret of wanting to stretch the journey back for as long as they could.

A berth with the seamen was allocated to me: I turned in at dusk and later told I slept solidly for more than twelve hours. Once awake, though, I went straight up on deck, and settled myself there for the rest of the following day.

We were particularly lucky that spring; the weather stayed fine and I was content simply to breathe in the fresh air. It hadn't been a game of skittles in the pressing tender's hold and, even though I had been unconscious for most of the time, the cutter's sleeping quarters were not exactly well ventilated.

But *Antelope* herself was a fascinating boat; I had seen several cutters before the one that Prettyman accounted for, and knew they could travel apace. The hull was surprisingly wide, and she carried sails for a vessel more than double her length. This was mainly achieved by the use of a reeving bowsprit, the length of which would have been illegal in any private vessel. To my eye, she was well armed, with broadsides of carriage guns that ran from stem to stern; doubtless a powerful privateer, or any ship of war might give her a seeing to, but the crew of a standard fishing lugger would have felt intimidated by such force.

I longed to feel her true mettle, see the reef shaken from her massive main, and the sail hauled in tight, then joined by square sails and, perhaps, an additional jib. But the commander was in no hurry, and we barely broke spray as the boat continued to meander along the Kent coastline. Life in Hastings had made me both philosophical and patient; I resigned myself to the wait and dozed in the spring sunshine while the rest of the crew yarned quietly and took surreptitious sips from small bottles I guessed to contain untaxed spirit.

By the time the sun started to fall, I was becoming stiff. It would be growing damp on deck soon, and thoughts of a stuffy seamen's mess were now not quite so abhorrent. I knew if the commander was determined to continue at such a leisurely pace it would be several more hours before we raised Hastings. There had been little other shipping up until then; certainly not the usual number of fishing boats: a shortage that could probably be laid at the door of the recent hot press. So when we spotted the lugger to the east of Rye, I stood up and wandered over to inspect. She was not fishing; in fact I would have taken her to be heading across the Channel, but then I was no expert.

Antelope's crew were however, and shared my opinion. They began making disparaging remarks amongst themselves about it being a likely runner although, as they were far from their own sector, none seemed particularly keen to do anything about it. The lugger was not travelling fast, and turned onto our course when we were spotted. In no time we had forereached on her and began to pass, less than half a cable off her beam.

Some of the Revenue men began to call out sarcastic remarks and mildly insulting comments, which were returned with interest by the lugger's crew. I got the impression of no illusion and little real animosity on either side; each knew exactly what the other was about, and were equally content that they should continue. Had there been booty visible on her deck, or a supply ship close by, I suppose the cutter's commander might have acted but, as a crime had yet to be committed, there was almost a grudging respect between the two. It was as if a gamekeeper had encountered a known poacher on neutral ground.

Nothing else of interest occurred, but I continued to watch idly from the starboard bulwark. The lugger appeared no different from the many hundreds seen before, and I was about to go below and investigate the possibility of food, when something brought me up short.

It was Nat. He was standing amidships and, although the clothes were different, there was no mistaking that phiz. I stood for a moment, just staring, and would have sworn our eyes met. Then the lugger's skipper shouted something to our commander, and there was laughter on both sides. I recognised him as the man who had worked with Ugly Joe to rescue us. Nat must have met up with him, and taken up the offer to join as a runner.

My attention went back to the figure amidships. Yes, he had definitely seen me and, as our two vessels passed, even raised a hand in vague acknowledgement. But the short distance between us only emphasised the gulf that had already appeared. Friends we may have been, but it was clear we were both now on opposing sides. I touched my forehead in an ironic salute, paused for a couple of moments, then finally turned away and took myself below.

Chapter Nineteen

Nat's story

Seeing Alex had given me the jitters as well as inducing a rare feeling of guilt. Logically, I knew there was absolutely no reason for the last emotion, which probably had more to do with my knowing him, and his background, too well. There had been no close friends in my life until then and I knew already that he would always be considered my best. But, in that chance and wordless meeting, I think both of us knew our history was exactly that, and we were now set on very different courses.

The thoughts and feelings stayed with me for some while, even though I constantly reassured myself that none of this was my fault: I had not done a single thing wrong, as such. At worst, it had been a series of small mistakes, some so infinitesimal as to make them barely worth the mention. But a line had definitely been crossed, and that strange encounter emphasised it perfectly: we were friends that had become foes. Little more than a day or so had passed between our sharing both a berth and a common fate, to him crewing aboard a Revenue cutter, while I sailed in a smugglers' lugger, and on a mission that was anything but lawful. The contrast could hardly have been wider, or come at any greater speed.

But once I accepted exactly where we both stood, a lot became simpler. And it helped that my personal position was not so very terrible. I had what amounted to an iron clad protection and, if luck continued to shine, would soon be making proper money. Enough to pay off anything the Bennetts might demand at least, and even claim Susan as my wife.

Alex could take his chance with the Revenue, but I doubted it would do him as much good. Britain was heading for another war; once that began, smuggling was bound to increase and probably become more lucrative as a result. And, though a few might be caught and even hanged, the majority of free traders led an easy and well protected existence, whereas life for a member of the Revenue was anything but. Preventive men faced danger both at sea and ashore; even when off duty, Alex would be at risk, to say nothing of his family. Some might well argue that he would have been better never to have left the pressing tender in the first place.

But still, as I watched him turn his back, it was with genuine sorrow. We had been a good team, and one that it was a pity to break up. But the body of water that separated us was already far too wide and growing by the second.

After a spell, the cruiser began to disappear into the setting sun and, as Jesse finally pressed the tiller, aiming our stem for the coast of France once more, I knew myself ready for whatever we were about to encounter.

Alex's story

There was no harbour at Hastings, and *Antelope* had a deep keel like most of her type, so was forced to stand off. I was taken in aboard a squat little boat the crew referred to as a galley. The tide was low, and they beached it on the sand, leaving me to jump into the well remembered surf. I pushed them back out as I had done a thousand times before with other boats, but now it all felt so very different. Only a matter of days had passed since my leaving, but this was still the longest period I had ever spent away from home and was returning as a very different person.

It was almost completely dark and the Stade was just as filled with boats as I would have expected. But a closer inspection revealed most were laid up. Masts had been taken down, tarred canvas covered the hulls and unusually heavy line and chain made sure all were properly secured. Even some of the runners' craft had been similarly treated, while five of the heaviest luggers, the big three-masters that spent most of the week at sea, and sat at anchor in the lee of the Piers Rocks when not, were also hauled up. I noticed old Ned Coglan's punt lying alone and apparently surplus to requirements. I trudged up the shingle beach in my damp boots and trousers, looking about for a friendly face, or even anyone who might know me, but all was deserted, and even the usually busy Rock-a-Nore lay strangely quiet.

As I drew near, I noticed *The Anchor* had lost the ensign that had been flying above the door last time I visited, and was now restored to its former usage. I stopped and, shielding my eyes with my hands, peered in through the salt stained windows, but there were no lights burning inside and the place was obviously closed. I could have knocked and tried to raise Tilly, but knew her parents not to approve of me. Besides, with my status as a provisional member of the Revenue unconfirmed, a very real risk remained that I could yet be pressed. Instead I moved on, and was soon opening my own front door, and walking inside.

It had been less than a week, but the front room appeared smaller. Our parlour furniture was still swathed in sheets of course; a practice followed by many families in the area and intended to preserve any good pieces for the rare occasions when they were used. But on that night the vast expanse of white cotton gave an ethereal quality to the place that I found quite disturbing. It was different in the kitchen, where the range was hot, and lamps guttered on the table and window shelf, but still there was no one to greet me. Movement could be seen through the back window, though, and I knew someone was in our tiny yard.

Drawing nearer, I made out my mother taking in the washing, something I had seen her do countless times, but now she also had apparently altered. Her movements were taut and jerky and the lamplight cast shadows that made her far older. I watched for some while before she sensed my eyes upon her and turned towards me. The expression was one of shock, as if something truly terrible had been spotted. Then it softened suddenly, and the current piece of laundry was dropped as she rushed inside.

"Alexander Combes, wherever have you been?" Her question came before she was properly through the door. "We were so worried!"

Mum was a tactile woman and hugged me most evenings, but this was more the Christmas or birthday version and I remember thinking how much thinner she felt.

"I was pressed," I said, with more than a little pride.

"Well yes, we guessed that. I sent a message to Mr Henderson at the Custom House, and he was very good: spent ages at the Medcalfs' place, but could not get you back. The Navy told him you was bound for the Nore."

"I was, but my plans got changed," I told her. "Where's Seth and Josh?"

"Now how should I know that?" she snorted. "Who'd tell a mother? They've been working late the last few nights, though the Dear knows where – herring season's been over for weeks."

News that my brothers were not present was disappointing. We had never been particularly close; they were very much a team, being only eleven months apart in age and so similar in size and temperament. They also suffered less from Dad's reputation: being older and always together meant that most of the unpleasantness was thrown in my direction. But they were still family and, with Tilly in her condition and my decision to join the Revenue still fresh, I would have preferred it had they been around.

"Have you heard from Tilly?" I could not help but ask.

"Tilly?" Mum was surprised. "Why should you be thinking about her? You haven't even told me how you got away from the press."

I said there wasn't time, that we must wait for the others to return, and maybe I should go down to the Stade and see if my brothers were there. It was nothing more than a ruse: I'd noticed Uncle Saul's boat laid up on the beach where it had obviously been for some while. Whatever they had told mum, it was definitely not going out that night and any work they had planned did not involve fishing. But I so wanted to see Tilly, and rather lacked the energy to explain why. It was strange: after waiting so long to return home, I could not get out of the place fast enough.

Mum wasn't happy I could tell, and there was the very real danger of a lecture brewing, so I ducked out of the kitchen and was through the front door again before it could begin. I didn't like upsetting my mother but, now that I knew the lay of the land, reckoned she would rather I was back, and being annoying, than still missing.

Nat's story

I had thought myself ready for whatever I was about to encounter, but nothing could have been further from the truth. Apart from my short period in the pressing tender, and the odd occasions when Ned and I had been caught by tides, I had spent relatively little time sailing at night and, as the darkness came, it brought with it quite a revelation.

The moon was not due to rise for several hours, and with Jesse's boat showing no lights, the world had become a strange and eerie place. It was a clear sky and we could see well enough by the light of the stars, yet there was no colour or depth to anything. With little breeze, the famed chop of the Channel settled to nothing more than a gentle roll. We were sailing on seas that might be filled with heavy oil and, though France was still our friend in theory, when her dark mass of coastline began to grow large above our prow, the sight chilled me.

It was sinister and altogether too close. I had been told there would be plenty in Boulogne keen to meet and trade with us. But, for much of my adult life, the French had been our enemies, and I could not escape the feeling that *Lucy*, together with all those aboard, was steering straight into danger.

"That will be Calais," Dan murmured next to me. There was no other shipping in sight but his voice remained low and I wondered if some of my apprehension was rubbing off on him. I stared forward, and could just make out a tiny bright point on the nearby headland. "At least when we sees that we knows there is no war," he continued, following my gaze. "French only keeps a light in times of peace."

"We'll stay on this tack until we draws closer," Jesse's voice was equally restrained and came from the stern, where he was manning his precious tiller. "There's no blockade, but I don't trust our Navy not to be about, and would rather stay in the shallows, if it be possible."

And so we closed with the coast. More lights became obvious, but these were from the town itself, and Nat kept them on our larboard bow. Then, when the first hint of breakers could be seen, we turned to the south-east, and began to follow the coast down towards our destination.

Alex's story

I found Tilly in the back yard of *The Anchor*. It was now quite dark; she was stacking empty crates by the outhouse and did not notice me for some while. She too looked different: even in the poor light I could spot a deep flush about her cheeks and she appeared oddly out of breath. Eventually I caught her attention, and the reaction was much the same as my mother's.

She came across and we found the missing plank in their fence that was convenient to talk through.

"Alex, I thought I'd never see you again," she told me. Close up, her face was definitely altered: it looked fuller and was really quite rosy, while her eyes shone clear and bright.

"I know, I was pressed," I confessed, as if it were some wicked indulgence. "But I'm free again now, and have come back for you."

She blinked at me for a moment, and I suppose it was a foolish thing to say. There was little I could do immediately in terms of taking her away, or even providing for our future. And with the damned fence between us, we could not even embrace. I pressed my lips up to the gap: she responded and neither of us said anything for a while. Then I asked the question that had been plaguing me for the past few days. "How's the baby?"

"Baby's fine," she whispered, looking suddenly cross. "Though no one knows yet, and it is best to stay so."

I nodded, but secretly wondered if such a thing were possible. To me, Tilly appeared very bonnie, and I would be surprised if her mother had missed the change.

"What are you going to do?" she asked. "How will we

survive?"

"You must not worry, I have a place lined up." It was a lie, but not a bad one. What I had told the Collector at Whitstable was quite right: I would have preferred to be in my father's sector but another idea had been festering in my head since then. "Tilly, I'm to join a Revenue cruiser," I told her.

She was silent for a moment, clearly digesting the information. Both of us knew there was no vessel based at Hastings; the shore just would not have accommodated one. So I would be moving on, which meant she must inevitably stay behind.

I could see her thinking this out, and was burning to reveal my dreams in full, however fanciful they might sound. The crew of the cutter had been definite: hands were relatively easy to come by. Even with the recent hot press, the Treasury's enforceable protections would give them sufficient whereas, if I went and saw Mr Henderson, he would find me something on land, of that I was certain. But my dreams now stretched far beyond being a simple landshark and, even from the brief time aboard one, I had decided there was no other place for me but as crew in a Revenue cutter.

If the boat at Rye did not need me, I would try Shoreham, or Newhaven, or one of the other stations until I found one that did. There was even the possibility of returning to Whitstable, but a cutter it would have to be.

"Won't that mean you movin' away?" she asked at last.

"Only for a while" I told her, and she nodded in understanding. There had never been the chance to discuss employment, other than I would have find some. She knew as well as me how working for the crown would make both our lives harder, but that must be offset by a regular income.

"*Stag* is the closest to here," I continued. "She's based at Rye, carries fourteen cannon and has a fine commander."

She winced slightly when I mentioned the guns, but I could see she was thinking the rest over.

"Tilly, the money would be so much better than anything I could earn on land," I implored.

"Is pay that good?" she was doubtful.

"More than they give a seaman in the Royal Navy," I replied.

"And there is always the prospect of reward." She nodded again, and still looked serious, but the idea was being considered.

"I can send for you as soon as I'm settled. The crew mostly sleep ashore: we can get a small house," I gushed. "Maybe not straight away, though I shall still be able to provide for you."

"But Alex, the baby will be here in a few months..."

She was right, it would be a close call; which meant I really should be getting along.

"Then I shall head for Rye tonight." I said, decisively.

"Rye?" she repeated.

"Yes, did I not say?" I was going to elaborate, but stopped when I noticed Tilly was now smiling. I looked at her quizzically and she explained.

"Rye is where Nat was heading, when he first arrived in Hastings."

I had forgotten that. In fact, so intent was I on telling Tilly my story, I had almost forgotten about Nat altogether.

"Are the Coglans all right?" I asked, more out of guilt than interest.

"Far as I know," she replied, a little distantly. "There was some trouble when Nat didn't collect the lugger – we'd all guessed he had been pressed as well. Most of the men folk round here were after all."

"What kind of trouble?"

"Both Bennetts were released almost straight away," she said sadly. "But then you'd expect that. They turned up at All Saints Street the followin' morning, wanting Ned to make a down payment; they said Nat had promised them a guinea."

"Does he have the boat?" I asked.

"Boat but no sails; they weren't included, 'parently, and Ned is hardly flush."

It was the sort of thing I suspected would happen, but still a shame: the Coglans might have their faults, but were basically good people.

"They still wanted the down payment, though and said it were set for a guinea a week from then on. It ended up with Ned scratching about until he finally produced a bean. The Dear alone knows where he got it – I never thought them to have two pennies to rub together. But pay up he did, and it'll keep the Bennetts off their back, though only for a few more days."

I was sorry to hear that as well, but there was little I could do about it. Perhaps if Ned had not been so stubborn, the two of us might have made a team every bit as good as him and Nat. I was still unsure why the old man had been so dead set against the idea, but there was no sense in thinking of it now.

"What happens then?" I asked, despite myself. "If he can't produce another guinea?"

"Then Susan starts working for the Bennetts," Tilly replied coldly. "They got a place in George Street 'parently; their own private little pot house. She says it will be like working at *The Cutter* though, between you and me, I rather doubt it."

I was amazed. Nat had told me a bit about the woman he had met at the Bennetts' place; it didn't sound like the sort of role that would suit the Sniffy Susan I knew at all. "But why would she want to do that?" I asked.

"I don't think she does," Tilly replied.

Chapter Twenty

Nat's story

The wind remained low: we reached Boulogne as dawn was starting to break, but were forced to await the tide, and finally entered port in broad daylight. The place was far larger and contained more warships than I had expected. Some might be ready to sail, with yards crossed and topmasts set up although most were obviously being held in reserve, and had canvas awnings spread above their empty decks. But the hulls still carried rows of gun ports; it was clear all were heavily armed and sobering to remember they belonged to our potential enemy.

There was no trace of animosity from the French people however. A small boat came out to meet us and two beaming men jumped aboard. They must have been the first foreigners I had met; émigrés were relatively common in England at that time, but none had made it as far as Ninfield, and I regarded them with cautious interest. One was dressed in a strange dark blue uniform and carried, rather than wore, a flamboyant hat, whereas the other seemed more the man of business. Both knew the Clarkesons and greeted them like old friends; the civilian even went so far as to hug Jesse which, I think, surprised him as much as me. They also spoke English: a revelation in itself and, apart from the physical contact, their appearance and behaviour was much as normal people. I'm not quite sure what I expected, but my sister and I had grown up with the concept that anyone not entirely British was bound to fall somewhere between a monster and Satan, with the French decidedly bordering on the latter. It was strangely disappointing to discover otherwise.

We were directed to a quay which also held a line of rather drab fishing boats, and promptly secured by two younger lads, who were every bit as keen to look after us as any British boy ashore. Not much was required of me, so I took the opportunity to look about.

Boulogne was indeed bigger than I had imagined, with countless tall houses of three or four storeys that stretched back in rows as far as I could see, as well as a vast number of extensive warehouses. There were several other separate quays and more than one basin, including a particularly large affair currently under construction just across from where *Lucy* lay. Work was still being carried out to either side, but the basin was already flooded and contained a small assortment of barges and lighters towards the centre. It was clearly intended for more, however; a good deal more: berths had been marked out and a series of mooring buoys were in place. This puzzled me; I'd not expected such facilities for what must surely be river craft, and wondered at their presence at a seaport. Dan was standing nearby and I could have asked easily enough, but was getting tired of always playing the coke, so let the matter drop.

The early sun was now shining brightly and, despite the novelty of our surroundings, I was hoping for the chance to take a decent rest. The passage had taken us far longer than Jesse predicted and, apart from the occasional doze, we had all been awake for most of the night. I had yet to learn the Clarkesons possessed endless energy, and assumed them to be equally tired, but was soon proved wrong. Before I was properly aware, they had jumped clear of the deck and, with Shiner following close behind, were walking down the quay, leaving the boat, and me, to our own devices.

I hurried to catch up, and joined them just as they were turning into a busy side street that everyone else apparently knew well. The two Frenchman were still with us, and simultaneously talking nineteen to the dozen. Both had strong accents, so I couldn't follow everything, but obviously much of great importance had happened since the last time *Lucy* visited, and all needed to be related loudly, and in the least possible time.

I followed, still wondering about the barges seen earlier. However busy river trade might be, to require such craft and provide what was apparently their own designated berth, was out of keeping. But then I reminded myself that, in time of war, the French coast would be heavily blockaded. For the town to survive without deep sea traffic, an alternative supply route must be found. Even ignoring the demands of a local population, the crew of any ships at anchor would consume a good deal on their own. Consequently, a high number of river craft would be needed to prevent everyone starving to death. The deduction pleased me, and I continued along the road feeling quite superior.

A couple of hundred yards further on, the Frenchmen led us off the road and into a yard, sheltered by two rather spindly trees. There was one large empty table set under their lee, where Jesse and the others sat down as if it had been their own home. Two older women came out; they wore dark, sombre clothing but pleasant expressions and I took them to be related to the Frenchmen. There was much laughing and general gaiety as they deposited heavy, wide mouthed cups in front of each of us, then filled them with a thick brown liquid that steamed in the bright, morning air.

I waited until Jesse and Dan had tried theirs, before sipping at mine. It was hot, and burned my mouth, but remained a fine drink and I almost drained it in one.

Setting the cup down, I looked about for more and noticed Dan regarding me, not unkindly, from further down the table.

"How do you like your first taste of France then, younker?" he asked.

I grinned, and wiped the residue of chocolate from my mouth. I liked it fine.

* * *

The surprises continued as we were given a generous breakfast. I'd heard much about the French and their fondness for nauseating food. Rumour had it, most of what they ate consisted of frogs, slugs and similar undesirables, all heavily seasoned, flavoured with garlic and served with stale biscuit and potted fatty liver paste. But there was nothing unpleasant about the quaintly shaped rolls that dissolved deliciously in the mouth, the crusty, warm bread cut from loaves of an extraordinary length, creamy butter and rich, fruit-filled jams. No porridge was on offer, or cooked meats, neither did they have eggs, sausage, bacon, or black pudding. But I had more than enough to eat and, after what had been a worrying time for my stomach, felt properly full when the table was finally clear.

Jesse and Dan bid their goodbyes to the two Frenchmen and we wound our way back to the boat at a slower pace. I walked next to Jesse, who seemed more relaxed and at home than when in Ramsgate or Rye.

"How long do we stay?" I asked, sensing this would be one of the occasions when he might consent to talk.

"We'll be gone with tonight's tide," he said.

"So soon?" I asked although, inside, was not sorry. France had come as a pleasurable surprise but, for all my claims of wanting to travel, I did not feel comfortable outside England.

"There ain't no sense in stayin' here: it only arouses suspicion," he snorted. "But we'll be back afore long. We takes a load at least once a fortnight; sometimes more, depending on how fast they needs the booty inland. What Joe Prettyman pays ain't riches, but is regular, and allows us to keep *Lucy* in trim and our bellies filled the rest of the time."

"But if war is declared..." I began the question in little more than a whisper; it did not seem polite to discuss such things while walking down our potential enemy's street. "If we find ourselves fighting the French again, what will happen then?"

"If war is declared, it won't make no difference," Dan interrupted from behind in a far more strident tone. "We have to dodge our own ships as it is, so we're used to that. And the French don't wage war on fishermen, or smugglers."

The concept of trading with an enemy shocked me for a moment: then commercial sense took over. I knew some foreign goods, such as brandy and lace, were not available while we were at war; consequently runners like Jesse and his son would have a virtual monopoly, and be able to fix their price accordingly. The thought pleased me, especially as I could foresee some of their profits finding a way into my own pocket. Then we were back at the boat, and I received yet another surprise.

"Well met, Jackie!" A decidedly English voice boomed out

around the harbour, and there was Ugly Joe Prettyman standing proudly on *Lucy*'s foredeck. If anything, his dress was even more flamboyant than before: a full length cloak gave a slightly piratical air, while the ornate bicorn hat was trimmed with gold lace and could almost have come from the Royal Navy. "You will see we have not been idle while you was a feastin'!"

Unconsciously, I followed his gaze. *Lucy* was low in the water and for a moment I wondered if some dastardly Frenchman had scuppered her. Then, as we approached, the reason became more obvious.

A crowd of heavily built men dressed in short sleeved shirts and loose-fitting trousers were standing on the quay, and most appeared both smug and slightly out of breath. We drew closer still, and could see that *Lucy* was literally loaded to the gunwales; her topsides being piled high with small round barrels as well as larger casks, chests, and rolls of what looked like cloth.

"Happy to see you, Mr Prettyman," Jesse said gruffly, although there was little genuine warmth in his tone. "An' folks call me Jesse," he added, with emphasis on the name. "I see we're filled, and with little to spare."

He stepped aboard his boat ahead of us, and it was far less of a stride than when we had left her just an hour or so before.

"You'll find the hold fair brimmed," Prettyman informed him. "Though we left much of the lighter stuff topside. I should not fear a wind at present, but would rather not lose you, or your vessel."

"Or his precious, bloody cargo," Dan whispered under his breath.

Even secured and in harbour, *Lucy* felt far more solid under my feet; I could not begin to guess how much fluid was being stored below, but her freeboard must have been several inches lower and I was glad of the good weather.

"Your manifest, captain!" Prettyman said, producing a sheet of paper with a flourish. "And I shall see you again in a fortnight or so." Jesse took the document and pressed the thing into his pocket unread. Prettyman then left without further ado, and to no word of farewell from any aboard *Lucy*.

The Frenchmen moved off also, and were soon absorbed in the

crowd that thronged along the quay, leaving the four of us standing alone in our laden craft. Dan and Jesse began to look at the stored goods, although neither made any attempt at checking or counting the cargo.

"Reckon there's more here than last time," Dan grumbled. "Just hope the old bugger's got a landing crew rigged and ready."

"He's never let us down afore," Jesse replied softly, if without conviction. "But we're tired; what say we take a caulk now and meets up again before high?"

"Evening tide's set for six," Dan agreed, then looked up to me and Shiner. "Either of you are welcome to sleep, or go into town as you will, but make sure you're back for four; we've only a couple of hours either side."

Shiner made a monosyllabic reply, heaved himself back over the side, and was soon lost to the town.

"Same goes for you, younker," Dan informed me. It wasn't the first time he had called me so, even though there could be little difference in our ages.

"There'll be precious little room below, but it's warm enough for a caulk on deck," Jesse added, overhearing. "Or you can take a gander about the town. You'll find a deal to see and the Frenchies are usually friendly enough. If you should get in a fix, just holler for the harbour master, and don't be afraid to mention Prettyman's name. As soon as they know you're with a runner's crew, you'll be looked after proper."

I was grateful for Jesse's advice, but the breakfast had been filling, and all I really wanted to do was rest. Both Clarkesons seemed set on staying aboard, and claimed the minute space at the stern. Meanwhile, I poked about the newly loaded stores, and found several bolts of cloth wrapped in thick brown paper. There was no way of telling what was inside; it might have been cotton, satin, or the finest silk. Any would make a good enough bed, however and, though we might be on enemy territory and carrying a boat-load of illicit cargo, I had done nothing wrong, and settled myself down to sleep the sleep of the righteous.

* * *

The sun was burning hot and heavy when I awoke and a prickling on my face and lower arms told me it had been doing so throughout the day. I stretched, then felt at my skin; both cheeks were tender and swollen while my nose was completely raw.

"Got quite a burn on you there," Shiner advised, with a distinct lack of sympathy. He sat on one of the small barrels nearby and was watching me with apparent interest.

"You could have woken me," I complained. Sleeping during the day always left me ill-tempered, and to know that someone had been awake and alert while I was frying in the sun hardly improved my mood a jot.

"I could, but then I weren't here," he told me, as if in revelation and I realised then that his voice was thicker than usual and he had been drinking. "Only just made it back m'self," he went on to explain. "Met up with those dockyard mateys from earlier. Hardly spoke a word of their lingo but, by the time we was finished, all were getting along fine."

Shiner's face had always been particularly dull and empty, but, as he spoke, it took on fresh life and performed several contrasting expressions in quick succession, as if trying to prove its true versatility.

"Will you be fit to crew us home?" I asked, artlessly.

"Fit to crew?" Shiner roared. "When have I been anything but? Why, I could take this little tub to China if I chose." He seemed disgusted, and I was genuinely sorry to have upset the man, then an idea took hold of him, and he began to point at me. "I heard of folks wakin' up in a bad skin, but never thought it were meant literal!"

As jokes went, this wasn't the best, although it tickled Shiner somewhat and he took to repeating 'in a bad skin' several times between bouts of hysterical laughter. I ignored him and, standing on the now crowded deck, stretched once more. My arms had been heavily tanned already so would heal in no time, but I had always worn a hat when sailing with Ned, and my face felt every bit as raw as it must have looked.

"There's tallow in the stern locker," a far more sober voice came from behind and I looked round to see Jesse. He must also have been asleep but, sheltered in the cabin, was not affected by the sun. "Some says it works on the sunburn, but I'm no expert," he continued.

"Well young Nat here will be in a spell," Shiner announced, and started to laugh again. The spasm turned to a fit of coughing that brought him to his feet before suddenly subsiding. Then, after curious look at each of us, he sat back down on the barrel, fell to one side, and slipped unconscious onto the deck.

"If he's been at the booty, there'll be hell to pay," Dan growled, approaching. He was rubbing at his eyes and clearly had been woken by the commotion.

"Maybe, but not by him," Jesse confirmed. For a moment he stared down at Shiner, then tutted softly. "If he's drunk what's aboard, we'll be putting him to bed with a spade."

I looked at them both in mild confusion.

"All this is over-proof spirit," Dan explained, pointing at the ranks of barrels. "Let it down with water and caramel, and you'll get twice the quantity, as well as a brandy fit for the king. But take it neat and it's poison."

"I think he was drinking in the town," I said.

"Then there's no knowing what he's taken," Jesse replied. "With luck he'll wake up with nothing more than a sore head, but it don't solve our little problem. It's a goodly jaunt to Fairlight; we have to make a quick passage, and *Lucy*'s loaded fit to sink."

"While Shiner here will be about as much use as a shortbread cricket bat." Dan added sadly, then looked up at me. "Reckon you'll have to start pulling your weight now, younker."

* * *

I did and, from that moment on, truly started to feel part of *Lucy*'s crew. More had been learned than I realised on the journey out and, tending to the mainmast on my own was actually easier than sharing the mizzen with Dan. We were free of the harbour mouth as evening was starting to settle, but the boat sat low in the water and made slow progress. With the fine weather keeping the wind in the east, it was growing darker by the time we picked up the light on Cape Gris-Nez. This was the headland that signalled our time to turn to larboard and start the dash across to England. All had been relatively quiet until then, with only two small fishing smacks and an East India packet for company as they passed us on their way into harbour. But, as we prepared to make our turn, more lights could be seen, and soon it was clear the sea was no longer ours alone to enjoy.

We were a good way offshore by then, and the wind had dropped for us, so Jesse let the lugger ride sluggishly in the gentle swell as we watched. At first, the lights were all we could make out; they shone bright and in a cluster that slowly widened with their approach. Then we began to see more clearly, and a spell fell upon the boat that even Shiner's vibrant snores were unable to break.

It was a fleet. There were a good many vessels: some were powered by their own sail, and others obviously under tow. I made out brigs and small warships mingling with what I took to be coasters as well as variously assorted *chasse-marées*. But amongst them were several large, wide, and surely unseaworthy barges, similar to those I had seen in the basin at Boulogne.

These varied in length, some being up to a hundred feet from bow to stern, others far shorter, but all would have been happier on a gentle inland lake or a wide forgiving river. Even in what was the sweetest of motions, they seemed precarious, while any degree of spindrift or spume would have seen them swamped.

None of us had seen shipping the like of them before: they were a truly amazing sight, although to what purpose they had been built, I still could not guess. Already I had rejected any clever theories about river traffic, and the need to keep Boulogne supplied in case of blockade. These barges were intended for something far more ambitious and, only as I thought further, did their true purpose dawn on me.

There could be no mistaking the French we had met were genuinely keen to help us. The fact that our actions, in smuggling, were undermining the British government might have been an influence of course but, even so, there was real warmth there.

These barges told a completely different story however, and I am certain none of us were in any doubt of their malevolence or intent.

"I think I shall put as much water betwixt us and that little lot as I can," Jesse said, as he pressed the tiller over. But the wind was staying close to the land and our turgid craft was left to wallow as the fleet continued down the coast.

I looked to Jesse, and then Dan, but both were equally in awe and uncommunicative, while Shiner remained oblivious, and continued making low humming noises from my former bed. Then, after we had observed them long enough, our wind finally picked up, and *Lucy*'s sails began to fill once more. Soon we were stubbing our prow deeper into the channel, and the strange sight was dwindling off our stern. But it was not forgotten, and we remained spellbound until Dan finally broke the silence.

"Did you ever see the like?" he asked his father earnestly and, experienced though the old man surely was, it appeared he had not.

Chapter Twenty-One

Looking back on it, the rest of the journey was pretty uneventful, even though I don't think I drew an easy breath until the English coast loomed out of the darkness. It was obvious that this was effectively a trial run; Shiner was still very much a mystery to me, but I figured neither Jesse, nor his son, held any great love for him. Therefore it seemed reasonable that, if I made a fair fist of things, it would lead to a permanent berth.

The overloaded lugger sailed like a brick, but Jesse helmed her well, and there were other factors in our favour. The wind veered and later grew, although not enough to raise too much of a swell, so our passage across the Channel was both steady and reasonably brisk. As soon as I sighted the Dungeness light tower, Jesse pressed the helm across and Dan was directed to set the mizzen topsail. Time, and the state of the tide, were becoming important, and we seemed to be falling behind. The extra canvas gave us slightly more speed, but Jesse remained tense and irritable as we approached the coast near Fairlight, while even I knew the moon was due to rise before long.

Shiner started to stir at that point but, apart from complaining about his head, did nothing to help, and I had no intention of giving up my post. Jesse plainly was intending to beach and reduced sail to the solitary jib, although it still felt that we were coming in far too quickly. Then, when the last remaining canvas was struck I braced myself for the impact.

This came sooner than anticipated, and almost threw me off balance. Dan plunged over the side and I followed, clutching the forward painter in my fist as I joined him in the surf. This also came as a surprise, being deeper than I was used to, and rising quite high on my chest. Between us, we hauled the boat further up, and were soon joined by two men who emerged silently from out of the darkness.

"What time do you call this?" one demanded, and another said we had been expected over an hour back, but there was enough to do to keep everyone occupied, and neither of us replied. *Lucy* was heaved up and, as the tide slowly left her, began to settle on the level shore. More bodies arrived and she was secured, then Jesse and Shiner jumped down, and the four of us waded slowly out of the water and up the shallow beach.

There were men to either side by then: well built and manifestly capable, they allowed us past without a word, while claiming the lugger as their own. Soon we reached the shingle, and were in the lee of what was indeed a mighty line of cliffs when Jesse stopped, and we all turned back to look.

It was an impressive sight. By the light of the stars and three small lanterns, two lines of men could be seen systematically emptying *Lucy* of her cargo. The assorted barrels and cases were being run up the beach, and already ordered piles had been formed at the base of the cliffs. We were apparently just in time; the boat was being lightened with the receding tide, which was now close to low water. If they worked fast, *Lucy* should be pretty near to empty when it turned, and then be able to rise with the flow. This meant she would have been beached and vulnerable for the shortest possible period. We were late, but there was still time before the moon rose; in fact the whole thing had been beautifully organised, and I thoroughly approved.

The landers were being watched over by a group of ten or more stoutly built men who carried heavy bats. They paced back and forth and seemed to have eyes everywhere. At first I thought them provided to encourage those tending to the lugger, but the work was being done swiftly and with rare competence. I was reminded of the manner in which the fishing boats had been brought in on my first afternoon at Hastings. All those unloading were aware of what had to be done, and worked in quiet concert with their fellows to see it carried out with the minimum of fuss.

A small dog began barking nearby, then came bounding across the beach towards what he must have assumed to be friendly activity. Passing close to the armed group, the noise stopped in a stunted yelp as a club was swung and the dog fell lifeless onto the shingle. Low, guttural, laughter followed, and I felt suddenly sorry for any preventive man who should be foolish enough to intervene.

We watched for no more than a couple of minutes, then the two Clarkesons set off once more towards the great expanse of chalk cliff that looked quite dark and forbidding in the starlit sky. I glanced at Shiner, but he was making himself comfortable on the beach and clearly intended to sleep. I considered joining him, but my clothes were damp from the sea, and with both face and arms sore from sunburn, the rough ground looked less than inviting. Instead I headed after Jesse and Dan.

The older man had collected a dark lantern from somewhere. To my coloured mind the smell of warm tallow made my mouth water, but I had already guessed there would be no time wasted eating, and we trudged up the beach together in silence. The light remained closed, and I stumbled over ground that rose steeply, and contained no end of small rocks and narrow crannies, all specifically designed to trap a tired and hungry soul. Then we were at the base of the cliffs, and had gone about as far as we could. Turning back I could just make out *Lucy*, still apparently alive with bodies scrambling about her. She was about fifty yards off, and a good fifteen feet below our level. To have come up here seemed senseless, and I looked around to ask one of the Clarkesons what we were about, only to find both had disappeared.

For a moment I was totally bewildered; they were gone and I stood entirely alone and in darkness. Then I heard a muffled voice that came from the rock behind me, and noticed a glimmer of light below. I crouched down and saw the chalk cliff was split from about four feet to the ground, and the fissure was actually the opening to a cave.

"Come, Nat; we haven't the time for dawdling," Jesse's voice was as gruff as ever, even though I suspected him and Dan to be playing some mild trick on me. Still I took it in good heart, and lowered myself down the hole.

Inside it was more of a tunnel than a cave. Jesse had uncovered the dark lantern, and I could see my surroundings a little better. The ceiling was about five feet high but, being sharply pointed, it was impossible to proceed without bending nearly double. The floor also sloped steeply downhill and was uneven.

"Do we store the booty here?" I asked, but Dan shook his

head.

"We don't stow nothing nowhere," he said. "We done our bit."

"Aye, it's all down to the landers now," Jesse agreed. "They might stash it where they likes, or send it on to London straight off, that's up to them. Come, you may as well see some more."

I followed them a little way down the tunnel, which became both narrower and lower after a while. Jesse and Dan were almost on their knees towards the end, and I wondered how a lugger-full of contraband would fit in such a small space. Jesse's lantern still burned brightly, but Dan was ahead of me, and his body blocked my view. Then the light disappeared, and once again I was in darkness.

This time I was prepared, and knew more about my environment. I could hear Dan scrambling in front and followed; before long the light from Jesse's lantern returned, although now it shone from a chamber off the tunnel proper. Once more I eased myself through a tight entrance and into a room that was far larger.

Jesse and his son were standing in a cavern roughly the size of a front room in a well-to-do house. The ceiling was slightly domed like that of a cathedral, and rose roughly twelve feet or more above us. There were several rough wooden shelves against what could only be described as the back wall; these were propped up on bricks. Elsewhere long, low platforms were placed in regular lanes about three feet apart. All in all, it was a tidy and extremely secret warehouse, and I was impressed. It was also empty, but likely not to stay that way for long.

"This is one of a good few such places, so you may as well get to know them," Jesse told me, with unusual loquaciousness. "Most of the cliffs are all but hollow inside and make ideal hides."

"And is this where the cargo from tonight will be stored?" I asked.

"Not necessarily." Jesse shrugged. "Like I said, it might just as easily be taken away. But that ain't our concern, and we don't ask."

"And if someone spots us, what then?" It was probably a foolish question but one I felt obliged to pose.

"A raid, you mean?" Jesse grunted.

"They would not be so foolish," Dan answered for him. "The

Clipping Crew are more than a match for a handful of dragoons, and that's all the Revenue can usually muster. You saw yourself how they dealt with the Deal cruiser. With things as they are, Ugly Joe's got the upper hand and ain't afraid of using it."

For a moment the words of the Shoreham based lander I had met aboard the pressing tender came back to me, but I said nothing.

"I'm not saying I approve of him, or his habits," the old man continued. "But times are harsh for all of us, and I won't sit back and watch my family starve. If it means taking *Lucy* over to France once a fortnight, I'm prepared to do it; but no more. I won't carry British wool nor gold to the French, and neither will I get involved in any fighting: Prettyman knows that."

"Don't stop him from askin' though," Dan smirked.

"He can ask all he wants, that's my limit," Jesse replied, before adding, "We may as well see if the boat's empty."

It was, and I sensed the landers were waiting for us to go. We left Shiner asleep on the beach where the piled up booty was about to be dispersed. The moon started to rise during the short trip back to Rye and, by its light, *Lucy* was secured at her proper berth. As I followed Dan and Jesse to their cottage, I had the odd sensation I was walking on air; boots, still damp from the sea, did not seem to be making contact with the ground while the late hour and strange light gave everything a feeling of unreality. My face still stung from the sunburn and I must have been hungry but, for once, the feeling of total exhaustion outweighed everything else. It was common knowledge that smuggling was a lucrative business, if one not without risks. But few spoke of the hard work, or long hours involved, and I was now of the opinion that any money acquired was earned the hard way.

Alex's story

I had actually returned home after speaking with Tilly. This was not through any desire to prevaricate but, by the time I reached

174

Rye, the Custom House would have been closed and I should have had to sleep rough. Far better to stay the night in my old bed and leave at first light.

But even that worked against me. Mum was unusually brisk and businesslike: apparently I'd missed my brothers; they and Uncle Saul had come and gone while I was out. All would be working now, and weren't expected back until much later. I thought it a strange schedule for fishing at that time of year, but when I expressed surprise, mother refused to say more. In less than a week the household had undoubtedly altered, and I no longer felt part of it.

Seth, Josh and Uncle Saul did finally pile in during the early hours of the morning. I heard them return, but pretended to be asleep. We had breakfast together just before dawn, which was the usual time in our house: my brothers were clearly tired and more than a little snappy: Uncle Saul didn't even make it out of bed. There was no talk of them taking the boat out that day, but I gathered they would be working again that evening.

I told Seth and Josh of my adventures, and they listened without comment. Then I learned the two of them had been lucky and at sea when the press descended on Hastings, although needed to beat a hasty retreat when a Navy brig gave chase to their lugger. I was known to be taken, however, and seeing me back in the house with some complicated story about pressing tenders, privateers and Revenue cutters seemed to disconcert them.

As did my decision to join the Treasury. Little of the bad feeling I regularly encountered in town affected them: both were far bigger and generally more popular than me, so it was reasonable to expect them not to suffer at the hands of bullies. To have two members of their family connected with the Revenue was apparently harder to bear, though. A father you could forgive: a dead one, the more so. But when a younger brother steers a similar course, they were clearly wondering if it might reflect badly upon themselves. Frankly I didn't care either way, and was glad when breakfast finished and I could start on my travels.

Mum had a small pack of lunch already prepared. She gave me another hug, and now appeared far more understanding, even though I knew she equally disapproved of what I was about to do. I had always considered her to be social and even over amiable but, when I thought about it, she actually had few proper friends who were not men. So much had been lost when dad took up the Revenue work.

Outside it was cold, and stayed that way for the entire journey. I reached Rye when the smell of breakfast was still in the air, and found my way to the Custom House. It was early, and the place appeared shut up, but when I knocked on the heavy oak door it did open. A slightly shrunken man met me; he had the stance of one who spent much of his time seated, but his welcome was friendly, and he ushered me inside.

"Looking for a position," he repeated. He had a wizened face with a squint and I noticed his fingers were heavily ink stained. "Landguard would that be?" he asked.

"I was hoping for the cruiser," I said, and was treated to a quizzical look.

"More of a need for men inland," he replied. "We can offer you steady work, and a good wage."

"I'd prefer to be at sea," I persisted, and he seemed to relent.

"Commander Travis may need an extra hand, though you might have to wait your turn. You can crew, I assume?"

"Oh yes," I said, and even went on to stretch the truth further. "Luggers, punts, everything up to small brigs."

The clerk appeared satisfied and directed me to a chair. "Well, he's due in this morning for the weekly review, and I wouldn't say it is going to be a good one," he added with a confidential air. "Were I you I should catch him on the way in, rather than out – wait, that could be him now."

The huge door opened admitting an equally large man, squarely built, and wearing a heavy boat cloak over a dark blue uniform.

"What ho, Bridley?" he bellowed. "Is the almighty in his heaven?"

"M-Mr Conway is certainly here, Commander," the clerk replied, ducking his head obsequiously. "But has yet to ring. There is a gentleman waiting to see you, if you have the time, sir." he added, indicating me.

I had already risen from my chair, but still felt at a distinct disadvantage as the bulk of Commander Travis heaved towards me.

"This is Alexander Combes, sir." Bridley indicated me with a discoloured hand. "He has a mind to join *Stag*'s people."

"Sailorman, are you?" Travis demanded, a quizzical look upon his face. "Tell me, have you experience of cutters?"

"Not of cutters, sir," I replied. "Though I have sailed in *Antelope* as supercargo. But luggers and the like a plenty. And I am John Combes' son," I added cautiously.

"Combes, eh?" The name apparently punctured his affability somewhat and he became serious. "A bad business, that," he said, almost under his breath. "Your father was a fine man. Nothing were proved, but we have a good idea who accounted for him."

I swallowed. Despite his strict enforcement of Custom Law, Dad had died a very mundane death, having fallen from the cliffs near Fairlight. It was on a moonless night and, such accidents being common, I had come to accept his loss as just another of life's injustices. But in a short space of time two prominent Revenue officers had cast doubt upon his death, confirming my inner suspicions.

"And what brought you aboard George Stile's little tub?" Travis continued, before I could follow that train of thought further.

"I took passage from Whitstable to Hastings," I replied, hoping he would not ask for more. I was unlucky though; his face remained set, and I found myself stammering out the story of how I'd met with Adams.

"It would seem as if you've a fair head on your shoulders," he said, when I had finished. "And are not afraid of a fight, which is rare in the young these days. What say you go down to the boat? You'll find her moored near the harbour; can't miss her, she's the prettiest thing afloat. Mr Lumsden is aboard and will be brewing tea at present, or I'm a Dutchman. Present my compliments and say you're the new lad, to replace Briers."

The large internal door creaked partially open and we all

turned as a portly, bald man poked his head through the space.

"Mr Bridley, I have been ringing this past age or more," he complained.

The clerk bowed slightly and went to speak, but Travis was ahead of him. "My fault entirely, Mr Conway," he boomed, unabashed. "Always did make too much noise, but there are worse things." The Revenue officer strode past me, adding a pat to my head for good measure as he went.

The door shut and there was silence for a moment before Bridley breathed out loudly. "It is always an event when Commander Travis calls," he said.

Chapter Twenty-Two

Nat's story

"The French have begun constructing a fleet of invasion vessels with a view to landing an army on our shores." The voice of Lieutenant Bryson was bold and authoritative, and all gave their entire attention to it, even though several in the room probably knew more about the subject than he did. I took a crafty glance at Jesse, but he was looking directly ahead, his expression totally blank. Bryson stood in front of a blackboard, on which the west coast of France had been chalked. He wore full Royal Navy uniform apart from the hat, which lay discarded on a nearby table, and was conducting the weekly Sea Fencible training day like a highly ornate schoolmaster.

"We have spotted craft under construction in various ports along the western coast of France and the Batavian Republic." He tapped on the board with his chalk, then paused, and gave a wry smile. "That's 'olland to you lot."

There was a murmur of polite laughter. Bryson was very much the king's officer and, as such, frequently the object of private ridicule amongst his audience of thirty or so practical seamen. But he was liked and respected as much as any man in a uniform could be, when trying to teach a bunch of old salts about the sea.

"It is clear the French are planning an invasion; it is something they considered and attempted several times in the last war, so we are almost used to it. But in the past their target has usually been elsewhere – predominantly Ireland."

There was a brief murmur of discussion, but Bryson was keen to get his message across, and spoke over it.

"That would have been bad enough in the late 'nineties and, since the Act of Union, must cause even more problems now. But this time we don't consider Ireland to be their aim." He paused, and looked at us far more seriously. "The shipping already completed is almost exclusively flat bottomed transport vessels with a dangerously low freeboard; candidly, I think they would be lucky to make it across the Channel: so we have to regard that, and our own shores here in south-east England, as their objective."

More intense talking followed. Bryson was quite right, all in Britain had lived under the threat of invasion for the past ten years or more. But to be given such detail, and by someone in authority, made the menace far more real.

"Now, this is where things start to get difficult." The lieutenant walked away from his blackboard and round to the front of the table, so that he stood that much closer to us. Then his manner changed to one that was almost informal. "You have to understand that we are not at war and the Navy can do little about any of this. Even if we are seen to be looking too carefully, the French might consider it a provocative act and, should they use it to declare war on us, many so called neutral countries may be persuaded to back them." There was now silence in the room; for all that they might despise the pomp and splendour of the Royal Navy, this was their particular expertise. Bryson was also a fighting officer, one of many who had kept the French at bay until then, and even the most pragmatic of seamen was prepared to listen.

"Obviously we are keeping an eye on matters, but there is still only so much that can be done. Each week, at least one of our brigs looks in at every major harbour and makes a full report. But it is very much as if a Frenchman were spotted off Spithead or the Nore: we wouldn't like it, and neither do they. Only three days ago, one was fired upon by a shore battery and, as I have said, we do not wish to give the French opportunity to name us as the protagonist."

I wondered how many present knew what a protagonist was, and only had the roughest idea myself, but let it pass. The lieutenant's expression was now growing far more confidential, and I felt something of even greater interest was to come.

"So, what we would like is for you to report for us."

There was a silence that lasted a moment or two, then men began to chatter again, and far more loudly this time.

What Bryson was suggesting stretched things rather. As he

had said, we were not at war and French ports were open to all for general trading. Ignoring the free traders, of which there were at least three full crews currently in the room, several men present visited France on a regular basis for totally legitimate reasons. Some were even fool enough to buy similar cargo to that carried in *Lucy*, and declare it through the proper channels. Then there were the fishermen who would drop a catch off at French markets, if they were staying out for any length of time, not to mention those carrying passengers or personal mail. But all this was done using the age old protection extended to civilians in private vessels; what the lieutenant proposed would take away that status. More importantly, any involved in counting shipping could only be regarded as military spies.

Bryson was leaning back against the table, and gauging the reaction of his audience. It was pretty clear they did not approve.

"Some of you may not welcome the prospect at first," he said above the growing rumble of protests. "Although I hope that, upon mature reflection, it will appeal to you in time. You may consider the point that an invasion would endanger you, your homes and your families first."

Silence returned.

"We believe the French are planning the largest collection of transports ever envisaged, and the more we know about it the better. Can I also remind you that, as Sea Fencibles, it will be us who shall have the pleasure of greeting them if they are foolish enough to land on our beaches?"

He was not wrong about the number of vessels involved; if what we had seen only a few nights back had been a fraction, it would be a mighty fleet indeed.

"Can we not just go in an' burn 'em?" Someone asked from near the front. "There's gonna be a war whatever, it may as well start now, an' with us takin' the lead."

"Burning is certainly an option," Bryson conceded with a look that might have been approving. "Several attempts were made when the threat came to our attention during the last war, and do not think that Britain will be slow in calling the French to battle when the time is right. But it must be right for us and, at present, that is not the case."

A sound point, but the room became divided by a dozen different discussions, with only Dan, Jesse and I remaining silent.

"So you want us to go a spying." Someone shouted out to one side of where we sat. "But what if we was caught? What if they sees us makin' notes, and haul us in? What then?"

Bryson, who was still resting back against the table, wriggled uncomfortably. "Then it will be the worse for you," he said, with commendable honesty. "I will not lie, the French system of justice is not as open as ours, and no mercy may be expected. But that has to be balanced..." He stopped as a roar of disapproval rose up to cover his words. "But that has to be balanced against the value of the information you would be providing."

Still there was grumbling and obvious discontent amongst his audience, and I could tell our dear lieutenant was starting to be worn down. "But if it came to it, we would be prepared to pay for such assistance," he said, in final desperation, and now the rumble of noise dwindled considerably.

"Pay, and pay handsomely, if that is required to ensure your loyalty," he repeated somewhat disconsolately. And order returned to the room almost immediately.

Alex's story

I found the cutter moored off the harbour approach. From way back I was expecting something larger; her topmast was set up, and seemed to tower as high as a frigate's main but, as I reached the low wall and looked down on the hull itself, there was little to it. Flush decked, with a wide beam, she hardly appeared inspiring. There were two broadsides of seven guns, but they looked like pretty small beer; four pounders – maybe six: enough to tackle an armed and heavy lugger, perhaps, but nothing more. Then I remembered *Antelope*, the cutter that carried me down from Whitstable. She had hardly more than ambled, yet the passage was made in remarkably quick time. The Deal boat had also been a good sailer. She may have fallen to the guns of Ugly Joe's brig but, even so, it was clear the power of a Revenue cruiser lay not in armament, but speed and manoeuvrability.

Three men sat on her deck and all were dressed identically, in red canvas shirts and blue trousers. One, who also wore a wide brimmed straw hat, was cross-legged and engaged in cleaning out a fiddle block, with the other two acting as his audience. I walked along to the break in the harbour wall and stood opposite them.

"I've been appointed to join you as a seaman," I said, feeling suddenly foolish. They turned to look at me and one of the watchers cocked his head.

"Is that right?" he asked. "Then you'll be the only one."

It was not the answer I had expected, and I was momentarily dumbfounded. Then the man's face relaxed slightly.

"Seaman is something you gets called in the Royal Navy," he explained. "Along with mongrel, bastard and lubber. If you can hand, reef and steer in the Revenue, you'll be a mariner – and it's a name to be proud of."

"Commander Travis said to come aboard," I told him, still feeling awkward.

"Then you better had," the hatted one replied, "and welcome."

Nat's story

"He's been part of the crew little more than a day or so, yet now he's tellin' us what to do."

Dan was absolutely right, there was no denying that, but what really got to me was his determination to make the most of the fact. It was as if he had been waiting for just such a chance to put me down. We certainly had only known each other a brief time but, after what had been a bad start, I was thinking us close to becoming friends, so the sudden change of heart was doubly disappointing. To my mind there is nothing worse than folk who let you down.

"I only said, if we were thinkin' of going back to Boulogne, it wouldn't do any harm to make a few notes." I protested, hoping the matter would be dropped. We were walking back to the Clarkesons' house after Bryson's lecture, and mine had been a chance remark; more for something to say than anything else. "But I'm not telling you we should," I stated, firmly. "Shall we forget I spoke?"

But Dan was rather too keen to remember, and I knew then how genuine his friendship had been.

"He's not to be trusted, Dad," he told Jesse. "We won't be able to leave him alone in the boat, nor let him off free to go round the town without us always being there with him. Shiner might have been a fuddle, but at least you knew he weren't going to stab you in the back."

"Look, this is becoming foolish" I declared, now a little angry. The journey back from France had been so encouraging, and I'd taken Shiner's place without any major problem since, on two fishing trips, so was beginning to consider myself an established part of the lugger's crew. "I'm not going to start writing things down, though it could hardly make much difference if I did."

"French justice is a mite different to English," Dan snapped back. "We have fair trials and punishments; if the frogs catch you, they'll just chop off your head, along with Dad's an' mine for good measure."

"There's right and wrong in both," Jesse muttered. "If you asks me, the guillotine's a better way to go than any scaffold. But Dan's correct; they wouldn't listen to reason. If a boat brings a spy into a French port, they'll seize it, along with anyone aboard; and no one's gonna care who it was what done the snooping."

"Can we just forget the whole thing?" I repeated, now almost pleading. It seemed a shame, when we had all been getting on so well. I glanced at them both: Jesse steadily pounding along the road with a set and neutral expression on his face, whereas Dan was flushed and white eyed and I knew would forever be a problem.

"If we can't trust you, I think we better had," he all but spat the words. "A man who's happy to betray his friends is not going to worry about who else he peaches on."

"But they're French!" I almost shouted, in wonder. However well we may have been treated in Boulogne, and whatever the trust Jesse and Dan might place in them, it didn't alter the fact that Ugly Joe was dealing with our potential enemies. "Why, they are actively making preparations to invade, or we wouldn't be speaking so."

"An' if they do come, who's gonna stop them?" Dan replied quickly. "A handful of fishermen with the doubtful back up of a few painted soldiers? When did we last win a battle on land? And what would be so very terrible about being ruled by Frenchmen anyway? Besides, they got the right idea about the value of a working man. Revolution is what we want, and they would give it to us."

It was like a bad dream where everyone behaves out of character and says the most outlandish things, while you are the only one to notice. I had known there were those in England who sided with the French; even some of our politicians came up with pretty radical views on occasion, but I never thought someone actually known to me would hold such thoughts. It was simply too hard to contemplate.

"A moment ago you were bemocking French justice," I reminded him, and heard his sudden intake of breath as the shot went home.

"Well I don't hold with no revolution," Jesse stated calmly, his still voice of reason interrupting what was in danger of becoming an outright scrap. "But there's a few in power round these parts what could do with shaking hands with Mr Guillotine. All this fancy legal talk of Enclosure and Consolidation Acts, when all they're really doing is robbing us of our right to live. If the French brought a measure of true democracy, I'd say welcome to them."

In the face of such heresy, there was little more to add, and we walked on in silence for a while. I supposed that Jesse and Dan might have a point; my family had never been greatly affected by the recent changes, and were relatively affluent. It still felt strange to openly embrace the country's potential enemy, but then the Clarkesons had been dealing with them throughout the last war, so why not the next?

"Would it help if I gave my word?" I asked at last, as the house came into sight. I was strangely keen to settle the matter; the disagreement had emphasised just how much being with the Clarkeson family meant to me. They gave me security, a common purpose, and what should turn into a viable source of income, all without any obvious effort on their part. But the most important benefit was far more subtle, and totally unintentional.

The Coglans had also been a family, and one I soon became a part of; although on a different basis. Ned was in charge, of course, but it was still my efforts that guided them, and even brought prosperity. But with the Clarkesons I was, and always would be, a minor cog. When surrounded by so much competence, experience and authority, there was no way I could make much impression. It was actually quite pleasant to be the passenger for a change, and I had suggested the intelligence work more as an act of bravado, to show them I could have ideas of my own.

"If Nat is willin' to give his word, that'll be good enough for me," Jesse said, as we were approaching the front door. "And it will be good enough for you as well," he added, looking pointedly at Dan.

"If so, then you have it," I said, greatly relieved, although also slightly contemptuous of Jesse for being so easy to fool.

Because it was a lie, and I knew it to be one even as I said the words. Now that the idea had been so soundly quashed, I felt able to think differently; think in the way I did when living with the Coglans. If the Clarkesons didn't want to take up such a prime opportunity, then maybe it was something I should consider entirely for myself? In my world, money was more important than anything else and, if it meant getting coin in my hand, the boat paid off, and Susan out of trouble, I didn't care how many words I broke. Besides, I could spot a good deal when it was placed before me, even if they could not.

Alex's story

Commander Travis joined us at the cutter within the hour. He appeared to be in a sour mood at first but, on boarding, and seeing me sitting easily with his men, seemed to perk up.

"It's the lad from *Antelope!*" he exclaimed loudly – I was soon to realise very little was said by our captain that was not delivered at a full blown roar. "Remind me of your name, son."

I told him and his expression hardened slightly.

"Ah yes, I was forgetting, we have Revenue royalty aboard; Alexander here is the son of John Combes, a prime landshark."

I felt myself blush; in the past my father's reputation had too often been the cause of shame or ridicule, so the looks of interest and even respect from the mariners was a pleasant experience.

"Well, what do you make of our new shipmate?" Travis persisted. "Needn't tell me to his face if it don't fit, but had you the mind to say something good, we may as well hear it."

"Lad knows his stuff," the hatted one conceded, and the other two nodded their heads in agreement.

"Well, that is good and no mistake. But saying and doing are different matters. The tide is right in less than half an hour; I think a little cruise may be in order."

* * *

It took all of that time to get the cutter prepared. Her bowsprit, a massive spar, more than half as long as the hull itself, had to be run out and there were sails to be stood ready and the bilges to pump dry. I got the impression she had not been at sea for a week or more, but did not have the time or opportunity to ask my fellow mariners.

There turned out to be about twenty of these: they seemed a friendly bunch, and genuinely pleased to have the extra help. I set out to show myself as no fussock, having long ago discovered such

187

an attitude popular with those who work hard themselves. Many of the specific duties were unfamiliar to me, of course, but I had all the basic seaman's skills and was a fast learner.

And then, almost before I was expecting it, Travis began to bellow from the quarterdeck. Bow and stern lines were released and, under jib alone, *Stag* eased smoothly out of her berth and into the channel.

We ran up the main gaff while still sheltering under the lee of the western promontory and, as we cleared the headland, took the wind at full force. *Stag*'s canvas tightened and she began to heel while her stem cut through the sea, producing a cloud of fine spray that might have been steam from some giant's kettle, and stretched back almost her entire length.

It was all so very different from the casual progress of *Antelope* or any other craft in which I had sailed. *Stag* seemed positively alive and, even though I had been aboard for such a short time, already I could feel her spirit and tendencies through the soles of my feet. Around me, my new shipmates were grinning with a common excitement. We ran up an extra headsail then, as Travis ordered us three points to larboard, set the square topsail.

I knew then I had never travelled so fast, either on land or at sea, and it was an exhilarating experience. The boat righted slightly with the turn, and appeared to leap from wave to wave, truly at one with the elements. The hatted seaman from earlier stood by me as I hung tightly to an iron hard shroud.

"So how do you find it?" he asked, shouting into the wind.

"Glorious," I replied, and received a look of shared enjoyment in return.

"Wait until we really get a pile on," he urged. "Then you'll know what it's like to fly."

Chapter Twenty-Three

Nat's story

Lieutenant Bryson had given me his requirements on a single sheet of paper. The invasion barges were expected to fall into roughly four classes, from the *péntche*, a lug rigged craft just over sixty feet in length to the *prame*, which was ship rigged, carried twelve heavy cannon and spanned nearly a hundred and twenty feet from stem to stern. In addition, there were a number of armed ships' boats the French were known to be using, as well as variants to the standard designs that accommodated horses, or additional ordinance. I was to note the number of each type, as well as any comments on their condition; whether they were ready for sea, undergoing repair or modification; whilst also looking out for fresh designs or innovations. He emphasised the value of my information would grow as it was added to; the rate of increase in numbers being almost as important as any one count. I drew the distinct impression there were others making similar notes, which was reassuring on one hand, but also meant I could not be in any way slapdash with my own figures.

But then I had no intention of doing anything other than a first rate job; this was probably the one task taken on since arriving in Hastings that I genuinely felt comfortable with, and I was determined to provide Bryson with the very highest standard of intelligence. Claiming a headache, I spent an entire evening in the tiny room behind the Clarkesons' kitchen that had been granted me, memorising the information until I knew it by heart. Then I burnt the sheet in the flame from my candle, stamping out the embers and rubbing them into the rough brick floor.

Quite how I was going to keep track of the barges was a potential problem. It was one thing keeping my observations from the French, quite another to hide them from Jesse and Dan. But then I had been blessed with both an agile mind and a memory to match. When young, I was quick to learn all my tables and could still recite the British kings and queens in order, as well as every book of the New and Old Testaments. And Bryson had agreed to pay me a guinea for each visit, so it should be no great problem to remember a series of numbers.

The Clarkesons visited Boulogne every ten to fourteen days, which meant I would be able to pay at least half the weekly instalments to the Bennetts, and had already worked out ways of getting the money to Susan. Were I paid in coin, a guinea could be concealed beneath the sealing wax of a mailed letter, if it were paper two postings, sent at differing times, might contain separate halves of the same bank note. Both were tried and reliable methods; all I lacked was the money, and no foolish scruples were going to stop me from getting it.

Staying on the right side of Dan and Jesse now became even more important. I felt the strain of taking what could be quite crude criticism from the younger man, but kept myself in check and when, eleven days later, I stood on *Lucy*'s prow, watching as the lugger made the difficult passage into Boulogne harbour, I was confident it could be carried off.

There were more barges than before, and the basin that held them was nearer to completion. The vessels within were arranged by size to some degree so, should I be able to engineer a way of going ashore, it would be relatively easy to take an accurate count. Nothing had been said since the tiff of a couple of weeks back: *Lucy* had spent several days fishing since then and Dan and I were back on something like speaking terms. But I sensed he would still be watching me, and even Jesse could not have forgotten the incident.

We had come in later in the day, to allow for the change of tides, and I was hoping a mid-day meal might have been arranged for us. But, despite being greeted every bit as warmly by the same two Frenchmen, they made no offer of food or hospitality and left us shortly afterwards. Neither was there any evidence of Ugly Joe, and we sat and waited in the boat for some while.

"About time too," Jesse grumbled when the first of the wagons finally appeared. "Tide will be right in under three hours, but there's no point in our staying here any longer." Along with the supplies, what was probably the same group of loaders were now walking towards us. Dan noticed them and added, in a lower voice:

"Well I ain't staying about, not if it means we have to act as free labour."

So saying he swung himself over *Lucy*'s low bulwark and landed squarely on the quay.

"Are you ripe for a stroll, Dad?" he asked his father. The old man looked from side to side, then shrugged his shoulders, before dropping down next to him.

"Come with us if you wish," he said, turning back to me. "Or stay with the boat. Your choice; though you'd be wise not to get yourself burned."

"I'll wait a while," I told them. "Then maybe take a walk later on."

Jesse nodded, and they were making to go when Dan swung round as a thought occurred.

"And none of that counting, do you hear?" he warned, pointing a finger in my direction. I shook my head seriously. Oh no, there would be none of that.

* * *

I left *Lucy* half an hour later, when the French loaders had all but filled her tiny hold and were starting on the deck. It took me half an hour of apparently aimless wandering to work my way round to the opposite basin, and when there, I resisted the temptation to stop. Still I couldn't resist casting an eye about the strange vessels as I walked slowly passed.

All were flat bottomed, and I wondered at their practicability: they had such a low freeboard as to make them vulnerable, even in an unloaded state. There was no doubt about their capacity, however; I guessed the smaller would take fifty or so men, and possibly double that in the larger. With the number amassed already, there was sufficient to transport a significant body of troops. But that was discounting horses, wagons and essential supplies, I reminded myself. I strolled on, counting the stubby bows where most housed one rather squat, but heavy, cannon. My eyes wandered freely, never settling on any one subject or vessel for more than a second. To anyone watching, I was simply a resting seaman taking in the pleasant spring sunshine but, before long, accurate numbers for all types had been noted, as well as their readiness for sea. Even the sprung strake on one of the *bateau canonniers* was not missed, and I was feeling suitably smug. Earlier I had carried out a detailed survey of the anchored warships in the approach and, though I held a ditty bag with the necessary writing materials, all the information was safely, but secretly, locked away in my brain.

I felt pleased with my labour, and the day in general; my face was almost healed from its previous burning, and the warmth of the afternoon was once more pleasant. With what I had to tell him, Bryson would hand over a guinea for certain, and that would buy the Coglans a further week's safety from the Bennetts. Then I heard the piercing scream of a whistle, and turned to see a group of men rushing towards me.

* * *

I ran also; it was instinctive. Even without the recent memory of being pressed, there was something primaeval about being chased. Thundering back past the barges, I heard laughter and shouts from all about, but a quick glance behind told me my pursuers were in deadly earnest, and not running for the good of their health.

My intention, if such a word was relevant in such a mad dash, was to head back to the lugger the way I had come, but I must have missed a turn and soon found myself starting on the leg of a pier. It would lead nowhere, other than the harbour itself, so I desperately threw myself down a series of steps before I was committed. But this only aggravated matters; I was surrounded by small, cheaply built, sheds and piles of rubbish that blocked my path and made further escape almost impossible. The men were tumbling down the stairway after me, and I could foresee being hemmed in. Worse: we were under the quayside and had disappeared from public sight. They could do pretty much what they wanted with me, and no one would be the wiser.

Then the first of them was on my level, and I could see by the look of triumph on his moustachioed face that my lot was definitely up. I turned, desperate to continue running, but there was nowhere to go. A line of empty barrels blocked my path with the gentle waters of the harbour lapping against them. I was a strong swimmer, and might have made my escape that way but, before I could even start, someone grabbed me from behind, and I knew myself taken.

* * *

The hand that held me did not belong to a Frenchmen. They were standing some way off: my captor must have appeared unnoticed from one of the sheds to seize me. I looked back along the arm, and straight into the eyes of Joseph Prettyman.

Ugly Joe was smiling in his usual benign fashion and his features were just as striking. This time he was bareheaded; the well kept mane of dark hair flowed over his shoulders without a speck of powder and, being as we were so close, I could trace more than a hint of his scent.

"The face I knows," he said, in assumed wonder. "But somehow cannot place it."

"N-Nat Audley," I told him hesitantly. "I crew for Jesse Clarkeson in the *Lucy*."

"So you do, by heavens!" he said, relaxing his grip. "And forgive me, but were you not present on our recent adventure with the pressing tender?"

I nodded.

"Recovered some valuable hands that night," he said, chuckling at the memory. "And many new friends were made. But you were not one, as I recall?"

"No, I joined Mr Clarkeson the following day."

"Then it were a wise move you made," he assured me. "Jackie Clarkeson runs a tight ship and is a dependable skipper." He turned to the waiting men and let loose with a barrage of French. One replied in a respectful tone, and there was a brief exchange of words before the group began to trudge reluctantly up the steps.

Ugly Joe's attention returned to me: I was treated to what felt like a dispassionate inspection that lasted several seconds and included my entire body.

"Our friends here say they saw you poking about the invasion barges, Nat," he said, almost sadly. "Thought you might have been a spying on them, and the French are sensitive souls; they do not take kindly to such things."

I selected my most earnest of expressions. "No," I said, emphatically. "It was nothing more than a brief stroll. We're currently lading and will be awaiting the tide; I was killing time more than anything."

"But of course," Ugly Joe agreed, and the smile returned. "I remember now – Jackie Clarkeson was due in late this morning was he not? I must step by and wish him well."

I nodded readily, although was unsure how Jesse would take to being addressed so.

"But first, I am certain you will have no problem in proving your story. No spy operates without notes so we will start with the bag and your pockets. Turn them out, if you please," he said firmly. "Then we shall examine every stitch of your clothing."

* * *

It lasted a good fifteen minutes and Ugly Joe was horribly thorough. My pockets and possessions were inspected in full, with every page of the writing tablet being studied. The same procedure was repeated with each item of clothing until I was left standing naked and shivering in the dappled light of the under-quay. He considered me for several moments longer than was necessary, then his face relaxed.

"Very good, lad; I never doubted you. And am glad to see you haven't let me down. What say you go back to Jackie and give him my respects?" His gaze travelled down my body one more time before moving across to the nearby shed. "Unless you would care to join me for a cup of chocolate and a yarn?"

"I had better return," I mumbled hastily, and began to collect my clothes.

I found my way back to *Lucy*, feeling both anxious and strangely unclean. The lugger had been filled with cargo much as before and Dan, who was on the foredeck, paid me little attention. But Jesse seemed to sense something. He looked up at my arrival, then watched me carefully as I climbed aboard and dumped my ditty bag down in a scupper.

"Been about the town, have you?" he asked, gently.

I said I had, while collecting my cow gown, the heavily oiled smock I favoured when at sea. I knew the tide would soon be right, and that Jesse liked to be prompt so as to clear Boulogne's awkward approaches before claiming the north-easterly current. And I also knew he was not so very fond of conversation, which made his current behaviour all the more disconcerting.

"Where did you go then?" he persisted.

I shrugged. "Walked about the harbour; no more."

"Did you look at them barges?" Jesse continued, although the tone remained almost friendly, and he didn't appear to be checking up on me.

"It would be hard to avoid them," I tried to raise a smile and looked across the harbour to the shipping near by. Perhaps my acting talents were not so good at that moment: the fact that something had sparked his interest was disconcerting in itself. "Didn't take no notes, if that's what you mean." I added hurriedly, even though the look on his face owed nothing to suspicion.

"No, son, I'm sure you didn't," he said, and now I found myself staring back. Neither of us spoke for a moment, and then I told him.

"I met up with Mr Prettyman." The silence continued; even Dan stopped what he was doing and looked over in our direction.

"Did you now?" Jesse asked eventually, but it was a rhetorical question and I felt somehow he had already guessed Ugly Joe was involved.

"He will be calling to see you," I said, and now the old man scowled.

"Then he will be disappointed." His eyes flashed over to Dan and then back to me. "We'll not be waiting about for that old molly to flaunt himself about the place. Tide will just about serve: we might as well stand off in the Channel if we has to, as waste time here." He finally took his attention away from me, strode aft and began to stare back out of the harbour mouth. "Single up to the stern cable," he said, his mind still apparently captured by the distant sea. "And let's show some canvas."

Alex's story

It was our second extended cruise, and we had been sailing eastwards for all of the morning. In the last three days, *Stag* had rummaged four Hastings luggers and a smack from Rye as well as heaving a stricken fisherman who had lost his masts off a lee shore. We also spent an entire night standing off and on a beach near Fairlight, to no avail. Whether this last escapade was an exercise, or us acting on some form of tip off, nobody knew: Commander Travis might have been a loud man by nature, but he shared very little with his crew. In either case, I could not help feel the time was wasted. The night had been clear and we were plainly visible. It would have been either a bold or extremely foolish lander who attempted a run under our very noses. The others saw little wrong in the practice however and, as I was the newest, youngest, and least experienced of them all, my opinions were kept to myself.

Being the greenhorn had few of the usual connotations, even amongst such a professional body of men. Despite having chalked up what was now a considerable number of days at sea, it was as if the other mariners were still trying to impress me with *Stag's* amazing sailing abilities. But this was no great undertaking; she was a remarkable craft and had already stolen my heart.

And I was learning quickly. The numerous exercises had already brought me up to measure with so many tasks: I was starting to trust, and feel myself trusted – an essential part of melding with any crew. I was also learning more of the duties expected of a Revenue mariner, as well as a good deal about our commander.

My earlier assumptions had Travis as a bold and charismatic figure who appeared eminently suited to his role. Whether or not his technical abilities were on a par with such confidence was less clear, and I was not convinced.

As a Revenue Commander, he had a good deal of autonomy over his vessel's movements; this was to enable a fast reaction to any intelligence that may be picked up, as well as making the cutter's movements less predictable to the smuggling community. Travis, however, was all too eager to fall into a pattern.

Though undoubtedly as fond of *Stag* as any man aboard, he tended to alternate between staying at sea for several days at a stretch, and letting her grow weed against the quay. Much of this was learned in quiet discussion with Honeysett, my straw-hatted friend of the first day. Honeysett berthed immediately next to me, and held definite ideas about our captain's future, which he was more than happy to share.

He had it that Travis was in the suds, and some form of ultimatum had been handed to him on the day of my recruitment: either he spend more time on patrol, or relinquish the post. I could not tell whether Honeysett was right, but we had spent hardly a day ashore since, and I, for one, was not sorry.

In between the odd professional incident, we had been put through a programme of extended exercise that seemed to include every evolution imaginable, from setting stunsails to the square main and topgallant. There was even a massive jib of Travis' own design that appeared determined to rip us up out of the water. I think I learned more about sailing a cutter then, than I did in all my later years with the Revenue.

On the evening we saw the lugger again, I was really starting to enjoy myself. There may have been problems ashore, but I was finally earning steady money which, though not a fortune, would be enough to take care of Tilly and the baby. Things might not have gone exactly as planned to that point, but I would soon be with my girl, and had found a job which was both fulfilling and respectable. And so it was that, when the boat first came into sight, I actually experienced an odd feeling of disappointment.

She had made such an impression that I knew her for what she was from the first moment, even though the boat rode low in the water. There was a good deal of sail being carried, so she was clearly in a hurry, though making little progress with what must have been a full load. And somehow, I also knew my old friend would be aboard.

None of the cutter's crew took any notice, although there was little to be surprised at in that. The lugger was coming from the north-east, and could have been fishing in any one of a dozen spots up-coast. And, if she was carrying both a full sivver and a bone in her teeth, was that so very unusual? A heavily laden fisher's crew could be expected to want their catch back and unloaded – anyone could see it had been a successful day for them.

But, to me, the boat had far more significance. Even ignoring my friend's involvement, as a fishing lugger she seemed to represent my old life in Hastings, with all its unpleasant connotations. And I was equally aware that, if she were running, there would be far more of interest within her hold than a few casks of untaxed spirit.

At that point we were practising setting up the topgallant mast, so most of the crew's attention was elsewhere, but I kept a wary lookout. As they passed by our stern, the elderly skipper could be seen at the helm. And then I recognised Nat standing by the mainmast.

Stag's spar was almost heaved up and would soon be secure. I knew that, greenhorn though I may have been, a word from me would see the cutter going into full flight; and we could be sweeping down on the lugger within moments. There was no doubt in my mind that the briefest of inspections would reveal them filled with contraband, and such a haul could do me no harm. I even opened my mouth to say something, but the words just would not come. All had their attention on the halyards; there was none to spare for the likes of me, and my mouth closed again, its job undone. I told myself, in a similar position, Nat would have spoken out, but was now well aware that he and I were very different beings. And, even when I thought about it later, I was glad.

Nat's story

I met with Lieutenant Bryson the following day. He had said to call at his lodgings in Rye on any morning before noon, and I was tapping at the door in Tower Street just after nine. The Clarkesons made no comment about my leaving the house early; we had been unloading until three in the morning and *Lucy* would not be going out again until the end of the week. As far as they were concerned, I was welcome to take the next two days as liberty.

It was strange how Jesse's attitude had altered since the incident with Ugly Joe; Dan was just the same, and Ma Clarkeson definitely no different, having complained about my tearing of a bed sheet which, in truth, had worn about as thin as muslin. But the change in the old man was undeniable.

It was as if he sensed something, and was almost protective towards me. I was even given a shilling and wished well as I left the house. I have always considered myself quite the judge of character, but people still manage to confuse me on occasions, and this was one of them.

But there was no thought for the Clarkesons as Bryson opened the door and grinned a welcome.

"I've information," I told him, matching his expression, and he nodded readily.

"We cannot speak here, I am sharing the room," he said. "Come, we shall take a walk." He reached for his naval uniform tunic that was hanging by the door. Then, thinking better of it, chose instead a plain woollen greatcoat that was far more anonymous.

We strolled easily along Tower Street then turned down the Rope Walk and on to a coffee house that sat to one end. It was all but empty inside, and Bryson led me to a table in the far corner where we could speak in relative privacy.

A pot of coffee arrived, and he poured a cup for each of us. I had never liked the stuff: it always tasted vile, bitter and burnt, and would have much preferred chocolate, but then we had not met for refreshment.

"Where have you been?" he asked, and I told him. "Do you have notes?"

"No, but I can remember," I said. On getting back to the Clarkesons' place I had considered writing everything out but decided against it. Despite the softening in Jesse's attitude, I did not wish to risk being found in possession of such information, and Prettyman's searching of me still left an unpleasant memory. Besides, my brain had never failed in the past and, I was sure, would not do so now.

And so it proved: Bryson brought out a small note book and began to write as I related my observations in what I have to admit was impressive detail. I had barge numbers and types as well as condition. Then for good measure, I reeled off the number and class of warships, together with their estimated readiness for sea. By the time we were finished, I felt mighty pleased with myself, and Bryson had filled two whole pages with notes.

"You are confident of all this?" he asked when we were finished and I nodded: I was quite certain. "Remind me again, what was the number of the *bateau canonniers*?"

I told him and, even though a lofty lieutenant of the Royal Navy, he had the grace to look abashed.

"Thank you. Thank you very much indeed," he spoke slowly, running his eyes over the hastily written pages once more. "I will be straight, no one has produced anything like so comprehensive an account, yet all have claimed their guinea."

I cleared my throat, and he came back to reality, hurriedly reaching into his pocket. The small gold coin felt wonderful in my hand. It was still early, there was time to raise Hastings, meet up with Susan, and be back in time for supper if I got a shake on. Knowing she was so easily in reach had suddenly made her even more important to me, and I longed to be off. But Bryson, it seemed, had more to say.

"When do you envisage visiting Boulogne again?" he asked, reading through the notes yet one more time.

"In two weeks." I replied. He looked up at me.

"You could not be persuaded to go sooner," he chanced. "And possibly other ports?"

"I don't think so," I replied. "Mr Clarkeson is not aware of what I am doing as it is, and would not be pleased were he to find out." Bryson seemed to understand. At no time had he asked the reason for our frequent trips to France, although I could not believe him so naïve as not to have guessed.

"It is the pity," he said, sadly. "You have a good eye for detail, and I would judge the Clarkesons' need for calling to be ideal for such work." He was smiling now, and then I was sure he knew *Lucy*'s purpose.

"Would they be ready to visit more often, and perhaps elsewhere, were we to arrange additional funds?" he enquired delicately. "What you have given me is undoubtedly worthy of a bean, and I could find more – if the information remained as comprehensive."

My mind raced: this had all the hallmarks of a first rate commercial opportunity.

"They would not," I said definitely. "But I may be able to organise something on a similar course, if reliable payment were promised."

His face brightened: "How so?"

There was no need to rush things, I had already decided on a gambit, but my inherent business sense told me not to overplay my hand.

"I have access to another vessel, and may be able to arrange to look into several ports a week, and on a regular basis; if that would be agreeable."

"It would," he told me eagerly. "And, providing the information were as fine as this, we should certainly pay. Would this be in league with the Clarkesons?"

I shook my head. "It would be my own craft, and brand new," I said, a little haughtily. "She is a conventional lugger, and will be used for nothing other than fishing. We may land a catch, obtain repairs, or simply stop by for refreshment; I shall not endanger the work by any other commitments."

Our eyes met in a look of mutual understanding. "Were that to be possible, I could make suitable arrangements to support you," he said.

I waited; we were both playing this equally carefully, not wishing to commit too much for fear the other might take advantage.

"Your listing as a Sea Fencible might stay," he began. "I could mark you as working independently, and there would be no one else to answer to on that score."

I nodded slightly, that was a major concession in itself and would grant me a shilling a week without additional effort. But there was more.

"And I will pay a guinea for every port you visit, provided such splendid intelligence is supplied."

I swallowed, very much aware that my ability to keep a neutral face was being stretched to the limit.

"It must be understood, however, that nothing could be attributed to the king," he continued in a whisper. "Were you to be caught, it would be entirely your own concern; no one could speak for you."

I nodded; that was quite acceptable; I had no intention of being caught. Obtaining the information should not be a problem either, and nor would providing the boat or, if it came to it, her crew.

"Just tell me again," I asked. "How much would you pay?"

Chapter Twenty-Four

It was early afternoon when I walked down All Saints Street again, and little more than two weeks since skipping out of the house and making my way to meet up with Billy Bennett. I'd come straight from Rye, and avoided both Rock-a-Nore and the Stade for fear of running into the press. My Sea Fencible papers were in my pocket but had yet to be tested. Besides, I had been carrying a perfectly good protection the last time, and was now rather of the opinion our splendid Royal Navy was a law unto itself. But there wasn't a trace of press gangs, ensigns or navy blue; in fact, apart from the very elderly, the place seemed deserted. Being a week day, I knew the fishing fleet would probably be out, but that hardly accounted for the lack of women or children.

Outside the Coglans' house, Ned's small rowing boat was still lying against the wall, and there was washing hanging in the yard. I knocked on the front door then, when no immediate answer came, opened it and stepped inside.

The first sight that met my eyes was Tilly Medcalf; she was dozing on a chair by the range and, on seeing me, jumped to her feet.

"My word, it's Nat. We'd heard you was taken by the press. Whatever brings you here?"

I could have asked the same question, but was rather more interested in Susan's whereabouts.

"She's with Ned and Jenny," Tilly replied. "They're gone to see some people but wouldn't say who. I gathered it to be important."

"Do you mind if I wait?" Whatever the reason for Tilly's presence, she was apparently part of the household now, whereas I was feeling very much the outsider.

"No, of course. I would make you tea, but we have none at present. There may be a drop of milk, though I think that was being saved for later."

I was actually quite hungry, and still had both Bryson's guinea and the Clarkesons' shilling in my pocket. But it was easier to say I wanted nothing and took a seat at the well remembered table. Having an empty stomach was no longer unusual for me.

"You'll be wondering why I am here," Tilly told me, and I admitted to being puzzled.

"Alex has me with child, and my parents are none too pleased. I were lucky the Coglans took me in."

The news shocked me on many levels, but her parents' attitude topped them all. I suppose it was a measure of their mistrust of the Treasury that any connection outweighed feelings for a pregnant daughter, but still I was appalled.

"But why did you not move into Alex's house?" I found myself asking.

"Because his mother is not always there," she said simply. "To be honest, Nat, I didn't want to be alone, and Ned Coglan said he would be happy to take me."

I thought it an unusually generous offer from the old boy, especially considering the family's current circumstances, although at that point I still had much to learn about him.

"Have you seen Alex?" I asked, even though I was slightly worried by what she might answer: my last sighting of him would be hard to explain. But the sound of the front door opening interrupted our conversation.

I stood and turned to see Jenny enter. She was followed by Susan then Ned. All looked slightly shaken, as if they had been through a particularly unpleasant experience, and Ned appeared to have aged a good ten years since I last saw him. Susan definitely registered my presence but said nothing, although her face went whiter still, and I thought she might faint. It was actually Jenny that broke the silence.

"Is that you, Nat?" she asked, her green eyes flashing in my direction.

"It is," I confirmed. "And with luck I have some good news for you."

"Both luck and good news are welcome strangers in this house," Ned told me in his usual gruff manner. "But it's a relief to see you safe from the press, lad," he added, grudgingly.

Susan approached almost cautiously, then seeming to have made a decision, reached out to hold me close, pressing the side of her face against my chest.

"Have you problems with the Bennetts?" I asked, rather awkwardly; this was the first time she had shown any affection for me in front of the family, and I was uncertain how to react, especially as she had yet to say a word.

"There's no good that will come of those two blackguards," Ned sighed. "Though I don't say it is your fault. You did what you thought was best, and I know it were meant for our benefit."

I reached inside my pocket and pulled out Bryson's guinea. "Will this help?" I asked. Ned looked at it cautiously, and Susan gave a sharp intake of breath.

"It will buy us a week, no longer," the old man barely whispered.

"I can get more," I told him, then added: "*We* can get more. It is perfectly legal, but will mean using the lugger. Is she ready for sea?"

"Hold fast there, boy," Ned raised his hand. "There is much to speak of."

"She's laid up on the Stade," Jenny confirmed, briskly. "But wanting for sails and a crew. Father can't afford one, and we haven't the other."

"Maybe not for now," I told them. "But I think I may know of a way."

* * *

The shilling bought more food than I think any of us had seen in a week. Jenny and Tilly took care of the buying, while Susan, Ned and I went down to the Stade to look over the lugger. And, I must say, the Phillips' yard had done a good job.

She was fully painted now, and finished in a smart, glowing red, while being payed and oiled inside. And she came with standing and running rigging, as well as ground tackle and mooring lines, though lacked sails. Ned said this was customary when buying or selling any boat, although I was still surprised at the omission. He thought he could beg or borrow enough to see her set but, even if not, I was now so full of confidence that no obstacle felt too large to overcome. The Clarkesons had not been so very terrible; I actually grew to be quite fond of Jesse towards the end, but there was no doubting the Coglans were my favoured family. And seeing Susan again was just so good that I kept finding myself smiling like the cat's uncle.

We came back and ate, and I don't think I ever felt so full. This was what I had wanted all the time: a chance to earn some decent money, and stay with the Coglans. Bryson wanted us to check at least three French ports a week, for which he would pay a guinea a visit. The first coin would cover the boat for all that period, with any more mounting up in reserve. Peace with France would not last forever and, as soon as war was declared, the money must stop as there would be no more need for us. But I still hoped to buy her outright eventually, and would put any extra aside. Meanwhile Ned and I could spend the rest of our time fishing and, with a boat the size and power of *Katharine II*, our catch should be correspondingly larger. One problem remained, however, we needed an extra hand.

"There's no one at liberty in all of Hastings," Ned told me, when I broached the subject after our meal. "Press snatched all the prime and likely seamen, an' most of the riff-raff: why even you was taken." he added gruffly.

"Dad's right," Jenny confirmed. "Several boats are rotting on the Stade for want of care, and half the London carts are going off light."

I winced; this was worse than I had thought. Hastings depended heavily on the City market; if such an outlet were not kept properly supplied, a different provider would be found, and the town must surely founder.

"What is the solution?" I asked and Ned shrugged.

"Women are putting to sea, mostly," Jenny nipped in quickly, before her father could speak, and Ned cleared his throat in annoyance.

"Though even that ain't putting matters straight," he grunted. "Not with no one left ashore to look after the young and the old."

"Well we have none of either in this house," I said brightly. "And will just have to do the same." I winked at Susan, knowing she was both willing and capable to hand aboard a small lugger, especially one as sound as mine. And it would be so good to work with her; already I could foresee the best summer of my life. But for some reason she looked uncomfortable, and would not meet my eye as Ned continued:

"There'll be no member of my family going aboard a boat." he declared. "Not if I am to have any say in the matter."

He had made similar statements in the past, but I never paid them much attention. Now though, his tone was deadly serious, and all my wonderful plans were in danger of coming to nothing, just because of one old man's stubbornness.

"Susan can hand," I said, looking from one to the other in desperation. "It's the only answer; you must see that." But clearly they could not, and my remark was met with silence. For a moment nobody spoke, then Ned took out his pipe as if the conversation was finished.

"Or Alex: he could crew," I said, desperately turning to Tilly, but she shook her head.

"One lugger won't keep two families," she told me sadly. "Alex is with the Revenue now, and will be sending for me shortly. I'm sorry for all the trouble I have caused, but having him here will not help and he was never a popular person in Hastings."

"I have no job at *The Cutter*," Susan said, cautiously. "And, if nothing else is found, must start working for the Bennetts next week. Given the choice, I should far rather go to sea, and would learn to hand quickly enough, Why I used to, before..." she left the sentence unfinished but raised her eyes to meet the old man's.

"Or is it better she sells herself to Rob and Billy?" Jenny added flatly. "Really Dad, we know why you are objecting, but can't you see it is the only way?"

Ned sat considering his empty pipe for a moment, then put it back in his pocket. "We could go back to sailing the punt." he said, looking directly at me. "Them were good days and we made a fair amount."

"The punt won't cross the Channel," I replied.

"So we don't," he brightened. "We forget all about the spying: stick to what we knows."

"And still have the lugger, and still have to find the Bennetts a guinea a week?" I asked, a little testily. "With me losing my Sea Fencibles protection, I could be back in the Navy in no time, and then all would be as bad as before."

It may well have been my fault we were in this fix, but at least I could see a way out, whereas Ned's continual objections simply made things worse. Principles were all very well if they could be afforded, but these were desperate times, and there could be no room for fine ideals. "In truth I find we have no option," I added. "If you can think of one, I should be glad to hear of it."

He shook his head sadly. "No, there is nothing else," he admitted, somewhat pathetically, and I could see he was finally beaten. "If what you says is true, and the king will pay for the information. I suppose it might work." He glared at his daughter and something of his old manner returned. "But you're gonna have to mind out particularly careful, young lady."

* * *

I was to travel on to Rye early the following morning. There I could confirm with Bryson, agree on which ports to reconnoitre first, then bid my farewells to the Clarkesons. With luck, I should be able to return to Hastings the same night and we may even take *Katharine II* to sea the following day. Meanwhile Ned and Susan were to see what might be done to acquire sails, and generally prepare the lugger. I could tell Ned was still not totally behind the scheme and felt more than a little guilty in thrusting it upon him. Had an alternative been available, I would have been more than happy to listen to it, but there was none: my idea remained our only option and I, for one, had no intention of scuppering everything because of one old man's finer feelings.

But it wasn't until the next morning that I learned the real reason behind his obstinacy, and by then was out of the door, and walking down the road with Susan, who was to see me to the edge of town.

"You must not think too harshly of him," she said, as we reached the end of All Saints Street and were holding each other for what might be the last time in possibly hours. I waited. There was a storm brewing and I had a good way to travel, but would have continued standing there forever if she had wished.

"I used to crew in the punt when I was younger," she told me eventually. "We all did, even mother." Then Susan paused, and looked away from me for a moment before adding, "and that's how she died."

* * *

Bryson had been delighted to hear my news, and we quickly arranged a schedule that would keep both Calais and Boulogne under reasonably constant surveillance, with the occasional journey further south, as time and tide permitted. There had been reports of further barges being built at several ports between Étaples and Flushing, so we would be keeping an eye on operations in general along the coast, and I could foresee little time for actual fishing. But I already felt I knew and could trust the lieutenant, and a guinea for every port visited would make good any losses we took on that score.

"Having a woman aboard may even turn out a benefit," he reflected towards the end of our conversation. "It makes all appear far more innocent, and is something I may suggest to the others."

"Others?" For him to consider Susan's presence an advantage was acceptable, if strangely annoying, but I did not care for what might be considered rival boats carrying out a similarly intensive watch. Were there to be a surplus of fishers cruising up and down their west coast, the French might become suspicious.

"For sure," he replied lightly. "I cannot rest the security of our nation on reports from one small lugger, but rather must keep my eye on the luff. Others will certainly be carrying out a similar task to you though, for the security of both, I shall not say who. You may rest assured that your information is by far the best, however," he added soothingly. "And will be valued above all others." So saying he passed a further guinea across the table which definitely put me in a better frame of mind.

It was a relatively short walk from the coffee house to the Clarkesons' cottage and I got there just as the rain set in. Ma Clarkeson was serving up lunch, so Jesse came to meet me at the door, and listened to my tale. I told him of the lugger, and my home in Hastings, but was careful to say nothing of any work for Bryson.

He seemed unsurprised, and even unbent enough to allow me an understanding nod. Then Ma Clarkeson came to the door and told him his food was ready, before fixing me with a look made entirely of thunder.

"I'll be there in a moment, Ma," Jesse told her. "This shall not take long."

She disappeared back into the kitchen, leaving me and Jesse staring at each other.

"I'm sorry things didn't work out," he said, and both the words and his softening of tone, took me further aback. "You're a good kid, and work hard if, perhaps, some of your ideas are not so sound."

I felt suddenly awkward and said nothing in reply.

"And you may be interested to know, there'll be no more Clarkesons dealing with Prettyman and his lot," he continued, as if confirming a fact agreed on long past. "That is something I am set upon. I don't say things are particularly easy at present, but we can survive without his shilling."

Mention of money seemed to trigger something inside his brain, and he reached into his pocket.

"Here, you had better take this," he said, thrusting two heavy coins in my direction. "You've earned as much, and more, though it is all I can pay, and don't rightly have to do that."

I took the silver crowns and thanked him. "What will you do?" I asked, and found I was actually interested.

"There's work enough," he told me. "Since the press robbed most of the fleet of its men, fish prices have never been so high. And I'm not adverse to a small amount of smuggling," he added, looking at me defiantly. "Not if it pays, and no one gets hurt. But I am careful who I run with, and you should be too." He considered me for a moment.

"There's some you can trust, and some you can't and Prettyman is one of those best kept away from; bear that in mind if your courses ever cross," he added, with emphasis. "Any offer he makes can only turn bad; see you refuse, and don't go back for a second try."

I shook my head; one encounter with Ugly Joe was more than enough for me. I had absolutely no intention of working for him again. Not in any capacity.

Alex's story

When I joined *Stag* she had been languishing in harbour for over a week, but Commander Travis' regime of conscientiousness was set to stay. In between the extended cruises, we sailed out on day runs: usually as soon as the tide permitted and often had to scrape out of Rye's treacherous harbour approach while it was barely navigable. On these local trips, our skipper was usually content to explore the coast, nipping into small bays, and often carrying out lengthy inspections or using creeping irons to drag an area he suspected might be hiding a crop of sunken booty. Other times he would organize drills covering everything from small arms work to great gun practice. Men used to trimming sails would be designated as boat's crew, and made to row the cruiser's tiny galley and, on one occasion, we were put through a series of evolutions, tacking, jibing, and heaving to, while the helmsman and most of the hands were shrouded in blindfolds, to simulate fog or absolute darkness. And there were times when he just used to revel in his little craft's stunning performance, a far off fishing smack would be selected and the cruiser ordered down upon her at the briskest possible pace. This was probably the favoured exercise for most: cramped, stuffy and damp she may have been, but *Stag* was built for speed, and performed so well when crewed by seasoned mariners who properly appreciated her virtues. On several occasions I was given the chance to act as second helmsman and experienced the thrill of feeling the boat's very soul through the warm and polished tiller. It was an experience I will never forget, and has spoiled me for other sailing craft since.

But on the day of the storm, Commander Travis clearly had something far more specific in mind and, as soon as we were clear of the shallow ground beyond our harbour, we were ordered to set all suitable sail and strike out deep into the Channel.

"Reckon the skipper's got a whiff of something," Honeysett told me, as we secured the second jib and felt the customary surge of power. "That or the breeze up his tail," he added with a smirk.

And there was certainly no shortage of wind; it blew strong and from the south-east, forcing *Stag* to meet it apparently head on as her quartermaster kept her close hauled and on the very edge of a luff. All aboard were well aware far worse could be expected, but Travis seemed to be enjoying himself right enough, and stood solid and beaming at the conn while the crested seas crashed about him, and our horizon steadily closed in. The sun that had blessed us for so much of the spring was soon blotted out by deep dark clouds, while the scent of storm was horribly apparent. And then the rains came.

With little time from the first spot to a torrent, we were all thoroughly soaked within seconds, but still the tiny craft beat out into the increasing chop of the channel. By now, all had guessed this was something more than a simple heavy weather exercise, as nothing extra had been called for from any of us, apart from close attention to the sails and a regular change of tack. But, if having his objective apparently in the eye of such a wind had upset our commander, he failed to show it, and remained stoically on deck, meeting our misery with rousing words and the occasional blast of resonant laughter. Then, after consultation with Lumsden, the mate, a solid man of many years' experience who unintentionally acted as a foil to his master's exuberance, we were finally allowed to heave to, and the tiny hull became a plaything for the gods' amusement.

Theirs, but not ours: the bucking deck was now a place of positive danger and, even with life-lines rigged and total concentration, keeping upright and in touch with the cutter was all most of us could manage. And it was at that point we received the order to clear away the great guns.

To date, gun drill had been mainly confined to dumb show, where the pieces would be worked and served in a manner simulating use. There had only been one live firing practice, and that had not gone terribly well: Dick Steven, one of the older mariners who should have known better, left a foot behind a recoiling cannon and was later judged lucky to have kept it. But now the peril would be far greater than simply dealing with high explosives.

Despite their comparatively small size, and our carriage guns were the lightest worthy of the name, they weighed in at over twelve hundredweight apiece. Ideally each needed four stout men to serve them although, with a total crew of little more than twenty, we had to make do with far less. Thus it was rare, if ever, that a gun was reloaded during action. A single, crisp broadside, with every piece fired by one gun captain, with a single assistant, was usually enough to frighten a lugger's skipper into surrender: were we to meet anything more substantial, we trusted our commander to use *Stag*'s exceptional speed to see us safe. The image of that bold and beautiful revenue cruiser being neatly swatted by Ugly Joe's brig remained with me. But I was young enough to strike such memories to one side, and look only to the future, which was certain to be glorious.

The carriage guns were kept loaded with round shot and charge at all times, but there was still sufficient for us to do, and it needed to be done in circumstances that were anything but easy. Honeysett, who acted as gun captain for two opposite pieces, locked his knees about the cascabels as he added fresh priming to each touch hole, while I instantly covered the dry powder with lead aprons. Then, together, we removed the transit frappings from the tackle that kept all safe whilst the boat was at speed. Our warranted gunner, who doubled as deputed mariner, brought up a round of slow match which was cut into seven separate sections and each was lit from the binnacle lantern. The burning ends hissed and glowed eerily as the gun captains selected a length and fitted it to their linstocks, and all was finally ready. *Stag* also carried smaller swivel guns mounted on stanchions within the bulwarks. These sat at regular intervals between her main armament and I had charge of two. But the range for their half pound shot was poor and, with the weather so foul, it appeared they were not to be used that day.

No sooner were our cannon ready than a call came from the masthead, and all eyes turned to the west. Nothing could be seen with such a dark and deadly sky, but our captain seemed to have found the clue he was looking for. We were ordered back to the wind and soon the prized pennant that gave us licence to enforce Custom law was run up, and blew out, stiff and straight.

Though cold, wet and, in my case, mildly apprehensive, there was no thought for comfort from any of us. Even under a single jib and reefed main, the cruiser's performance was every bit as spectacular, but now she was sailing in earnest and heading into what we could only assume to be action.

"No knowing what the skipper's heard," Honeysett muttered next to me. "But you can be sure we ain't here on no pleasure cruise."

"Brig to larboard! Fine on the bow!" The cry came from Johnston, the forecastle lookout, and we all rose slightly and peered forward. Sure enough, there was a two masted vessel just emerging from a squall, and running before the wind, under reefed topsails.

"Port your helm: take us three points to starboard!" Travis' massive voice rolled out above the din of the storm and could be heard by every man on board. Honeysett grinned:

"The old man's been practising that bellow his entire life," he said.

And then, Lumsden, the mate, added: "Gunners to larboard!" and it all became far more serious.

There was too much going on for me to be fully aware of the details, but I could guess what our commander was about. By turning to starboard, he had drawn more speed, and was intending to gain the ultimate position off the mystery brig's prow. The cruiser settled on her new course, and we peered into the rain to see what the enemy would make of us. Until then, I was merely aware we were fighting a larger craft. Such a vessel may well be

214

armed and probably foreign, in which case action was unlikely, as Britain was not in a state of war. But, when the silhouette of our adversary became clearer, a cold feeling of dread rose up within me. I had seen this particular brig before. More than that, I knew the chances of her opening fire to be better than even. And I was also uncomfortably aware that the results could be utterly devastating.

Chapter Twenty-Five

"The brig you see before you is the *Jessica*," Travis boomed from his customary position next to the helmsmen. "And for those who do not know, she is owned by Ugly Joe Prettyman: moon-curser, coxcomb and all round nubbing cheat." The statement was sufficient to elicit a chorus of boos, hisses and catcalls from my fellow mariners and I was oddly relieved that both the vessel and her owner were well known to all.

"Word has it that friend Joe was planning a run tonight, and had hoped that this charming weather would be enough to put off any interference. But then that little dandy was not counting on *Stag*, and the men what man her!" Now laughter replaced the jeering and the crew's reaction was heartening in itself.

"So what say we meet him half-way?" Travis continued. "And maybe deliver a dose of iron to mix with any booty he may be carrying?"

Stag sliced through the dark, crested waves, aiming at a point that should put her before Prettyman's solid little brig, with every man aboard shouting or waving a fist. A dandy he most certainly was, but I may have been the only one who knew quite how lethal Ugly Joe could also be.

"Stand by your guns. Ready larboard battery!" Travis again, and now his voice was in deadly earnest. Honeysett and I moved to our larboard piece, and I reached forward and removed the watertight tompion from the cannon's mouth. The view of *Jessica* was getting clearer by the moment: we could see the line of guns that punctured her side; all run out, and all trained on us.

But we had the heels of her, that was another thing that was becoming more and more obvious. In most sailing vessels the bows are considered an especially vulnerable area, so it is every captain's aim to cross his opponent's prow with his own broadside. Prettyman's brig would have to perform some fancy tricks if she were to avoid receiving nearly thirty pounds of iron landing upon her hawse. In such a situation, even *Stag*'s mild armament could do considerable damage. I was watching the brig and considering this when Honeysett said something to me and gave a smile. I did not catch his words but instinctively grinned in return, which meant I missed the moment when Prettyman swung *Jessica*'s helm across, and the brig turned savagely to starboard.

The manoeuvre had been both violent and sudden, and must have taken her a good eight points to the east, yet *Jessica*'s sails were trimmed with commendable efficiency. I drew in my breath, and most about me began cussing at various levels of profanity, but there was no sound, or obvious comment from our commander. It had been horribly neat, and marked Prettyman out as a skilled tactician, while the painfully simple plan Travis had envisaged was revealed as such, and lay in total tatters.

Prettyman's brig, now a definite threat, settled on her new heading and, though she might lack the speed and intention of closing on our own bows, the hull of a revenue cutter is known to be eggshell thin, and no such advantage would be necessary.

"Take her to starboard!" Travis shouted as it dawned on him that discretion had suddenly become the better part of valour. It meant missing our opportunity to fire a shot, and turning tail on the enemy, which had been the last thing on his mind until a few seconds ago. But there was still a chance *Stag* could put a decent amount of sea room between her and what was bound to be a devastating broadside.

Our trimmers were ready at the nearby headsail sheets and waiting for the moment when the hull began to turn when a cry went up. Glancing across, I caught the end of a ripple of fire that had begun at *Jessica*'s stem, and was now reaching her stern. The midst of a storm was hardly ideal conditions for small cannon fire; a good distance separated us, and most of Prettyman's shot went wide. But those that told were heavy, well placed, and proved quite sufficient.

A twelve pound ball smashed though the larboard bulwark between two of our guns, breaking down a stanchion and knocking both half ports into one. Beside me, Chalky White gave out a sharp yell of surprise as he looked down at his right arm that suddenly appeared unusually short. A further round shot struck us somewhere lower, and the hull itself reeled from the blow like a pugilist might when landed with a lucky punch. A third hit us aft, and there were splinters and line apparently flying all about, while shouted commands and cries of alarm merged seamlessly with the less ordered screams of our wounded. The wind was to larboard and we had been carrying a heel, but suddenly the cruiser righted, became sluggish, and then began a slow roll in the swell.

"Starboard battery prepare!" The call took me by surprise and I looked out to leeward. In what seemed like no time at all, *Jessica* had worn round, and was now heading back on the opposite tack, clearly intending to deliver a second broadside with her larboard guns. I was no expert but could tell from our feel that *Stag* had taken significant damage and was already wallowing. Another drubbing from Prettyman would probably see us finished and, as yet, we had not fired a single shot in return.

Honeysett's hand urged me roughly over to the opposite cannon, and I swiftly removed the tompion and apron. He squinted down the barrel at Prettyman's brig, which was now just off our starboard beam and in a perfect position to fire. I was ready with a handspike should some degree of aiming be called for, but he shook his head. Then one of our aft guns spoke, and soon all of *Stag*'s puny broadside had rolled out.

The range was closer than before, although the cruiser's broadside weight was still considerably less than a quarter that of Prettyman's vessel. But either one of the Revenue's gunners was an expert, or fortune remained with us that day, as the brig fell off the wind shortly after our shots rained down upon her.

"Someone's got the bugger's rudder!" a man next to me shrieked with glee, and there was little doubt the larger craft was in a fix. With the sudden lessening of pressure, her hull was being turned further to windward, throwing every sail into a tangle of confusion, and removing the threat of another deadly pounding from that larboard battery.

"Stroke of luck, that," Honeysett shouted, as he joined me. We had watched our own shot go wild and clearly he had no confidence in any of the other gunners.

"Can she close on us?" I asked, as the brig began to disappear into the gloom of the storm.

"Na," Honeysett replied. "And it's the pity, for she could have been taken with ease, were we not wounded ourselves."

I felt no regret at all, and was merely glad the action was over, but Honeysett had more to say.

"She'll be filled with booty, mind. There's a tidy sum for us all out there, were we only able to claim it."

I looked at the retreating brig with fresh interest as he continued.

"They say *Bee*, the Newhaven boat, got eighty guineas a head when they took down the Horsebridge gang's brig a year or so back."

It was the first time I realised how seizer money could be so quickly earned, and my spirits rose. Eighty guineas might ease a lot of my problems but, as *Jessica* finally faded into the mist, I felt little true remorse. The fight had been short and savage and I was only too aware how close we had come to sharing the fate of the previous Revenue cutter Prettyman engaged.

A call came through for men to attend the pumps, while someone else began to shout for sail trimmers and the boatswain. Judging by the amount of line that already lay about our deck, there was extensive damage aloft while, beneath us, our hull felt heavy and torpid.

"Well, the Clipping Crew'll have their work cut out afore they see harbour again," Honeysett told me, as if in consolation. I looked about at the damage and confusion caused by just a few of *Jessica*'s shots. We had certainly been lucky, both in the damage received from Prettyman's brig, and that delivered by us in return. But the wind remained strong and the rain still fell in sheets; I guessed we too would be having a busy time of it before finding shelter.

Nat's story

It was actually three days after I returned to Hastings that

Katharine II finally saw open water. In the meantime, Ned had managed to acquire a complete suit of sails and the rig was also adapted. When last viewed, she sported a similar arrangement to the Clarkesons' *Lucy*, with the same preponderance of spars and lines. Ned, who was in charge of the fitting out, spoke with someone at Phillips' yard and now, rather than the eclectic collection of topsails and heads the lugger was originally equipped with, she boasted two simple lugs, with a small jib for the bowsprit. It was a similar rig to Ned's punt, and I immediately assumed he had specified the changes to allow for my inexperience.

I should have been aware of the danger jumping to such an assumption could bring; this was not the first time it had happened, after all. But Ned's calling me a lubber still stuck in my gullet, and I was furious. Admittedly, when first arriving in Hastings, I had known little of seamanship or fishing in general, but felt much had been learned since. Why, I'd even had sole charge of the mainmast in a far larger lugger, and felt more than competent to crew what was, after all, my own boat.

"Why the change of rig, Ned?" I asked, as the two of us gathered round her. Dawn had only just broken, we had the Stade pretty much to ourselves, and should really have been thinking about how to launch the beast with so few people, rather than quibbling over her tophamper.

"Standard set up for a boat this size," he grunted. "Don't want no dipping lug, or to be bothered with too many fancy tops'ls, heads and stays."

"But we want her to be fast," I countered. "And I am experienced enough to cope with a little extra canvas, whatever you may think."

I remember his look: as direct as always, but this time he seemed genuinely angry, and I prepared myself for an outburst. But he must have had a change of mind and, when his answer came, it was far more reasonable.

"Tops'ls can be rigged later, as can additional heads, but they will cost. Elsiver Phillips took our spars back in exchange for the sails you see here; not brand new, but they will serve, and I considered it a fair deal. Especially as he threw in a second-hand trawl with weights."

There was little I could say; his logic and commercial sense were impeccable. But more was to come.

"You may have come a long way, but a couple of trips across the Channel hardly makes you a foremast Jack," he told me. "Even if you was, Susan, for sure, is not. And, if it comes to it, I have no wish to skipper a new boat, with a raw crew, and still keep track of a cat's cradle aloft." His expression mellowed further as he added. "So why not think less about yourself, and what folk might be making of you, and more of those who also have a say in matters?"

Susan joined us shortly afterwards and was reluctant to meet my eye. It was the first time I'd seen her in an oilskin smock, sou'wester and sea boots, but to me she never looked finer. With that, and the strain of tempting a twenty-four foot hull into the sea, all complaints of the lugger's rig were soon forgotten.

Once she hit deep water, *Katharine II* truly came to life, and I don't think I have ever been happier. The running bowsprit and mizzen outrigger were set, and soon we were thrusting out to sea with a comfortable south-westerly just forward of our beam. She sailed well; lighter than *Lucy,* and probably not so solid, but I did not doubt she would be ideal for what we had in mind, and a far better sea boat than Ned's old punt.

Susan handled the lines well enough, but soon took the helm, which was to become her permanent position. No sooner were all the sails trimmed to perfection than Ned ordered us east, and we began to follow the coast for a spell. With the wind more or less on our quarter *Katharine II* became far more lively, and I inwardly conceded that Ned was right to simplify the rig. It was a reasonably strong wind, and we might feel the need for extra canvas on still days although, with the work I had in mind, I did not foresee speed or power as being so very essential.

And I was at sea, in the sunshine, in my own boat, sailing with my own girl, and with prospects ahead that suddenly looked impossibly bright. I found myself glancing back at Susan who, guessing my thoughts, smiled in return, and then we both began to laugh.

Hearing us, Ned turned his customary po-faced expression full upon his lunatic companions, which only fed our mood. Soon the two of us had tears running down our cheeks; I was having difficulty breathing while Susan clutched at the tiller in an effort to stay upright. And then the unthinkable happened, and the old man began to laugh also.

Alex's story

The journey back to Rye Harbour turned out to be one of the most miserable of my life, and took all of eight hours. *Stag* was holed just above the waterline; constant pumping and a subsequent patch kept us afloat but, with our gaff damaged, and only questionable support from the larboard running and standing backstays, we could not manage any appreciable speed. The rain continued to fall throughout and, while our wounded moaned below, those who were able rigged an auxiliary stay, and took their turn with the pumping. Mercifully, we reached the harbour approach with sufficient water beneath our keel, but that was about the only element in our favour. The cutter was laid up against the harbour wall, and we were turned down until repairs could be effected.

This inevitably robbed me both of income and lodgings. My home, in *Stag's* cramped mariners' mess, was soon invaded by the shipwrights and carpenters who appeared to take her in hand. I might have begged quarters in Stag House, the single storey red brick building that sat next to where we berthed. The place was not large though, and already held all but three of the cutter's married men, as well as their extended families. Lodging elsewhere would cost me money I did not have, as no pay would be due while the boat was laid up, and Tilly must soon be needing funds.

They estimated a week as being the likely time needed to put *Stag* back into service, and I was at a loss as to how to amuse myself for such a period. Tilly was no more than ten miles away but the last letter told me her condition was now generally known, and I had become an even less popular person with her family, and others in the area. The line had made me laugh; since Dad took his posting with the Revenue, the Medcalfs had been distinctly unfriendly and, although it was my home, I felt little inclination to return to Hastings.

I had already sent ten shillings for her needs from my first two weeks' wages, and now was left with less than two to see me over the next seven days. Consequently, when Bridley, the Custom House Recorder, mentioned a possibility of work with the landguard, I seized the opportunity.

It meant lodging with John Musgrave, a local riding officer with a reputation for drinking too much and keeping a poor table, while his horse should have been retired years ago. But I could continue to draw my mariner's pay, and was prepared to put up with a good deal of discomfort, if it ultimately meant being with Tilly.

Bridley assured me there was much I might learn about smugglers from the old soak, and presented me with two heavy pistols. The weapons would be of limited use against a group of determined landers, but I comforted myself with the thought they might at least bring in reinforcements, even if it came in the form of a tipsy old man on a lame horse.

Nat's story

The port of Boulogne felt quite familiar to me by now; those tall and brightly painted houses that appeared so striking on my first visit seemed almost mundane, and the massive harbour itself altogether less threatening. I noticed Susan and Ned taking more than an interest however and felt agreeably superior as we approached on the very edge of high water. Our passage across had been uneventful. I had been ready to advise Ned on tide and currents, the proper observance of which could halve or double a crossing time, but he declined all help and, even though he had not visited the French coast in twenty years, steered a fine and economical course that took full advantage of the elements.

This was our fourth day of sailing together and already Susan, Ned and I felt very much a crew. We had fished on the two previous days, and brought back reasonable catches; now we were confident, both of the boat, which had exceeded all expectations, and each other. It had been fair weather sailing, however. After that one, terrible, storm a few days back the fine spring of 1803 had resumed. Quite what would happen when *Katharine II* experienced her first harsh conditions was yet to be seen, of course, and we were in no rush to find out.

So, for the moment, we were content to creep slowly into Boulogne harbour with the wind at our backs and a warm sun on our faces. There was the sound of seagulls and the far away noise of workmen; in all it was little different to any port in any country, and there was nothing to be feared.

I confidently directed Ned over to the strangers' wharf that Jesse had always been directed to. It lay to seaward of the main fishing quay and had accommodated *Lucy* well enough. I knew we could use it to await the arrival of the French officials and, while doing so, I might even make my first cursory inspection of the basin.

Yet again there were more barges than before. Even the briefest of glances revealed at least two new arrivals, both of the larger class, while the number of warships had also grown. There had been two extra frigates in the roads, both with topmasts set up indicating they were either newly arrived, or about to put to sea. I was getting better at identifying ships, and knew these to be relatively light for their class. Even without counting ports, an eighteen pounder frigate lay at anchor close by and was far more substantial in frame. It was disquieting news, especially considering the short space of time since my last visit, and I was keen to return to Bryson to pass the information on. But before I could investigate further, my attention was drawn to the quayside, where someone was speaking French, and loudly.

Ned had apparently grown restless and stepped ashore; I could see him, standing some way from the lugger, and looking bewildered. Around him three men, two of whom were dressed in elaborate uniforms, were all shouting at once. As their protests grew, I could tell Ned was becoming angry. I looked about for Susan, and we both clambered over the lugger's bulwark, landing on the quay together. But our arrival seemed to annoy the Frenchmen even more.

The two uniformed officers turned to Susan and began expostulating noisily before simultaneously losing interest on realising her to be a woman. But she was more than a match for them, and produced a piece of paper that was waved boldly in their faces. This was our crib sheet, copied out the previous night by one of Ned's cronies who claimed to speak the tongue. One of the officials took it with both hands and studied the thing for a moment before passing it to his colleague with a look of derision and a brief expulsion of breath. Susan turned to me with defeat on her face.

"Salt," I said loudly, while waving my hands in an attempt to demonstrate the mineral. "We come to buy salt." It was something we had decided upon as convenient. Salt, although taxed, was rarely smuggled, yet remained in constant demand by most fishermen. The best by far came from France, and would be denied us when war broke out. Buying a supply now was an excellent cover: we could be intending to avoid tax, or not, but either course should have avoided the attention we were currently attracting.

A small crowd of interested onlookers started to gather. Some began making what might be suggestions or comments, but none were well received by the officials. Instead, one opened fire with a barrage of French that left me reeling, and soon the other two joined him. I looked warily to Ned, then Susan, before the three of us started to back away for our boat. We had seen a good deal and already I had information to give Bryson, but this did not auger well for a return trip.

"Nathaniel, is it not?" The voice was at once familiar, welcome and utterly terrifying. "You appear to be in something of a bind, dear boy: perhaps I might help?"

I turned to see Ugly Joe appear from out of the crowd, debonair as ever, and now also wearing a concerned, but friendly, expression. The officials melted into compliant silence on his approach and willingly gave up the paper when he extended an elegant hand in their direction. Prettyman glanced at it briefly, before pulling a wry face, then muttered what I assumed to be an explanation. This was taken fully, and with obvious respect; the two uniformed men turned away without so much as a glance in our direction. Prettyman beamed back at me in triumph.

"A simple misunderstanding," he exclaimed. "You should know that war is likely and might come at any moment, so our friends are especially sensitive."

He handed the paper to me while the crowd about us began to disperse in silence. "What you have here is French in parts, but would serve little use, it being mainly made up of a folk song which is considered rather rude by most. I can provide something more suitable if called upon, though suspect my help might come in a far more practical way." He smiled, showing us his immaculate, white teeth. "See, the lovely *Jessica* lies close by; perhaps the three of you will join me for some refreshment?"

Chapter Twenty-Six

The brig was indeed moored several berths up from our lugger, and appeared to be the source of the noise we heard earlier. A small stack of fresh wood lay piled on her quarterdeck, lengths of which were being sawn to size by two shirtless men, while a stage set lower down held several more workmen currently involved in ripping out damaged timber. A strong smell of marine glue permeated the air and, as we mounted the short gangplank, there was the sound of frantic hammering.

"You will forgive me," Prettyman said, indicating the activity. "*Jessica* is undergoing essential repairs, and my quarters are not fit to be seen. But the day is warm; perhaps we would be comfortable enough on deck?"

There was no objection from me; indeed, even in company of Susan and Ned, I had no wish to go below with our host. But, as chairs and a small table were produced, and we sat stiffly together on the brig's main deck, I still felt unaccountably awkward. Ignoring our last encounter, it was as if two completely diverse parts of my life had been thrown together, and my mind felt to be racing in several directions at once.

Jessica was a far larger vessel than I had reckoned from my brief inspection while aboard the pressing tender. A few months back, any thirty foot lugger appeared substantial to me, yet this was more akin to a ship. The sombre lines of cannon that surrounded me were also impressive, although in a completely different way. I remembered the damage they had dealt out to the Revenue cutter and felt a chill inside.

Other thoughts occurred as a pot of coffee, china cups and plates of small biscuits were brought out by a lad far younger than me who was overdressed like a flunky. We were evidently about to be well looked after and I grew increasingly uneasy. By now Ugly Joe may well have heard the Clarkesons were no longer in his employ, and the last thing I wanted was for him to suggest any form of smuggling to the Coglans.

Ned was still not entirely happy with our new venture; having his precious daughter crewing aboard a boat was bad enough, while skippering the same craft himself, when it was not his property, did not make the situation any the easier. Knowing that I, at least in name the owner, was heavily in debt to a pair of hoodlums multiplied the sin many times over, while our current occupation must have felt as alien to him as the port he had just sailed to. Even to be seen sitting and drinking coffee, or in his case not, with a stranger that looked like something between the Prince of Wales and a Drury Lane dancing master was possibly a step too far: were he offered the chance to run illicit goods, I could not have answered for the consequences.

But Prettyman was important, even Ned could see that. Despite his fancy dress, there was the look of power in his eyes. And he was no fool: another thing that became immediately obvious. He spoke with charm to Susan, respect to Ned, and addressed me as if we had been trusted friends for many years. And not once was contraband mentioned, even though a potential replacement for *Lucy* was apparently being handed to him on a plate.

It was soon decided any immediate supplies we required could be obtained from himself, though, and the hundredweight of salt we had settled upon would be delivered to the quay before the evening's tide. We returned to our lugger as soon as the constraints of politeness allowed, and I noted that Susan and Ned were quick to retreat to the lugger's pat: the small and marginally more private area at the stern.

"You know I must check on shipping," I told them simply, after giving a decidedly vague outline on Joseph Prettyman. "What say you to a stroll about the harbour, Susan?"

"Go, if you wish, girl," Ned grunted. "I shall be content enough to remain with the boat."

"I shall stay also, Nat," she replied, and I could see she was every bit as uncomfortable as her father. "But know your work must be done, and ask only that you return soon, and safely."

Our eyes met. "I am sorry for the confusion," I said, a little awkwardly. "And the more so if Mr Prettyman worried you."

"Sure, he was our saviour," she replied lightly. "And apparently a fine man; I would think he means us no harm."

Her reaction was just another in a series of surprises that day, but she had more to say.

"But do hurry back, Nat; this does not feel like a healthy place to be for long, and I would rather be quit of it."

* * *

More than seven hours would have to pass before that could happen and I resolved to get my private work done as soon as possible. I was careful not to stray too close to the flat bottomed barges this time, but actually found much could be seen from a distance. Then I wondered if wandering a little deeper into the harbour complex might procure additional information which Bryson would find useful. I was by no means a boot catcher, but the lieutenant already held me in good esteem, and I had never been known to pass up any chance of raising my status further.

The number of invasion craft had certainly increased and I recorded the new figures, while mentally wiping the old from my brain. I also noted signs of increased military activity. Building work was well underway to the east on what looked likely to be a huge barracks, and the town itself seemed even busier, with a greater proportion of military uniforms in sight.

With the fresh figures in my head, I was on my way back to the boat when I saw Ugly Joe for the second time that day. On this occasion there was no surprise; I sighted him from some distance. He was standing at the end of the quay that held both our vessels and apparently waiting for me with a smile that might even have been genuine on his face.

"Well met, Nathaniel," he said, although by now I was certain that little in Prettyman's life occurred by chance. "Perhaps you could spare me a moment of your time?"

I eyed him warily; obtaining the salt, securing the berth: indeed all our negotiations with the French had turned out to be far harder than we envisaged. There was no doubt that Ugly Joe had saved the day for us on every count, but Jesse's words came back to haunt me and I was determined not to be placed under any obligation to the man. "We have already spoken, Mr Prettyman," I said temporising.

"Yes, but I gauged your companions would not care to discuss the particular favour I had in mind."

I tensed. "They are good people, and will have nothing to do with contraband goods, or free trading," I told him. "If you could not speak before them, I will not have you do so now."

"Indeed, I judged them to be of worthy principles," he said, with apparent sincerity. "And always value a man by the company he keeps. However, I have suffered from several misfortunes of late, and am in urgent need of a friend myself. *Jessica* cannot travel to England for a spell, and my previous courier would seem to have turned against me. Yet a commitment remains outstanding, and I find I must take delivery of a small package in as little time as possible. I believe I have performed several favours for you in the past, Nathaniel; would you deny me a single one in return?"

I had not considered the point before; even ignoring that morning's assistance, Prettyman had previously saved me from what might have been another awkward incident in this very harbour, to say nothing of indirectly providing employment with Jesse and Dan. And there was the not inconsiderable matter of my release from the pressing tender in the first place. Without him I might be aboard a Navy man-of-war right now, with the Coglans left to the mercy of Rob and Billy Bennett.

"Your help has been appreciated in the past, Mr Prettyman," I replied, cautiously. "And will gladly be repaid. But I cannot commit to running dutiable goods." Even afterwards I was pleased with my reply which, though a mite prissy, should surely have sewn him into a neat enough corner. But the flamboyant appearance disguised a sharp mind at least the equal of mine.

"Then I would indeed be glad of your help," he said, his face relaxing into that well remembered expression. "There will be no loss to the government as this is an untaxed item, and such is the size that you may carry it without your worthy friends being in the least aware."

I was momentarily aback, but there was more.

"And I can promise you something in return; a single trip for me will earn you far more than can be made in any of Lieutenant Bryson's little spying ventures."

* * *

"Spying ventures?" I had been taken totally off guard, and probably stood open mouthed for a moment before replying.

"Indeed, my dear Nathaniel," Prettyman said, extending one hand in my direction. "Come, don't look so aghast, lad. 'Tis a wicked world: there are few we can count upon and even less that might keep a secret."

"But Lieutenant Bryson..." I began, foolishly. What was I to say? That he was a king's officer? That I had trusted him? All sounded absurd now, as did the plans Susan and I had built upon his word.

"Lieutenant Bryson has nothing to do with the matter," Prettyman told me candidly. "I have never met the cove, but am certain he is as upright and trustworthy as any man should be who wears a Navy uniform."

I regarded him cautiously as he continued.

"But, if the officer has a fault it is undoubtedly in his choosing of subordinates. *Jessica* has been in for repairs a bare two days, yet in that time you are the third small English boat to have called in, ostensibly for supplies and to wait upon the tide. I obtained the story from the first; who were only too keen to tell all, and would doubtless have done the same to the French, had they asked firmly enough. After that, it was but a simple matter to spot the second and watch as the poor fools began swarming over the dockyard with their paper and pens. They were seized by the authorities almost immediately, of course, as you yourself would have been, not so very long ago."

Our eyes met, and I could tell he was remembering that encounter.

"Sadly, I was not able to intervene in their case, and the unfortunates are being held, while their boat is impounded. Whether or not they live to see England again is doubtful, but the

French are no fools, and will definitely be on the lookout for any person following their example."

He drew his face closer to me, and I had to brace myself to avoid reeling back from the familiar fragrance.

"So be very careful, Nathaniel. Take the Navy's guinea on this occasion, do, but in future, sail for me. Why, your friends need never know; you may even say you are still collecting information for the good lieutenant, while we pass the occasional package to each other in such a way that is totally private."

"What would I be carrying?" I found myself asking.

"Gold." He barely whispered the word, while holding me with his hypnotic stare. "It need take up no more than the smallest of packages, yet will bring in a return far higher than any tea, spirit or baccy."

I remembered the Clarkesons mentioning something a while back, but was still unsure of the exact procedure.

"And we would be taking it to England?" I was doubtful.

Prettyman shook his head. "No, the bullion must be collected near Hastings; you then bring it here, to me in France. The French are paying an ever rising premium at present, and there is greater ease, and far less risk, than running contraband from east to west. I shall see to it the authorities know what you are about and do not detain your craft in any way," Prettyman paused, and set me again with his stare. "Although it would be wise if you were not to pay too much attention to their shipping."

I swallowed. "How much would be the load?" It was as if someone else entirely was having the conversation.

"What say we start with a small amount?" he asked, as if deciding which particular card game we might play. "Three hundred guineas; my venturer will supply the goods, all you must do is hand them over. Reimbursement would normally be in booty, but in this case I will pay ten English guineas for your trouble."

As in the past, I was certain the proposal had a flaw, but could not see it. Suitably packaged, three hundred guineas would make a small enough parcel that should be almost impossible to find. Besides, why should anyone wish to rummage an empty lugger travelling to France? We would then sail from their coast under

French protection and, with no dutiable goods aboard, must have nothing to fear from either Revenue or the Royal Navy when returning home. In addition, with my sharp eyes and exceptional brain, I was reasonably certain of being able to satisfy Bryson with at least a good approximation of the state of play in Boulogne harbour. Deceiving Ned and Susan did make me feel a little guilty though, but what they did not know could hardly hurt them. And they would not find out: of that I was certain.

"We shall try one trip," I said, greatly condescending. Prettyman's eyes flashed wide as he beamed.

"That is astoundingly good news, Nathaniel," he said. "I shall make the necessary arrangements, and send word of where the money may be collected."

It was a measure of the confidence I felt that, even when it was decided, there were no last minute feelings of regret or doubt. But then Prettyman had more to say, and I found time for both.

"I shall pay you on receipt: why, one trip will keep your boat safe for two whole months from those Bennett robbers."

My stomach went cold and, yet again, I looked at him in astonishment. But once more his eyes flashed.

"I did tell you, Nathaniel. This is a wicked world, and there are few who will keep a secret."

* * *

We left at the first opportunity and were all of a similar disconcerted state, although Ned and Susan grew more cheerful once we had cleared Boulogne. Feeling the late evening wind on their faces, and knowing we were heading back to England – it had been agreed to leave the intended trip to Calais for another time – seemed to lift their spirits, but I remained both uneasy and probably a little tetchy. There was only the hundredweight of salt in our forepeak, and there would be time to kill before being able to approach Hastings on the sand, so it was decided to try a small amount of fishing.

That did not go so well, though. Susan argued with her father, and we tangled the lines. By the time all was stowed away again, there was nothing to show for our efforts, and we were actually late running up onto the beach. The three of us walked back to the small house in All Saints Street in glum silence; it had been a long and eventful day

* * *

The note had been left for me at the Phillips' yard and was singularly brief; I was to present myself at a house near Fairlight to meet with Ugly Joe's venturer. This was the man who would supply my gold, and was probably the financial force powering Prettyman's empire. The place was a good way from Hastings, but an easy enough road, and one I had taken before.

Leaving Susan behind was not easy, however. Despite us being together for the past few days, she was oddly keen to stick with me, wherever I was bound. As a consequence I set off late, and not in the best of moods. Probably the fact I was intending to deceive the Coglans did not help, but I reassured myself it would be done for the right reasons. If Ugly Joe was willing to pay ten guineas for one trip, we might own the lugger outright in less than a year, even ignoring the money I still hoped to make helping Bryson, and any return from fishing. At that point it felt things were finally on the up and up and, if by some quirk of fate the Coglans did discover what I was about, I was quietly confident they would understand and even be grateful.

Evening was approaching, and the weather had been changeable all day. We had spent most of the time trawling off The Hards and returned with fifteen boxes of flats; more than enough to pay our way. But now the sky was darkening, I had a good few miles to walk, and then must find a place to hide Ugly Joe's gold.

By the time I had located the house, a dingy little cottage that sat quite alone, it was raining in earnest. I trudged up the brick path while the dark earth to either side was swiftly being turned to mud by giant rods of water. The front door lay slightly ajar, but I had been taught always to knock, and did so, despite the torrent of rain that fell about my head and shoulders.

A particularly well set man appeared, and I gave him my

name. He was mildly startled at first, then regarded me suspiciously through his bovine eyes before, almost reluctantly, allowing me in. There was no hall: the door opened straight into the front room.

"It's the lad you was expecting, from Hastings." My guide addressed someone seated in front of a moderate fire with his back to me. "But he says his name is Audley," he added with a smirk.

The figure rose slightly as if in surprise, and light fell upon his face. For a moment we stood and simply looked at each other, with no sign of welcome or greeting on either side. My mind reeled: it was as if everything I had ever believed in had turned out to be totally false; everything I trusted, a cobweb of lies.

This was the man I felt I knew better than most, and also the one I had discounted as a wastrel, a sluggard and a lounger. Yet now he seemed to be revealed as the financier of a major smuggling operation. I don't think anything could have shocked me more, although any amazement I felt was clearly matched, if not surpassed, by that of my father.

Chapter Twenty-Seven

"I had no idea," I told him, when we were finally seated and facing each other, with the fire between us starting to steam the water from my coat. But quite what I had no idea about was unclear, even to me. He had already dismissed his heavy companion; we were quite alone and free to talk, yet neither of us said anything more for some time. We just continued to stare at one another. Father and son we may have been and, until a few months back, had even lived in the same house, but we both seemed equally fascinated by the other, and there were no words that needed to be exchanged.

"Annie will be pleased to know you are well," he said at last. "She worried when you just disappeared – no note, or message."

I did not reply; to me, my step-mother's view on matters was totally irrelevant, although the fact he expressed no pleasure at finding me alive certainly registered.

"So, now you're with the free traders?" These were also his words, but they might as easily have been spoken by me.

"Only in part," my voice cracked slightly as I hurried to assure him, adding, "I also have my own boat – a lugger, and a thriving fishing enterprise," in a stronger tone.

"Then you have done well for yourself," he said, with a complete absence of approval. "So what brings you here? Why are you risking your life to carry my gold?"

I suppose the second question put everything into perspective. However I might dress my status, I was definitely intending to break the law and, if caught red handed, would face the gallows. And carrying his gold – yes: if my father was indeed the venturer, that was exactly what I would be doing. Naturally I tried to justify my actions as much as possible; after all, I had come to this remote cottage with no intention of working for him – it was something I was determined never to do.

"Mr Prettyman will pay me well," I said simply, and thought he would accept this as a simple commercial statement. But instead he began to laugh.

"Ugly Joe has no money other than that which I choose to allow him," I was told, when he had recovered sufficiently. "The man is nothing but a dandy and a coxcomb as well as being something of a pederast. It is me who owns and runs the Clipping Crew, and has been so since you were nothing but a child."

There was a pause: I had nothing to say.

"And you are little more now," he continued, as if in reflection. "While, if you take this gold across to France, Nathaniel, you shall be working for me, just as he is."

It was the best reason yet for getting up and walking out of the room, and I was sorely tempted to do so. But something made me stop, something far too strong to ignore.

However disagreeable it was to discover my father at the centre of everything, the deal remained a good one. More to the point, without it, I would find continuing to work for Bryson almost impossible. Prettyman was bound to make it hard for me to enter Boulogne again and, for all I knew, might see me clear of Calais as well. We would be back to trying to scrape a living on fishing alone, and remain at the mercy of the Bennetts.

"So, I have the money here," he indicated a small canvas packet next to his chair. "We usually require some form of security on a first journey, but I think may dispense with such formalities, considering the circumstances. Do not deceive yourself, however: should you let me down or turn whiddler, I will have no hesitation in reacting in the harshest of manners."

I'm not sure if I gave any answer to that; my mind was still so caught up in the ramifications of what had just taken place, and was about to happen.

"Do you intend to take it?" he asked, eventually. My eyes went from him, the father I had always detested, to the gold that could unlock a future, not only for me, but Susan, and the rest of her family. Really I had no choice.

Alex's story

They had reckoned on *Stag* taking a week to repair and all was done in that time, almost to the hour. My spell with the landguard had also been limited to seven days but I learned a good deal more than expected and, on the last one, old man Musgrave let me go early. I reckoned there was time enough to head into Hastings and still be back to join the cruiser for the next morning.

It was my first visit since joining the Revenue, although Tilly wrote regularly and I had learned of her moving in with the Coglans. Had it not been for the rain, I would have made the entire trip in daylight, but the path was muddy and it was almost dark when I trudged down All Saints Street. I was cold, tired and very wet; only the knowledge that I would shortly be seeing Tilly again, and had nine shillings and sixpence in my pocket for her, kept me going.

I felt no desire to return home, but made straight for the Coglans. It was ironic, and not a little sad, that I should gauge the welcome to be warmer at Ned's house than my own.

Tilly was there, twice as lovely and even more bonnie than usual, and the two Coglan girls were kind enough to leave us alone in the back parlour for the evening. Of Ned there was no sign so, when the front door opened later, and a half drowned man washed in, I assumed it to be him.

But no, it was Nat. I was well aware he was also living with the Coglans, but somehow the thought we might run into each other had not entered my head. So much had happened in the short time since we parted and, knowing he now associated with the free traders while I was a confirmed Revenue man, made the distance between us simply too great.

He gave a rather sticky smile, but did not shake my hand, and something in his manner made me suspicious. In the past week, Musgrave and I had spoken with a good few folk, many of whom were confirmed smugglers. Under the old boy's guidance, I learned the minor clues a man might give when spinning a yarn, or not giving the exact truth and, even in the course of our brief conversation, Nat revealed himself continually. I also suspected he had suffered some form of shock, as his words were clumsy and repetitive; not like the cocksure, businesslike cove I had known, and liked, so well.

I already knew about him and the Coglans sailing the lugger, but listened to his version of the story with interest and told him I was glad. As far as Tilly was concerned, their arrangement was entirely above board, and I would have expected nothing less of Ned, or Sniffy Susan if it came to it. But there was definitely something not quite right about Nat.

I tried to analyse my thoughts as he rattled on about what they were to do, and the money he would surely make. But, however bold and credible his words, I knew him too well to be convinced. Nat had always been something of a dreamer, but now there was an odd evasiveness about him I had never known before. That, and a complete failure to look me in the eye, gave doubt, while the indisputable fact he was trying to hide something within the folds of his coat was the final clincher.

Susan appeared shortly afterwards, and was followed by her sister. Then Ned turned up; apparently he had been in his upstairs room all along, and the six of us sat rather awkwardly about the kitchen table.

I remember Nat asking how I liked working for the Revenue, and him being especially keen to hear my answer. Wearing my cutter's crew clothes, I actually felt quite smart in such surroundings and gave an accurate report of what indeed was becoming my chosen profession. Nat still clung to his coat throughout. It must have been thoroughly sodden, but he refused to give it up, even when Susan became quite cross. I could tell this wasn't going to be a sociable evening and, as I had already spent some time with Tilly, soon stood up to leave.

But it was Nat who saw me to the door, and afterwards stepped outside and walked a little of the way down All Saints Street with me, despite the rain that continued to fall. He was still awkward, but it was somehow easier, just the two of us. For all that had happened, and however much our paths had divided, we were once good friends and, I think, still trusted each other in a strange way.

"So, you're enjoying being cutter's crew?" he asked, and I could tell there was something on his mind.

"I like it fine," I replied; it was almost the same question as before and my answer differed little.

"That is good to hear," he said, without feeling. "Though if you ever decide not, I have a plan that might suit." In the darkness I could see his eyes shine out white as he watched me, hoping, I could tell, for a favourable response.

But I was safe in my first regular paid employment and, with a baby on the slipway, there was no room for any of Nat's wild schemes: I stopped him before more could be said. It was common knowledge that the majority of business enterprises on the south coast were in some way compromised, and my former friend's behaviour that evening was hardly reassuring. I remember his face falling at my refusal and realised, with something of a shock, how much he still depended upon me.

And I suppose I did him, to some extent, at least. Despite my Revenue connections, I was finding life in Rye far better than Hastings: in a place without roots, there were few to betray me, and I enjoyed a certain amount of security from living in the cutter and mixing mostly with my fellow mariners. But Nat had been as good a friend as I had ever known; we learned a lot together and there would always be something between us that no change of status or role could destroy.

I thanked him, and we finally shook hands, if only briefly, before turning away to walk back to our own respective homes and lives. Nothing had been said, but to me it was obvious he was still involved, either in smuggling itself, or something equally nefarious. That being the case, we were very definitely on different sides and probably always would be. If ever we met again, it must surely end up for the worst for one and I think, at that moment, both of us hoped we never would.

Chapter Twenty-Eight

But they'd done a cracking job on the old *Stag*. I arrived in the early hours of the morning, slung my hammock and dropped into a deep, dreamless sleep. At first light I woke instantly, though, and joined the other mariners on deck to properly inspect what, to many of us, was our home.

She shone like a new pin, with little evidence of any previous damage, and a good thick, if slightly tender, coat of marine paint which gleamed in the crisp morning sun. Fresh line had been reeved for the gun tackles, and some of the standing rigging, while the metalwork, and what small amount of brass we possessed, was burnished to perfection. The boatswain, carpenter and gunner, along with most of their mates, had stayed with the boat throughout, and now indicated small points of specific interest with assumed modesty, while those of us who had left the work to them, nodded our heads and made appreciative noises to hide our secret guilt. The undeniable feeling of excitement and expectation lasted as Travis and Lumsden came on deck to announce a short patrol. Our bowsprit was run out once more, canvas raised, and the immaculate *Stag* was carefully guided back to sea.

At no point did any of us think that the work would have little long term benefit. The very reverse, in fact; *Stag* had simply been through a minor refit and, now she was sound again, was setting off for what would be no more than a cruise. Three, maybe four, nights at sea; in that time several boats and perhaps a few ships would be rummaged. We might snag a spot of booty, and maybe earn some seizer money – I was especially interested in the last point – or there could be a run ashore, possibly to interrupt a landing. And all with a reasonable chance of actually firing at least one of our newly serviced guns. But, as we scraped out across the dangerous ground off the outer harbour, and set our prow for the Channel, none of us guessed we should find ourselves fighting a desperate action before the day was out. Or that Rye Harbour itself would never look upon such a magnificent sight as our freshly polished *Stag* again.

Nat's story

The package of gold was small, and weighed about five pounds. I spent the night with it under my pillow in my old place before the fire, the promised front room having long been given over to Tilly, and went off to the boat at first light to find a place to hide the thing. There were still the eight cases of Prettyman's salt in the forepeak from our last trip to France. I eased the top from one and emptied a good deal of its contents out onto the beach. Then slipped the dense bundle inside, and covered it with the rough grains. The supply was unlikely to be broached until the start of the herring season, which was a good few months away yet, and I would be unlucky for it to be discovered during a rummage. But still the fact of the gold's concealment worried me and, as I stomped back to All Saints Street and ate a meagre breakfast, stayed heavy on my mind.

The weather had cleared, and it was already decided we would sail for Boulogne again that very day – this time with a definite intention of continuing on to Calais, as Bryson had been particularly concerned about developments there. But there was none of the excitement from Susan and Ned that was obvious when we last set off for France. Neither enjoyed the previous trip and, even though both knew that to go must keep the Bennetts from our door for at least another two weeks, either would have done anything to stay behind.

Susan and I were barely speaking, and I suspected my somewhat distant behaviour of the previous night and over breakfast was partly to blame. I did consider telling her of the gold; thinking perhaps the knowledge that a further ten English guineas, or two whole Bennett-free months, would actually be earned in the next couple of days might reassure her, but was still worried she would not see the wisdom of my actions.

And so we set off in sullen silence and even the bright

morning sun, such a welcome contrast to the atrocious weather of the previous night, could not lift the mood. The recent storm had played havoc with the wind, which was sitting obstinately in the north-east. It meant we could not take full advantage of the prevailing current, but neither of us chose to comment or even, apparently, notice.

As soon as the boat was launched and underway, Susan took the helm, as had become the usual way of things. Her eye was sharp and she had a sensitive hand, while having her effectively in command left Ned and me free to tend the rig. But, on that particular morning, she was the only one to have anything to do and, under a strong and steady wind, *Katharine II* was soon eating up the distance between us and the French coast.

I have to admit to still being a little upset about Alex not joining us. Meeting up with him had been a mixed experience in many ways. So much about the cove came back to me, and I was reminded just how I missed having him as a friend. But his stoical, I would say obsessive, preoccupation with the Revenue was not so welcome. The Alex I had known would not only have been good company and support aboard *Katharine II,* but was bound to understand my arrangement with Ugly Joe. With him alongside for support, I could have told the Coglans exactly what was going on, and felt confident they would see sense and accept it as the right and proper thing for us to do. Even after what was a relatively short space of time, keeping such a secret from Susan and Ned was starting to tell on me, and might even have been a cause of our current silence.

But by mid-morning, when the sun had grown to being undeniably hot, and our home coast was fading into the distance, things did begin to ease. I turned back and found myself smiling at Susan as we both, simultaneously, threw off the heavy fisherman's smocks, and allowed our bare arms out in the fresh air and tender rays.

"We should make Boulogne by mid-afternoon," I told her. Ned was also in shirt-sleeves and dozing quietly forward, so we could talk in relative privacy.

"And shall we stay long?"

"No more than is necessary," I reassured her. "I need only to check on the transports, and deliver a small package to Prettyman." I had been tricked by the warmth of both the sun, and her proximity: the words escaped before being considered, and Susan was instantly suspicious.

"A package?" she asked. "But you promised we would never deal with the fellow."

"And we are not," I said, with as much sincerity as I could conjure. "Sure, it is just a favour; something he requested from England that I was asked to carry for him. We are already in his debt, and this may even remedy the situation."

"What is it?"

"I would not know, and did not ask," I lied. "But it is so small as to be purely of personal value."

She nodded and did not pursue the matter. I suppose there was actually little to draw her attention as it could surely not be smuggling. The best known commodity to travel from England to France was wool, and I could hardly have contained more than a skein in the parcel that held my father's bullion. Only a few would realise the difference in value gold commanded in the two countries and Susan, for all her natural cunning, was not particularly informed on world affairs.

But for all my apparent confidence, the worries returned, and we spoke no more. Partly I wondered how to explain why a perfectly legitimate package should be hidden in one of our salt canisters, and partly felt ashamed that I had so readily lied to her.

After a while I was able to justify my actions, to myself at least. A lugger, halfway across the Channel, is no place to ponder on ethics, but I remained convinced my actions were for our common good. Once a few more trips like this were completed, we would be safe for the rest of our lives. And there would always be time to tell her the whole truth later.

Stag met all our expectations and more. She sliced through the dark waters with even greater panache, and could tack and jibe on the proverbial sixpence. Even when Commander Travis grew tired of throwing the cruiser through her paces, and simply piled on speed, the north-easterly filled our oversized rig, and brought a general feeling of contentment. We were at sea again; our natural element. And were sailing in what we considered the fastest, and most weatherly craft afloat, so was it any wonder none of us could keep from grinning?

We held a southerly course for some while, with the wind comfortably on our quarter and England growing ever more distant over the taffrail, before being ordered round and running for the south-west. All aboard were accustomed to our captain's little ways, and knew this may easily be nothing more than a pleasure cruise. Alternatively, he could be working on information acquired, and at that moment we might be heading to intercept a homeward bound runner, or even a foreign supply vessel. But I don't think any of us cared; it was just so good to be free again. Whatever our destination turned out to be, it would suit us fine.

Nat's story

We saw the Revenue cutter at mid-day and guessed it to be Alex's. The usual cruiser in those waters was *Hound*, the Shoreham based boat, but she was slightly smaller and carried fewer guns. With the wind on her tail, the craft made a wonderful sight and, as she headed to cross our bows, I was even hopeful we might get a closer view, despite my little pot of deceit secreted in the forepeak. The sullen silence of earlier was almost forgotten, but still we watched without speaking, although now this was more the result of having nothing to say. There was little other shipping to distract our attention and, ignoring any connections we might have with the cutter, just the sight of a craft so eminently suited to the task in hand was enough to raise the spirits of anyone associated with the sea.

Slowly the two vessels drew closer, with the cutter still half a mile or so off when she swooped gracefully across our prow. I told myself there was nothing to fear, the Revenue men were clearly intent on other prey, or nothing at all, and it seemed likely this would be as near as they would come. Then, with a turn that was both sudden and elegant, the cruiser swept to larboard, and began to head away from us, but on a similar course, and one that would also take her to the French coast.

"Must've caught the scent of something," Ned informed us laconically. "That or the gobblers fancy a taste of French brandy. However smart they might dress, them's all a bunch of dudders."

"Except Alex," Susan said stoically from aft, and Ned had the grace to incline his head in recognition.

"Aye, he may be the exception," he agreed.

Alex's story

We sighted Ugly Joe's brig just after noon. She had the wind on her beam and was undoubtedly heading for England. Even ignoring the damage she had previously caused us, the vessel was a known runner and worthy of investigation but, when Commander Travis ordered us round, and on a course to intercept her, we all knew there was more to this than simple Revenue business.

"Master gunner, how are you loaded?" he bellowed from aft and Pickering knuckled his forehead.

"All great guns charged and loaded with round shot, sir," he reported.

"Very good, clear them away and see to the swivels as well. Break out small arms and bring up the surgeon's chest; I think we may be about to teach Mr Prettyman a lesson."

246

In a craft such as *Stag*, this was as close to clearing for action as it came. The swivel guns were rarely used and never kept loaded. One of my many duties was to serve a pair on opposites sides, just aft of the larger guns I assisted Honeysett with. In theory, these were for me to fire as well as serving the carriage pieces, but it was unlikely a warship like Ugly Joe's would allow us close enough for their meagre range. Still I went to work with a will, and had both guns charged, primed and ready for use, before turning my attention to Honeysett and his cannon.

About me, others were readying the boat for action; some sprinkled damped sand on the decks, or broke out the half barrels that would contain seawater for dampening sponges and fighting fires. *Stag* had become a mass of activity, with each man entirely dedicated to his own tasks, and all the time we swept steadily nearer to the small, but potent, brig that had dealt us so much damage in the past.

Nat's story

The Revenue cutter had been drawing away at speed for some while when she suddenly turned to starboard once more. Soon she was heading back with the wind on her beam, spray steaming from her bows, and steering a course that was bringing her closer to us by the second.

"Gobblers have had a change of heart," Ned said evenly, as we watched the cruiser apparently bear down on our lugger. It had been an extreme move, and one that seemed unlikely to be merely a diligent commander exercising his crew. The customs pennant was blowing out stiff and straight from her masthead; she was sailing with intention, but I remained confident we were not the prey. Then, as we watched, the cutter began to take in sail, and her speed decreased.

"Perhaps there is a vessel beyond," I said slowly.

"P'rhaps there is," Ned agreed. "If so, we'll soon be knowing about it," he added and we both looked up at our own sails. They were board stiff and drawing well; we must have been making a good six knots and be closing on the cutter at considerably more than double that.

"Do you think we should let her fall off to starboard?" I asked at last, but Ned shook his head.

"They ain't going to run down a tub like this," he said with certainty. "Should a cruiser want us to stop, we'll do so right enough, but they got bigger fish to fry, and we won't be thanked for chasing our tails."

That made sense to me; even a lithe and handy Revenue cutter needs space to manoeuvre, and a twopenny lugger steering an erratic course would only complicate matters.

"What can you see?" Susan's voice came from aft, and I walked back to join her.

"Cutter's coming back on a broad reach," I said. It was an unnecessary statement; Alex's boat was firmly in sight and growing larger all the time.

"Are they after us?" she asked; it was a strange question from one who should have nothing to fear, and I noted the look of doubt in her eye.

"We think not," I replied, with slightly more confidence than I felt. "Your father reckons they have another target in mind."

Susan nodded, but said nothing and I was feeling more and more disconcerted. Could it be she already knew about the gold? That I was more involved with Prettyman than I had said? Perhaps she suspected I was carrying out some other knavish scheme that was being kept from her? Or was it simply that she no longer trusted me?

Alex's story

Prettyman's brig had not changed course, and was still heading stoically for England. We had almost twice her speed at our command, and I think all aboard *Stag* were expecting Travis to sweep down upon her prow, in a similar manner to before. It was a logical, if hackneyed move, but one that served us badly last time, so I think we were all relieved when our commander showed himself to have another shot in his locker. It was only when this was revealed that the doubts returned.

"Take in the tops'l and prepare to spill!" The order was clear enough, but it took a second or so for his intention to sink in. We already knew *Jessica*, Prettyman's brig, was heavier, and better armed than us: the only advantage *Stag* held over such a vessel lay in her speed, and we were about to sacrifice that, seemingly on a whim.

But orders are to be obeyed, and our way fell off significantly as the canvas was taken in. By now the brig was almost exactly on our stern, and starting to forereach visibly. There was a fishing lugger off our larboard bow but, apart from that, no other likely vessel in sight, so Travis could not have been attempting to lure Ugly Joe to certain capture by a Navy ship.

"Ready larboard battery; carriage guns only, lads: this will be long range work."

Then his intentions became clear, and we ran to our appropriate posts eager to deal out a measure of what we had previously received.

I joined Honeysett, and together we ran the gun out. The only thing in our line of fire was the open sea but, by now, all knew what the commander was about, and waited in silence for the expected order.

"Starboard the helm, lay her over!" Travis roared, and *Stag* lurched violently to larboard. The deck heaved, righted, then began to dip and roll in the swell, but Honeysett was already peering down the iron barrel, his linstock ready to hand.

"Make sure of your target, then fire as you will: this ain't the Royal Navy!"

The commander's words drew a murmur of laughter as the seven gun captains concentrated on their work. *Jessica* was a good five hundred yards off – long range for small calibre guns such as ours, but with seven shots, one at least might make contact.

The enemy opened fire with their bow chasers, just as our first gun spoke, although no one was quite sure where either shot fell.

Our broadside rattled out over the space of several seconds, with Honeysett's piece being the last to fire. But the range was too long to be certain of a hit, and there was no visible damage to Ugly Joe's craft.

"Secure your pieces!" The commander's voice rolled out without a hint of disappointment. "We'll collect a little way, then try again with the starboard battery."

Honeysett and I were now under pressure. Two men was far too small a crew to handle even a gun as light as ours, but when *Stag* had come back to the wind, and was keeping pace with Prettyman's brig once more, Freeman, one of the trimmers, came to assist.

It was all happening far too quickly. No sooner had the larboard piece been loaded, primed and secured than we were crossing the deck to ready the starboard. Freeman left us once more to attend the sails, then *Stag* was falling off, and we were viewing the oncoming privateer over the starboard bulwark.

This time the range was slightly shorter, and we were in time to catch the first of two shots from the brig's bow mounted guns. It drew a splash well to one side which cheered us all, but the second landed squarely on the galley, that was upturned amidships, and the small boat was smashed into her component parts.

For several seconds splinters of wood and iron seemed to be flying everywhere: a few of us were cut, and one quite badly. Our broadside was also delayed so, in the time it took for us to return to the guns, the brig had drawn closer still.

This time our gun was the first to fire, and I was reasonably certain scored a direct hit on the enemy's prow. Others were just as successful and, when the brig's jib finally fell in a confusion of canvas and line, it drew a rousing cheer from most of the crew.

It was the first worthwhile thing we had done; our blood was up and, at that moment, I think we would have tackled Prettyman's lot with our bare hands. But, despite his normal bonhomie, Travis was not satisfied, and bellowed for us to stop performing like girls. And so we set to, and the business began once more.

Exactly what the Revenue cutter was about soon became obvious. We could see both her, and the smudge of grey that quickly grew into *Jessica,* well enough – could hear the sound of gunfire, and almost smell burning powder as the two vessels took pot shots at the other. Even with the cutter's reduction in speed, and her frequent yawing to either side, we were steadily creeping up on her: so much so that I was concerned in case any wild shot might endanger us.

"Closest splash is still a cable or so off," Ned said dismissively as I raised the point. "But if they continues as they is, we'll let her fall off to starboard," he added, almost in consolation.

Frankly, I thought him mad. As soon as the first cannon fired I had been trying to contain the need to piss and, for us to carry on towards what was becoming a pitched battle, could only be senseless in the extreme. The sight of that earlier Revenue cutter being so neatly disposed of remained fresh in my mind, and I had no wish to be on hand should it happen again; especially as my own boat, and life, were concerned. I glanced at Ned, but he was wearing the same set expression I had seen too often in the past. He knew the story of the last cutter almost as well as I did and had even met with Prettyman so, to some extent, understood the kind of man he was.

"In an action like this, there's likely to be men in the water, and no one with the time to save them," he said, as if such a feeble excuse could explain his determination.

"But we are in danger," I reminded him. "And Susan is aboard." Probably it was a low shot but the old man took it without flinching.

"I am aware, and have already made my feelings known," he said, firmly. "Susan is an intelligent woman, and will say if she wishes us gone." Then he did turn and meet my eye. "If that be so, she will speak her mind and not blame her thoughts on anyone else. I would recommend you do likewise."

It was a long speech for Ned and the point was lost on me

until later. But I knew then there would be no shaking him.

I wandered back to where Susan stood, equally solidly, at the helm. She was still wearing the tattered canvas shirt and, with her auburn hair broken free and trailing in the wind, looked far more attractive than she had a right to.

"Your dad thinks we should draw nearer," I told her airily. "Not that I mind, but things might get a little rough later and I wished to be sure you were happy with that."

Her eye switched from our mainsail to me, and then immediately back again.

"I think we should close also," she snapped.

I gave what was probably a wet smile. "It might be dangerous," I suggested.

"It probably will be, but Alex is aboard that cutter: Tilly would never forgive me if anything happened, and we did nothing to save him." Her eyes caught mine again. "Besides, he would do the same for you."

There was little I could say to that: I felt shamed, and truly did not have an answer.

"And he is my brother" she added, more softly.

Chapter Twenty-Nine

Alex's story

We had fired two broadsides from each battery and were deafened, brittle and exhausted, but the enemy brig was appreciably closer, and things were starting to become serious. *Stag* had been hit twice by Prettyman's chase guns; apart from the rowing boat, number six larboard gun was now lying carriage-less on the deck, with Barrows and Crosby badly wounded. Both were below, and in the hands of the carpenter, who was as close as we came to a surgeon. All aboard knew it was just a matter of time before Ugly Joe turned his craft's full broadside to meet us and, as soon as he did, our commander would have to pile on the canvas and make a run for it. But, however fast *Stag* responded, we would be bound to face at least one solid broadside on our vulnerable stern, and that was not a pleasant prospect.

For now though, we were once more beam on to the advancing privateer, and Honeysett was as diligent as ever as he squinted along the warm gun barrel. I watched as he carefully pressed the wooden quoin deeper, raising the cascabel slightly to lower the aim then, standing neatly to one side, plunged his linstock down on the touch-hole.

The gun erupted with its customary crack, and probably left the deck when it recoiled, although our attention was set solely on the flight of the ball. Other shots from *Stag* were striking as well, but the tension of battle, mingled with what experience I had gathered over the last half hour, allowed the path to be followed reasonably easily. Therefore, when *Jessica's* foremast was struck, soundly and with force, I knew for sure our gun was to blame.

Prettyman's craft had been in the act of turning, and the hull continued to move slightly even as timber, line and canvas cascaded down about her forecastle. We could see she was in total confusion, while around me our men were cheering with primaeval gusto.

"That were down to you," I told Honeysett, breathlessly. "It were one hell of a lucky shot."

Honeysett gave me a toothless grin. "Aye, it were," he agreed. "An' you know it seems the longer I go on firing cannon, the luckier I gets."

Nat's story

By then, we were almost upon the cruiser and Ned had relented enough to direct Susan to let the lugger fall off a little. Still, we had a grand view of the action, and saw the broadside strike, and *Jessica*'s mast fall. A shot from the brig had hit the Revenue cruiser seconds before, and splinters of wood landed perilously close to us but, apart from taking in the main, and spilling wind from our head and jigger, neither of the Coglans looked like retreating further.

And neither did I want them to; for some inexplicable reason I had apparently lost all fear, and was only intent on the drama playing out before me. The full effect was only temporary, although I did not return to being quite so hen-hearted later. Neither did I feel the need to continually boost my standing with grandiose schemes and wild commercial ventures, although that might be pure coincidence.

But for whatever reason, I found myself able to analyse the battle, rather than be frightened by it. And, with my newly acquired perspective, was quick to realise the brig would still be a difficult capture. She may have been damaged but even a badly aimed broadside from those devastating twelve pounders could finish Alex's cutter in seconds. And Ugly Joe was bound to have her well crewed. I had no idea how many *Stag* carried, but her opposition would certainly fight. Having already fired upon a king's vessel, they were doomed to meet the gallows if captured, so victory offered their only true chance of life.

The cutter was underway again, and we watched as she eased herself across the wind, finishing in irons, but with her starboard broadside facing the brig's prow. Again the clatter of *Stag*'s guns rolled out, and again the shots did visible damage to the privateer: *Jessica*'s best bower was shot clean away, and her jib boom sagged when the dolphin striker was demolished. But the brig's crew were making headway on the earlier wreckage and, despite damage to the bowsprit, a tattered headsail had been rigged to the stump of the foremast and was already starting to draw. Soon their vessel was showing signs of life again and, far more sinister than that, had begun to turn.

She went with the breeze and slowly; the damaged prow seeming to need persuasion. Then the wind caught more strongly, until the full broadside of Prettyman's powerful little brig was brought to bear on Alex's cruiser.

Alex's story

I don't think Travis expected the enemy to be able to move again, either that or simply had not planned beyond the last broadside. But, for whatever reason, when the brig's prow begin to creep round there was more than a moment's indecision from our commander. Honeysett and I were mainly occupied with loading our gun but, while I helped him sponge out the barrel and cram in fresh powder and shot, my mind continued to race. Freeman, along with the other trimmers, had been called to attend the sails, even though we remained square in the eye of the wind. And all the while our commanding officer stayed uncommonly silent.

As she turned, the brig's broadside was slowly, but inexorably, being brought round to face us; in no time those twelve pounders, three times the size of our little popguns and far more numerous, would be spitting their vengeance our way. And all we could do about it was stand and wait.

"Starboard battery, prepare to fire!" Finally the voice of our captain rang through, but the order was futile. Hopelessly undermanned, our gun crews were still less than half way through serving their pieces, and could not have responded if they wished.

Then, with a series of flashes that stood out, even in the bright sunshine, Prettyman's brig released her first proper broadside.

The two vessels were less than eighty feet apart, and the hot iron had already begun to strike as we registered their thunder. The drift rail next to me dissolved into a thousand pieces, and Honeysett rolled to one side, clearly injured. Beneath my feet, I felt the deck vibrate as hits were taken in various places and it seemed as if the very hull itself might burst apart.

Men were wounded; some lay screaming, others suspiciously quiet, and there was the smell of what could only be burning. A series of shouts made me look up, and I saw with horror that a ball had struck our gaff, and the mainsail was collapsing in a heap of canvas and line. We were facing almost dead into the wind and the jib flapped wildly. There would be little fancy sailing from the old girl now. Even ignoring the damage below, our wings had been very neatly clipped.

All was not without hope however and, as the dust and confusion cleared, command began to be restored. Lumsden's whistle cut through our deadened ears, calling us to attention. Orders were shouted by various heads of department and any not specifically instructed, took to sorting whatever damage was nearest to him. I kicked the remains of the splintered drift rail over the side, then looked about for further employment. Honeysett had heaved himself up on all-fours and was clearly stunned. I reached out to him, but he brushed me away, so instead I turned my attention to the gun we had been tending.

Despite the partially wrecked bulwark, the beast was still secured by ring bolts set deep into the cutter's frame. It was also filled with shot and powder; only priming was required; that and to run her up into the firing position. As more capable men were cutting away wreckage, and bundling up the remnants of our mainsail, I concentrated on what I knew best, and checked the gun tackle. Beside me, Honeysett rose shakily to his feet and began examining a mighty bruise that was already spreading down most of his right arm.

"We must reply," I all but screamed; to me it was the most logical thing in the world, and almost as important as attending to our damage.

There was no knowing how practised Prettyman's men were; the Royal Navy claimed to fire consecutive broadsides barely minutes apart, whereas five was the best we had been able to achieve in *Stag*. It was likely to be as long before *Jessica's* battery was reloaded, which gave us that much time to prepare, and even one shot from us in the meantime must slow them down.

Honeysett was undoubtedly dazed, but registered what I was about, and began feeling for the priming horn that still hung from his waistband. After tapping powder into the touch hole, he looked for his linstock. It had fallen to the deck, but was missing the slow match. I glanced down and saw the length of smouldering line lying nearby. Honeysett took it from me as if in a dream, then between us we ran the gun up on its tackle.

Once the cannon was secured, I waited as he sighted down the barrel. It was quickly done, for the two hulls were now closer than ever. Then, without a word, he plunged the glowing end down, and the gun spoke yet again.

There was no way of telling how badly damaged our hull might be; for all we knew, water was flowing in below and we would soon be swamped. And if *Stag* failed to move in the next five minutes she would be sunk for certain. But we had returned fire, and that single note of defiance seemed well worth the effort.

Nat's story

I saw the Revenue cutter fire back and wondered slightly at her temerity. There was work going on aloft as well; the wrecked main was being tended to: men on her forecastle were desperately spreading out her jib, while the helm was across, although it still felt hopeless. But Ned had other ideas.

"Cruiser's in irons," he grumbled, from his position near the prow. "The runners will knock her to pieces unless she gets back on a wind."

There was no arguing with his logic: broadside to broadside, the cutter was at a definite disadvantage. Even ignoring her frail timbers, *Stag*'s cannon were nothing compared to *Jessica*'s larger, and more numerous, twelve pounders.

"Dad, we have to do something!" Susan's plaintive plea came from aft, but must be in vain. She should have known, as well as any of us, that nothing could be done: the situation was hopeless.

Then Ned asked, "Do you wish that?" and I was astonished.

"We must," Susan replied. "I won't have Tilly bringing up the child alone. I'm taking us to larboard of the cutter!"

Her words took me by surprise, although Ned apparently accepted them as inevitable and went to hoist the mainsail once more. As soon as he had, Susan put the helm across and the two of us tended the sheets.

Actually Susan's move was quite astute: positioned so, our lugger could not have come up between the two vessels. Even attempting such a move would place us as much in the eye of the wind as the cruiser, to say nothing of exposing *Katharine II* to Prettyman's broadside. We could, however, claw back to larboard, passing the Revenue cutter on our starboard beam, then work up towards her, as near to the wind as we would lie.

I guessed the intention then would be to bring the cutter over to starboard, and felt such a plan might work. Alex's boat should be back on the wind in no time, and might even close with Prettyman's brig before the expected broadside. But the danger to us would be far more subtle. To tow the cruiser's head round would mean our lugger sailing almost straight for *Jessica* and, when Prettyman saw what we were about, I doubted he would take it calmly.

Ned and I remained fully occupied trimming the two huge lug sails but, in no time we had captured the breeze, and were underway on the fresh tack. As we passed the cutter's stern, the old man looked up to them.

"We're passing you a line for'ard," he roared. "Secure it and we'll haul you back to the wind."

There was a wave of acknowledgement from a uniformed figure as we drew away from the cruiser's broad hull, still on the starboard tack. Then, once we were a good distance off, Susan pulled the helm back.

The time spent tacking seemed to go on forever. *Katharine II* actually manoeuvred well for her type, and came out of irons quickly enough, while we were relatively safe, with the cruiser between us and Prettyman's brig. But every second wasted was bringing the next broadside closer and it was only as our bows finally came round and the lugger caught the wind once more, that I felt able to breathe again.

Then, with both sails iron hard, we began to bear down on the cruiser's long bowsprit and *Katharine II* actually appeared to be travelling too fast. Ned had rushed aft and was standing next to his daughter, a coil of weighted two inch sisal in his hand. It was light stuff for such work, but there was no time to roust out anything heavier; besides, all we needed to do was move the cutter's head a matter of feet; once she was back on the wind, she could look after herself.

Susan was steering a perfect course, one that would bring us as close to the cutter's prow as the bowsprit allowed, but there would only be time for a single cast of Ned's line. Once past, we would have to completely box the compass in order to set ourselves in a similar position, and by then *Jessica's* broadside was bound to have been fired.

I was no judge, but Ned seemed to leave it too late although, when he did finally hurl the line, such was the energy that our boat rocked for several seconds afterwards. The three of us watched as the sisal snaked neatly over the cruiser's tiny forecastle. There was a brief confusion of bodies aboard the Revenue cutter, then someone on board waved an arm, and the tow was secured.

"Take her further to starboard," Ned cried, and Susan eased the helm back. We were clear of the bowsprit now, but *Jessica* was in plain sight. Slowly, the tow line came under tension, and eventually rose, dripping and taut, from the waves. Prettyman's Clipping Crew would know for certain now what we intended and, being as our boat was well within range, revenge could be expected at any moment.

I stepped back and joined Ned and Susan at the stern; this was in no way to avoid being hit by the brig's fire, but more in a final spirit of unity. Susan kept hold of the tiller while kneeling as low as she could, and Ned and I wrapped our bodies about her. The sun felt hot on our shoulders, and it was surely far too pleasant a day on which to die. There was a series of slight plops, as if someone was lobbing pebbles into the sea a few feet off, but none came nearer to us, and neither did the brig's cannon fire. I glanced behind; the Revenue cutter was definitely being moved into the wind. Then, even as I watched, her jib began to fill.

"Keep her as she is," Ned ordered, as he broke away and released the tow. It ran out and was soon lost, but our boat picked up speed immediately. Soon, we were almost flying, although the course was inevitably bringing us nearer to the brig.

Now there were more of the same strange splashes, and I realised them to be small arms fire. Several bullets struck the hull but none came close to us; either *Katharine II* was moving too fast for Prettyman's snipers, or their attention was being distracted by the cutter that was coming steadily back to life. I looked back; she was both drawing ahead and starting to turn: soon she would be bearing down upon the brig.

The angle was fast becoming such that, even if Prettyman had fired, some of his heavy cannon would not have been able to train on Alex's boat. *Jessica* was being turned in an effort to compensate, and the three of us watched in horrified silence as the two hulls began to revolve slowly about the other, as if embroiled in some drawn-out and gigantic waltz.

The cutter had the sleeker hull, either that or her lack of weight gave more speed but, for whatever reason, she was slightly the faster of the two; while some trick of either wind or waves was also drawing her steadily closer to the privateer.

I reckoned later it must have been a good ten minutes since the brig's last broadside: had Prettyman's men been up to snuff, they should have been ready with the next long since. But only one shot came before the two hulls collided, and the dance ended with them grinding together, as if in one final and loving embrace.

Chapter Thirty

Alex's story

At that point I had only a scant idea of the fishing lugger's intervention and none of who was aboard but, when our prow began to be hauled round and into the wind, I certainly breathed a sigh of relief. Then, as the plucky little boat came into view, I saw Nat and the Coglans sheltering in her stern, and everything was explained. The tow could not have been in place for more than a minute, but rescued us from the dead spot that held *Stag* in irons. Soon she took up speed and drew closer until Prettyman's brig lay only yards off. But *Jessica* had turned also, and was drawing abeam: were the broadside to come now, we would be sunk for certain.

A single gun aboard her did fire, but only one, and it was not properly trained: even at such an incredibly short distance, the shot went wide. Still we all knew that, if Prettyman's men had been able to serve one cannon, chances were strong that others might also be ready, and we must board without delay.

As we stood in a line by the remains of our starboard bulwark, I remember holding my freshly issued boarding cutlass and thinking how weighty the thing felt. I was probably tired from my exertions with the cannon, and this was the first time I had carried such a weapon, but it felt too heavy and agricultural for combat use. There was a crowd of men on the brig's deck, and some might have been serving the guns, but most were standing as we were, and appeared keen for a more conventional fight.

From down the line, one of our lads roared out an obscenity, and soon each side was cursing and swearing at the other, as if in some ancient battle rite. From the bow came the crack of one of the swivels, and I hurriedly went to my own, discarding the boarding cutlass in the process. I had used the swivel several times during practice, but it had misfired more often than not. Still, I took rough aim at the approaching brig, and tugged the firing line. The flash took, and my little gun erupted, belching smoke and grit into the wind. It was loaded with canister and there was no way of telling where the shot had fallen. I felt I had done my bit, though, and collected my sword from the deck where it had been lying. Then the two hulls grew suddenly closer and, with a final rush, were swept together.

It was our intention to board and take the brig, but Prettyman's Clipping Crew had the same design on our cutter, so the two forces met and began to slug it out over the battered sides of both vessels. They had a slight advantage, in that the brig's freeboard was a good foot or so higher than ours, but that was more than offset by *Stag*'s men being the better armed. I had never used one before, but soon realised what a good weapon the standard boarding cutlass was: balanced, soundly built, and actually exactly the right weight, it felt like an extension to my arm. I quickly despatched my first victim who seemed almost ready to fall, and offered only a puny little hunting sword up as defence.

Looking back, I should have been terrified. Years of bullying and intimidation had tempered me to any form of physical violence, though. And on previous occasions, I had always been the target: now there was less need for defence, in fact I soon found a spirited attack would clear much before me, and was actually one of the first to board Prettyman's brig.

Travis was close by. I could hear his roar even as I clambered up and over *Jessica*'s top rail, then we laid into a group of somewhat bemused runners together. Almost immediately I felt a stab of pain in my arm, and knew myself wounded, but was strangely confident that nothing was actually going to stop me. The two of us were quickly joined by more from the *Stag* and we slashed and hacked our way deeper into the crowd, with the cheers of those behind urging us on. I was aware of an odd sensation: not exactly pleasure, more a feeling of satisfaction. It was as if I were paying back for all the hurt and pain of the last few years, and I think at one point I may even have been laughing.

Nat's story

Ned, Susan and I watched the battle in grim silence. This time there really was little we could do, and I was still reeling slightly from the extent of what had already been done. Or, to be more precise, what the Coglans had achieved, and in support of Alex. They surely owed him nothing. I could not see why either of them had put themselves out, risking their own lives, and mine, to help. There must be another reason for their action.

Then Susan's words came back to me although, in the terror that was currently unfolding, I doubted if I had heard correctly. For Alex to be her brother, and presumably Ned's son, seemed simply too incredible. But then, neither had I thought my own father capable of involvement with the Clipping Crew. In fact, when taken alongside other recent events, Alex being a Coglan felt like just another for the list.

There was one thing I was still sure of, though; Ned would never have any truck with smuggling, and detested Prettyman and his like. I was in complete agreement on the last point. My freedom from the Navy was down to Ugly Joe and he might have been a route out of poverty and obligation to the Bennetts, but I had more than enough reason equally to despise the man.

Not that I wanted him dead, or anyone else for that matter although, in the intense desire to slaughter that had apparently possessed all before us, the choice was hardly on offer. Men were being wounded and doubtless dying on every quarter, yet all we could do was stand off, watch for any that fell overboard, and wait for the madness to end.

And then I noticed Prettyman himself and, more to the point, he saw me. Our lugger was still a good thirty yards off to windward, and almost level with the cutter's prow when he came into sight on the brig's stern. He stood there, hatless, and looking unusually dishevelled, but there was no mistaking him, or his intention.

"You there, boy!" he bellowed, pointing in our direction. I could have been in no doubt as to whom he was referring, but still looked about, in the hope that someone else was required.

"Nathaniel; draw near to me." Then, switching his attention to Susan: "At the tiller, there! Come alongside!"

I knew the Coglans by then: no command from him would be obeyed, and guessed that even I would have no more influence over them.

"A hundred guineas if you take me off," he bellowed again. "Two hundred, to see me safely back to France!" He looked round at the horror that must have been unfolding behind him, then took on fresh energy. "Or you may keep the three hundred you have already," he added, as if clinching the deal beyond doubt, "Now come alongside, lad: and be quick about it!"

But the boat did not move and soon he disappeared from sight.

Chapter Thirty-One

A Navy frigate rescued us in the end. Like a shark to blood, the warship had been drawn by the sound of gunfire, and brought a measure of sanity, with her smartly dressed officers, modern tackle and rigid command. But by then the action was over, and Prettyman's brig taken. It had been a bloody battle and, of the three vessels the fine king's ship encountered, our lugger was the only one in any way seaworthy. *Katharine II* had also landed her biggest sivver of all: nine men, variously wounded, were crammed within our gunwales while Susan, Ned and I did what we could to tend their injuries and give comfort.

Within minutes of the frigate's arrival, capable seamen were surrounding us by the boatload. Those of the Clipping Crew who might still cause trouble were swiftly secured, while pumps were brought across for the waterlogged Revenue cutter, and a jury mast raised on the brig. Then, as the first signs of evening were starting to make themselves known, our small flotilla set off for England, and safety.

The Coglans and I could have gone some while before; once our wounded had gone to meet the wonders of a modern medical department aboard the frigate, there was no cause for us to stay. But stay we did; after undergoing such an experience we felt a certain connection and, of course, we were concerned about Alex.

We met with him just as *Stag* was being taken under tow for what was to be her final journey back to Rye. Susan brought *Katharine II* close enough under the wrecked cutter's counter for a few snatched words. There was a grey bandage strapped about his left arm, but he made light of it, and said to tell Tilly not to be worried.

"Say also the capture's filled to brimming with booty," he added casually. "Seizure money will be paid, and I shall be back to claim her in no time."

* * *

The following morning, Tilly left for Rye, taking Ned and Jenny with her, and leaving Susan and me unusually alone in the house on All Saints Street. It was a situation I had dreamed about in the past but, after the horrors of the previous day's action, both of us still felt mildly stunned. The otherwise empty building was also forbidding. We were so used to it being a family home, and Jenny's ever ebullient presence still permeated the place to the extent that indulging in any amorous play would have been akin to laying bets on the Sunday reading. And so we sat in silence and sober contemplation, hands touching across the kitchen table, but our thoughts many miles apart.

"I don't know him to be my brother, if that's what you're thinking," she said at last. My mind had actually been on the gold still stored in *Katharine II*'s forepeak, but I did not contradict her. "It is something Jenny and I have discussed over the years," she continued. "Sharing a room is liable to bring on such fantasies: you would barely credit the conversations two sisters can have at night."

I nodded, but said nothing as my mind adjusted to the subject. On the face of it, for Ned to be Alex's father did indeed sound like the product of adolescent girls' imagination. There were simply so many factors against it.

"It was the red hair that first gave us the clue." She was still not looking directly at me, but preferring to stare at the table instead. "Both his brothers have jet black, and straight, as did his father, yet dad was like a carrot top when younger. And their build is so similar, yet different again from Seth and Josh."

"I have known children to have unexpected red hair, and the other way about," I suggested. "My teacher, Mrs Bredshaw, had a child with brown curls when she and her husband were both ginger."

"Everyone says Dad was distraught when mum died," Susan carried on, as if I had never spoken. "She were washed from the boat, and he always blamed himself."

"Did your family know the Combes then?" I asked.

"Everyone knows one another in Hastings," she replied

simply. "But yes, mum and Mary Combes were good friends, and stayed so, even after her husband joined the Revenue. Dad never got on so well with him, but then neither man was known for being sociable. As I say, it was all so very long ago, but I understand the two women were together a lot, and Mary has stayed close since mum died. There's not many who'll mix with the Combes, and not many who get on with dad, so we have a lot in common."

"And Alex's uncle lives in the house now..." I commented.

"Yes," she agreed, a little sadly. "But he's not a real uncle: you were aware?"

I was, but couldn't think what else to call him.

"Saul Robbins is not the first to take that title," Susan continued. "Her husband might not have been especially popular, but Mrs Combes is one of those who makes men friends very easily, and has never wanted for male company."

"It still does not signify," I said defiantly. For some reason I felt protective about the Coglans; their taking me in as part of the family meant a great deal. And, even though Alex was my best friend, I felt vaguely uncomfortable about him becoming a member; almost as if I were afraid he might usurp my position. "If Ned knew himself to be Alex's father, why did he not take him out on the punt?" I asked. To me it seemed obvious; when I had first met him, Alex had been more or less unemployed, whereas Ned was equally struggling without any help.

"That was a major factor in making us think it true," she replied. Her eyes were still set on the table, but she smiled suddenly, and I felt a small shiver run down my back. "When mother died, dad swore never to take another member of our family to sea with him again. A few years later I could easily have helped out, but he wouldn't hear of it, even though it was obvious one man could not handle a punt on his own. Alex was the obvious choice: being young, he wouldn't even have been entitled to a full share, and we have all seen how an extra hand can increase the sivver. But dad was adamant, and refused to even consider having Alex aboard. When you know my father well, it was all rather obvious."

"But he did agree to you crewing," I reminded her. "I admit, he was not keen at first, but allowed it eventually."

"When it was a choice between that, and me selling myself to the Bennetts, you mean?" she asked, almost laughing. "But no, you are right; I think he would have allowed it anyway. And we have you to thank for that as well." Her gaze rose and those wonderful eyes finally looked directly into mine. "Indeed, you have changed this family in more ways than you will ever know."

I don't remember much in detail about the rest of that conversation: my mind was racing elsewhere. In those days I knew precious little about human nature and am hardly an expert now. But, even then, I could fully understand why Ned should have sought comfort from Mrs Combes, following his wife's death. And if he had, and if, for all the trouble it would have caused, he chose not to recognise the son that was subsequently born, was it really anyone else's concern? But it was her last remark that had really started me thinking.

It appeared that, for all the impression of needing to almost break into the family, my arrival was far more welcome, and made more of an impact, than I could have guessed. Not only had I brought a measure of wealth and stability, Susan thought I unintentionally showed Ned the error of his ways. The two of us did so well with the punt, it emphasised the mistake he had made in rejecting Alex. They could have benefited from working together, even without any acknowledgement of being father and son. As it was, his stubborn attitude meant both had been on the breadline.

"And you had taught him more in other ways," she continued, stunning me further. To my mind there had been only one student, and one teacher in the arrangement. "You showed him that looking to himself, and the past, did not make for a future, while being obstinate was hardly a measure of strength, and could actually be self-destructive."

At that time we still had the Bennett brothers about our necks, Ugly Joe was in custody and, for all I knew, willing to implicate all and any about him, while I would be in the suds with Bryson for not coming back with a report on the current state of Boulogne. If I had taught Ned anything, it must surely have been to keep his head down, and not challenge the *status quo*. But I thought of her words often then, and still do now: as far as life changing experiences were concerned, that was mine.

* * *

They came for my father the very next day. I read about it in Bryson's newspaper, just two weeks later. It gave his full name, and described him as a Ninfield man who was considered to be a stalwart and respectable member of the community. The same edition later made it as far as Hastings, but no one associated him with me. There were some advantages in living in a small community; to all about I was simply Nat, never Nathaniel, and my surname didn't matter. I was also becoming as much part of the town as those born on Rock-a-Nore, and few remembered, or even cared, where I had come from.

Besides, his crime was not of the highest. It had been reported as financing the free traders which, to most on the south coast, placed him on a similar level to that of a poacher. Even using such a euphemism proved the lack of severity with which the offence was regarded. My father was effectively accused of bringing cheap liquor, tea and tobacco, as well as other such luxuries, within the reach of the common man. In the eyes of most, to have grown rich from such endeavours was completely fair, and his only true transgression lay in being caught.

But then the public have a right to be ignorant: when I read later he was sentenced to seven years' transportation to New South Wales, I wondered quite how much the authorities knew, or were willing to forget. Certainly, if they had been aware of the gold Dad had been freely exporting, nothing was said. And, to my freshly altered mind, that was far worse a crime than any evasion of taxes.

For it was gold going to France. Gold, to finance an army already setting its sights on England. Gold, the lifeblood of our country, yet bled to nourish our closest enemy. Had that been revealed, he would probably have joined Joe Prettyman in taking the morning drop at Newgate. But either he failed to tell, or those in authority did not want to know. And I stayed quiet, both about

269

my father's involvement, and his three hundred guineas that spent the next few weeks concealed in the forepeak of *Katharine II*.

Actually it was not until the June of that year, and after a new state of war with France was properly in place, that I broached the case of salt once more. By then my father was well on his way to the other side of the world, Ugly Joe had died a dismal, but honourably mute death, and it seemed likely the rest of the Clipping Crew were either arrested, or unaware who actually held the money.

The former included Rob and Billy Bennett: it was with no great surprise that I discovered the pair to have also been working for my father. Still, I made four payments of fifty golden guineas, a week apart to their lawyers. Each was fully receipted, and made on the understanding that *Katharine II*'s papers would be presented upon my final instalment.

Which they were. I think knowing the brothers were likely to be absent for some while acted as a sobering influence on their legal advisers but, for whatever reason, the boat was lawfully mine by summer. And, by autumn, so was Susan.

* * *

We had seventeen happy years together, and she bore me three healthy sons before dying, in childbirth, with the fourth. She is buried in the churchyard of All Saints at the end of our old road, if anyone cares to look. The grave is next to that of her father, who followed a year later, although not until he had given his older grandsons a first rate grounding in the fishing. But, for all the time that Susan and I were together, no mention of the gold was ever made, and I was never completely sure if she, or Ned, had even registered Prettyman's last remark.

The whole thing was muddled slightly by our receiving a share of the seizer money. This was far less than that needed to pay off the Bennetts, but did at least confuse the issue, certainly as far as Ned was concerned.

And so it became yet another matter that was laid to one side, and never referred to; even if it actually made little difference either way. Susan and Jenny could be wrong: Ned's concern for Alex might have been nothing more than that felt for any fellow human being. It was not typical of his behaviour perhaps, but people do alter. Even I had realised that by then. I also knew the reason for change might be spectacular, or subtle: public or private, and the alteration itself, for good as well as evil – it all depended on the person, and the circumstances.

In my case the change was for the good, and most certainly welcome. When the first of the boys appeared, Susan and I moved from the old cottage on All Saints Street and took one of the new houses that were part of the building expansion further to the west. Jenny who, true to her prediction, has never married, stayed behind and looked after her father. She did become a mother later however, if only by proxy. After Ned's death, she followed us to Middleton Street where the two of us raised the fourth lad together. Jenny still cares for, chases after, loves and disciplines the boys now, even though all but one tower mightily above her, and regularly make play by hiding her knitting.

I gave up the fishing even before Susan passed, but never lost my love for the sea, and invested the last of my father's gold in the Phillips' yard, at the end of Rock-a-Nore. With my funds, Elsiver Phillips' son was able to put the business back onto a sound footing, and now I draw a small income that meets my needs adequately enough. But it was through my connection with the yard that I ran into Jesse's son Dan once more, and came to the conclusion that, whatever the circumstances, some folk don't change a bit.

He came to me with no thoughts of the past, only a future which, for him at least, appeared extremely rosy. Gold was still at a premium in France and a third could be made without even trying. Many of the south coast free traders were doubling their profits by effectively carrying cargo both ways. The authorities were becoming wise to the fact, of course, and even outward bound vessels were regularly rummaged and impounded. But Dan, it seemed, had come up with a scheme that would put an end to that, and it actually turned out to be almost foolproof.

His vision was for specialised boats; they were to be long, at least forty feet from stem to stern, narrow and powered only by a great number of oars. Each would carry up to twenty men and, properly managed, were predicted to cross the Channel in under five hours. It would be exhausting work, but reasonably safe; the boats being faster than anything similarly powered and sitting so low in the water as to be almost invisible. They also had the added advantage that, if a Revenue vessel did spot and try to stop them, they only needed to steer into the wind, to remain totally invulnerable. He envisaged the yard building several, which would provide regular trade for my business. And I was also welcome to invest, with a single trip netting an estimated five to six hundred pounds profit for anyone wise enough to do so.

The plan proved successful and for several years guinea boats, as they came to be known, were both plentiful and prosperous, while regularly humiliating Revenue and Navy vessels alike. But I was not involved.

By then my standards had changed significantly, and any commercial opportunity with the faintest taint of illegality was given a wide berth. I was a respectable man with a family and even more determined not to follow in the wake of my father. Besides, such a course would almost have been a betrayal, when my best friend was the mate of a Revenue cruiser.

Alex seldom comes to Hastings now, but our families regularly meet up at his smart little house by the harbour in Rye. And sometimes the two of us go line fishing together, despite the fact that I still can't stand the creatures. The chance that Ned might have been his father has never been mentioned: even after the old man passed, it felt like an unnecessary invasion of their private worlds. Our friendship continued, however, and lasts to this day. Certainly I would never have compromised it by actively supporting smuggling; something that still causes him so many problems. Besides, I have already owned a guinea boat of sorts: and that proved more than enough for me.

Author's Note

The luggers mentioned in my story can be described as such, being vessels powered by lug sails. However the term, when used by a latter day native of Hastings, is more likely to refer to the far larger, three masted boats that became common between 1830 and 1860. These were very different affairs, and often spent many weeks at sea, travelling the length of the country. Nat's later acquisition was indeed a lugger, but a Hastings resident living in 1803 would have probably refereed to it as a "bog", and the day fishing vessels as "big boats". I have used the more conventional terms as constant references to bogs and big boats gave the narrative a slightly juvenile air.

In a similar vein, when speaking of the rig I usually refer to the forward mast as the main, it being the principal mast. Once more, a purist might disagree and call it the foremast (and refer to the mizzen as the jigger). The lugger rig described originated from a three masted layout. In time the central mainmast became redundant, however, and was removed, or foreshortened and used for other purposes. Many local fishermen retained the former name however, and 'foremast' is still used in Hastings to this day. But I feel the majority of readers would expect it to be referred to as a main, and I have done so in the hope of avoiding confusion.

All Saints Street has been in existence since 1450, although many residents did, and still do, refer to it unofficially as Fisher, or Fish Street. Again, I have steered for simplicity.

Selected Glossary

Anker	Cask holding from six to nine gallons. See half-anker and tub.
Back	Wind change; anticlockwise.
Backstays	Similar to shrouds in function, except that they run from the hounds of the topmast, or topgallant, all the way to the deck. Serve to support the mast against any forces forward; for example, when the ship is tacking. (Also a useful/spectacular way to return to deck for topmen.)
Backstays, running	A less permanent backstay, rigged with a tackle to allow it to be slacked to clear a gaff or boom.
Bat	Lander's weapon, usually made of ash and up to six feet long.
Batman / Batsman	Lander armed with a bat to defend a landing.
Bean	(*Slang*) A guinea.
Binnacle	Cabinet on the quarterdeck that houses compasses, the log, traverse board, lead lines, telescope and speaking trumpet.
Blab	(*Slang*) A gossip.
Block	Article of rigging that allows pressure to be diverted or, when used with others, increased. Consists of a pulley wheel, made of *lignum vitae*, encased in a wooden shell. Blocks can be single, double (fiddle block), triple or quadruple. The main suppliers were Taylors, of Southampton.

Boatswain	*(Pronounced Bosun)* The officer who superintends the sails, rigging, canvas, colours, anchors, cables and cordage, committed to his charge.
Bog	*(Hastings Slang)* A decked fishing boat between 20-24 feet in length.
Bone (in her teeth)	*(Slang)* Commonly used to describe the prominent bow wave of a vessel travelling at speed.
Bottom	*(Slang)* Strength and fortitude.
Boot Catcher	*(Slang)* A servant employed to clean boots at inns or other commercial establishments.
Bower Anchor	Anchor carried at the bow, usually in pairs – "best" and "small".
Box the Compass	Officially the act of reciting all 32 points of the compass both clockwise and anticlockwise, but often used to describe a full 360-degree turn.
Boy Ashore	*(Hastings Slang)* A fishing boat's shore worker.
Braces	Lines used to adjust the angle between the yards, and the fore and aft line of the ship. Mizzen braces, and braces of a brig lead forward.
Brig	Two-masted vessel, square-rigged on both masts.
Bulkhead	A wall or partition within the hull of a ship.
Bulwark	The planking or wood-work about a vessel above her deck.
Canister	Anti-personnel shot used in cannon, similar to but smaller than grape.
Cartwheel	*(Slang)* Early British penny, first minted in 1797. Cartwheels were in circulation for several years, yet all carried the 1797 date.

Cascabel	Part of the breech of a cannon.
Caulk	*(Slang)* To sleep. Also caulking, a process to seal the seams between strakes.
Chawk	*(Hastings Slang)* Lower a boat down a beach.
Chopbacks	*(Hastings Slang)* Hastings Fishermen.
Chub	*(Slang)* A fool; from the fish that is supposedly easily taken.
Cleat	A retaining piece for lines attached to yards, *etc.*
Close hauled	Sailing as near as possible into the wind.
Coaming	A ridged frame about hatches to prevent water on deck from getting below.
Coke	*(Slang)* Fool (from the character in Bartholomew Fair).
Collector (of customs)	Chief customs officer responsible for a port or sector.
Conn	The act of commanding a vessel: the captain, pilot, sailing master, officer of the watch *etc.* is said to have the conn, or be standing at the conn.
Counter	The lower part of a vessel's stern.
Course	A large square lower sail, hung from a yard, with sheets controlling and securing it.
Cove	*(Slang)* A man. Often used in a mildly derogatory fashion.
Coxcomb	Originally a fool, but came to mean one who was permanently over-dressed.
Cow Gown	*(Hastings Slang)* Tanned smock, usually very long.

Creeping Irons	Revenue tools for detecting and recovering sunken contraband.
Crib	Cribbage. A card game that utilises a dedicated board for scoring.
Crimp	*(Slang)* One who procures men for the Royal Navy.
Crop	*(Slang)* A cargo of contraband.
Crows of iron	Crow bars used to move a gun or heavy object.
Cruiser	*(Slang)* a Revenue cutter.
Cull	*(Slang)* A man.
Cutter	Fast, small, single-masted vessel with a sloop rig. Also a seaworthy ship's boat.
Cut Purse	*(Slang)* A form of pickpocket.
Deputed Mariner	Member of a cutter's crew with powers to seize contraband and carry out official revenue work.
Dished	*(Slang)* Ruined.
Ditty bag	*(Slang)* A seaman's bag. Derives its name from the dittis or 'Manchester stuff' of which it was once made.
Dry goods	Literally non-liquid contraband.
Dudder	*(Slang)* A cheat or a fraud: one who sells shoddy goods.
Eighty-Four	*(Slang)* A common term for transportation was seven years, or eighty-four months.
Fall	The free end of a lifting tackle.
Fetch	To arrive at, or reach a destination. Also the distance the wind blows across the water. The longer the fetch the bigger the waves.
Flasker	*(Slang)* One who smuggles liquor.
Flukers	*(Hastings Slang)* Large plaice.

Flush	*(Slang)* Wealthy. (Or used to describe a deck, on one level, stretching from bow to stern.)
Forereach	To gain upon, or pass by another ship when sailing in a similar direction.
Forestay	Stay supporting the masts running forward, serving the opposite function of the backstay. Runs from each mast at an angle of about 45 degrees to meet another mast, the deck or the bowsprit.
Freeboard	The height of a ship's side above the water line.
Free trader	*(Slang)* Popular euphemism for a smuggler. (Also fair trader.)
Fuddle	*(Slang)* A drunkard.
Fussock	*(Slang)* Literally a donkey, but usually used to describe a stupid or lazy person.
Gobbler	*(Slang)* Euphemism for a Revenue official.
Groat	Small British coin worth fourpence.
Gunwales	The upper reinforcing band to the sides or edges of a vessel.
Half-anker	Cask holding about four gallons; often referred to as a tub.
Halyards	Lines which raise yards, sails, signals etc.
Hawse	Area in bows where holes are cut to allow anchor cables to pass through. Also used as general term for bows.
Hawser	Heavy cable used for hauling, towing or mooring.
Heave to	Keeping a ship relatively stationary by backing certain sails in a seaway.
Hide	Safe place for concealing contraband.

Horse Pistol	Heavy calibre firearm usually held in a holster, for use whilst riding. Often supplied in pairs.
Hussy	*(Slang)* Originally an abbreviation of housewife, but later used as a term of mild insult.
Jack	*(Slang)* Colloquial term for an RN seaman.
Jape	*(Slang)* Joke.
Jib-boom	Spar run out from the extremity of the bowsprit, braced by means of a martingale stay, which passes through the dolphin striker.
Jibe	To change tack with the wind coming from astern. (Also known as to wear, a term more commonly used in square-rigged vessels.)
Jigger	*(Slang)* Mizzen mast.
John Company	*(Slang)* The East India Company.
Jury mast/rig	Temporary measure used to restore a vessel's sailing ability after damage.
Landshark	*(Slang)* Popular euphemism for land-based Revenue officers.
Landsman	The rating of one who has no experience at sea.
Lander	*(Slang)* Member of a smuggling gang principally responsible for unloading contraband.
Landwaiter	Revenue officer responsible for recording imported goods or contraband.
Lanthorn	A large lantern.
Larboard	Left side of the ship when facing forward. Later replaced by 'port', which had previously been used for helm orders.

Leeboards	Similar to a centreboard in operation, leeboards are set to either side of a vessel and help maintain stability when sailing with the wind forward of the beam.
Leeward	The downwind side of a vessel or structure.
Leeway	The amount a vessel is pushed sideways by the wind (as opposed to headway, the forward movement).
Let down (to)	The act of diluting over-proof spirit.
Linstock	The holder of slow match which a gun captain uses to fire his piece when a flintlock mechanism is not working or present.
Lubberly/lubber	*(Slang)* Unseaman-like behaviour; as a landsman.
Luff	To sail closer to the wind, (intentionally or not) perhaps to allow work aloft. Also the flapping of sails when brought too close to the wind. The side of a fore and aft sail, laced to the mast.
Martingale stay	Line that braces the jib-boom, passing from the end through the dolphin striker to the ship.
Mitch	*(Hastings Slang)* Support for a boat's lowered mast.
Molly	*(Slang)* General term for homosexuals; from the Latin meaning soft or sissy. Also used to describe female prostitutes, many of whom were from Ireland (and were often called Molly).
Nub	*(Slang)* To hang, as a method of execution. Nubbing cove – a hangman.

280

Nugging House	*(Slang)* A brothel.
Owler	*(Slang)* One who smuggles wool.
Pat	*(Hastings Slang)* Area to the stern of a fishing boat.
Palarum	*(Hastings Slang)* Small hold or area to store a catch.
Pay – paying	To preserve wood with oil, pitch, tar or resin.
Peach	*(Slang)* To betray or reveal; from impeach.
Pederast	In the 18th and 19th centuries, the term usually referred to male homosexuality in general.
Phiz	*(Slang)* Face.
Privateer	Privately owned vessel fitted out as a warship, and licensed to capture enemy vessels. The licence allows a greater number of guns to be carried than would otherwise be allowed.
Protection	A legal document that gives the owner protection against impressment.
Punt	*(Hastings Slang)* Two masted open boat between 14-16 feet long (in the 1800's)
Quarterdeck	In larger ships the deck forward of the poop, but at a lower level. The preserve of officers.
Queue	A pigtail. Often tied by a seaman's best friend (his tie mate).
Rag Water	*(Slang)* Gin (or Hollands).
Ratlines	Lighter lines, untarred and tied horizontally across the shrouds at regular intervals, to act as rungs and allow men to climb aloft.

Reef	A portion of sail that can be taken in to reduce the size of the whole.
Reeving (Bowsprit)	Alternative name for a running bowsprit; one that can be extended or retracted. The length of a bowsprit was governed by law; only a Revenue cutter being allowed one of such a length in proportion to her hull.
Riding officer	Shore-based customs officer, usually mounted, detailed to search for smugglers and hidden or abandoned contraband.
Rigging	Lines that can usually be divided into standing (static) and running. (moveable). Or *(Slang)* Clothes.
Roast	*(Slang)* to arrest.
Rock-a-Nore	*(Originally Hastings Slang, but officially adopted in 1859)* An Area between the east cliffs and the Stade.
Rondy	*(Slang)* The *Rendezvous*: where a press is based and organised.
Rummage	*(Slang)* To search.
Running	Sailing before the wind.
Running (Bowsprit)	A bowsprit that can be extended, usually on leaving harbour. See also reeving.
Scragged	*(Slang)* Hanged.
Sammar	*(Hastings Slang)* Fine weather.
Scran	*(Slang)* Food.
Scupper	Waterway that allows general drainage.
Sennight	A week.
Seizer Money	An allowance given to revenue men for the confiscation of contraband goods.

Sheet	Line that controls a sail.
Shrouds	Lines supporting the masts athwart ship (from side to side) which run from the hounds (just below the top) to the channels on the side of the hull.
Simkin	*(Slang)* a fool.
Sivver	*(Hastings Slang)* A catch.
Smack	Vessel similar to a cutter in rig.
Smoked	*(Slang)* realised.
Stade	The area of Hastings beach dedicated to fishing boats, nets and equipment. It has been used thus for over a thousand years and is currently home to Europe's largest fleet of shore based fishing boats. The name comes from the Saxon for landing place
Stay sail	A triangular or quadrilateral sail, hung from under a stay.
Stem	An extension to the keel that acts as the forward part of a vessel's bow.
Stingo	*(Slang)* Beer.
Strake	A plank.
Suds (in the)	*(Slang)* To be in trouble.
Tack	To turn a ship, moving her bows through the wind. Also a leg of a journey relating to the direction of the wind. If from starboard, a ship is on the starboard tack. Also the part of a fore and aft loose-footed sail where the sheet is attached, or a line leading forward on a square course to hold the lower part of the sail forward.
Tattletale	*(Slang)* Gossip.

Tide waiter	Officer responsible for searching any newly arrived, or impounded vessel.
Tophamper	Literally any unnecessary weight either on a ship's decks or about her tops and rigging, but often used loosely to refer to spars and rigging.
Trick	*(Slang)* Period of duty.
Trug	A traditional open basket common in Sussex and usually made in Herstmonceux.
Trull	*(Slang)* Actually a soldier's female companion, but can be used more freely as a derogatory name for a woman.
Tub	A small cask, or half-anker, the main purpose of which was for smuggling.
Tub man	Smuggler employed to carry tubs inland, usually two tied about the neck, one in front and one behind.
Veer	Wind change, clockwise.
Wearing	To change the direction of a ship across the wind by putting its stern through the eye of the wind. Also jibe – more common in a fore and aft rig.
Whiddler	*(Slang)* One who betrays a fellow gang member.
Windward	The side exposed to the wind.
Yard	Spar attached to a mast from which a sail can be hung or set.
Yellow George.	*(Slang)* A guinea.
Younker	*(Slang)* Youngster.Able Seaman One who can hand, reef and steer and is well-acquainted with the duties of a seaman.

About the Author

Alaric Bond was born in Surrey, and now lives in Herstmonceux, East Sussex. He has been writing professionally for over twenty years.

His interests include the British Navy, 1793-1815, and the RNVR during WWII. He is also a keen collector of old or unusual musical instruments, and 78 rpm records, is a member of various historical societies and regularly gives talks to groups and organisations.

www.alaricbond.com

About Old Salt Press

Old Salt Press is an independent press catering to those who love books about ships and the sea. We are an association of writers working together to produce the very best of nautical and maritime fiction and non-fiction. We invite you to join us as we go down to the sea in books.

www.oldsaltpress.com

More Great Reading from Old Salt Press

A fifth Wiki Coffin mystery

"Combining historical and nautical accuracy with a fast paced mystery thriller has produced a marvelous book which is highly recommended." — David Hayes, Historic Naval Fiction

The Beckoning Ice finds the U. S. Exploring Expedition off Cape Horn, a grim outpost made still more threatening by the report of a corpse on a drifting iceberg, closely followed by a gruesome death on board. Was it suicide, or a particularly brutal murder? Wiki investigates, only to find himself fighting desperately for his own life.

ISBN 978-0-9922588-3-2

Thrilling yarn
from the last days of the square-riggers

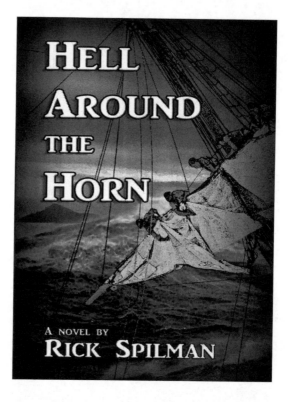

In 1905, a young ship's captain and his family set sail on the windjammer, *Lady Rebecca*, from Cardiff, Wales with a cargo of coal bound for Chile, by way of Cape Horn. Before they reach the Southern Ocean, the cargo catches fire, the mate threatens mutiny and one of the crew may be going mad. The greatest challenge, however, will prove to be surviving the vicious westerly winds and mountainous seas of the worst Cape Horn winter in memory. Told from the perspective of the Captain, his wife, a first year apprentice and an American sailor before the mast, *Hell Around the Horn* is a story of survival and the human spirit in the last days of the great age of sail.

ISBN 978-0-9882360-1-1

Another gripping saga from the author of the Fighting Sail series

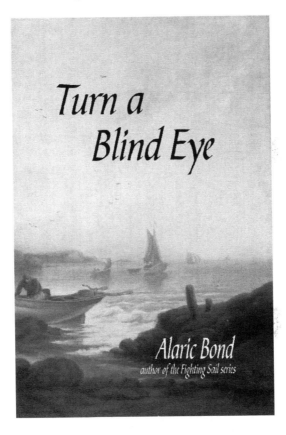

Newly appointed to the local revenue cutter, Commander Griffin is determined to make his mark, and defeat a major gang of smugglers. But the country is still at war with France and it is an unequal struggle; can he depend on support from the local community, or are they yet another enemy for him to fight? With dramatic action on land and at sea, *Turn a Blind Eye* exposes the private war against the treasury with gripping fact and fascinating detail.

ISBN 978-0-9882360-3-5

A romantic adventure from the days of wooden ships and iron men

A small, audacious British frigate does battle against a large but ungainly Spanish ship. British Captain James Blackwell intercepts the Spanish *La Trinidad*, outmaneuvers and outguns the treasure ship and boards her. Fighting alongside the Spanish captain, sword in hand, is a beautiful woman. The battle is quickly over. The Spanish captain is killed in the fray and his ship damaged beyond repair. Its survivors and treasure are taken aboard the British ship, *Inconstant*. ISBN 978-0-9882360-6-6

"Not for the faint hearted – Captain Blackwell pulls no punches!" - Alaric Bond

The repercussions of a court martial and the ill-will of powerful men at the Admiralty pursue Royal Navy Captain James Blackwell into the Pacific, where danger lurks around every coral reef. Even if Captain Blackwell and Mercedes survive the venture into the world of early nineteenth century exploration, can they emerge unchanged with their love intact. The mission to the Great South Sea will test their loyalties and strength, and define the characters of Captain Blackwell and his lady in *Blackwell's Paradise.*

ISBN 978-0-9882360-5-9

He can save the ship and the crew, but can he save himself?

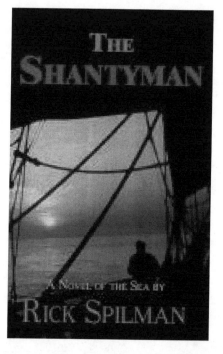

In 1870, on the clipper ship *Alahambra* in Sydney, the new crew comes aboard more or less sober, except for the last man, who is hoisted aboard in a cargo sling, paralytic drunk. The drunken sailor, Jack Barlow, will prove to be an able shantyman. On a ship with a dying captain and a murderous mate, Barlow will literally keep the crew pulling together. As he struggles with a tragic past, a troubled present and an uncertain future, Barlow will guide the *Alahambra* through Southern Ocean ice and the horror of an Atlantic hurricane. His one goal is bringing the ship and crew safely back to New York, where he hopes to start anew. Based on a true story, *The Shantyman* is a gripping tale of survival against all odds at sea and ashore, and the challenge of facing a past that can never be wholly left behind.

ISBN978-0-9941152-2-5

"A very satisfying conclusion to the Blackwell's Adventures series, with lusty escapades tempered with amusing side passages, lively characters and a lovely ending." - Broos Campbell, author of the Matty Graves series

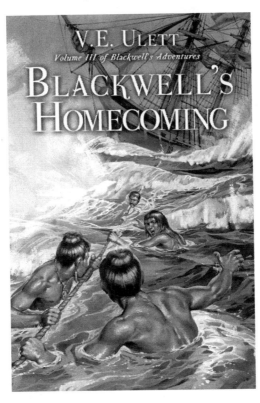

In a multigenerational saga of love, war and betrayal, Captain Blackwell and Mercedes continue their voyage in Volume III of Blackwell's Adventures. The Blackwell family's eventful journey from England to Hawaii, by way of the new and tempestuous nations of Brazil and Chile, provides an intimate portrait of family conflicts and loyalties in the late Georgian Age. Blackwell's Homecoming is an evocation of the dangers and rewards of desire.

ISBN 978-0-9882360-7-3

Britannia's Shark by Antione Vanner

"Britannia's Shark" is the third of the Dawlish Chronicles novels. It's 1881 and a daring act of piracy draws the ambitious British naval officer, Nicholas Dawlish, into a deadly maelstrom of intrigue and revolution. Drawn in too is his wife Florence, for whom the glimpse of a half-forgotten face evokes memories of earlier tragedy. For both a nightmare lies ahead, amid the wealth and squalor of America's Gilded Age and on a fever-ridden island ruled by savage tyranny. Manipulated ruthlessly from London by the shadowy Admiral Topcliffe, Nicholas and Florence Dawlish must make some very strange alliances if they are to survive – and prevail. ISBN 978-0992263690

Lady Castaways by Joan Druett

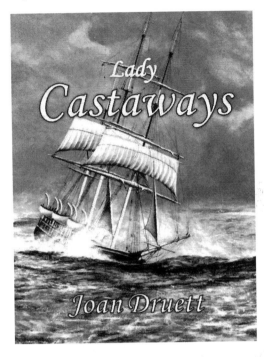

It was not just the men who lived on the brink of peril when under sail at sea. Lucretia Jansz, who was enslaved as a concubine in 1629, was just one woman who endured a castaway experience. Award-winning historian Joan Druett (*Island of the Lost, The Elephant Voyage)*, relates the stories of women who survived remarkable challenges, from heroines like Mary Ann Jewell, the "governess" of Auckland Island in the icy sub-Antarctic, to Millie Jenkins, whose ship was sunk by a whale.

Due for release shortly.

The sixth book of Alaric Bond's

Fighting Sail series.

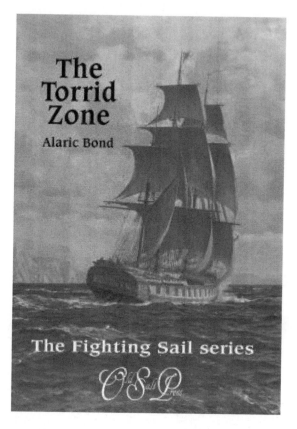

A tired ship with a worn out crew, but *HMS Scylla* has one more trip to make before her much postponed re-fit. Bound for St Helena, she is to deliver the island's next governor; a simple enough mission and, as peace looks likely to be declared, no one is expecting difficulties. Except, perhaps, the commander of a powerful French battle squadron, who has other ideas.

With conflict and intrigue at sea and ashore, The Torrid Zone is filled to the gunnels with action, excitement and fascinating historical detail; a truly engaging read. ISBN 978-0988236097

Made in the USA
Middletown, DE
08 September 2015